HIS
FINAL MISSION

HIS
FINAL MISSION

William Clifford Brown

HIS FINAL MISSION

This book is written to provide information and motivation to readers. Its purpose is not to render any type of psychological, legal, or professional advice of any kind. The content is the sole opinion and expression of the author, and not necessarily that of the publisher.

Copyright © 2019 by William Clifford Brown

Printed in the United States of America.

ISBN   978-1-64552-041-2   (Paperback)
ISBN   978-1-64552-042-9   (Digital)

Lettra Press books may be ordered through booksellers or by contacting:

Lettra Press LLC
18229 E 52nd Ave.
Denver City, CO 80249
1 303 586 1431 | info@lettrapress.com
www.lettrapress.com

Contents

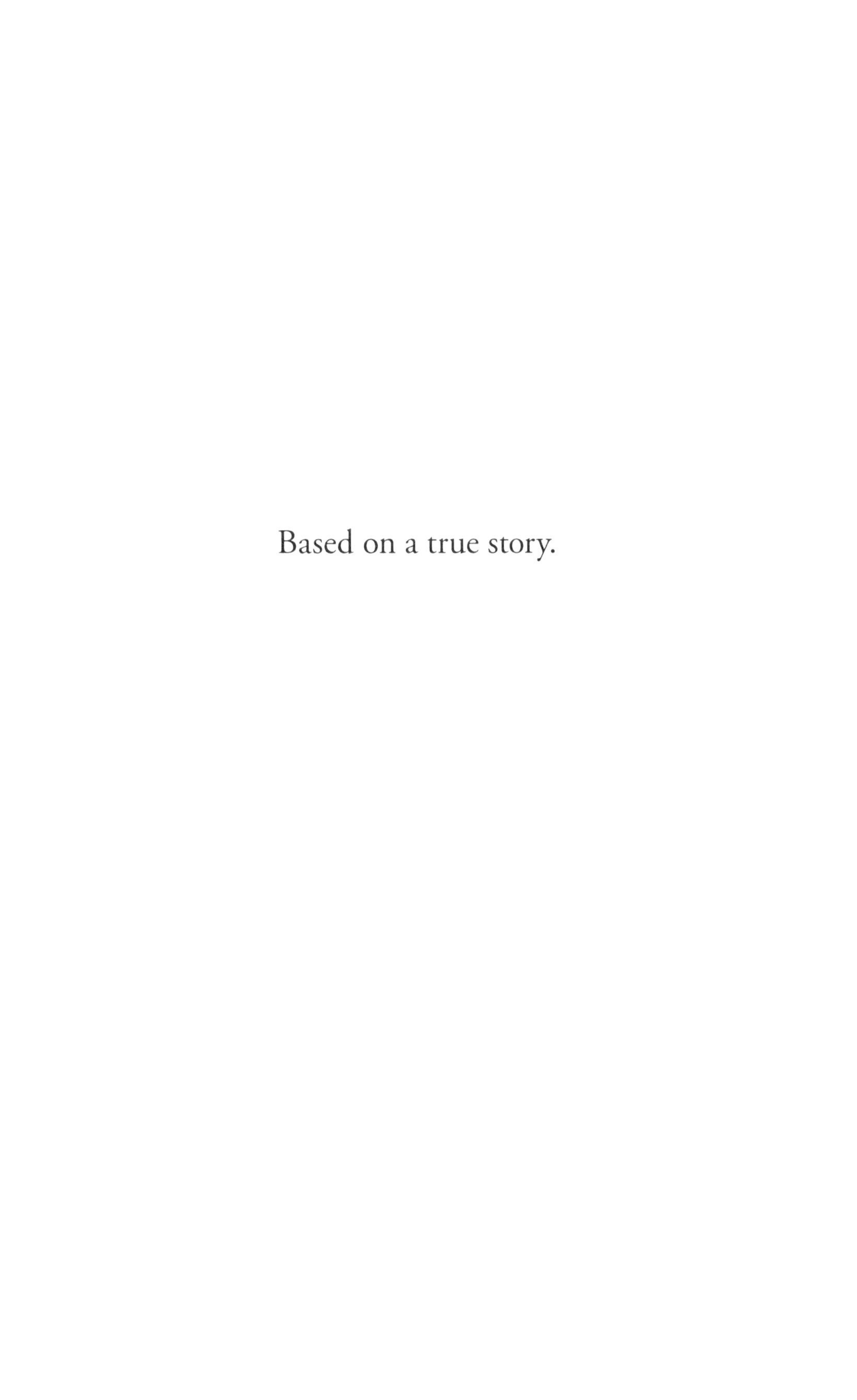

Based on a true story.

The author grew up in those sometimes magical times after World War II during the Fabulous Fifties in a small town in the Midwest. It was evident each time he returned and felt the strong camaraderie at one of his class reunions, that those who grew up in a small town in the West shared a truly unique experience. Those who had moved away and traveled to the far ends of the world and those who went to war found very little evidence of anything like it…because nothing compares to "the old hometown." The town was Sikeston, in the Southeast corner of Missouri, an area known as the Bootheel.

The central figure of this story is Will Brandon, and the starting point is his returning home from Vietnam to his class reunion during a time of war. This story is about events that lead up to that reunion, the catalyst that blended Will and his friends into the soup of their shared past. As if they had never parted, the years and distances seemed not to matter as they were thrown back to a time when the world was far less serious, when childhood friendships were more like holy covenants than relationships. It's the story of such alliances, boys from different family backgrounds, different sides of the track, and the girls who made Sikeston High the wonderful experience that it was. It is also a story of war and death and a small town boy's struggle as he grew into manhood to cope with both.

Although it encompasses the author's childhood, this story also depicts how boys become men during times of war. And it's the story of lifelong friendships, for without them, the soup of their life would not be as rich and flavorful.

The time is 1968–75, and like all stories, events prior to the rising curtain shape the characters and the circumstances. The Tet Offensive had a devastating affect on morale and support for the Vietnam Conflict here in the United States. Militarily, the Tet Offensive had been a bigger disaster for the North Vietnamese than Little Big Horn was for Custer, but it had some very unintended consequences for the United States. Many years have passed, but the memory of that national struggle is still with us, part of the long ending stretch of eternity that is gone forever except in our minds. If you can relate to that memory, perhaps you can relive some of it now.

Saying Good-Bye to SF Camp 222

When Will Brandon walked into his class reunion at the Sikeston Country Club, the shock of having been fighting a war just just a few hours earlier in a jungle a world away and now strolling into a big party as if nothing was happening overwhelmed him. The first person he met shook his hand and asked him what he had been doing since they graduated. If he had told him, Will thought to himself, he might not have wanted to shake his hand. It was a hand that had brought death and destruction on his enemies time and time again. It was unclean.

Some of Will's friends were waiting outside to greet him as if the party was for him alone. He felt like the prodigal son and was embarrassed by all of the attention they bestowed upon him. There were many of his best friends: David Bailey, Don Baker, Sam Bowman, Edward Malone, Alan Stewart, Nicholas Walker, Bobby Crawford, just as he had imagined they and the reunion would be. It was more than he could take in at one time, seeing them there together again. It was as if he had never been away. They seemed to be thrown back in the days of their youth and his heart was warmed as he listened to the stories they told about their past, most of them he had long forgotten, others he had hoped to forget.

It occurred to him that the joy he was feeling was heightened by the fact that this was the first real joy and peace he had felt in years, and it was such an unusual feeling that he didn't really know how to cope with it.

Friends who had married spouses from outside the area brought them by to introduce them to Will as the DJ began to play recorded music from their high school days. "In the Still of the Night," a reminder of those hot star-filled summer nights when Will and his friends would drive around Sikeston and the countryside enjoying their friendships, dreaming about the future, and thinking about their favorite sweetheart. Now, here they were together again and he marveled at how different his life had become compared to what he expected it to be when he graduated from high school. Thinking back to the war, his thoughts took him back to that last day.

It was raining hard now as Will's eyes searched the jungle surrounding the landing zone and the lake that had formed around the base of their helicopter gunship alert to drops of rain that might not be rain at all but, instead, incoming rifle fire. The UH1-C gunship, which had taken off a few minutes earlier, hovered high above them, waiting to provide support in the event they ran into resistance as his Special Forces Team abandoned SF Camp 222, one of twenty small team outposts that had been set up as backup to villages where Green Berets had been teaching local villagers modern methods of sanitation, agriculture, and animal husbandry.

Platoon SF 22 was the last fire team to leave Camp 222, and none of them would breathe comfortably until they were out of rifle range. That morning, patrols had been called in due to the increasing enemy activity reported by their spotters in preparation of departure. Visions of the firefight the night before were much too vivid. Will knew the enemy would not soon forget what his Special Ops team had done to a platoon size contingent in retaliation for their merciless torture and murder of the villagers of Doc Tran.

Expecting the Americans to be in pursuit, the enemy could not have known that through the night, Will and his Special Ops team had run around the perpetrators to set up positions along the pathway they were expected to be following. All of Will's team had lost friends who lived in that Montagnard village called Doc Tran, and their deaths were just the incentive they needed to endure an all-night run. Some highly trained yards, the slang word for Montagnard tribe fighters had also joined them to run down the enemy. Many of their relatives had also been slaughtered so they gladly had taken part. It was a complete surprise to the VC, and they walked right into their trap. The Green Berets made sure none of them escaped.

Streaks of rain slithered past the curved window of the Huey as they prepared to lift off from the compound for the last time. There was a very high level of anxiety felt by the soldiers in the chopper. Will observed his comrades; his South Vietnamese counterpart, Tom Vo, was having trouble holding a lit match to a cigarette dangling from his lips while the youngest trooper in the platoon gave every indication he would fill a barf bag at any moment. As for Will, he knew everyone was observing his composure, looking for a crack in the wall of his psyche, so he remained the macho guy everyone thought he was. But underneath it all, his mouth was so dry it reminded him of the dryness he experienced while driving a combine through the fields of dust as they harvested soybeans and wheat on his grandmother's farm.

Sitting on the opposite side of the aircraft was his buddy Larry Stockton, a friend he had met at Fort Bragg when they were in jump school. Will and Larry, who was also from Missouri, became close when they attended Special Forces School together. These past two years, Will had been effective in controlling fear using the mind control tactics taught him by the CIA. But all of the team knew that dying in the final minutes before leaving the Vietnam battlefield was always a possibility and would not be cool, especially since according to rumors, the war might soon be over.

It was unusual how he and Larry ended up in Vietnam. It wasn't by any direct route, and it took years of preparation. The path started at Jungle Survival School in Panama just after they had finished Special Forces training. When the course was completed, both of them were selected to be instructors, and it wasn't long before they were expecting a new assignment to Langley, Virginia, and the CIA Operative Training Program they had applied for. One night while sleeping, Larry and Will were set upon by armed men who had broken into the school compound in the early hours and abducted them, forcing them to run though the night to some unknown destination. Because they were being tested to qualify for assignment to the agency, they assumed that this was part of the drill. That was until Will caught a foot in his face when he tried to resist. With hoods placed over their heads and their arms bound, they ran through the jungle for what seemed hours, taking a rest only when it looked like they couldn't continue.

Speaking Spanish, their captors had no compulsion about beating them vigorously about the head and back until they could feel the blood soaking through their shirts. They were not allowed to talk and were deprived of sleep, food, and water for two days. Early on the third day, they arrived at a camp fatigued, and except for a latrine break, only stopped a few times to rest. It was fortunate that they were in good shape and could keep up with the rebels. Upon arrival, their hoods were removed, and they were separated to opposite sides of the camp for the night.

By the time the forced run was over, Will and Larry had come to the conclusion that this must be a Panamanian rebel camp as they recognized the Indians who were present as Embera people, a very primitive tribe of Indians that were known to fraternize with rebels in eastern Panama. It remained a mystery why they had been taken unless they were to be hostages for ransom or to be killed to revenge some American atrocity. Either way, they knew they were in a lot of trouble.

Just when Will and Larry thought they were going to get a few hours sleep, they were abruptly awakened, given a cup of water and a strip of meat that Will believed to be dried rat, and marched to a mine on a hillside some distance away. Speaking in broken English, they were given shovels and told to dig for jewels. The target appeared to be opals, turquoise, and emeralds. The question they couldn't find the answer to was why they had been taken. The ransom or revenge ideas didn't add up. Will knew that there are emeralds and gold in Panama, but he had never heard of them finding opals or turquoise there.

Larry, who understood and spoke some Spanish, began to question the guards about the feasibility of digging for something that didn't exist, started an argument with one of them who promptly knocked him off his feet, kicking him hard in the stomach. Will then saw that same look on Larry's face that he had seen at the Enlisted Club at Fort Bragg a year prior, when some guy tried to hit him with a sucker punch only to find himself being thrown across the bar. He knew Larry wouldn't put up with this treatment for very long.

Arriving back at camp exhausted just before midnight, they all but crawled the last fifty yards. Will became disgusted when they were served skewered grebes on sticks roasted over a fire, some with the feathers still on them. But it didn't matter, they were starved and they ate them anyway before being separated for the night.

During the early morning hours, the sounding of an alarm signaled something major had occurred. Larry had escaped and the guards were furious. Will was brought out of the hut and led to a circle where everyone had assembled. The leader of the group stepped out of his hut and for the first time, in perfect English, informed Will that he was Col. Robert Price, commander of the Delta Force's Escape, Survival, and Elude series (DESE), the army's elite testing program for personnel especially selected and scheduled for positions within America's intelligence agencies and who may face the risk of being captured if they were assigned foreign service.

"You and Corporal Stockton were chosen by a federal agency to be recipients of this test," Col. Price said, "but your friend somehow overcame his guard and is somewhere out there on the run. We will find him and bring him back and the testing and training will continue until completed. If either of you try that again, we will forget we are all part of the same team." With that, Will was taken back to his hut to await Larry's capture and the next phase of their testing. He was relieved to know that he was not going to be killed by a terrorist group, but he also knew there was a lot left to endure; the course wasn't over, and it was evident Col. Price was going to make sure this ordeal was as realistic as possible. Their captures had gone to great lengths for realism even to the extent of speaking Spanish and to the physical abuse they were experiencing. Their purpose was to weed out the weaker individuals, and from those that survived, certain assumptions could be drawn to determine their fitness for the missions the government had in mind for them.

Larry was found the following day, brought back to the camp, and for two weeks, they were starved, tortured, and abused. They were beaten, hung by their wrists, and made as uncomfortable as possible. No bones broken, but they found out later their guards were authorized to break small bones if it would add reality to being a prisoner of war. And sleep deprivation continued day after day.

One morning, they were stripped of all clothing and made to stand in front of female cadre who pointed to and made fun of their genitals. To increase their stress and anxiety, Col. Price showed up one day with their personnel records and informed them that their next of kin had been notified they had been killed in the line of duty. This didn't bother Will because he had very little family left anyway, but it did bother Larry when they gave him proof that his family had, in fact, been notified. Knowing the kind of soldier he was, Larry knew his loved ones would believe the military.

After a while, Will and Larry lost count of days, but sometime into the second week, it all came to an end as abruptly as it started when a group of high level government officials flew in by helicopter, congratulated them for having survived the course without coming apart, and informed them that they had been accepted into foreign service with an intelligence agency later to be named. One of the men they were introduced to was Cecil Tighe. From that day forward, Cecil became their up man at the CIA.

For certain assignments, trained operatives remain outside the purview of Langley and other intelligence stations remaining autonomous to the agency population tied only to the up man for guidance, control, and command. It is from this contact person that operatives like Will and Larry get their orders, instructions, and support.

A month later, after they had recovered their weight and strength, they were assigned missions in a number of countries starting with Africa, Central America, and the Middle East. Their assignments were for the purpose of training foreign nationals in airborne tactics and Special Forces techniques. On occasion, their assignments varied from guarding dignitaries, diplomats, and their dependents to surveillance and courier work.

It became apparent, however, that they were being groomed for Southeast Asia when they were sent to language school to learn Vietnamese. Will was excited about the prospect of joining in the fracas in Vietnam. After all, this is what the last four years of training had been all about. It seemed a long time ago, those years of preparation, those years of deployment. But now, it was all over; he was going home, unless they got shot out of the sky.

Intelligence from Airborne Command patched through from high altitude reconnaissance aircraft had indicated a large force of Viet Cong heading in their direction. The enemy had suffered heavy losses because of SF 22, so it was time for them to go. Air support they were normally provided was occupied in other sectors, so it made no sense for the team to stay even another day. Charley was out there waiting for any indication that they were vulnerable. Results from his probing actions would quickly be relayed back to their commanders, and it wouldn't take long for them to find out they were missing aerial support and begin monopolizing on that vulnerability. The problem was that in this last day, this last moment, Will found himself wanting to stay. Trying to analyzing it, he realized that he hadn't exacted the toll on Charlie that he deserved. Too many innocent people had died at the hands of the VC, and some of them because of their relationship with him.

It was amazing how his thinking had changed. When Will first came to Vietnam, it was repulsive to kill a human being, and it caused him considerable shame and guilt. But that was before he had witnessed all the pain and suffering dealt out by his adversary. He felt differently about it now. He realized that the shame and guilt he was feeling was brought about because he didn't believe he was doing enough. Revenge had taken on a heightened urgency, a sinister prospective, and not just an eye for an eye, but even beyond a pound of flesh. And therein lay Will's problem.

On the other hand, as distorted as Will's thinking was, he wasn't crazy enough to believe he could kill them all. He also knew it was primordial to live like he had been living the past year, going through the hardships and constant threat of death. But he was out here doing what he did best, kill VC. He was mindful, however, of others he had known that had been out here too long, killing the enemy until they thought they were invincible, a very dangerous mind-set that could get a warrior killed.

The SF 22 unit Will and Larry had been attached to was extremely unique. The team had been chosen by the CIA from the Army's 82nd Airborne and from Special Forces units. Most of them had trained as rangers in jungle warfare, airborne tactics, and in several Southeast Asian languages. Some of them including Will and Larry had been psychologically trained, more commonly known as brainwashing, or perhaps the better word is brainwashed, to have no fear. Of course, Will knew the term "no fear" is relative. He knew that you always have an occasional twitch of concern, but having no fear to the extent of believing you were invincible is scary as hell, which within itself is an oxymoron.

For Will and Larry, their training stopped just short of invincibility, that special mind-set that starts to develop later after a long period of close encounters where the enemy loses.

Interrupting supply lanes, destroying bridges, sitting up ambushes, striking with small five- to fourteen-man fire teams, hitting the enemy while he slept and whatever the hell else they could do to bring havoc to the VC had been the order of the day for Special Forces Group 22 since they had sat up the camp.

Whenever Will looked back and contemplated his tours of battlefield service, he found it disturbing to realize that his sole purpose in life the past few years had been to eliminate VC and NVA. He had no other purpose. Considering this, he knew that out here on the edge, it takes strength to defend your position or to take theirs. And more than physical strength, it takes mental strength because in the process, you find yourself doing ungodly acts of brutality far beyond what you thought you were capable of. On the other hand, a soldier still has to be human, lest he loose all sense of reality or decency. Was he there yet? Had he lost his humanity?

The sense of reality came to an apex the night Will's unit was overrun during a rainstorm at Camp 222. More than a dozen times, their fortification had been attacked from the same direction and never from the south. Although the camp was fortified against attack from any bearing, they expected it to come from the same direction it always had. However, it came from the south this time, and it caught everyone by surprise. Ever since the Tet Offensive had begun, everything was more chaotic, unsure, and in this case, surprising. As a result, a number of their comrades paid the ultimate price that night. It was an expensive lesson prompting SF 22 to throw the rules to the wind. The firefight was so intense, so swift, Will's team used every weapon available. Grenade launchers, pistol fire, 50-caliber machine guns, M-16s, even Bouncing Betties—those crazy mines that detonate in the air to increase casualties were part of the ordinance, so dangerous as they could take out their own team members. But it was that kind of an attack. Had it lasted longer they might have even called in an airstrike on top of themselves, but it ended before that became necessary.

But now, Will was going home. Looking down at the camp, he wondered how long it would take the VC to set this place ablaze, this patch of clay mud and debris carved out of the steamy jungle that had been his home off and on for the last year. Well, Charlie could have it now, Will thought, because he was out of there. No more rice and snails and no more nervous nights of one- eyed sleep. No more leeches sucking his blood in private places. Soon, he would be sleeping in a safe place, in a comfortable bed, in an air-conditioned room, where he'd be praying that he would have no more visions of the massacred people of Doc Tran.

Glancing around the chopper, Will observed his closest friend Larry Stockton peering out the other door at the ground below. Originally from Kansas City, he reminded people of a gunfighter out of the old west, his sidearm slung low, his swagger as he walked. Traveling with Will to Phnom Penh, Cambodia, and as far as Bangkok, Thailand, he would make connections to Hawaii for a little R&R. Knowing Larry, he would be returning to Saigon long before his leave was over because it would put him close to the war zone, the only place he was at peace.

Assessing the situation, the theatre of war and their mission had shifted recently. Terrorizing the enemy and destroying their supply chain was no longer so important. With the pace slowing down, *Intelligence* had other activities in mind for this Special Op's team. Regardless, their mission was over. Will needed to get away from the theatre of war, to think things through, and to get a hold on reality again…if that was possible.

It was before they abandoned Camp 222 that the condition of Will's mental status became of concern to Larry brought about by his obvious delight anytime they scored large on Charlie. Without telling Will, he radioed a friend of theirs, Pastor John Rowe, to let him know they were leaving Vietnam, asking him to pay them a visit before they left the camp. John was a missionary who had come to South Vietnam long before the war began to manage a Christian aid station and mission within the sector SF22 patrolled.

Knowing all the humanitarian things John was doing for their people, the Viet Cong had chosen to permit him to stay, but he knew that could change at any time. There had been several anxious moments when the VC stormed through the mission grounds unexpectedly, roughing up John and the nurses. But regardless of their warnings, he chose to stay on. He had become very close to the poor peasant farmers who had come to rely so heavily on his medicine and upon his God. It was the same closeness Will's team had for the people at Doc Tran before the massacre.

When John stepped out of the Cobra ship as it landed at Camp 222, it caught Will by surprise. They hadn't seen John since the day he came to help bury the massacred villagers of Doc Tran mainly because it was too dangerous. He also observed several more bullet holes in John's aircraft that weren't there before.

It didn't take long for Will to realize why he had come. "We need to talk, Will," John said, taking him by the arm and walking him outside the hearing distance of the other troopers.

"Larry tells me you've been making some weird statements of late. Something about having second thoughts about going home, is that correct?" Will had to smile at that remark until it dawned on him how ridiculous that might sound to an outsider considering the stepped-up activity by the enemy the past month. When Will didn't answer him, he immediately probed a little deeper. "What's your thoughts about the job you've been doing out here? Do you feel you've done all you could do, or do you think you should have done more?" "If you are asking me did I think I should have killed more gooks than I did, the answer is maybe. If you think that I have a need to kill more, the answer is no." Will knew his questions originated from the psychiatric training John had gone through before he became a missionary, trying to determine if he had a screw loose. He lied when he said no and suspected the pastor recognized that he had. But Will also knew that because of the atrocities he had seen committed by the VC, John wouldn't have blamed Will one bit if he wanted to kill a few more.

Convinced that Will wouldn't take out a shopping center full of people when he returned to America, he bid them farewell to fly back to the aid station where he had committed his life to helping the poor. As he waved good-bye, Will was prompted by some internal spirit to say a prayer for John and the dedicated people at the mission, with the feeling that God had put him on hold for some time, but he just might take this prayer since it was for one of his own.

As Will continued to watch Tom Vo keeping a careful watch out the door behind him, his 30-caliber at the ready, he wondered what was on Tom's mind, knowing that he would be reassigned to another one of the CIA's elite Special Reaction Units and returning to the battlefield. There would be no vacation for Tom. He had been fighting this war long before the Americans got here, and he would be fighting it till it ended, if he lived that long.

Looking down at the endless rice patties separated only by an occasional strip of jungle, Will reached into his shirt pocket for the envelope with the announcement of his class reunion. He'd been carrying it with him ever since it arrived two months before. The event was to be held in his hometown at the Sikeston Country Club in July, the very same week that he was scheduled to arrive home. It was a strange feeling to be an active participant in a war and, in the same moment, contemplating attending a party back home at a country club scheduled for that same week. There seemed to be something bizarre with that picture, he thought to himself.

Thinking of the upcoming reunion, the first person he thought about was Mary Ann Muldune. Would she be there? Had she changed? How would she receive him, the guy that made promises but didn't bother to write for all those years? It occurred to him that she might have gotten married. Why not? After all, she was the most desired girl in his class. But whatever relationship they had, it had been broken by Will's failure to respond to the many letters she had written over the years. Closing the door on the girl of his dreams had been difficult, but when he took the oath of the agency, he knew he would never be able to tell her where he was or what he was doing, nor would she be able to communicate with him even by mail. In order for Will to do his job, follow the code of silence, and keep his sanity, he had to put her out of his mind. But now her image was reawakened.

The first time Will saw Mary Ann she was sunning on a lounge in her front yard. She had just moved into town and was living a few blocks away from Will's house. Riding his bicycle on his way to the public swimming pool where he worked as a lifeguard, he spotted this gorgeous Amazon. From that very first day, he knew she was the one for him. Now, he found himself praying that she would be at the reunion and still be single.

Images of other reunions began to emerge, like the time he and his classmates destroyed a local sports bar that started a party that didn't end until Will returned to Vietnam. Up until the day he left, he expected the local gendarmes to knock on his door at any moment. Because of these images, he was certain that like before, all of those classmates that had played such a prominent role in his life would be there. For them, there was no reason to be anywhere else.

Will knew that it was definitely time for him to leave this part of the world. His memories of Vietnam were not fond ones, and he felt he had lost his sense of purpose since the fall of Doc Tran. This land that he once thought beautiful had taken on an ominous, menacing appearance and sleep became increasingly interrupted by foreboding nightmares too terrifying for him to recall. Man's inhumanity to man had found its zenith here, and he had been a participant. His hands were unclean…he knew he had baggage that he might never get rid of.

In addition, Will also found himself thinking more frequently about all of his comrades he had sent home in body bags, close friends that were willing to die for each other and some who did. On the night they were overrun, they lost sixteen paratroopers out of sixty-five, four rangers, and an observer from the agency. They filled a helicopter floor to ceiling with bodies; the smell of rotting flesh was overwhelming. This was the worst thrashing they ever experienced, yet it seemed to increase his resolve to punish the enemy even more.

For Will, it was time to go, to think of things other than killing and death. The question he kept asking himself was could he? There seemed to be no clear-cut answer, only images racing through his head during those moments he felt the most relaxed and perhaps the most vulnerable. The images he saw spoke to him, but in visions rather than words. Dozing off, he began to imagine what it would be like to be a normal guy, but it was difficult. Each thought of the future brought a nightmarish vision from the past. Finding the villagers of Doc Tran massacred and the innocent children like Mei Rai butchered so violently impacted his psyche beyond sanity.

There had been times when his dreams were so disturbing that he dreaded falling asleep, so he stayed awake as long as he could. Visions in the back of his mind came twisted and convoluted, and even now as he dozed off, there they were:

> Viet Cong running from him through the brush…a little brick rambler on a cul-de-sac, with a driveway leading to a double car garage.

> A grenade dropped down a tunnel and the enemy scurrying for their lives…a wife greeting him at the door after a hard day at the office.

> Mei Rai begging Will not to leave her and her family unguarded at Doc Tran…Will's "yet to be conceived" children running to him with outstretched hands.

The children of Doc Tran squealing with joy each time he returned…the smell of supper prepared for him as head of the household.

A napalm air strike and the smell of burning flesh…a glass of wine just before dinner.

The feeling of numbness after killing the last Doc Tran perpetrator…a feeling of peace.

Utter destruction…harmony. Reality…patriotism.

Will wakened with a start, not knowing that he had fallen asleep. As he oriented himself, he became disturbed and troubled because he believed that his dreams might be a reflection of an inner perversion, a mental torment as if he had slipped away into some deep dark pit from which there was no return. It was the dungeon of hatred, and if he had ever been frightened before by what he had become, he certainly was now, brainwashing or not. There it was in all its ugliness and horror and it wasn't going to go away.

Something had to change, he knew that. He could not go on thinking the way he had in the field, experiencing pleasure from his ungodly deeds and having no remorse for his actions. It could cause him to go beyond caution to fulfill those desires.

Perhaps returning to the place of his birth, he reasoned, to that other world he once called home, where people were civilized, where every day was a normal day, that even he might find peace. That was his prayer.

To keep a grip on reality, Will tried to picture himself doing simple things his friends at home would be doing, the day-to- day stuff, and some of the pleasurable routines, like spending weekends at the lake fishing or entertaining friends. Maybe, just maybe, he could be a normal person again. Why not? Isn't it possible, he asked himself, that his life could become normal again, that every evening after work he'd go home to a hot bath and a good night's rest and be able to sleep through the entire night without worrying about a possible overrun of his position or a night of mortar attacks?

Other questions came to mind. Would he again feel comfortable in his church where he had been a member since he was old enough to walk, and would he be able to face those good people without fearing they could read in his eyes the ghastly atrocities he had participated in and even orchestrated?

The reality was that he hadn't slept in a bed, had a hot bath, or ate a home-cooked meal in longer than he could remember because he'd been in the field without a break for over six months. Daily sustenance was primarily from C rations with an occasional can of fruit and a K bar. Showering required the use of that same fruit can hung overhead with holes in the bottom followed by unceasing sweat and misery. He had been sleeping so lightly that a change in the decimal level of the crickets would bring him to full alert because out here, Will knew you can never relax. He also knew that other than his closest comrades, no one really gave a damn.

As the reality of heading home to the United States sank in, he began to think more clearly about the town where he had spent the first twenty-two years of his life, Sikeston, a farming community in Southeast Missouri. Most of Will's buddies were still there, probably living the same way they were when he left. He remembered their faces always laughing, joking, and enjoying life. They had a philosophy, "Every day was a holiday, every night a party." Some of them hadn't gone anywhere farther than St. Louis or Memphis. There was no reason to; it was all there. Their futures were secure because their parents owned the local Ford dealership, perhaps the bank, a service station, a steel factory, a funeral home, or maybe one of the massive plantations on the outskirts of town.

Of course, there were those who were more international, who traveled to the islands or the ski slopes of the Rockies or the beaches in South America because their parents had given them credit cards with unlimited reserves. But for the most part, it was all happening for them in their world, Southeast Missouri. Where do kings and queens go? They stay close to the castle. There is no security like the walls of the kingdom.

Will was pretty certain David Bailey would be there, his buddy from across the street. Davie, as he was called, had been drafted in the army but had never been a real soldier because he played football most of the time. That experience was a good tune-up for the four years he played at Missouri University that earned him a business degree. Upon graduation, he returned to Sikeston, opened an insurance agency, and became a very successful businessman.

Will's good friend James Peter Malone, who friends called Petey, would surely be there too. Will and Petey had been friends since they were kids. Petey lived with his grandparents, the Bakers, and their grandmother was a very close friend with Will's. The Bakers lived on a five thousand acre farm on the edge of town called Burn Brae, a true plantation that had it all, including a southern style mansion with tall white pillars and a barn even bigger than the house. Will didn't consider it Tara from *Gone with the Wind,* but it was close.

Petey was in the very dangerous occupation of aerial crop dusting. With the accident rate in that profession as high as it was, no one thought he would last more than a year. The last time Will heard, Petey had exceeded 20,000 hours in the air in fifteen years, flying almost every day of his life. Then there would be Edward "Buddy" Malone, Will's hunting companion and mentor. Will had heard that he was working at Walmart, managing the sporting goods department, a perfect place for a guy that loved hunting and fishing.

In the past, one of the first things Will would do when he went home was to visit the graveyard with his grandmother. It wasn't something he looked forward to this time as there would be one more grave in the family plot and he would be going alone. The second thing he usually did was to go by the old homestead. Both had played too much a part of his life growing up not to pay them the respect of a visit. Will imagined the massive oak trees surrounding the house he grew up in, some dating back to pre-civil war times. With twelve rooms, it was an exceptionally large home for just him and his grandmother. Envisioning the immense dining room with the long table and chairs, twelve in all that were always filled during the holidays, he could almost smell the lavish holiday dinners prepared exquisitely by his grandmother and hear the joyful laughter somewhere in the back of his mind.

Other memories of his grandmother emerged. When Will was three years old, his grandmother took him to raise after his mother died because his stepmother felt he would always remind his father of his mother. He called his grandmother Mam, a mixture of Mother and Grandmother. Her early years had not been easy growing up on a farm along the Mississippi River miles from nowhere. She was a proud Christian lady who lived her life as an idealist, never faltering from a very strict code of ethics. The Bible was never far away, and when Will lived at home, he could usually find her on her knees in prayer. She loved Will like he was her son, and although they always seemed to be in conflict, he loved her like she was his mother.

Going home was starting to make Will apprehensive. He had only been there a few times in fifteen years, the last time when Mam died. He harbored a lot of guilt about not being there when she needed him. Will was all she had, but he thought trying to save the world was more important than sitting around Sikeston, Missouri, being a chauffeur, cook, housekeeper, or nurse catering to an old woman's needs. He wanted to see the world, go where the action was, and to be all he could be. But he found out he was wrong. He hadn't made the slightest difference in world affairs. In the meantime, she died lonely and disheartened by his seemingly coldhearted indifference.

Mam loved aprons and welcomed every opportunity to wear one. Will could still see her in a flowery apron sitting close to the TV, her small folding table loaded down with cups, glasses, knitting, newspapers, mail, pills…all close-at-hand conveniences for an elderly woman who had been hobbled by age. In the midst of all of this was a small rubber banded stack of letters from Will that she must have read over and over.

From the few letters that reached Will, he had learned about Mam's illness from her best friend who told him that she had cancer and that he should come home as soon as possible. Having been wrapped up in his work as an agency operative, he had taken very little time off in the last five years. But the summer before Mam died, he flew home vowing that this was one visit he would devote entirely to her.

Intentionally, Will hadn't told anyone he was coming because he knew his friends would do their best to toll him away. But he vowed it wouldn't happen this time.

She was sitting in her usual high-back swivel chair in an apron, with the TV blasting away. Even when her hearing aid was turned up, it was hard for her to hear every word from the tube. Although her eyesight was failing, she was still able to recognize Will's 6'5" frame silhouetted against the door, opened with the key he had carried all those years. "Oh my God! Oh my God! I can't believe it! Oh my God!" she said, arms outstretched as she stumbled to her feet to meet him in the middle of the room. She was completely surprised, and it was such an emotional moment that Will would always remember the warmth of that meeting.

She was all he had. He painfully had to ask himself, why had he been so oblivious of how important he was to her or she was too him?

In the past when he came home, he usually spent most of his time with friends who lived as though they were still in high school, totally unconcerned about the war that was taking thousands of our country's young lives every year. If he had stayed home, would he have become as apathetic as well? Perhaps that is why he'd spent so little time with her, so he could forget about Vietnam by raising hell with his buddies. All he knew was that on previous trips, most of his time had been spent riding around the local hangout, the Bulldog Inn, bragging to his buddies about all the places in the world he had been and all his exploits…at least the ones he could tell them about. "But for what?" he asked himself, realizing that he hadn't grown up much either, deluding himself into thinking that being a paratrooper, Green Beret, ranger, jungle survival trainer, a spy, or whatever the hell he was meant he was a mature man of the world. He now knew how foolish a man could be.

Remembering that last visit with Mam, he began to choke up on the thought that she would not be there this time or ever. Thank God he had spent that special time with her that last visit instead of carousing around with his buddies. At that moment, above the noise and wind from the rotors, Will asked himself that obvious question: how could he have been that heartless, that indifferent to the only person in this world that really mattered? With heartsick sorrow, his conscience answered the question.

Thinking about that last visit, Will realized that he and his grandmother hadn't really done anything special, at least it wasn't special to him. He drove her to the grocery store in her 1956 DeSoto Adventurer, and it gave her great joy. There are only three major grocery stores in Sikeston, and they visited them all. But all she bought was bread, some fatback bacon, a watermelon, and a six-pack of cream soda. Will recalled it vividly because this was the first time he began to realize that she wouldn't be with him much longer and how important this time was for the both of them.

As they usually did when he came home, they visited the graveyard where they pulled weeds and replaced the wreaths on each of the tombstones. But above all, it was the freedom of doing it with out being hurried or hassled that she appreciated. Later in the afternoon, they stopped on the edge of town and bought fruit, vegetables, a cantaloupe, and some fresh catfish so that she could fix her grandson a home-cooked meal. It may have been the thing that she loved to do the most, above anything else. As she bought from the roadside market that sits on the Sikeston ridge, he remembered staring down on an otherwise flat plain as he waited for her in the car and seeing the sand dunes off to the north where he used to search for arrowheads. Off to the east was the rodeo stadium and to the west the old barn and corral, the same one where he had boarded his horse Nevada, a good friend he would always remember.

Six months later, Will was called home for her funeral. As they lowered her in the grave next to his grandfather and his mother, the loneliness of knowing he was the last living member of the Malone/Brandon clan cast a dark and foreboding shadow over his spirit. At that moment at the gravesite, one of her friends took his arm and said, "She used to tell all of her friends that her grandson was out there fighting to make the world a safer place, she was so proud of you," innocently driving the nail of guilt even deeper into his soul.

Flying Home

Above the noise of the helicopter rotors, Larry Stockton, who was sitting between Tom and Will, shouted, "Think you'll miss Camp 222, Will?" facetiously, rolling his eyes. They had been like brothers, Will and Larry, the past few years, having been recruited by the nation's top intelligence agency. Larry had been recruited because of his pilot experience. He could fly everything the army could put into the air. Will qualified because of his jungle warfare and survival training experience. His superiors recognized that he was a little different because, unlike the majority of the troops, he liked living in the jungle, so they made him an instructor. When the camp took a break for siestas, Will would be out in the swamp, looking under rocks for something to eat. He was the only one that ever gained weight at the school.

Will always felt that Larry was far better adapted to the Southeast Asian war scene than he was. Originally from Kansas City, he joined the army when he was very young, became a paratrooper, and served his time. When he returned to Kansas City, he got into trouble with the mob, something to do with a nightclub where he worked as a bouncer. When Kansas City became too hot for him, he reenlisted and returned to the 82nd Airborne at Fort Bragg, where they required that he go through jump school again. After that, the military sent Larry to fixed wing flight school, and Will was assigned to jungle survival school in Panama. Six months later, Larry was sent to Panama where the two were reunited and were trained for assignments with the Defense Intelligence Agency and later to the CIA.

The agency sent Will and Larry on separate terrorist missions, but by an act of providence or God, they were reunited two years later when the CIA picked men for a special warfare intelligence team, with the acronym SWIT. The team was to be deployed in Vietnam, working hand in hand with the South Vietnamese Commandos and a contingent of Special Forces warriors under direction of the CIA. Most of those selected came from the 82nd Airborne or Special Forces and the agencies other curriculum, which included ranger training, at least one foreign language course, and the CIA's fear suppression program, the controversial psychological program that fostered the book and movie *The Manchurian Candidate*, albeit for another reason. In this case, the program was to train men to have no fear because the team's mission required asking soldiers to do what their better judgment told them not to do.

For Larry and Will, the agency's training was terminated just short of invincibility. The danger comes when a soldier starts to own indomitable after a long period of close encounters with the enemy, especially where the enemy loses.

One of Larry's greatest assets was his ability to get into the mind of the enemy, postulate what his next move would be, and be there ahead of him. He was strong and quick, especially for a guy 6 feet tall and 220 pounds. The harder conditions became, the better he thrived. Today, he was on his way to Hawaii, but Will suspected he got more pure enjoyment out of killing VC than relaxing on the beach. He enjoyed his work and, unlike Will, had no intention of permanently leaving South Vietnam. Two years earlier, he had been shot down and sustained damage to his inner ear, making it difficult for him to fly full time. Instead of going home, he harassed the big brass into reassigning him to a Special Forces unit, which was fortuitous because the agency was looking for a pilot to round out their Special Warfare Intelligence Team. His three Purple Hearts were not enough, he wanted five.

When Larry and Will traveled throughout South Vietnam, villagers thought they were Europeans because of their blond hair and blue eyes. Their military counterparts referred to them as the Vikings when they were together. Larry's liability was his willingness to respond at the slightest grievance. An example was the night a couple of Marines made a comment about their hair at the NCO club in Saigon. Will was willing to overlook it, let it slide. Larry was not. The camp emergency room became a little crowded that night. The only reason they didn't end up in the brig was their connection to the agency. So to some degree, they felt that they were above the law, at least while they were assigned to the unit under the agency's command.

The danger Will and Larry had shared made them come dependent on each other. But today, they would be saying good- bye, one of the few times since they took the oath. They had become a very effective team, a force to be reckoned with, at least that's what they liked to think. Saying good-bye saddened Will. He felt like one of his appendages was about to separate from his body. He wondered who would watch his back, but then he remembered, why would he need his back protected where he was going?

The din of the rotors made Will drowsy, and he closed his eyes as he thought about all the time he had spent with Larry. Contemplating their relationship reminded him of another close friend. Will's mind went back to his early childhood and he began to think of Davie again, the kid who lived across the street when he was growing up.

David's life, unlike Will's, was very normal. His father was an attorney, and his mother had graduated from Missouri University.

Both had PhDs from Purdue: his father's in law, his mother's in advanced education. Both of them were brilliant, his father was the chairman of the board of education, his mother head of the state Republican Party. From Will's point of view, Davie had inherited his parents' size, for he was always a big kid, but not his parents' brains. At least, Will thought that at the time because he could talk Davie into anything. His parents believed that the crazy things Davie did were his ideas, like smoking corn silks in the rafter hut they built in the garage, putting the cat in the freezer, or jumping off the second story roof of his house with an umbrella in each hand pretending to be a paratrooper. How ironic. Will thought about that the first time he went out of the 35-foot jump tower in jump school at Fort Bragg.

Their helicopter rolled heavily to one side as they flew through stiff turbulence, giving them occasional glimpses of the jungle passing quickly below. Between the low-lying clouds that drifted lazily across the landscape, Will could see the rain-drenched trees and lines of refugees escaping the advancing communist forces.

Once they crossed over the border into Cambodia, they no longer had to be concerned about taking fire from the hilltops, and their pilots began to descend. But Tom and the other members of Merciless

Vengeance (MV), the name they had given his fire team, had problems relaxing. They had been at it way too long.

It was still difficult for Will to believe that he was heading home after being away so many years or that he'd be saying good- bye to a friend that had been like a brother, a blood brother. But with a little luck, he thought, he'd soon be seeing his original blood brother, Davie. Will wondered if he had changed. Would they still be as close as they had been when they became blood brothers the Indian way?

As the turbulence subsided, he closed his eyes and thought about the life he shared with Davie. One exploit he remembered vividly. It was a particularly cool, early fall Saturday. Will and Davie had just been paid $2 for running cattle at the auction barn where they worked. This was a lot of money for two boys only eight and nine. They had gone to see a Western movie about a mountain man and his Indian friend. In those days, movies cost a dime, popcorn a dime, and coke a nickel. This left them enough money to run the eight blocks across town to see the other Western movie and to go again Sunday afternoon if they wanted. Sikeston was a small town.

In the first movie, a mountain man became blood brothers with his Indian friend by cutting their wrists and letting their blood intermingle. It seemed like a really neat thing to do so they decided to do the same. Unable to get their hands on a knife, they found a jagged piece of glass behind the garage, and there, being older, Will went first. After sawing away for several minutes, the glass finally broke the skin and a small faint trace of blood appeared on Will's wrist. Suddenly, he could hear the sound of Indian drums far off in the distance and the chant of a medicine man. He could feel the early fall winds as it whipped up dust and leaves, adding to the mystery of the moment. Will's imagination had no bounds in those days. Davie took one look at Will's one drop of blood, squealed, and ran for home. Obviously, he hadn't heard the drums or the old man's chant.

"Come back, you traitor," Will hollered, but Davie never looked back. This was the first indication to Will that maybe Davie wasn't as dumb as he had thought. In fact, maybe Will was the dumb one. The boys didn't speak for two days, but that was as long as either one of them could stand it.

Saturdays were always the same for Davie and Will. From a very young age, they worked doing various jobs at the cattle auction located in a huge barn on the edge of town about two miles from their homes. Of course, they never would have been hired as young as they were if it hadn't been for Davie's Uncle Bob who was one of the owners.

Each Saturday, the boys would ride their bikes to work past Slade's Pool Hall, located just a few blocks from the barn. Slade was an older man who used his pool hall for an illegal gambling front. It was located across the street from the Frisco railroad depot where Will's grandfather, Tom Malone, had been stationmaster for thirty years. Due to their mutual love of baseball, these two men had been very close until Will's grandfather passed away.

Minors were normally prohibited from entering pool halls, especially those establishments that served alcoholic beverages. However, Slade saw Will and Davie peering in the window one day, recognized Will as Tom Malone's grandson, and invited them in, which indicated temerity on his part. It was a lesser infraction of the law considering what went on the back room.

Slade loved to tell stories, and Will loved to listen, especially if they were about Will's grandfather who, as an avocation, managed a semi-pro baseball team. Will never knew his grandfather, as he passed away the year Will was born, but because of his friendship with Slade, Will spent a lot of time at the pool hall listening to the wonderful stories that made him proud to be the grandson of Michael Thomas Malone.

By the time Will was ten and Davie nine, they learned to be excellent pool shooters. Many of the characters who came into Slades, and there were some pretty shady ones, enjoyed teaching them tricks with cards, pool, and other games of chance. But no one dared to harm the boys in anyway; they knew they would have to deal with Slade. Will had seen him in action, so it was easy to understand why.

There was also another element that frequented Slade's: ladies of the night. Had Will's grandmother known what went on there, she would have barred him from ever going there again. But these women of ill repute were gracious and motherly to the boys.

One in particular, Elizabeth Beechum, was especially kind, loving, and protective. At that age, the boys had no understanding of the arrangements that took place between these women and their frequent guests. They could, however, sense the presence of immorality by the attitude the men took toward the ladies.

But Elizabeth B, as she was affectionately called by her friends, was different. She must have heard the story about Will's mother dying of pneumonia when he was three because she was always trying to mother him. It was a pleasure to have this beautiful woman pressing his face to her soft and warm breasts. Will had heard that she never had children, but he knew that if she had, she would have been a loving mother.

Will could see that Elizabeth B was different in other ways too. There was something classy about her. She seemed to be well educated and did not use the language commonly spoken by the other women. But there was talk that she was the county hi-sheriff's private property.

His name was Lonnie Maxwell, and according to his reputation, he was not someone to cross. Will's father knew him well; they had played football against each other. He had heard his father say that Lonnie was on the take and abused his position as sheriff by shaking down people like Slade. As it happened, Will was there the day Lonnie stormed into Slade's and slapped one of the girls around for holding back on him. When Elizabeth stepped in, he picked up a spittoon and slugged her in the head with it, sending her to the floor unconscious.

This is where they got to see Slade go into action. With the speed of a samurai warrior, Slade swung a pool stick across the side of Maxwell's head. First on his right, and then on his left, leaving Lonnie out like a lightbulb but still on his feet. Finally, he wilted into a pile of humanity, and for about fifteen minutes, the people just left him there on the floor, stepping over him on the way in and out of Slade's. He was not well liked.

When Elizabeth came to, Will was the first thing she saw. Smiling at him with a little grimace of pain, she pulled him close and said, "If you were as big as your daddy, you would have helped me, wouldn't you, darlin?" Will wondered how she knew his father or that he was big?

Slade's provided a unique education for Davie and Will. They were the only kids in town who were proficient at pool, trained at hiding the pea in the shell game, knew how to pad roll and palm dice, and cheat at cards. These all important skills to get one through life.

Occasionally, Will would see his friend Edward Malone's father passing through on his way to the back room. It was no secret that he was a professional gambler; everyone in town knew it. Edward would also join Will and Davie early on Saturday mornings to play pool before the auction would start. His house was just a short distance away on a farm owned by W. R. Lewis, whose son Billy was also a close friend of Will. Many times, they would go to Edward's house after the auction ended to enjoy his mother's cooking and admire his father's gun collection.

Their first job at the auction was to run sale tickets from the weight scales to the front office. Later, as the boys grew older, they herded cattle from the back feed lots to the auction ring, first on foot and later on horseback. Many of the horses and cattle had been brought in from the open range. Most of them had never been in a barn and were never very cooperative.

The older boys that hung around the barn taught Will and Davie how to make whips from old rope or hemp. They became experts at plucking flies off the rumps of cows, and the cracking noise of the whip was usually enough to frighten off aggressive bulls or stallions, but not always.

Pen 55 had been built to hold the most dangerous and destructive animals brought in from the range. Seldom did the boys draw that number because the manager knew they might run into more trouble than they could handle. However, on this particular Saturday, the two of them inadvertently drew pen number 55.

It was an especially muggy morning and the stench of cattle manure hung heavy in the alleys. Steam rose up from the freshly dropped dung, giving the covered runways a surrealistic effect. The swarms of large green flies that buzzed around fresh droppings would harass the animals as well as those who worked around them. To counteract the flies, management would bring in a tractor trailer load of sawdust and spread it generously in the alleys and pens, making it difficult to walk without having it spill into their shoes. The sawdust was supposed to absorb the manure, but occasionally, it rolled into their shoes anyway.

Since it was the policy of the Auction Company to keep difficult to control animals in pen 55, they decided it best to go into the enclosure together. Davie ran ahead to the gate, avoiding the large piles of cow and horse dung as he skipped from side to side, sawdust flying here and there. Swinging the gate open wide, he walked into the pen and came face to face with a nasty Black Angus bull standing defiantly just a few feet away. He was big and he was mean, and they were about to find out just how mean. Davie immediately bolted for the fence, but it was too late.

As he jumped, the big Black charged, catching him by the seat of the pants and wiping his body down the side of the fence. Will ran into the open gate and, as soon as he was close enough, lashed out with his whip he was dragging behind him. With a snort, the bull turned and headed Will's way. He jumped to the fence but only managed to climb halfway up as the black beast flashed by at full speed, swinging his horns to the side and upward. One of them slashed through Will's jeans, cutting his rump and sending him over the top rail into the next lot.

Climbing back over the fence, Will saw the bull turn toward him again. He charged, but he was only partially interested in Will…it was Davie he wanted. Davie was laying still, hoping the bull would ignore him, his mangled body curled up on the edge of the lot near a light pole. Will went for the fence, but this time, he dropped back into the lot, striking out with his whip as the black went past. The whip, cutting as it went, wrapped around the side of his rear and circled his testicles and the snapper on the end of the whip struck against his most tender organ with a loud crack that brought a bellow from the bull, sending him sliding to his knees in the dirt and filth of pen 55.

Running to Davie, Will helped him sit up, blood beginning to flow from his nose. With a dazed expression on his face, he looked at Will and whispered, "Help me, Will. Is he coming back? Get me out of here." As they walked by the black beast, his tongue was hanging out and he was breathing laboriously, steam lifting up from his nostrils. It was hard for Will to believe that one swing of his homemade whip had brought this black devil down. Leaving pen 55, Will became nauseous, not knowing if it was from the fear of the black bull or the sight of the injury his homemade whip had inflicted.

As they walked Davie back to the infirmary, Will remembered the story of David felling Goliath, and he wondered if David might have had that same sick revulsion when he looked down at the giant Philistine. Within a few hours, the black beast was back on his feet, but it would be some time before he would become amorous with the ladies again.

Here, several hundred feet above the Cambodian jungle in a military aircraft, Will thought back on that day and the infirmary at the auction barn and the older country women on staff that cleaned Davie up, dressing his cuts and bruises. How he reveled in the attention he was getting and was unaware of how fortunate he was there were no broken bones or worse. Will couldn't help but think that of all those wonderful ladies who were so kind and motherly to them back then would probably be gone now as time marches on.

Both ships were flying closer together now as they continued on over the rice fields and jungles of Cambodia. The rain had stopped and the sun began to dissipate the clouds, giving a clear view of villages here and there along their route. The roads were full of people as they went about their lives. Some were running from the terror of war and others were oblivious of the fighting taking place next door in Vietnam. Looking around the aircraft, Will noticed most of the men, particularly their Vietnamese counterparts, were smoking. He and Larry had never picked up that nasty habit possibly because they wanted every edge they could have. On the other hand, maybe that's why they were always so hyper while their MV friends often seemed calm, even in the face of extreme prejudice.

From that mental picture, Will contemplated the change his emotions had undergone since he had come to Southeast Asia. No longer was he squeamish about bringing pain or death to the enemy. No, on the contrary, how would this affect his life as a civilian? Would it show? Would people see it in his face? Was there a mental sickness lurking in his psyche, an unholy exigency needing to be satisfied?

In late afternoon, they arrived in Phonon Penn. They cleared the ammunition from their M-16s and handed them over with full magazines and grenades to their helicopter crew. Saying their farewells, all of their comrades from Merciless Vengeance loaded a troop carrier bound for Saigon. In their business, there was always the possibility that they might be seeing their friends for the last time. Will and Larry had tickets waiting for them at the carrier's ticket counter, and within an hour, they were aboard a shuttle flight to Bangkok.

The next flight reminded Will of an old movie taken in Central America where local natives boarded their plane with chickens and pigs. Like the movie, they clucked and oinked the entire trip, making sleeping on this flight near impossible. An old one-eyed gentleman peasant farmer kept eyeballing Will with his one good eye, unnerving him a bit. There had been no screening before this flight and he wondered what atrocity this old fella might want to set right.

The chicken noise and smell also reminded Will of another chicken experience. As he was growing up, his grandmother kept chickens. Why, he never knew. It was such a nasty, smelly arrangement, especially when it was cheaper in those days to buy eggs at the store. Maybe it was a carryover from her days of being raised on a farm.

Although Will still owned the family farm he had inherited from his grandmother, he had never lived there; they had lived in town. They were "city farmers," his grandmother used to say.

Frank Sewell, his grandmother's father, was first generation German and an industrious farmer with the ability to transform river swamps and backwaters into productive farmland. Mam and her Irish mother lived right on the edge of Old Man River and could watch riverboats passing from their front porch.

From the time Will was very young, he had heard the infamous stories about his great-grandfather, Frank Sewell. His exploits included stories about how he had worked year after year raising horses, cattle, cotton, and corn and when the riverboats would arrive in late October, load everything aboard, and embark downriver to New Orleans, they assumed. Months later, when he had run out of money, he would return to start the whole process over again. It appears that Will's great-grandfather was a gambler and a sporting man. His adventures were not the stuff of conversations heard around the dinner table in a Christian home like Will's. The rouges that hung out at Slade's knew the legends, however, and retold the stories with reverence, admiring the escapades of Frank Sewell and a lifestyle they could only dream about.

As immoral as he must have been, Will found him to be a fascinating character with none his equal. To have survived on the river during the late 1800s and early 1900s was no small feat. Even soldiers returning home from the great Civil War were not safe traveling along the river. Murderers, criminals, fugitives, and ex-cons controlled large sections of the river and preyed on unsuspecting travelers. Many times, travelers would disappear somewhere along the river only to be found with their throats cut or a bullet in their head. It would have been essential for travelers to have a close relationship with riverboat captains to assure their safety or have their own private bodyguards.

One can only imagine the attractions aboard the river gamblers, especially for a man who had never seen more than his wife's petticoat. The loose, young, perfumed ladies, plentiful whiskey, music, gambling, and excitement were enough to draw Frank Sewell back to the river year after year.

But Will suspected Frank Sewell was more complex than he was given credit. At one point, he owned 5,000 acres that he had cleared of the richest river bottomland in the Midwest. But there came a time when he chose to split it with a local widow who was in a family way to avoid a scandal that would have brought dishonor to his wife and the Sewell family. This was the traditional way to handle this kind of problem as it must have occurred often in those days. It was in that disgrace that Frank disappeared, and for twenty-two years, no one in Will's family knew where he was. But Mam never gave up looking for him, half expecting him to walk in the door at any moment. In all that time, she never heard a word from him.

When her mother died, she desperately began to search for her father. It wasn't until she hired a private detective was he found, living only fifty miles away and farming a tract of land he had drained and cleared just like before. He had remarried, this time to an Apache Indian, and together, they had raised two sons who grew up and went away to college in California.

As straitlaced as Will's grandmother was, she was willing to overlook her father's disgrace and the fact that he had deserted her mother, remarried without obtaining a divorce, and had abandoned them for all those years. It was even more astonishing that because he was approaching ninety, she convinced him and his wife to sell their farm and to come live in the apartment she had on the side of the house. Welcoming her father with open arms, she accepted his wife as one of the family. Will knew her as Dough Dough, and for many years, she was like a nanny to him. The thought of chickens triggered pictures of his grandmother's chicken coop. It was always a mess out there, and the neighbors complained about the noise and the smell. But Mam never gave in until she became too old to take care of them. So that responsibility fell on Will. It was his job to feed them and bring in the eggs every morning. This meant running the gauntlet of rats that infested the wooden walkway leading to the chicken house. Because Will was very young, the rats knew how scared he was and would run out of their burrows, making noises to frighten him. They succeeded.

Later, as he grew older, he found a way to get even with those monstrous little devils. Lying on the roof of the chicken house, he would wait for the nasty rodents to stick their heads out to grab the bait he had set for them. First, they would test for danger, darting in and out until they were certain it was safe. With a spear Will had made with a hunting knife tied to a broom handle, he would try to pin them to the wooden walkway. It required that he time his downward thrust just right, and sometimes, he missed. But many times, he didn't.

That thought reminded Will to reach down to feel the survival knife he kept strapped to his ankle. It had been a source of comfort to him for many years now, hardly the same knife he used on those pests, but certainly a more efficient weapon that cut both going and coming. Like most survival knives, the top of the handle had a screw-off cap that was a compass, and in the hollow handle were fishhooks, line, matches, and a small tube of antibiotic. Some Delta Force fanatic once told Will they had cyanide pills in their knife—just in case. Of these items, only the compass had proven useful to him thus far. The blade on the other hand was a different matter; it was made from the highest quality Spanish steel. Will tried not to think about its deadly past, but those thoughts came anyway. It had not been easy to forget those flashes of light that reflected off his knife that signaled another life coming to an end.

It was a dark period of his life in more ways than one. For several months, Will's team lived almost exclusively in the dark. He contemplated those months of darkness where they seldom saw the fully risen sun because they were out all night whacking Charley while he slept. Their assignment had been to interrupt the enemy's supply lines by destroying bridges, setting up ambushes, and hitting the enemy where it hurt him the most, and whatever the hell else they could do to rain havoc on good old Charley.

So standing orders were altered a bit, taking the command, "Unless otherwise directed" to a new level. Operating near the Cambodian border, he and Larry came up with a new way to strike fear on the

Khmer Rouge. It was a form of role reversal. The enemy had been booby-trapping American dead and their weapons along many of their most heavily traveled pathways through the jungle. A lot of young American troopers had been killed or wounded by these clever traps. Now the enemy was getting a taste of their own medicine.

So Will and his comrades turned the trick on the VC by doing the same thing to them, only in areas far removed from where they expected GIs to be. Moreover, the team expanded their methods of terrorism by brazen acts that they knew would catch the enemy's attention. On several occasions, using night vision goggles provided by their agency contact, Cecil Tighe, they were able to quietly enter the enemy's camp and discover the entire compound sound asleep.

Larry came up with the idea to leave evidence that they had been there, but to let them live. They would leave small mementos such as a G.I. handkerchief, for example, or something more exotic like an ear or an empty C ration can. Larry claimed there was power when the enemy realizes that American Special Forces team could go and come anytime they pleased with impunity and could have killed them anytime they choose, a harrowing thought for the black pajama boys just before they go to sleep.

Every time memories like these came creeping back into Will's head, he would wonder what his dear friends at the class reunion would think of him if they knew about those late night forays of death into the enemy's sleeping camp, the confirmed kill tally, or the horror Will created with his cherished friend, the Spanish stiletto.

To keep a firm grip on reality for fear of going over the edge, Will knew he had to concentrate on more pleasant memories. For some unknown reason, the old chicken house roof kept coming back. It had been the scene of many other great adventures. There were just enough tree limbs hanging down over the roof to provide a great hiding place. From his lofty perch, he would launch raids against the neighbor's fruit trees or pretend that he was Tarzan or a pirate boarding a doomed ship as he swung down from one limb to another.

This haven also provided rations for Will and his buccaneer companions. It was a pecan tree and was always loaded in the fall with the tastiest pecans he had ever eaten. It also offered a great view of his neighbor's bedroom, which but for the grace of God could have given

Will a twisted mind on the sexual relationship between a man and a woman. He watched them playing a strange kind of game reminiscent of a circus act, with trapeze and costumes, or an animal trainer's act, with whips and chains. It was a lewd and obscene game bordering on hilarity.

The chicken house roof and the pecan tree were not his only perch as a boy. The mulberry tree between the sidewalk and the street provided another great hiding place. It grew next to a light pole from which a street light hung, with a shade that darkened the limbs of his hiding place above.

At night, Will and Davie found it great fun to play bombardier with eggs stolen from the chicken house. Will's imagination had no bounds. Pretending they were flying a B-17 over Germany, they would drop their payload of eggs on the unsuspecting motorist Krauts passing in their cars below. Many times, drivers would stop their cars, get out, and look around, but the light shining down was so intense that they couldn't see into the black void above. That was until Mr. Schell from down the street came by in his pickup truck and caught a couple of eggs on his windshield. Ironically, he was German and spoke with a heavy accent. He had left his country a few years before the war, but Will always thought that Mr. Schell would certainly have made a great Gestapo officer for the Third Reich. The truth was that nobody really liked Mr. Schell. Whenever there was a controversial issue in Sikeston, he would be in the middle of it and usually on the wrong side.

Screeching to a halt, he backed up, turned on his side- mounted spotlight, and trained it on the two monkeys in the tree. "Okay, Will Malone," he said, "you and little Davie come down here now." *Little Davie*, Will thought to himself, *for gosh sakes, I'm only a year older than him*. Mr. Schell had called Will Malone because he lived with his grandmother and, like so many other people, assumed Will's name was the same as hers.

Up to the front door of Will's house they went. As he banged on the door, Mam opened it, saying, "Yes, Mr. Schell, what's happened?" "Your boy and Davie here splattered da eggs on my new truck. I tank you ought to punish dese boys properly. After all, I could have had an accident cause I couldn't see out of der vindshield." He went on and on, and Will could see that Mam was getting a little perturbed, listening to him tell her what she should do with her grandson.

Finally, she interrupted him, saying, "Mr. Schell, if these kids have broken anything on your truck, I'll pay for it. If not, I think you've said enough. These kids were just having a good time. They are not criminals. Good evening, sir. Davie, you go on home now, and, William, you come in this minute." Will knew he was in trouble and would get punished, but Mr. Schell had done him a favor. She was now more upset with him than with Will. "I never really liked that Mr. Schell," she mumbled, as she turned off the porch light. She was a hard taskmaster, but was not about to be told how to discipline her grandson. Not by the Gestapo anyway. Will and Larry had a two-day layover before they could get reservations out of Bangkok, so Larry called a pilot friend of his, John Cavanaugh. John had an apartment overlooking the bay area and invited the two of them to stay as long as they wished. So they kicked back and tried to relax, something they had not done in over a year. And for the first time in many months, Will came face-to-face with a stranger looking back at him from John's bathroom mirror. He hardly recognized himself. Not only had he aged, there was a sinister look in that face. A look of pain or was it evil that reflected back at him? Whatever it was, it was not a happy face, and during their stay with John, he caught himself going back to that mirror several times a day just to see if that face had changed. It had not.

It was enjoyable for Will to see Larry let his hair down a bit and hear him rehash funny war stories with John. They had both been spotter plane pilots assigned to the same unit in Vietnam before Larry was reunited with Will, and they began to reminisce about their exploits. Both of them had been shot down and in Larry's case, three times.

As required by the US arrangements with South Vietnam, one of their people had to be along on all spotter plane combat flights as advisers. However, a number of American pilots that had been shot down were found with bullet holes in the back of their heads, and the advisors were missing. This caused great concern among our airmen. The first thing Larry would do when they saw they were going down was to disarm the guy in the backseat. If they managed to land safely, the adviser was sent on his way and a helicopter would pick up the pilot.

It remains a mystery how many times the advisor would beat our boys back to their base.

But the best story they told that day was when Larry had been taking ground fire each time he flew over this one sector, so he talked ordnance into letting him take a box of grenades on his next reconnaissance mission. Then when he would receive fire from a defined area, he would fly off, making the enemy believe he had left for good. Moments later, he would come flying in at treetop level, catching the VC out in the open scrambling for cover and their rifles. Pulling pins from grenades, he would toss them left and right, raining havoc down on the enemy. By the time they could train their weapons on his plane, he had disappeared over and behind the trees.

On one occasion, as he was dropping grenades as fast as he could pull their pins, he heard something heavy hit the floor of his aircraft. Thinking it was a live grenade that had been dropped inadvertently in the floorboard by the spotter in the rear, he instinctively pulled the stick straight back, putting the plane in an almost vertical position. When asked why he executed that maneuver, he said, "So the grenade would roll to the back of the plane." Will and John roared with laughter when they heard that. They laughed because they knew that the explosion might not have killed him, but the crash caused by stalling the plane and blowing the tail off certainly would have. As it turned out, the thud that he had heard was the spotter dropping his army .45 and that maneuver ended his ambition to be a bomber pilot.

THE FIRE

As a lightning storm passed over and the rain subsided, Will contemplated going home again as he watched the water droplets slide off the leaves of the banana tree just outside the window. John's apartment reminded Will of the apartment on the side of his grandmother's house, the one his great-grandfather and his wife Dough Dough lived in for a short time. That in turn made him think of the lowest point of his childhood: the fire.

The grade school Will attended was located just two blocks from his home on the other side of Davie's house. One cold winter day, Will was at the school window sharpening a pencil when he noticed smoke spiraling up from beyond Davie's house. Thinking it was someone burning their trash, he never gave it a second thought until the principal, Mr. Hunter, came out during Will's recess period and motioned him over.

There was a light cover of snow, and he was certain Mr. Hunter was going to punish him for throwing snowballs. Pretending he didn't see him, Will ran and hid in the hollow of a tree. There he was, feeling safe in the security of the hollow of an old tree when Mr. Hunter found Will anyway and called out "William, we just got word that your house is on fire. You don't need to go home because they have everything under… William! William! William!" Will didn't hear anything after that as he struck out for home at full speed. A number of his buddies disobeyed Mr. Hunter's calls to come back, and they arrived together to see the destruction that had taken place.

It was below freezing and the water from the firemen's hoses streaming down from the roof had flowed out the front door and down the steps, giving it a frozen stream effect of water cascading over rocks. The chandelier that had once hung in his grandmother's house on the farm when she was a young girl was connected to the ceiling and floor by the stream of frozen blue water that had poured down from above through the light fixture, creating the appearance of a solid ice waterfall. And as much as Will hated to practice the piano, he begin to choke up with emotion as he beheld the old upright player on which he had first learned to play and on which his mother and grandmother had started their musical experience so many years ago.

No one that Will knew had a piano so exquisite. It was priceless. Not only did it operate flawlessly and with great tone, but the wooden cabinet that housed this ancient music maker was hand carved in beautiful cherry wood into the figures of horses, farm houses, and mountain scenes. In addition to the piano, there was a matching music cabinet with doors on both sides permitting each one to swivel open, revealing its treasure of sheet music. Only the top of the cabinet was burned, and they were later able to have a craftsman replace the part that was damaged. But the piano was another matter. Stuck in the middle of the front cabinet was a fireman's ax, and lying about the floor were the family's cherished paper rolls, the ones with tiny holes that the pneumatic action used to determine what notes were played. Lying nearby were many old music sheets that his grandmother had so meticulously protected from the ravages of time. The name of Sarah Malone, Will's mother's maiden name, written in ink at the top of each front page was smeared by the water from the fireman's hoses, leaving stains and obliterating the titles. They had been so important to Will; it was like a thread or connection to the past and the mother he never really got to know. They were worthless now.

Although the roof was missing over most of the house, the dining room table, chairs, hutch, and crystal cabinet had only suffered a few burns. It was unbelievable! The significance of this was that this extremely large dining room set had come to be a symbol of grief in Will's life because of the many members of his family that gathered there in years past. They were gone now, but this symbol of grief, the dining room set, was still with them.

After the fire, Mam and Will moved in with neighbors while repairmen worked to shut off three rooms that had been spared the fire. Subsequently, this apartment became their temporary home, and they thanked God that they had a roof over their head. It was also the apartment that Will's great-grandfather and his wife would live in and where Will later got the bright idea that he thought would make him rich.

Will and his grandmother survived that winter living in those three rooms, and the house was almost totally rebuilt by the end of spring. During the summer, they moved back into the rest of the house and kept the apartment separated from the main part so it could be rented. After that, Will's great-grandfather and his wife Dough Dough lived there until he passed away a few years later.

During the summer, Will's favorite sport, other than misappropriating fruit and vegetables from the neighbor's gardens, was the game of hide-and-seek. And all the kids knew that the best games were always played in Will's yard because it was bigger and darker with more neat places to hide. Nobody could beat Will at hide-and-seek because he had the greatest hiding place. His buddies had to beg him to come out of from where he was hiding so they might have another chance at a new game. The reason it was great place to hide was because he had discovered a hole his dog had dug under one of the bushes in the backyard. It was near the house where the dog could stay cool during the heat of the day. Will would race around the house while his friends were counting to ten, dive under the bush into the hole, and practically disappear.

During that time, his grandmother's only source of income was from the one remaining farm, so she decided to rent the apartment. After her father, Frank Sewell, died, his wife Dough Dough moved into one of Mam's guest rooms and lived there for several years until she became so homesick for her boys, she moved to California to spend her remaining years there with them.

To Will, how he and his grandmother managed to get along as well as they did remains a mystery to him to this day, but it must have been because Mam was so great at managing money. Her banker told Will later on in life that if she had been a man, they'd have been rich. Anyone who hadn't heard of her business prowess would come by the house to try and sell her their products such as refrigerators, stoves, pots and pans, rugs, magazines, encyclopedias, or insurance. But they would never try a second time. Oh, she would buy all right, but on her own terms and usually at her price. She was tough! Will always thought the town folks sent people they didn't like to his house just to get even with them.

The first thing she would do was to nitpick their products apart, always finding a flaw, a discrepancy, or an error, drawing the value of the product down. By the time she got around to discussing price, they were almost willing to give it away.

The first renters of the apartment were three telephone operators, three girls just out of high school and away from home for the first time. To a twelve-year-old boy, they were the most beautiful women in the world.

The most gorgeous of the three was Betty Jean Thomas, or B. J. as she was so aptly called. To Will, she was definitely a nine on a scale of ten where tens were a figment of a boy's imagination. Her long blond hair was contrasted by her olive complexion, and she moved like a movie star. Joan Harvey had the best figure of the three, and Patsy Evans filled the biggest bra. There were no losers here. He would have been proud to bring any one of them home to Mam had he been old enough.

Will and his friends would sit on the curb to flirt with the lovelies when they came home from work. What a thrill it was to hear the girls call them naughty boys. Will even mustered up the courage to sing to them the first and only line of that ribald classic, "She's got freckles on her butt, she's pretty," which always produced a giggle out of them. This was spicy stuff and much more risqué than even the older boys were accustomed to. Will felt intimate with them, and he began to see himself as a "man of the world."

The boy's curbside watch got a little crowded when the girls were due home from work as Will's friends lined up to greet them. They envied him because these beauty queens lived in his house. During a game of hide-and-seek on a very dark moonless night, Will dove into his usual hiding lair under the bush and began waiting for the searchers to come. Several times, they walked within a few feet of him, but as usual, they gave up and walked back to the front to wait under the street light for Will to come out and claim victory.

Because of an overcast sky, there was very little of the usual starlight that their part of the country was noted for. Will always remembered this night as it was the night his get-rich scheme was hatched. As he was about to stand up to leave his secret hiding place, his security of total darkness disappeared. A light emanated from the windows behind him, shining out across the bushes into the backyard. The windows were open, and Will could hear laughter. The girls had just returned from working the evening shift. He froze, afraid to move, knowing that if he got up to run, they would see the bushes rustle. And if they came to the window and looked down, they would see him, think he was a Peeping Tom, and he would never be able to face the girls again.

Then it dawned on him that the sheer curtains that covered the windows reflected light back into the room, making it impossible to see out. He knew this because his room had the same type of curtains.

Slowly, he stood up and was stunned to see all three nymphs running around in their underwear. His view allowed him to see the entire bedroom, including their bed that lay against and parallel to the window. Before long, they began to play tag, chasing each other around the room, across the bed and back again. It was a sight to behold, and it was taking place just a few feet from Will's face. He remembered asking himself, "What am I suppose to do, be a good little boy and ignore what was going on here, to run from this place and never look back?" No, he was not about to do that. He had just discovered a new game: hide and peek.

To understand the impact this had on Will, one would have to understand that he had never seen a woman in their underwear before. The only woman he had any closeness with was his grandmother, and she was in her late fifties. Suddenly, he had three luscious full-bodied women in his sights. It was almost more than this twelve-year-old could stand. He must have watched for five minutes but finally left in fear of being caught. By then, his buddies had given up and gone home.

Will didn't sleep more than a couple of hours that night, astonished by what he had seen. Ladies were definitely built different than guys, he concluded. Many more curves and far less body hair than older men he had seen in the swimming pool locker room. And there was this matter of breasts. He had been taught that what he had just done was sinful, but how was he supposed to learn about the opposite sex?

It was during this very long and sleepless night that Will had his first stroke of evil genius. He realized that his friends had never seen anything like that either. There was no doubt in his mind that they would pay anything to see what he had just seen. His imagination began to work overtime as his plans for financial success unfolded.

The subjects worked a shift that caused them to arrive home at the same time every evening after dark. Will's mind was racing at warp speed now. Could he be sitting on a gold mine? Now all he had to do was stay out of trouble long enough to mine it, which was not one of Will's greatest assets.

His buddies drove him nuts, begging him to tell the story over and over, but he told them only enough to whet their appetites. He agreed, for a nickel, to let them in on the sight of a lifetime. First, they had to bring a wooden soda pop crate or milk carton to sit on, promise to be perfectly quiet, and pay in advance. Furthermore, there would be no credit extended.

Will began to formulate his plan. The first night was to be a sneak preview, by invitation only. How appropriate, a test viewing if you will. But not for free. The first guys to be invited were Davie, Petey, Calvin, Jerry, and Buddy. They set out soda cases theater-style, facing the windows as Will collected their nickels. It was an especially dark night, and the boys kept bumping into each other. It was only after Will threatened expulsion that they quieted down. Will looked at his Mickey Mouse watch. It was show time.

As if on queue, the bedroom lights suddenly came on. It was so blindingly bright that for a moment, the boys panicked. Forcing themselves to remain perfectly still, not believing that they couldn't be seen, they watched the girls cavort about the room. Will glanced over at the guys and almost blurted out with laughter as he saw the expressions on their faces lit by the light from the bedroom. Together, they looked like a snapshot frozen in the eerie glow from the window, chalky and surreal. The show went on that night full scale, a duplicate performance of the night before.

As soon as it looked as if the girls were about ready to turn in, Will hustled the guys out of the backyard, their soda cases dragging behind them. He counted the spoils. At this rate, he could make a small fortune. He envisioned the money being used the same way he and Davie had used the money they earned from the auction barn. It took 0.25 cents to get into two movies with a nickel left over for a bag of popcorn, or you could buy two comic books and still have a nickel left over. No more would he be dependent on Mam's mood swings for show money. He was independent now. No more knocking on doors to do chores that no one else would do. He was flush. Will could see himself as the first kid from Sikeston to become a tycoon. Wait till the sharks at Slade's get a load of him.

On the south side of town, the word of Will's little theater spread. Ticket sales grew by several cases a night. Petey became his assistant, helping him keep order for which he had the privilege of seeing the performances free. Out of fear of ruining a good thing, Will began to limit the viewing to two or three nights a week. But that required policing the area on the off nights or poachers would try to sneak in for a freebee. In addition, he didn't dare open on moonlit nights, fearing they would be discovered, opening only on very dark nights. He also had a money-back guarantee so that if the girls didn't come home until it was too late for the boys to be out, or if they changed their schedule, a rain check would be issued. He had thought of everything.

One night, Will caught two of his buddies who couldn't come up with the money for a ticket, sitting on their cases in the alley watching through binoculars. It was disgusting. Will wasn't getting a minute's peace. Now he knew how the farmer felt, trying to guard the henhouse from the fox.

There was no doubt in Will's mind that the day would come when all this would end. His grandmother kept asking him what was ruining her garden back there, finding candy wrappers scattered around the flowerbed and the majority of her plants flattened. "Those darn cats, Mam," Will told her. "I hear them fighting every night." She believed that lie, mainly because she took her hearing aid off when she went to bed, relying on Will's good hearing to alert her if something went wrong.

But before that day arrived, Will was loading all his hiding places with cash. This was a key element of his operation because if Mam found any of the money, she would think he had stolen it. He was now up to "folding" money, cashing in the change at the local grocery store for dollar bills. With all this cash, he was loaning money at exorbitant rates just to get it out of the house: a quarter for thirty-five cents, a half a dollar for seventy-five cents. He wanted to buy the new bike he was admiring, but what would he tell Mam?

Just as he suspected, the stuff hit the fan late that summer when all of his fears were realized. B. J. had brought home a boyfriend, and it looked like the boys were in for a real treat. Suddenly, Calvin's father, Mr. Hopkins, came around the house and caught them cold.

At first, he was very considerate about their little indiscretion and didn't create a scene, only a warning, until after he had taken ten minutes to see for himself what they had been watching. Then, he gathered them all under the street light, lectured to them about the virtues young men should have, and sent them home feeling disgraced.

Unfortunately, their minor infraction was nothing in comparison to what was to come. A few weeks later, Mr. Hopkins was arrested for being a Peeping Tom. His name was splattered all over the front page of the local paper, including the location of his immoral transgression: Will's house! He knew that if it had been his name plastered on the front page of the *Sikeston Standard*, his grandmother would have skinned him alive, and he would have been the talk of the town instead of poor Mr. Hopkins. He could see the headlines: "Police Catch Peeping Willy."

The boys knew that they had dodged a bullet, and it was now time to close this little enterprise and look elsewhere for recreation. The young ladies in the apartment were now shutting their blinds every night anyway. Years later, Will received a big surprise when he ran into B. J. She told him that the girls knew all along that the boys had been watching their escapades and that they had enjoyed teasing him and his naughty little friends. She also told him that because of their names being in the paper, their social life had taken a big jump. All the older guys were anxious to meet the Gladys Street Trio.

Years later, at one of Will's previous class reunions, some clown told him he had brought his milk case and asked when the next viewing was scheduled. Everyone had a good laugh, except Will.

Will and Larry began to feel cooped up in John's apartment after having lived in the open for so long. "What do you say, sport?" Larry asked him. "Want to step out on the town a while this evening? I hear the ladies will make you forget about going home." It sounded like a good idea until John brought them back to reality by telling them that a North Vietnamese terrorist group, operating in the Bangkok area, had assassinated several American military advisers in a Bangkok tea house. The city was a perfect place to catch GIs who let their guard down, thinking they had left the war behind.

"If you decide to go out in the evening, let me know. I have a small arsenal here and you can take your choice of weapons." They decided against it after hearing that story, but they asked for weapons anyway.

After all, who might have watched them arrive and followed them to John's house? And who might want to make a name for themselves by taking down three Americans, unarmed and unaware of the danger. In addition, they were too close to getting out of this war to tempt fate at the eleventh hour.

Thinking about danger and trouble, Will had to ask himself if there had ever been a time in his life that he hadn't been in trouble. Even as a kid growing up, it seemed trouble was always close by. Anytime his grandmother told him not to do something and he did it anyway, he usually ended up in the soup. Like the time she told him not to climb the giant magnolia tree in Davie's yard, but he did it anyway. Sure enough, he fell out of the top and nearly broke his neck, not only once, but three times in two years. To Will, it became personal between him and that stupid tree.

After the first two falls, anytime he was about to make a climb, his friends would spread the word around the neighborhood and they'd come just to see him fall. Not one of them dared climb this giant of a tree themselves. Oh no, too many had tried and failed. That tree was a killer. It was at least seventy-five feet tall, and the limbs were slick as glass. But it was a challenge for Will, like so many other events in his life.

The desire to reach greater heights stayed with Will all through his childhood. He climbed every hill, silo, grain elevator, water tower, and fire tower in Southeast Missouri. He even tried to soar into the blue by swinging in the school swing set until he reached the highest possible apogee and then bailing out over the edge of the hill below. Will liked to pretend he was a paratrooper dropping into France with Gen. Slim Jim Gaven, who was the commander of the 82nd Airborne during World War II and who was considered a hero by the American people. Davie tried to outjump Will for height and distance but lost two of his baby teeth when his face and knee met. This high altitude jumping was serious business and not for everybody.

Will was to find out later in life that the landing jolt after bailing out of a swing was nothing compared to the bone-rattling collision with the ground after a jump with an army T-10 parachute.

It was ironic that years later, he had the honor of serving under Gen. Gaven who was commander of the 18th Airborne Corp, a command that included all of America's airborne forces at that time. Late one night, when Will was on duty in the war room of the 18th and things were quiet, Will tried to engage the general. He told him the story about the school swings, and the general responded by asking him if he were playing with a full deck.

When Will first arrived at the 82nd airborne jump school, the first person he met was Sgt. Frank Pennington, a veteran of the Korean War and a warrior who had served two tours of duty in Vietnam. His experiences had hardened Pennington, making him bitter and mean as hell. He constantly rained havoc on new jump school students under the guise of preparing them for the war that was still raging in Vietnam.

Rumors were that Pennington was one of only eight paratroopers out of 300 that had survived the massacre that occurred at the Chosin Reservoir where a battalion of Marines were surrounded and cut off from escape. Pennington's unit was air dropped to open an escape route for the Marines. They said he had only survived, after being shot several times, because he ran faster than everybody else. He was tough, and he showed no mercy. His experiences had taught him that the only way you survive in battle was to be tougher than your enemy, both in mind and body.

It was the first day of training on the 35-foot tower that Will had his run-in with Pennington. When the sergeant called for a volunteer to be the first trooper to jump from the tower, Will made the mistake of volunteering. When he shuffled to the door, he stumbled over Pennington's shinny boots. The sergeant was insanely proud of those boots and, growling like a bulldog, grabbed Will's riser straps and kicked him out the door backward. As he bounced up and down out in space, the risers came up between his legs, causing excruciating pain as he swung down to the end of the cables and hit the dirt mounds on his back.

But that wasn't the end of it. During the four weeks of jump school, Pennington at any moment would call out Will's number, number 68, as numbers were placed on every troopers helmet and shout, "Number 68, give me 10 to the east, 10 to the west, 10 to the south, and 10 to the north." Will would drop to the ground and start doing pushups. This went on right up to the last day of school, which was the day the class made their fifth jump that qualified a soldier to graduate. As they came off the drop zone and scrambled into the trucks, the sergeant called Will's number again, only this time he ordered him to lay out a full-field display, that senseless exercise for which the army was noted. This required Will to display the items that all troopers carried in their backpacks. There in the dusty drop zone, Will complied.

"Graduation will be at 1300 at the division parade field. See you there," the sergeant said. And with that he got into the truck with the men and left Will there standing alone. The drop zone was eight miles from the parade field, and it was almost 1100 hours at that moment.

Will felt the anger build up as he contemplated his situation. It was obvious the sergeant didn't want him to graduate. The more he thought about what the sergeant had done, the madder he became. He was not going to let this SOB defeat him! He was going to make it there somehow. So he started running.

The temperature was hovering near 100 degrees as he ran down the road leading back to Fort Bragg. Several cars and trucks came by; he tried to hitchhike, but no one would stop and pick him up. His uniform became soaked with sweat, his legs and lungs ached, but he kept on running. He called upon the only one, his Creator, to help him overcome this dastardly deed perpetrated on him by Pennington. He knew he had to get there; all these last four weeks would have been for naught otherwise.

As he came into the division area, he passed classmates on the way to the parade ground for graduation, all sharp and spotless in their clean uniforms. Stumbling into the barracks, he splashed water on his face, quickly changed into his uniform, and dashed off to the parade field. Will arrived as the class was being called to attention, and he slipped into the end of the formation. There on the podium among the bevy of officers was Sergeant Pennington who saw Will join the formation, and it was apparent he was taken aback. As they called the name of a graduate, he would step forward, walk up to the podium, and accept his diploma. Will's name was called in order, and he moved forward. His hatred for Pennington was eating away at him, and he thought of all the things he would like to do to him to get even. As Pennington handed Will his diploma, he grabbed Will and pulled him close and whispered in his ear, "You son of a bitch, if I ever have to go to war again, I want you there with me in the foxhole. You are one hell of a trooper, young man. Congratulations." And all of a sudden, all the dastardly things he had been thinking about Pennington vanished.

ROLPHENSTEIN

As Will watched the fan on the ceiling turn lazily above his head, he remembered reading a book where the main character was in a hotel room, watching an overhead fan, and his opening line was "Why, when I am here I want to be there and when I am there I want to be here?" It also reminded him of a similar scripture line from the Bible that he couldn't recall, so he asked John if he had a Bible and was surprised when he said, "Of course, I have a Bible, Will. What kind of a Christian would I be without a Bible?"

After searching though the book for several minutes, he came upon the lines he was looking for.

> I know that nothing good lives in me in my sinful nature, for I have the desire to do what is good but I cannot carry it out. For what I do is not the good I want to do; no, the evil I do not want to do—this I keep on doing. Now if I do what I do not want to do, it is no longer I who do it, but it is sin living in me that does it.

Another rainstorm crossed over the area and Will lay there, listening to the thunder roll, contemplating those ancient texts, thinking how apropos those words were to his life. All the killing, the taking of human life, was not what Will wanted to do. But it wasn't long, especially after Doc Tran, when it became what he wanted to do.

Will read on.

> So I find it to be a law that when I want to do right, evil lies close at hand. For I delight in the law of God, in my inmost self, but I see in my members another law at war with the law of my mind and making me captive to the law of sin which

dwells in my members. Wretched man that I am! Who will deliver me from this body of death?

To some degree, Will was intrigued to see that the author must have found the peace he was looking for when he read the final words of his text: "Thanks be to God through Jesus Christ our Lord!"

Again, the question arose in Will's mind: would he ever find the peace he was looking for?

As he continued to think about his hometown, he thought of the people and the places he would be seeing again, things he hadn't thought about for quite some time like jumping out of swings to jumping off a roof. But there was one memory involving a roof that had stayed with him until this day. It's a memory of something he was never very proud of, and it involved another childhood friend, Gary Roberts.

Gary lived just a few blocks from Will, and he and Davie played with him when he wasn't working in his father's landscaping business, which was most of the time. Living in a cottage behind Gary's house was an alcoholic who looked just like Boris Karloff of Frankenstein fame. He seemed to have his seasons mixed up, wearing winter clothes in the summer, summer clothes in winter. If you looked closely, you could see that his shirt and pants were usually inside out. Like the movie monster, he appeared to walk stiff legged, arms extended. It was probably because he was blind drunk most of the time, and his arms were extended to keep him from running into things.

On several occasions, Mam gave Will orders to stay away from this old derelict. He was too strange for her to feel comfortable about Will playing in Gary's yard. But did he listen to her?

His name was Rolph Moline and the boys called him Rolphenstein. Never to his face, mind you. This guy was too terrifying. He would stumble around his little cottage drunk, talking to himself in gruff, indistinguishable mutterings that sounded like the monster himself. Why they had to harass this poor old man Will never knew, but they did, continually and mercilessly.

One evening, they went too far. Situated just above Rolph's bed was an old flue, used years before when the only heat in the house was a potbelly stove. When natural gas came to Sikeston, the stove was no longer needed, and the flue was closed off with a round tin sealer.

Some mastermind came up with a scheme to drop a cherry bomb down the chimney while he slept. So Gary and Will climbed up the tree growing next to the kitchen, stepped onto the roof, and quietly crawled over to the chimney. They thought of themselves as commandos, about to blow up a German ammunition dump. Will lit the cherry bomb Gary was holding over the opening, and he dropped it. They could hear it bounce around and come to rest against the tin sealer. They ran for the tree, but neither of them wanted to take time to climb down, so they jumped into the soft garden below just as the explosive went off.

The concussion of the blast blew off the sealer, sending years of soot into the bedroom and all over Rolph who was asleep below. When he opened the door in rage, they couldn't believe what they saw. Except for the whites of his eyes, he was black. His face was covered with soot, which was rolling out from behind him like a dark ominous cloud.

By the look on Rolph's face, there was no doubt in the boys' minds that it was now time to run for their lives. In the past, it had always been the three of them throwing stones at Rolph. But now, he was throwing stones at them. He chased them all the way to the railroad tracks until one of his stones glanced off a track and a piece of it hit Davie in the cheek. This prompted the boys to take a stand, and they began pelting the old man until he finally turned and ran for home.

When they took Davie into Gary's house to tend to his barely bleeding wound, Gary's father was shocked by their wanton act of cruelty. So much so that he sat them down and told them the tragic story of how Rolph had come to be the man he was.

Thirteen years before, Rolph had lost his wife and two children in a fire that destroyed his house and almost cost him his life. Worst of all, it was determined that the fire was caused by improper wiring in a clothes dryer that he had just repaired, causing Rolph to feel responsible for their deaths.

Hearing this story, shame rolled over Will like great ocean waves as he began to see this old man in a different light. He no longer saw him as the monstrous Rolphenstein. Instead of being hated, he was to be pitied.

The day after the incident, the three boys knocked on his door and asked him to forgive them. He was sober that morning and told them they were forgiven, which increased their shame even more. Gary's father suggested they offer to clean up his house, but Rolf declined the offer, saying he had already taken care of it. Rolph died the following summer, and only ten people showed up at his funeral. Gary, Davie, and Will were three of them. Of all the rotten things Will had done in his life, he had more regret about the way he treated this tragic old man than any thing else…until Vietnam.

With sweat pouring off Will like he was lying in the rain, he shifted uncomfortably in the guest room bed, glancing absentmindedly at the army .45 lying on the end table. Its presence made him feel safe and secure. He knew that he wasn't invincible, but from the first day he was forced to use a weapon, he lost his fear of things that go bump in the night and other men.

Yeah, going home was definitely making Will nervous. There were two reasons he dreaded going home. The main one was that Mam would not be there. Secondly, that he would find that Mary Ann Muldune was no longer Muldune, that her last name would be her husband's if she had a husband.

Will's thoughts and feelings were mixed. There was a feeling of joy as he thought about cranking up Mam's old 1956 DeSoto Adventurer and taking her places the last time they were together. It reminded him of *Driving Miss Daisy*. The DeSoto was the first car he had driven over 120 mph, and it brought back an unending stream of memories. It was in perfect shape with very few miles, as it didn't get driven very often because Mam's eyes had gotten so bad, she had failed a driving test.

Will thanked God for that last visit. It meant a lot to both of them, and it let him see what he had failed to see before: that life is short and that she was more important to him than he had ever realized.

The second reason Will dreaded coming home this time was because of Mary Ann Muldune. Maybe dread was not the proper word. Perhaps apprehension is a better choice because as he thought of her, the uncertainty made him feel apprehensive. Had she gotten married? If so, did she have children? And would she be at the reunion? He had to stop thinking of her negatively. He wanted desperately to see her, but what if she had gotten married? He tried to think of Mam again, of the good times, and of his childhood, most of which had molded him into what he was today. Then that same question popped up again. "What in the hell am I?"

It was daybreak now and hawkers were selling their bananas and other items on the streets of Bangkok. He couldn't remember if he had slept or not, but he knew that this was going to be another stifling day in Southeast Asia.

Mam was back in his thinking again as the sweat poured off him into the mattress. He thought about how she barked orders like a drill sergeant. One of her orders was to not go swimming at the railroad trestle when Will's friends invited him to go, but it was a hot July day so he went anyway. Being the "dare me to do it!" kind of guy that he was, he ended up with a six-inch gash in his foot after a twenty-foot jump from the trestle into only six feet of water. His foot came down hard on a broken bottle, and it left a perfect imprint visible to this day.

Amazing how some kids get into trouble any time they're together. This was the way it was with Will and Edward Malone; they seemed to think alike. Like Will, there wasn't anything Edward wouldn't try. He was the one who taught Will how to skip school and get away with it—that is until the time they went swimming in the water tank on the Frisco railroad.

It was a beautiful spring day in early May. The wind was brisk but the sun was warm, so they skipped school and went down to the railroad where the locomotives filled up their steam engines. The top of the water tank was open, and they knew that once inside, no one could see them. It was a great place to swim and play because it was in the sun but out of the wind.

The only problem was the green algae that had grown extremely heavy on the inside of the tank that spring. When Will and Edward dropped down over the side into the water, they found themselves unable to climb back out because of the slime that had accumulated on the walls of the tank. They tried every possible way to get out, but it was no use. The walls were too slick.

As they bobbed there, wondering what to do next, Edward got a funny look on his face. "Do you feel something touching you under the water?" he said, his voice quivering. Suddenly, Will felt it too, something bumping him from all sides. And it was slimy, whatever it was. "I don't know what it is, but we'd better find a way to get out of here and fast," Will replied.

Just before they began to panic, heads began to pop up out of the water all around them. Frogs by the thousands! The warm spring sun must have induced them into coming out of hibernation at the same time. For Will, it was horrible, bobbing in water filled with millions of slimy amphibians.

As they flailed around in the water to make their escape from this watery trap, the frogs begin to crawl up on top of them, trying to find a place to sun themselves. The boys screamed and thrashed around, but it only stirred them up the more. After what seemed an eternity, a worker at the railroad station heard their cries and within a few minutes, climbed up the ladder outside the tank. His face appeared over the edge and Will could see it was Mr. Jennings, the stationmaster. Will's grandfather, Tom Malone, had been the stationmaster of that same Frisco station for thirty years, and when he died, Mr. Jennings took his place. He loved Will's grandfather and had received all of his training from him. Had it not been for this relationship, they would have made the front page for sure. At that moment, it wouldn't have mattered. Anything would have been better than frogs.

Contemplating the way he always seemed to get into trouble, Will remembered another incident that occurred about that same time. He had always thought of himself as one of the good guys, the one in the white hat, until what he called the Buick ring caper occurred. Returning from the movies one night while walking through a parking lot, Will stumbled against the hood of a 1949 Buick Roadmaster, pushing the hood ornament with such force that it broke the chrome ring surrounding the center rocket-like spear that distinguished Buick from other cars.

When he tried to pull it back in place, it broke off in his hands, revealing that the ring was not one solid piece of chrome but two that swiveled into what appeared to be a bracelet about the size of a person's wrist.

Wearing it to school the next day, it caught the eye of a female classmate who admired it so much that she talked Will out of it. Within a few days, almost every girl in school wanted one. Desirous of pleasing them, he began nightly forays into parking lots to fill all of the requests. Before long, most of the girls were wearing this distinctive ring. You couldn't walk the halls of Sikeston High without seeing one. The word was out: Will Brandon was the man. Over night, he became the most popular guy in school. Too popular as it turned out because one of the girls, June Cathy, happened to be having supper with her family one night when her father spotted one on her wrist and demanded to know where she got it. The ring on his Buick was missing.

The following day, as Will was entering school, he noticed a police car sitting in front of the main entrance but thought nothing of it as there was always someone getting into trouble. He continued on to his first class. Within the hour, the superintendent of schools, Tharon Stallings, entered the classroom and interrupted the teacher by asking Will to come forward. As he stepped out the door, he was handcuffed by two police officers and led away like a common criminal. He was mortified.

Once in the superintendent's office, Mr. Stallings and the officers, which now included the county sheriff, began to discuss Will's fate. It seems that the insurance companies that had to replace all these hood ornaments were not very happy with Will Brandon and wanted to see him punished. By this time, he was really scared.

It was finally decided that if Will would return all the Buick rings, they might drop the charges. But if he didn't, he would be put away for an undetermined length of time, would then have a record, never get a decent job, own a gun, or be allowed to vote, in short, be an outcast of society forever. He was given one week to bring in the rings or else, and according to their records, the number was fifty. Will tried to explain that he had never taken more than twenty, maybe twenty-five, but they were adamant. Where in the world was he going to get fifty?

When he started asking girls for their ring back, he suddenly changed from the most popular guy on campus to the most hated. He was called an Indian giver as well as other less flattering names. Some of the girls said they would never give them up. But they did, and eventually, life got back to normal.

Will and Larry said good-bye to John and left Bangkok early the next morning bound for Manila. There were thunderstorms on the horizon, and it was a rough ride all the way. Will shifted uncomfortably in his seat, dozing off late in the afternoon, amid thoughts of his friend Edward and wondering if he was still living in Sikeston, or had he moved to the mountains of the far west where he said he would live someday.

The Pond and the First Hunt

Edward, whose nickname was Buddy, was born at least a hundred years too late. Being the outdoors man that he was, he would have been better suited for the frontier days. Will learned later that Buddy felt like an alien, never fitting in like the rest of the boys his age. His folks were not farmers, but they lived just outside of town on the Lewis farm. His father, Edward Malone, Sr., was the grandson of Earl Malone who was one of the early mayors of Sikeston. Some of Edward's forefathers were true frontiersmen, having traveled west with Daniel Boone.

Buddy's father, however, had become a professional gambler and was the black sheep of the Malone family. This was not only because of his gambling but also because of whom he married, a woman from the wrong side of town. Although she was a wonderfully kind lady to Will and Buddy's other friends, the Malone clan looked with disdain upon his parents. Perhaps this is why Buddy always felt like an outsider and why he became the consummate outdoorsman that he was. Whatever the reason, as far as Will was concerned, Edward "Buddy" Malone Jr. was the greatest hunter Sikeston had ever known. He would have fit in perfectly with what Will had been doing these past few years, he thought, although he might not have had the stomach for the taking of human life.

Weather never seemed to affect Buddy. The worse it was, the better he seemed to function. He had great natural attributes and abilities like his uncanny eyesight. His friends used to say that he could spot a gnat on a hawk's bill. He was always the first to spot geese or ducks off in a distant sky or a deer that blended in with the scenery. Although Buddy was of average height and weight, he was extremely fast on his feet and tough as a pine knot.

Buddy's father had a poker or crap game going several times a week. Once they started, they played for days. His mother served food and drinks to their guests and cleaned up their mess while Mr. Malone cleaned up their money.

Will thought about the first time he went to visit Buddy's house on the Lewis farm; he was only nine years old. It was unusual that Mam would let him go anywhere overnight, especially to a house where things went on that were a step or two below her approval. Although his grandmother was a Malone, she was not related to them and had known most of the Malone family, having socialized with Buddy's grandmother for forty years. She had always felt sorry for him, and when he called and invited Will over, she gave her permission. She was like that. Hard as nails yet soft as jelly when it came to kids and injustice.

Buddy's parents always treated Will as if he was one of their own. After Will's mother died, his father remarried and left Will with Mam. Consequently, he never knew what it was like to have a real family, even though his grandmother tried to be both his father and mother. By her letting Will visit the other Malones, it gave Will a taste of what it was like to live with parents. It also caused him to realize, for the first time, what he was missing by not having a mother or father.

Will was awestruck when he saw Buddy's room, which was decorated with his father's gun collection and hunting trophies. It was an incredible sight for a young man dreaming of being a big game hunter someday. He had collected game from all over the world. The Grand Slam of sheep is a well-known and a difficult achievement for hunters. It requires bagging five trophies from seven species of sheep scattered throughout the world. Many hunters spend their lives pursuing this goal and most fail. Edward's father had two Grand Slams.

Protected by his grandmother like he was, Will had never been hunting. Edward, on the other hand, had been given a 410- gauge shotgun on his eighth birthday, and hunting had become old hat to him.

There was a small pond on the Lewis farm about two miles from his house where Buddy spent a great deal of time during his childhood. Ducks and geese could be found there any day during the fall migration. But it was a long walk, even longer in the winter, or so it seemed.

When Billy Lewis, who lived just a short distance away, heard that Will was visiting at Billy's house, he came over to see what they were doing. When Buddy told Billy he was going to take Will on his first hunting trip, he ran home to get warmer clothes and a shotgun. So on this cold November morning, the three of them bundled up and struck out for the pond and Will's first hunt. Buddy's dog Cooney took the lead, wagging his tail ahead of them, constantly looking back full of anticipation. The walk to the pond was rough that day, but nothing like they were to experience coming home against the wind with the temperature dropping rapidly as the sun fell.

The stand of trees that marked the pond's location was like an oasis off in the distance on an otherwise flat plateau of farmland. When they were within 100 yards of the bushes that lined the water's edge, Buddy and Billy stopped and bent over, walking as low as they could without crawling. Watching the other two, Will fell in behind them and did the same. When they were within twenty-five yards of the pond, they began to crawl, looking back to make sure that Will was on his knees too. Once they reached the bushes, Buddy slowly rose up to peer over and through the brush. He popped his head back down with a smile on his face that let the other boys know they were on to something.

"Four," he whispered, "just a few yards out and off to the right." Will could see the excitement in Buddy's eyes as he checked his gun to make sure it was loaded. He reckoned he'd better do the same, although Buddy had loaded it for him earlier. "When I rise up and say, 'Go,' you guys get up with me. I'll shoot at the ones on the left. Billy, you shoot down the middle and, Will, you go for the ones on the right." Will's breathing picked up, his heart began to race. His hands and knees began to shake. This was it, the moment of truth. Will suddenly felt mature, even manly because for the first time in his life, he had a gun in his hand and it was loaded. That vivid imagination that continues to this day began to work overtime as he saw himself as a western pioneer stalking buffalo on the Great Plains, and now with the power of life or death in his hands. He moved up closer, watching Buddy as he poised himself to go for his share of the game. To him, this was the moment of truth.

"Go," Buddy shouted. They jumped to their feet, but before Will could see where the ducks were, the other two boys had fired. As one duck fell, he could see Billy out of the corner of his eye, reloading his single shot 20-gauge. At that same moment, Will saw them moving straight away from them no more than ten feet off the water. Will lined them up, squeezed the trigger, and what seemed like a mule kicked him hard in the shoulder. Not only did it kick him in the shoulder, it glanced off his shoulder and mashed his nose.

Bam! Buddy's 12-gauge automatic fired again, going off in Will's left ear as he let out a yelp that signaled another hit. Will couldn't find a shell in his pocket, and when he finally did, it was all over.

At his master's command, Coney hit the water, grabbed the first bird, and swam it back to Buddy, dropping it at his feet. He signaled the dog back into the water, and he was off again for the second bird, which had drifted out quite a distance.

Buddy didn't embarrass Will in front of Billy by asking if he had shot anything. He knew Will had missed. In fact, he did his best to make Will believe that he had shot the second duck, but Will knew better and it bothered him. The other two boys had proven themselves, and Will could think of only two things: when would he get another chance to redeem himself and what his nose and face must look like? Under the roots of a fallen tree at the pond's edge, they sat down out of the wind and marveled at this magical place, so far removed from civilization and parental supervision. Will felt the presence of some higher force here in the wilderness, and without realizing it, the hunter instinct had been imprinted into his memory forever.

The waves off the pond lapped lazily at their feet and the cattails and pussy willows swayed back and forth, creating a shushing sound that seemed almost holy. They were in their element, and Will's bloody nose and face became secondary to the magic of the special place, that special moment. Like so many hunts to follow, Will always felt that he was with the Father of it all, sharing his great creation, closer now than he had ever experienced it before.

As Will sat there in the aircraft so far removed from home, contemplating those early hunting years and the camaraderie he shared with his friends; it caused him to marvel at how different it was from the kind of hunting he had been involved in the past few of years. He was light-years away from the pleasant days of boyhood spent with good friends sharing nature, and he wondered if he could find his way back to the presence of the Father of it all?

As he adjusted the airflow in the airliner from above his head, his thoughts raced back to that day so long ago, remembering how the sun fell rapidly behind the horizon, leaving the sky a mixture of colors from orange to dark gray. What seemed pure and peaceful began to feel ominous and menacing. "I guess we'd better start back," Buddy said. "It'll be dark before we get to the house now." After Coney had retrieved the last bird, they struck out for home.

At first, it wasn't snowing, but it might as well have been because snow was blowing in from across the plains, stinging their faces and blurring their vision. Several times, they crawled down in ditches beside the fence line to get out of the wind, curling up with Coney and placing their frozen hands in his wet fur to thaw them. Coney loved those little intervals.

As the northwestern wind picked up, it started to snow intensely. They began to lose feeling in their hands, causing them to throw down their guns near a very large oak tree and jog to stay warm. The steel barrels had made their hands that much colder. At that moment, Will remembered thinking about Mam, home by her warm fire with no idea that her nine-year-old grandson was out on this terrible night in the wilderness with a shotgun and a busted nose.

They had been following a fence line but in the darkness strayed from it several times. Billy disagreed with Buddy, insisting that they were going the wrong direction. He was so convinced that he was right that he threatened to leave them and take his own route home, but the dog caused him to change his mind. Coney knew his way home, and occasionally, they would lose sight of him, but he would always return barking to get them to follow him.

Buddy said his folks would have the back porch lights on and one of the lights would be green. This was the landmark they used to identify the house for new gamblers looking for the action. The boys strained to decipher the green light from the multitude of farmhouse lights that formed a broken blinking line across the horizon, but with the piercing wind in their eyes, all the lights looked the same.

Behind those blinking lights were families enjoying their warm homes, totally unaware of the drama taking place in the snowstorm just a short distance away.

They had slowed down almost to a walk, gasping for air, when Buddy cried out, "There it is, over there." They then began to run again but not as fast, realizing that it was still a long way to the house. But it was comforting to spot that green light and to know that they were moving in the right direction. It was like a beacon that would guide them safely home to warmth and security. As the snow subsided, the stars shined crystal clear in the heavens, and Will remembered saying a prayer to those blinking stars in the sky, thanking God that Mam would not lose her grandson this blustery night.

Passing the old barn, they could see Mr. Malone bundled up in his arctic coat, coming toward them with a gas lantern. What a relief it was to know that they would soon be safe in the warm house. He wrapped blankets around all of them, remarked about Will's bruised face, and led them into the yard and onto the porch. "Only two things between you boys and the North Pole tonight," he said. "What's that, sir?" Billy asked. "Two strands of barbed wire," he answered with a chuckle. They dumped their boots and, with Coney, ran to the fire that was roaring away in the fireplace.

Will thought of the pond often since that time and of all the experiences he shared with Buddy there. He was with him the day Davie accidentally shot Coney's eye out with a .22 rifle. He was firing at a rabbit the dog was chasing. The three of them cried remorsefully, thinking their hunting companion would die, but somehow, he survived. Davie never forgave himself and, as far as Will knew, never picked up a gun again.

Will became a proficient hunter and outdoorsman during the years that followed, but he knew he could never compare to Buddy. He often thought that if we were ever to go to war, he's the guy he would want in the foxhole beside him. It was a prophetic thought that came back to haunt Will, long after he grew up.

Thoughts of the pond continued. It was while hunting there one day a year or so later that he met a boy that would have more of an influence on his life than any other childhood acquaintance. His name was Curt Gregory. Curt was a hunter and equally as accomplished as Buddy. Will had seen him before because Curt was a high profile guy, a natural athlete who stared in basketball, baseball, swimming, diving... there was nothing he couldn't do. And he was ubiquitous, particularly where sports were concerned. Although Will had never officially met him, he had always envied his athleticism.

Perhaps time can dull a person's memory, play tricks with it, twist it, even build it into fantasy. Conversely, it can also enhance one's true recollection. Will knew this was a fact because it happened to him one day when he went to find his aunt's house in Bismarck, Missouri, after not having seen the house in over twenty-five years. His Aunt Annie and Uncle Tom had raised twelve kids in that house, and Will knew he would have no trouble finding it because he had visited his aunt and uncle every summer as a child. He remembered how huge the old country house was until he returned many years later to discover, after passing up the house several times and not recognizing it, how small it had been all along.

Some of Will's happiest moments were spent in that house, living as the thirteenth and youngest child during those much too brief periods each June. Uncle Tom was a locomotive engineer and like his wife, Annie, was a fine Christian. He always reminded Will of a beardless Santa Claus until he grew a beard, and then he didn't look like Santa at all.

The stories his Uncle Tom told around the fire place as he smoked his pipe, about Jessie and Frank James, the Daltons, Tom Bass and Belle Starr, and Quantrill's Raiders kept the young Will Brandon spellbound. Most of those exhilarating stories had been told to his Uncle Tom by his father who, as a locomotive engineer, had his train robbed by the James gang. These stories were handed down to Will's uncle and then on to his children and the next generation. What was truth versus fiction didn't matter; it was exciting and real to Will, especially since it had taken place in that same part of Missouri.

One evening as Will was walking home from town in the dark with his cousins on the old cobblestone road leading to the farmhouse, they heard a band of horsemen approaching. The noise was resounding, sonorous as the steel horseshoes clanked against the cobblestones. Fearful of what they might do, they jumped off the road and hid in the bushes and witnessed the most unusual phenomenon. As the galloping horsemen approached and passed them by, the sparks from steel against stone was so bright that it lit up the roadway. It was like their horse's hooves were on fire. The stories of raiding outlaw bands became even more vivid in Will's mind, and he knew that this was Jessie and his gang or some other band of desperados, coming to do them harm.

As soon as the horses were out of sight, Will and his cousins ran for home where they were greeted by his Uncle Tom. Seeing their fear, he sat them down and proceeded to tell them the real story of Quantrill's

Raiders and how they were no different than many of the Northern raiding parties who believed they were fighting for what they believed to be a patriotic cause. They were also fighting for their homeland that was being invaded by both the Kansas Jayhawkers and the northern Federal army. Although Uncle Tom assured them that they were not going to be shot by some raiding party, it was difficult to sleep that night, expecting Jesse and his brother Frank to appear at the door any moment.

Will's Aunt Annie was one of the most righteous, kind, and humble women he had ever known. He would always cherish those summers spent with Uncle Tom and Aunt Annie Tinsley up in the mountains of Missouri. He had tried to stay in contact with most of his cousins who had made his trips to Bismarck the happy, unforgettable moments that they were, but the war had changed all that. Regardless, he vowed that he would visit them when he returned.

As to the mind and memory, thinking back again to Curt Gregory, he had to ask himself, is it possible that he was not all the things he remembered him to be? In Will's mind, Curt was world-class. Yet as good as he was and as many awards as he earned, including All-American in several sports, he never advanced beyond local college status. He was to find the answer to these puzzling question years later, thanks to conversations he had with Curt's father and with teammates Sam Bowman and Don Baker at one of their class reunions.

Thinking of that first encounter with Curt, it brought back the memory of how he and Edward had run from Edward's house to the pond so many times that they could run the two miles in fifteen minutes, and that was with guns and gear. It was on one of those runs that they saw this lone hunter sneaking up from the far side of what Will and Edward considered to be their own private pond. They slowed down to a walk and watched as the trespasser stood up, took aim, and fired at a flock of geese as they rose from resting on the water. He fired three shots, and they watched with envy as three magnificent Canada geese fell, one by one, into the pond. The six remaining geese, which were out of sight hidden by the tree line on the far side of the pond, finally reappeared off in the distance as they rose above the horizon.

The hunter was Curt Gregory. He didn't seem too surprised when they approached him, and Edward asked, "What do you think you're doing?"

"You boys look bright enough, figure it out for yourselves," he replied, with a smirky little smile on his face as he went about collecting his kill.

"Listen, smart guy," Edward fired back, "I live on this farm, and I'm the only one that has permission to hunt on it except the owner's son, Billy Lewis. What's your name anyway?"

"Curt Gregory," he responded. "And no, you're not the only one with permission," he said with brashness. "Old Man Lewis told me I was welcome to hunt here anytime I pleased. I suppose you know who he is?"

Will glanced at Edward, and he could tell by his expression that they had a problem. "Crap! Mr. Lewis is the owner of this farm," whispered Edward.

"Don't tell me we have to share this place with this punk," Will whispered back.

"Okay, lets talk," Edward said louder, with a note of distaste in his voice.

They were in the middle of a heated debate when Will caught movement out of the corner of his eye, on the horizon off to the right. When they saw them, wings cupped, heading their way, Edward half-shouted, "Get down, they're coming back." The three of them hit the ground, laid perfectly still, and listened to the sound of the wind over wings and an occasional half-muffled honk as they glided overhead and landed on the water beyond.

Suddenly, it no longer mattered who had permission. Three hearts beat in unison as they worked themselves up to the brush line and stared through the tall Johnson grass. It was one of the most beautiful sights a hunter experiences. There they were, so close, no more than thirty yards out. *Six of them, two for each of us*, Will thought.

Edward hand-signaled Will to the right, Curt to the left, and they spread out just wide enough to blanket the entire pond with firepower. The geese became spooked and rose to the air, but the boys were up and firing. Geese began to fall. Will emptied his shotgun, then reloaded as the two remaining geese were flying away in opposite directions, Edward running after one, Curt the other, firing and reloading, firing and reloading.

Finally, it was all over and deathly quiet. They had bagged them all. Will felt weak, knees shaking, hands trembling, yet at the same time, he felt strong and confident. Without realizing it at the time, Will was now a part of what was to be a great hunting team, a team that would hunt all types of game for years to come. As Will thought about those wonderful days out with his buddies, he also thought about those who thought killing game was cruel and anyone who hunted was sadistic and heartless. As a young man, he thought about it a lot. But what those people didn't understand was that killing is not the important issue in hunting. It's communing with nature, the stalking, the stewardship, and the camaraderie that goes with it, not the killing. Bringing home the game was like bringing home the evidence. Will had concluded that it's something primeval that lies within all men. All he knew was that he felt closer to God as a youth when hunting then any other time. So he tried to experience it as much as he could.

Now Will was leaving the land that was taking a deadly toll on young American soldiers. Some of those gallant men could be dying as he sipped his drink in an air-conditioned aircraft at 35,000 feet, trying to relax enough to fall into much needed sleep. He couldn't help but wonder if he would have survived out there in the enemy's backyard had he not grown up with a weapon in his hand?

The aircraft hit a wave of turbulence, causing Will to wake from a dream. He imagined he was asleep back in Bangkok, waking up to the sound of confusion in the street, lying on the sweat-soaked mattress. Someone had been caught stealing chickens from a neighbor's chicken house. He tried to clear his thoughts and sat up straight as he reoriented himself to his surroundings.

The first thing he saw sitting across the aisle by the window was that same old one-eyed gentleman he had seen in the other aircraft. He had that same expression of distaste, causing Will to remember another character, Eagle Eye Flegal who had that same look, straight out of Li'l Abner.

The hostess saw that Will's glass was empty and immediately came over with another to take its place. Even that simple gesture was pleasurable to a trooper that had been doing everything for himself for so long. So Will took a few minutes and asked her about her life. The problem was it didn't take long for the conversation about her life to turn around to Will's life, with her asking about what it was like back there. At that point, Will found a way to cut the conversation short. Why did he feel embarrassed by this young lady's question?

Taking a sip from his drink, he returned to thinking about embarrassing moments when another incident came to his mind that had been hard to live down. This unforgettable moment occurred on one of his usual hiking trips to the sand dunes, which are just east of town. Indian artifacts could be found both at the dunes and at the Indian mounds. The only difference being location; the mounds were much farther from town.

On a hot summer day in Southeast Missouri, there was always plenty of roadkill. Kids from the country love sail rabbits, those lifeless flattened objects that, when peeled off the highway, sail like Frisbees. There was always a wide variety to choose from, like sail mice, sail rats, sail squirrels, sail chipmunks, and occasionally, a sail skunk. Of course, no one in their right mind would pick up a skunk...the smell seems to last forever.

But Davie did, and his mother, after giving his hands a bath in onion juice, tomato juice, and every other known solution, made Davie sleep outside on the screen porch for a week. The one time he entered their house, it started to smell like skunk, permeating through it for days.

But on this particularly hot summer day, Edward and Will picked up a sail coyote, carried it to a big ravine, and let it fly. It must have sailed a quarter of a mile, landing near a herd of horses, scaring the daylights out of them and causing a stampede. They laughed long after the herd disappeared over the horizon in a cloud of dust.

As the boys continued on to the dunes, it required traversing several streams. One was a drainage ditch that ran beside the city sewage treatment plant. During periods of heavy rain, the city would permit the overflow of untreated sewage to flow into the ditch, creating an odor that would fowl the air for miles. On this particular hike, Will and his friends arrived to see Sikeston's excrement overflowing the banks of the stream. The smell was so strong, it took their breath away. Normally, they could jump across, but this day, it was impossible.

Being the leader, Will had to come up with something. That's when he got the idea to pole vault across the stream to save walking to the nearest bridge several miles away. After all, he was a pole-vaulter on the track team so this was no big deal. They began to look for a pole long enough and strong enough to vault each of them across this black stream. Eventually, they found a sapling that was just right for the job, but nobody had the courage to try it first. The smell was so putrid all Will wanted to do was get over it and move on, so he volunteered.

After walking off the runway, trampling down the grass, making sure there were no rocks or holes that might cause him to stumble in his approach, he was finally convinced he could make it so he began to run, first at a jog, then at half speed, and finally at full gallop. Thrusting the sapling out as far as he could, he lifted off the embankment. As the pole swung him out over the middle of the stream, it stopped, and Will began to slowly sink.

And there he was, hanging on the pole just above the water. There was nothing he could do, he was going down. Climbing the pole to the top was no use. Will was about to go swimming with Sikeston's waste. Seeing himself sinking, he threw his baseball hat, wallet, and watch to his friends and disappeared into the slime of mankind. Will's friends told him that when he came up, he was speckled with remnants of toilet paper, and his clothes and body had turned a greasy tar-like black.

As it turned out, there was only about two feet of water in the stream but five feet of sewage sludge, an oily substance that sticks like glue and stains everything which it comes in contact. Will thrashed his way to shore, trying to keep his mouth shut, but he couldn't close his eyes. Consequently, his eyes as well as his ears were decorated with sludge. His usually blond hair turned green, and his shoes were filled to overflowing with the slime. Worst of all, there was no place nearby to wash. He had to walk back to town covered with the stuff, which dried in the heat. And naturally, he walked alone as his friends walked fifty yards ahead to stay upwind. Judging by the looks people gave him along the way, he thought he must look as if he had been tarred and feathered without the feathers.

When they were a few blocks from home, the guys ran ahead to warn Mam of what had happened so she could be prepared to deal with this black gunk-encrusted wretch. When Will arrived, she had several buckets of hot soapy water ready and waiting that, after stripping him down, were generously poured over him, then she sprayed him with a hose. His clothes had to be thrown away because they looked worse than a roustabout's clothes in an oil field. This stuff was so staining that it took six months for his hair to turn blond again.

Knowing what he knows today, it's hard for him to understand why he didn't come down with some exotic illness. Most city sewage contains practically every disease known to mankind including the bubonic plague. Will thanked God the he didn't get sick, not even a cold. He also thanked God that no one had a camera that day either. There was only one thing that could have made the day worse than his vaulting folly, and it happened. His father showed up. He was the last person Will wanted to see him looking like he did. Even worse, his father had his sister with him, Will's Aunt Bertha.

Bertha was his favorite aunt. His memory of her goes back many years to an earlier age, perhaps his fourth or fifth year when she was in her late teens. She would come and get Will to spend the weekend with her in Charleston, a sister community to Sikeston, where she lived with one of her friends. It was always a treat for Will when she would take him to the local drugstore, Salibas, for a fountain coke and a chocolate sundae. It is amazing how little things from childhood are remembered as special events.

Although Will was a very good swimmer, he wanted to be a diver. There were no instructors around in those days, so what he learned, he learned by trial and error. Error usually means pain. These errors were commonly described as belly flops, and he had his share of them. He had just about given up any hope of becoming proficient on the three-meter board until Bertha volunteered to help him.

Bertha was very athletic: an excellent swimmer, diver, and tennis player. When she took Will to the Charleston pool one day, she witnessed one of his high board belly flops and said, "It's possible that you could become a pretty fair diver, Will, since you've got the courage to try. Would you like to learn a few secrets about diving?"

"You bet, Bert," Will replied. That was the summer he mastered the high board learning approach, style, form, and many other techniques that would later help him win many trophies. He was one of the few reasonably proficient springboard divers in Southeast Missouri. There was only one person better, Curt Gregory of course.

There was a lot Will didn't know about his Aunt Bertha. Her relationship with his father and his brother Uncle Jimmy bothered Will.

He never thought they treated her right. He had no real basis for that feeling; it was just something he sensed. Somewhere along the way, he heard that she had fallen in love with someone who Will's father and Uncle Jimmy didn't approve, and they had intervened, causing Bertha and her lover to separate. As big as Will's father and his uncle were, they could be very convincing.

That summer, she moved to St. Louis and never married. Will loved her dearly and always had fond memories of the time they spent together. This flight home would take him into St. Louis so he made plans to see her before traveling on to Sikeston.

The Phantom and the Flood

Their plane landed in Manila after dark, and two hours later, they boarded a 737 for the big island of Hawaii. Larry caught the eye of their hostess once they were in the air and motioned, as if he were lifting a glass to his mouth, for a drink.

It reminded Will of his father. He made that same gesture when he'd be at a restaurant or bar, which was all too frequent.

When Will was growing up, his father would, without warning, drive up in the driveway or be waiting outside after school in his government pickup truck. Every time he showed up, Will thought his heart would stop. He was so proud of Clifford Elbert Brandon and wanted all the other kids to see that he actually had a father. It was difficult for Will to understand why they had to be apart. He was later to learn the answer, but even then, he never understood it.

What a joy it was when Will got a chance to spend just an hour with his father. He was such a huge man, tall, handsome, and strong, always smelling of aftershave and hair tonic even after he had worked all day. He had a presence that drew people to him. When he came to visit, he usually took Will out to the South Y, a barbecue drive-in on the south edge of town owned by his father's good friend Jack Lancaster. Jack's great-grandfather had been one of the founders of Sikeston and, like the Malones, had a rich family heritage. Jack and Will's father had played football against each other in high school and had become closer over the years than their own teammates.

It was always exciting for Will to hear them talk about their playing days. His father was a very big kid even in grade school and played five years of high school varsity for Charleston, Sikeston's long-time rival, starting when he was in the eighth grade. They would laugh robustly when they told the story of how his father had broken his nose three times in five years playing center. It was from this heritage that Will was to later want so desperately for his father to see him play and perhaps earn a scholarship to college.

Jack's favorite story involved a player named Tuffy Crain, who would go out of his way to step on any hand or limb with his sharpened cleats, regardless of who it was, even his own teammates.

It was incredible how high Will's emotions would soar and how low they would plummet within just a few short hours. The hard part came when his father would drop him off at home and say good-bye to return to his wife and her relatives. Clifford was like the Phantom, appearing and disappearing throughout Will's life. He told himself that as bad as it hurt, it was better than not seeing him at all. Even now as he sat aboard the aircraft heading home, contemplating that period of his life so long ago, Will knew that he was right.

On a few rare occasions, he would take Will home to spend the weekend with him when his wife was out of town. Her name was Beechy, and she resembled Lana Turner, the movie star. Even as a young boy, he recognized that she was an extremely attractive woman. The problem was Will looked too much like his mother, or so he was told, and she didn't need him around to remind his father of Sara Malone Brandon.

Clifford's job required that he move every couple of years, usually within a seventy-five mile radius of Sikeston in an area of Southeast Missouri known as the Bootheel. Mam loved Clifford and hated him at the same time. She loved him because her daughter, Will's mother, adored him. She hated him because she held him and his wife Beechy responsible for her death. How could that be, Will would ask himself? She died of pneumonia when Will was three years old. When she became ill, Dr. Presnell, their family physician, informed Will's grandmother that she had lost the will to live. Over the years, Will would ask the question why? After all, she had a reason to live: her son. It bothers him even now, high in the clouds somewhere over the Philippine Sea. Mam never let Will forget how his father remarried just six weeks after his mother's death. Regardless, he loved his father with all his heart. He was Will's hero, and all that other garbage meant nothing to him. Sitting next to the window, he looked down at the glistening vastness of the ocean. It was a beautiful Asian night...you could see forever, so the expression goes. Off in the distance, the black outline of an island appeared on the horizon. He suspected it was the island of Guam as he had flown over the Marianas several times before.

Approaching the island, a few signs of human occupation could be seen. The military base, a few primitive roads, and a river were the only distinguishable landmarks. The river widened into a delta, flooding a large area of the island. Will thought about the inhabitants and the bombardment this island took during World War II. It had suffered tremendously, and because of the flooding, it was probably suffering again.

Floods were part of life back home in Southeast Missouri, and they usually occurred in the spring. High water levels were announced like tornado watches by the local media. To Will's father, nothing could be more serious than rising water as he was responsible for the preservation of the hundreds of miles of levees that held back the Mississippi river. From Missouri to Arkansas, from Illinois through Kentucky to Tennessee, there was always the risk of levee failure during flood times. Floods were not alien to Will, he grew up with them, and they were his father's business. Although floods occurred every year, one flood and the incidents that followed are very vivid in Will's memory. It was an extremely warm spring, and while he was attending a Boy Scout meeting, an announcement came over the radio that caught everyone's attention. "We have just been informed that the levee north of New Madrid at mile post 165 has been breached, and the river is pouring into surrounding farmland unabated." Everyone stopped what they were doing and moved closer to the radio. "I've just been handed a bulletin that indicates that members of the US Corp of Engineers emergency flood team who were on site when the levee broke were swept into the flood water about 6:20 p.m. Their fate or identities are not known at this time. People are being evacuated from low-lying areas and emergency rescue teams are on the scene." All eyes were on Will as everyone knew his father was a member of the Corp's flood team. The Scout meeting resumed, but he became anxious and left the meeting early, feeling uneasy and afraid.

When he arrived home, Mam was at the door to meet him. "Have you heard the news?" she asked, her concern showing in her tone of voice. "Only that there was a levee break, and some people were lost," Will replied. "Your dad was one of them," she answered quickly. He suddenly stopped at the foot of the steps. "They just announced on the radio that several men from Washington, who were inspecting the flood damage, were also caught when the river broke through and swept away the levee where they were standing and sweeping them into the spillway. They also mentioned that your father was one of them."

For the rest of the night, Will and his grandmother sat by the radio, listening to flood reports, but news was vague concerning the fate of his father and the other men. Will finally fell asleep, and around 7:00 a.m., Mam woke him, saying, "Listen." The radio was announcing, "All the men who washed into the river last night when the levee broke above New Madrid have been recovered safe after a harrowing night in the water. Our man at the scene reports that had it not been for the heroic efforts of Corp of Engineers District Levee Engineer Clifford Brandon, one or more of the visiting officers from Washington would surely have been lost. It appears Brandon was able to keep them afloat until a rescue boat could get to them. They were found miles from the break, and as dark as it was, it is truly a miracle that these men survived the cold rushing waters of Old Man River."

Clifford Brandon was given a commendation by the Corp, but he never wanted to talk about it. He was an unassuming, humble man, and all of this notoriety was an embarrassment to him. The commendation metal was put away in a drawer, and Will never saw it again while his father was alive.

As Will thought about his father, he contemplated how much life is like a circle. We start at one point, travel great distances sometimes, and somehow find ourselves right back where we started. When Will's father died, he found himself right where he started. The comparison of life to a circle began when his friend Don Baker's father died. The boys were very young, and death was a stranger to them. Just before he died, a call went out for blood donors, and because Will's blood matched his, he gladly donated. He did this not only because of his respect for Mr. Baker, but because he knew Don would do the same for him. As the circle turned, there came a time when he did. When Don found out Will's father needed blood, he was the first to donate. That's why the two of them had remained such close friends. What could possibly draw two friends closer than that, Will contemplated.

Will reflected on the circumstances of his father's death. He had been called home from Panama by his agency contact after his grandmother called the emergency number he had given her when he began his training for the CIA. It was then arranged to have a fighter jet waiting when he returned from the jungle, and he was flown home in an F-104. Will also remembered the stark terror in his father's face when he saw his son walk into the hospital room. He knew he was in serious trouble, or they never would have brought Will home. His stepmother, Beechy, gave him the details of how he had complained of abdominal pain, had been diagnosed with appendicitis, and taken in for an appendectomy only to find his abdomen full of peritonitis, a deadly poison that had been caused by ileitis. So they closed him up and waited for him to die.

In the last few hours before Will's father went into a coma, they had an opportunity to say what they needed to say to each other. It wasn't long before the pain management drugs they had administered kicked in, but the few things they were able to say were priceless. Will thanked God for that special opportunity to make things right between them.

After several hours of watching his father slipping away, just before the doctor pronounced him dead, Will became so emotional that he had to retreat to a silent place, the hospital stairwell. There all the grief and all the disappointment of all those childhood years when they were separated exploded in him, and he cried out once more to the god of mercy for a little of it. And then, his father passed into eternity.

There were other fathers that played a part in Will's childhood. One of them lived across the street from him. He was a doctor, and his last name was Sargent. He never really liked Will because to the doctor, he was the neighborhood rowdy. Will was seen as a threat to his dog and his daughter Becky, who was two years younger than Will. His disdain for him started when Will decided to do something about his dog Thor.

For years, the doctor's Doberman terrorized all the kids and animals on the block. The dog's favorite trick was to wait until the hottest part of the day, gather a few of his friends, come flying into Will's backyard through the gate that was usually left open, and catch his grandmother's cats, lounging under a tree or out in the open. It was great sport for Thor. Will hated that dog, but he feared him at the same time.

One day, Thor and four of his friends hit Will's backyard at full gallop while Will was sweeping the back steps. Out of desperation, he swung his broom at that black devil, and you would have thought Will had shot him. Thor actually tried to climb the tree that stood in the middle of the yard. He whacked Thor's rear end good, and the dog took off for home, almost getting hit by a car as he raced across the street. Will smiled. He now had that dog's number.

As it turned out, the doctor observed the whole scene, and not knowing what had transpired in Will's backyard, assumed that he was being mean to his dog. Will knew he would really be in trouble if he ever had to go to the hospital while Dr. Sargent was on duty. His daughter Becky was a cute girl but still carried a little baby fat on her legs and rear. She always wanted to join Davie and Will in their garage hideaway, but that of course was out of the question. After all, she was a girl, and no self-respecting club member would violate the rules by permitting a girl to even see into their clubhouse, much less be a member.

Becky and her girl friend Sherry Lynn liked to play in the garage below the hideaway when the boys weren't there. Will knew they were up to something but couldn't figure out what it was until one day, through a peep hole, they spotted Becky and her girl friend heading toward them. "Let's be perfectly still, Davie, and see what they do in here," Will whispered. And through holes in the floor, they watched as the girls began to sing and play on an old sawhorse Davie's father used for doing household repairs. Straddling the sawhorse, facing each other, Becky reached over and kissed Sherry Lynn full on the lips. This was not just a peck on the lips, this was a long passionate kiss, like in the movies. Maybe they were practicing for that boyfriend somewhere in the future, but whatever the reason, Davie couldn't suppress his laughter any longer and blurted out a howl. This so surprised the girls, they immediately jumped down from the sawhorse and ran for Becky's house. Being the jerk that he sometimes could be, Will hollered after them, "I saw that, Becky. Wait till I tell the Doc," never really ever intending to tell him anything.

After that, anytime Becky saw Will coming, she would run for home. Her father noticed her reluctance to face him and figured he had either done something terrible to her or, at the least, had terrorized her into being afraid of him. This gave him more reason to despise the boy from across the street. The doctor would have a chance to get even in the not too distant future.

The hostess dimmed the lights and announced they were starting a movie. Will couldn't believe this. He's trying to get war out of his mind, and what do they play? They play a war movie, and most of the people aboard had just come from the battlefield. He switched his headset to a classical music channel and closed his eyes.

As the hostess came by with her cart of drinks, Will asked if she could put something on the screen other than war movies. "How about an African safari flick?" she replied. It brought back memories of an African assignment Larry and Will had when they were attached to the Congo military in Kinshasa.

Rebels had been killing, raping, and pillaging small villages in the Congo, and they were sent with a team to hunt them down.

Although they were successful in rooting them out and taking most of them prisoners, the thing he remembered mainly about the mission occurred when they first started searching for the rebel camp. Informants had given the location, which was later confirmed by pilots who overflew the area. Traveling up the Luapula River, they landed about three miles from their suspected encampment in a riverside clearing void of trees, so rare for that part of the jungle. Outside the clearing, the jungle was so dense it required clearing a path for the entire trek, making progress extremely slow.

As they moved forward, the view of the sky disappeared, blotted out by the canopy of trees above then. This created a menacing, ominous atmosphere enhanced by the low-hanging fog that lay just above the forest floor. This suffocating advance of the jungle and tropical heat caused the entire squad to feel uneasy and concerned that something might happen at anytime, perhaps an ambush.

Then the wind seemed to pick up, and what sounded like a distant tornado brought with it a cool rush of air so unusual for the jungle, heightening their state of alert. The canopy above began to sway back and forth, revealing the deep blue sky intermittently above. As the sound grew stronger, Will realized that it was not the wind at all but rather something material, something alive, bringing all the men to a halt and to full alert as they raised their weapons to firing positions, ready to fire on command at whatever might be coming toward them.

Suddenly, swinging down out of the trees and heading straight at the men like a freight train was a tribe of baboons, destroying everything in their path. Acting as one body, there were over a hundred coming through the brush, teeth bared, tearing and ripping as they came, bounding over each other as if trying to be first to participate in their encounter with the soldiers.

"Fire!" came the command from the sergeant leading the team, and in unison, they let their weapons of death do their job, dropping them like charging Watusi bent on destroying everyone in their path.

Combining the firing of their weapons with the tribe's screaming, barking, and hollering, the jungle seemed to amplify the sound, making it deafening to everyone's ears. They were everywhere now, jumping, tearing, and biting. It was at this moment that Will felt they might not survive this onslaught. A grenade was thrown in the midst of the beasts, expecting the blast to scare them away as body parts were blown in every direction, but they were not deterred. Will could feel their hot blood streaking across his face as he fought them, first with his M-16 rifle and then with his Spanish knife in one hand, a .45 in the other.

The attack lasted for several minutes, and Will could see that they had barely made a dent in their numbers. It was apparent that to escape and to avoid destroying them all, the team needed to retreat to the river and their boats. Picking up the wounded, they slowly backed down to the river, continually firing and slashing at these demons to avoid any more injuries.

Looking back on it, Will doubted that he would ever feel comfortable again in the primate exhibits of a zoo or watching an African safari flick.

Covenants of Youth

With his headset tuned to a classical music channel, he closed his eyes again. This time, his thoughts turned to his comrade in arms.

So often, friends are bound by events they experience together. It can be mundane or breathtaking. It might be a hardship experience or a life-threatening experience. Larry and Will were bound by both. There was rarely a day that went by since coming to Vietnam they didn't have a threat to contend with, some danger to work their way through, and they did it together. Sometimes, it's being together at the scene of something unusual, such as the day Buddy Malone and Will got into trouble together, an episode that thrust both of them into the spotlight at South Grade school.

It started the day they were caught throwing spitballs in Mrs. Utterback's class. Being the smallest teacher in the school, this poor woman was never able to control any of her classes and Will's class was no exception. During the school year, Will and Buddy had systematically replastered the room with spitballs, especially George Washington's picture that hung above the blackboard. Chewing up Kleenexes until they were nice and soggy, they would toss them at George when the teacher turned her back to write on the board.

Because the picture was hung tilted away from the wall, it rocked back and forth, making noises when they scored a hit. Mrs. Utterback was never able to determine where the noise was coming from, and of course, when she would turn to see what had happened, they were like angels looking for Madonna.

After chewing up a dozen or so tissues, Buddy reared back and let this super colossal mush ball fly just as Mrs. Utterback turned to write on the board. Only this one began to disintegrate in its trajectory and pieces fell into Margo Hunter's hair. When she reached back and felt the slimy spitball on her head, she jumped straight up and, with a twisted look of pain on her face, let out an *eeyoo* that sounded more like a kicked dog than a girl's voice. This was a major problem because Margo was the principal's daughter.

They had no idea, when Mrs. Utterback told Will and Buddy to stay after school to scrape off the dried spitballs, what was coming next. A student from one of her other classes, Buddy Sinclair, the colossal of grade school, had just been released from juvenile detention and ordered by the court to return to school. Whose class did he get assigned to? Yep, Mrs. Utterback's. Like Buddy and Will, he had been kept after school, but in his case, it was for making profane remarks to the girls. To say that the teacher was in over her head would have been a major understatement.

After several years of being in serious trouble, kicked out of school, and being detained in a house of correction, he ends up back in the sixth grade. Only now he's fourteen going on twenty- one with hair on his chest and a breath that every morning smelled of cigarettes and alcohol.

Sinclair had other nasty habits, like bringing those little pornographic eight-page bibles as they were called, to school. Showing them to the girls gave him sadistic pleasure just to see the look of shock on their faces as they witnessed the overly accentuated body parts of the comic book characters. Only his big mistake this day was giving one to Margo who marched down the hall to her father's office to show him what he was passing around in class. About that time, the bell rang, and Mrs. Utterback released all of the class except the three bad boys to await the arrival of the principal.

Will had never heard the sound of a charging rhino, but the thunder coming down the hall must have been a close resemblance, as all eyes in the classroom were fixed on the door. As they sat there in fear of the approaching storm, Will looked over at Sinclair to find that fool was laughing. Who laughs when a tornado is about to strike? When Jack Hunter came through the door, he struck it with such force, it came off one of the hinges and swung to the side, banging into the edge of the backboard and sending a crack across the full length of one panel. No tornado here, just a small earthquake.

Immediately, he reached down and with both hands, jerked Buddy to his feet saying "Okay, you perverted freak, let's take a little walk." Hardly had his feet hit the floor when Buddy threw a right cross that hit Mr. Hunter in the nose, sending him reeling backward, blood leaking from one nostril. Mr. Hunter took one long swipe at his nose with his arm, leaving a streak of blood on his white shirt from his elbow to his wrist. A devilish smile came on his face and he said, "I'm going to fix you so your momma won't know you, punk." With the force of a bull, he picked up Sinclair, who was at least six feet tall and about 170 pounds, and slung him over the desks on top of the other two boys, sending them sprawling across the room. But Mr. Hunter wasn't finished. While Sinclair was trying to pick up the dunce stool to use as a weapon, Mr. Hunter kicked him full in the chest and Buddy went down gasping for air, his cigarettes and lighter bouncing across the floor.

It was pretty much over after that. Mr. Hunter took him by the collar and dragged him down the hall, and that was the last time any of them saw Sinclair back in school. They heard a week later that Mr. Hunter's house had mysteriously been set afire and the prime suspect was Sinclair, but the fire did minimal damage before being extinguished. Shortly thereafter, he was picked up for stealing a car and put back in the slammer, and that's the last they ever heard of him.

As exhausted as he was, it was difficult for Will to sleep because of the jet noise. Where he had been sleeping these last few years, it was either extremely quite or loud as hell. The creatures that interrupted the silence of the night would clam up whenever Charley was on the prowl, and the sudden cessation of their calls usually brought Will to his feet. But that was yesterday, this was today. Being awake on the aircraft gave him time to think and contemplate the upcoming reunion. If it was to be anything like he expected, there would be speeches, introductions, classmates talking about life at old Sikeston High, the school record of five years of undefeated football, the legendary stories of Curt Gregory, dancing, and lots of food and drinks.

Will was smiling to himself when the hostess returned with the beverage cart. Drinking had never been his thing, but as badly as he wanted to sleep, he asked for a beer to help him relax. Watching her select a German brand, he caught a glimpse of the guy on the bottle in a pair of lederhosen. Instantly, he was reminded of a very good friend that he hadn't thought about for years. His name was Alan Stewart, a great guy that he hoped would be at the reunion.

The first time he saw Alan, he laughed out loud. Will was walking down the alley one morning when he sees this kid standing in his backyard wearing a pair of lederhosen, those short pant coveralls with shoulder straps. Will thought he looked like a nerd in those britches! He was aiming a BB gun at a bird in a tree and was missing it every time he pulled the trigger.

Will had seen Hans, as he was later nicknamed, who had just moved from St. Louis into the neighborhood a few months earlier with his parents. His nickname came because he looked so much like Hans Christian Anderson in those funny lederhosen. His father had opened a small steel plant, but before moving to St. Louis, they had lived in Europe where he picked up those stupid-looking britches.

Will walked over and said, "Let me try that," reaching for the gun that Hans quickly handed over. In a blink, the bird was tumbling down through the branches, landing at his feet, dead without a peep. "Wow!" Hans whispered. Will handed the gun back to him and went on his way. When he reached the end of the alley, he looked back, and Alan was still standing there, looking at Will with his mouth open. Will laughed again. *Those stupid lederhosen*, he thought.

You could tell he really wanted to be a part of the neighborhood gang, but how could they accept a member who wore lederhosen? When they found out his father was installing a tall antenna to bring in television reception from St. Louis and Memphis, they decided maybe there might be room for just one more member. For in those days, none of their homes had a television. In fact, some of the boys had never even seen television before.

It wasn't long before Hans' parents got tired of the gang hanging around to watch television and told Alan not to bring more than one friend home at a time. Shortly thereafter, it was "Don't bring anybody home at all." Like beggars, the boys would gather outside the house at night when they saw the flickering light of the tube and watch through the windows. So here was Will, looking through windows again. The problem was that they couldn't hear anything, but who cared. This was new age stuff. This was the future.

The Sandlot

I t would be summer when Will arrived home, and summer meant baseball. Every kid he knew played ball or wanted to in those days. Great memories here, and they came bouncing out of his brain like a baseline hit. The one that he would never forget was the most vivid and a joy to relive.

It was during his eighth grade year. The summer league was made up of more than a dozen teams scattered about town, and everyone thought their team was the best. It was sandlot baseball personified. Will's team had the perfect diamond; it was Baker's field at Burn Brae, except for the cow pies. They presented a special hazard to the outfielders who couldn't see them lurking in the high grass. The fresh ones were the worst, those dark-green, goopy ones that were often so big and so deep that if you stepped in one, you could lose your shoe. And if you recovered it, you would now have one green shoe to accompany the white one. What the cow had eaten for dinner that day dictated the variety of colors and aromas of the outfield. Dark green with wild onion and a hint of garlic was a deadly combination that could quickly ruin your day.

It was about that time that Will came into his own as a catcher and was extremely proud to catch for John Bloomfield, the star of the local high school team. He normally had his high school team catcher, but fortunately for Will, that catcher had been hired by the Missouri State Highway Department for the summer, making it impossible for him to play in the summer league.

It was a Saturday game in mid-July at Baker's field, and it was the classic rivalry between the South Side and the North Side, the most heated rivalry in disorganized sports. John would always call ahead to give Will a game plan. It was rich boys against poor boys. Will and his buddies hated those guys who lived in fancy houses with heated swimming pools who belonged to the one and only country club and drove fancy cars.

Slim Yeager, another high school star, played first. Big Nasty Boardman played second, another high school star who was the best tripper the South Side had. Their opponents hated rounding his base when they played the South. Lee Snyder, probably the most talented guy on the team, played shortstop. The rest of them were rejects from the high school program or those like Will who were too young to play varsity ball.

When their rivals from the North arrived, Bobby Crawford, who was playing third, ran over to Will as he was putting on his catcher's equipment and said, "Look who just showed up with the North." It was Curt Gregory. As much as they loved the guy, they knew he was going to cause them big trouble. Baseball was just another excel sport for him.

Petey Malone who covered center field came over to make the same comment, but Will stopped him in midsentence, saying, "Yeah, yeah, I know."

The sky was perfectly clear, and the temperature hovered at 100 degrees with a gusting wind that occasionally picked up dust, momentarily destroying one's vision. There was an unwritten rule that a sufficient supply of Pepsis had to be iced down for both teams by the host. A nearby horse trough was perfect for the job, packed with bottles and ice. After a game, Will could easily wolf down a half a dozen sodas himself.

That day, John and Will got in a groove. Everything Will asked for, John threw. He was an artist. With every pitch, Will moved closer in to the plate as his confidence level increased. The opposing pitcher was no match for John and the South moved out ahead by three runs in the second inning. When Curt finally came to bat, he hit a triple but couldn't get home when two of his teammates struck out. If it hadn't been for Curt's outstanding defensive play at shortstop, throwing several double plays in the next inning, the South would have been uncontrollable.

It was late in the seventh with the South ahead, 6–2, when it happened. Will called for a fast ball with a slight break to the inside when Cudda Martin, the biggest guy on the field, foul tipped the ball.

In those days, face masks only went halfway up the forehead. The ball hit Will just above the mask, careened off his noodle, and came to rest in the brush about fifty yards behind him. And that's the last thing he remembered.

Will later learned that bringing in a new catcher screwed up John's game so bad that he walked three straight batters. Wouldn't you know, Curt Gregory came up next and hit a bases loaded home run, tying the game at six all? They played until dark but agreed to call it a tie as many of the players worked their parent's farm, and there were chores to be done at nightfall.

Those hot, dusty summers would not have been remembered with such fondness had it not been for those exhilarating ball games on the sandlot at Burn Brae.

Burn Brae

Will and Peter Malone were always friends, Will couldn't remember a time when they weren't. Peter lived with his grandparents, the Bakers, and the boy's grandmothers were close friends. They lived on a five-thousand acre farm on the edge of Sikeston called Burn Brae. The plantation had it all, including a huge Southern-style mansion with tall white pillars and a barn even bigger than the house. It wasn't Tara, but it was close.

Will had very little contact with black people growing up, but the ones that worked at Burn Brae had an everlasting effect on his life, especially Velma who ran the mansion and George who supervised the farmhands. The two of them taught Will things about people and life that he would always remember.

After the Civil War, most of the blacks remained and sharecropped a part of Burn Brae, and their descendants followed suit. The rest of the acreage the Bakers farmed with the help of men relatively new to the area who lived in the Sunset Addition on the west edge of town. Peter's mother Virginia was one of the Baker's five children that grew up there. Because of their wealth, they were more cosmopolitan than most of the town's people.

The meeting of Peter's mother and father always intrigued Will. His father, James Malone, was an early barnstormer who flew the mail between St. Louis, Missouri, and Memphis, Tennessee. On one of his flights, he developed engine trouble and was forced to land in a field. He walked up to the nearest farmhouse, and the girl who answered the door became his wife. That girl was Peter's mother.

The marriage of James Malone and Virginia Baker was a stormy one that seemed to be doomed from the start. They moved to St. Louis where James pursued an aviator's career, doing air shows and flying the mail. Eventually, he became a test pilot for McDonnell Aircraft, which caused him to be away from home frequently. In her loneliness, Virginia, who had studied music, became a cocktail pianist and worked at many of the major hotels around St. Louis.

When Petey was born, his parents' marriage was already in disintegration, and on his sixth birthday, they sent him to Burn Brae to live with his grandmother to avoid exposing him to the war at home. His parents separated shortly thereafter, and except for several brief stays with his mother, Petey grew up in Sikeston. He was also Don Baker's cousin, his mother and Don's father were siblings.

Peter picked up the nickname Petey from his canary that looked like Petey Bird from the Warner Brothers cartoon. Since both of their grandmothers were close friends, Petey and Will spent a lot of time at each other's homes from an early age. Staying overnight at Burn Brae was a real treat for a young boy because there was always so much to do and get into.

Although tractors had long since replaced horses and mules on the farm, Petey's grandfather, Grover Baker, always felt obligated to take care of the old animals. Their barn was always full of pigeons, and on Will's frequent visits, they would climb the ladder to the loft and start shooting at them with their BB guns. Both their fellowship and hunting pigeons were great fun. They became fair marksmen in the process, but then came the day of the stampede.

Normally, these horses and mules were safe to be around, and the boys knew each one by name. The mules were Old Frank, Hattie, Smokey, Blind Jack, and Lucie. The horses were Jessie, named after Jessie James, Pop Eye, named because of the white ring around one eye, and Thunder. Why Thunder? Will never knew the answer since he was the oldest and most even tempered of them all, but maybe that was why the named him Thunder.

The animals seemed to know the boys were small and fragile and seldom showed ill temperament around them. Consequently, Will and Petey were not afraid to mingle in with them when they were stalking pigeons. They were usually very peaceful as far as horses and mules go.

On one particularly hot summer afternoon all of the animals were in the barn, Will was on the floor level with them, sneaking around, trying to catch a bird asleep in the rafters. As Petey was climbing the corral fence, he accidentally pulled the trigger of his loaded BB gun and fired a pellet into the rump of Old Frank. As old as he was, he jumped a good five feet into the air and, with both back hooves, kicked Thunder broadside. Thunder began to buck in a circle, colliding with Lucie, who was not known for having much patience. Then all hell broke loose.

There Will was, right in the middle of all these crazed animals running all over him like he wasn't there. He was bumped, knocked down, stepped on, and kicked. Somehow, he managed to cover his head with his arms to avoid being kicked in the head. By this time, the animals couldn't see Will for the dust that clouded out their vision, as around and around in their frenzy they went. George was in the tack room when he heard all the commotion coming from the barn. Jumping into the fracas, he grabbed Will's arm and dragged him to the fence. At the same time, he chased off the animals that had kicked down a gate as they excited the corral. Will could still remember how George picked him up, cradled his broken body in his arms, and said words that calmed him down from his hysteria. His caring actions let Will know the he was safe. What a gentle person this giant of a man was, Will recalled.

Luckily, there were no bones broken, but there was hardly a place on his body that wasn't bruised or bleeding. George had saved his life, and Will knew it. After that, he followed George around like a stray dog, but it never seemed to bother him. On the contrary, he appeared to enjoy it. Will learned a lot from that old black man, and it gave him a very positive outlook on black people even when his own family felt otherwise.

Many of the blacks at Burn Brae resented the city blacks from St. Louis that visited Sikeston to recruit marchers in the civil rights struggle of the 1960s. George ran off the NAACP contingent after a heated argument about treatment of blacks at Burn Brae. Although most blacks in Southeast Missouri were treated as second-class citizens then, George knew that life for the farm-working black man at Burn Brae was far better there than anywhere else, especially during that period. Looking back on it, Will recognized that George could have been pretending to enjoy his work there and his life as farm manager. After all, wages were low and housing was poor. But he had grown up on the farm and had worked his way up to foreman, no small feat. George was treated with respect by everyone who knew him, especially the Bakers. There was security at Burn Brae. As far as they were concerned, he was family, and they proved it when he was old by providing him a comfortable retirement. They supported him in respectable comfort to the ripe old age of eighty-nine. As foreman of Burn Brae, the Baker's entrusted George with their money, credit, and property, and that seemed to be enough for him. After all, honor and respect were hard to come by for a black man in those days.

One evening, sometime after midnight while Will was staying over with Petey, they heard a knock on the kitchen door. His room was near the back of the house, so they got up to see who it was. There, standing at the door was George, sweat pouring down his face. "Massa Petey, would you ask Massa Baker if he would comes down here for a minute… ah needs him." Petey ran for his grandfather as Will helped George to a chair, his legs beginning to shake. It looked like he might fall on his face any minute. It was then that Will saw the ice pick embedded in his back. There was very little blood, but he was in deep pain and about to pass out. When Mr. Baker came in, he immediately called Dr. Sargent. The doctor advised against pulling out the ice pick and told him to rush George to the hospital where he would meet them.

From what they were told, George had caught a hired hand by the name of Foster stealing one of the sharecropper's cotton from the storage area, and George had fired him on the spot. When he turned to walk away, the guy stabbed him in the back and ran.

The next day, George came home bandaged with one arm wrapped to his body. That evening, the other blacks had caught Foster and brought him up to the big house where George was being cared for. "Give the word, George, and we'll hang this nigger here and now," one of the leaders called out. George paused to let the man know that he was seriously thinking about it, and then he stood up, walked down the steps, and stood face- to-face with him.

Foster had the fear of facing death in his face, and in fact, he was. Mr. and Mrs. Baker, Petey, and Will were on the veranda watching all of this, and Will wondered why Mr. Baker said nothing. But he never interfered with his workers in matters such as this. "You've got one minute to get off this property," said George, "and if I ever see your ugly face again, I'll let my friends have their way with you. Now get!"

In a flash, Foster had covered the distance from the house to the main road, and that's the last they ever saw of him. It was a moonlit night, and Will remembered with the negro community they had their own justice and, in some cases, their own punishment.

Will often wondered how Petey would have grown up had it not been for Velma. Part of her duties at the big house was to help raise him. She could be tough at times, but Petey and Will always respected her. After all, she had raised three children of her own; the oldest grew up to be a preacher at a local Baptist church, her daughter became a teacher, and her youngest joined the army just before the end of WWII where he earned a commission after several acts of heroism in the South Pacific.

Velma also seemed to have a soft spot in her heart for Will. He assumed she felt sorry for him being a motherless child, so he got a lot of mileage out of that throughout his childhood. Regardless of how late he arrived at Burn Brae, she always made sure he had something to eat. If he got real dirty, which was frequently, she would wash his clothes to make certain he went home in clean ones. Velma reminded Will so much of the Aunt Jemima lady on the syrup bottle.

Just before bedtime, she would tell the boys stories her mother had told her about life as a slave before and after the Civil War. She loved Abe Lincoln, and because of the stories she told about him, so did Will. He was always amazed how she had learned all those great stories about Lincoln when she had never gone to school.

The story about Abe that Will loved the most was how the president grieved to know so many people hated him including the time a politician whom Abe highly respected had criticized him intensely by calling him the ugliest man he had ever seen. But Abe, being the gentleman he was, had such high regard for the statesman, he simply replied, "I guess with his knowledge, he must be right."

But the story that etched the most vivid vision of Abe Lincoln in Will's mind was the tragic story of his son's death and how he had grieved for weeks on end, unable to function as the president. Finally, a very close friend, former minister, and politician told Abe that his son was not dead. Abe rose to his feet from behind his massive desk and said, "Have you come to mock my son's death, sir?" His friend replied, "Oh no, Mr. President, heaven forbid. But are you a Christian, Mr. President?"

"Yes," he answered.

"Then you must know that he is not dead, but alive with Christ. He lives, Mr. President, just as our Christ lives. And just as we will live with him again someday." He then placed his arms around Lincoln and prayed as the president wept.

As the story goes, Abe Lincoln seemed reborn after that day and was once again able to function as our president. Will often wondered how Velma knew these wonderful stories when Will's schoolteachers didn't.

Waco

After a few drinks, Will began to really relax. He could feel the effect of the alcohol, but he was far from being drunk. The numbing effect was welcome as the aircraft's engines continued to drone through the night. The movie then being shown on the cockpit wall was about a boy who was constantly being harassed by a bully. Will wondered if his nemesis would be at the reunion. As a boy, Will attended South Grade School, and it had its share of bullies, and he had his own personal one. He was called Waco. For two years, he ran Will home from school, pelting rocks off his noodle, and calling him names. Names that no fourth grader should ever hear, nor should sixth graders for that matter since he terrorized Will well into the sixth grade. And not just Will, but Davie, Jerry, and anyone else he could lord over.

Will could outrun Waco, but he didn't always see him coming or waiting in ambush just around the corner of the school building. The next thing he knew Waco would have him by the collar, whaling the stuffin' out of him and in front of the girls too. The shame of it all was almost more than Will could bear. Something had to be done. But what?

Several times, Will would arrive home crying and bleeding, but he never let Mam see him in that condition. Waco wasn't that big, but he grew up with two brothers who boxed his ears on a continuing basis. This gave him the desire to take it out on Will and his friends. Waco was especially cruel to a retarded fellow named Wally Lee. Wally, who must have been at least seventeen, lived near the school, but didn't attend because he had the brain of a four-year-old. He lived in a fantasy world of war, carried a stick rifle, and wore a plastic helmet. When he passed through the schoolyard, he would run from tree to tree, bush to bush, pretending he was assaulting the enemy. The school kids had discovered a long time ago that if they hollered, "Hit the deck, Wally

Lee!" he would instantly dive face-first into the dirt, avoiding imaginary enemy aircraft or the enemy on patrol.

Waco loved to follow Wally around and yell, "Hit the deck, Wally Lee!" near a mud hole or on the hard surface of the street. And as expected, Wally would dive face-first into whatever happened to be there. The poor guy never learned, but Will learned an important lesson.

One day, with a few of the school kids watching, Waco coaxed Wally into walking over near the foot of a small hill close to a pile of boulders. When he had Wally in position, he yelled, "Hit the dirt, Wally Lee!" and sure enough, Wally dove face-first into that pile of rocks. To the witnesses, it was appalling. It was so devastating that some of the girls left in tears.

Always before Wally would freeze in the prone position for a few seconds, then jump up and holler "Charge!" before chasing after some unseen foe. But this time, he was slow getting up and gave no exclamation of "Charge!" He just raised his head and looked Will's way, with his pitiful face looking like hamburger. He tried to speak, but nothing came out, appearing to be in shock. The cruelty of this act made Will sick, and he remembered feeling as though he would throw up. How mean can one human be to another, he wondered? This was the beginning of his first thoughts of retaliation.

One day, Will received an unusually brutal thrashing during which Waco laughed the entire time calling Will "Momma's boy without a Momma." Getting up, he ran to the safety of his room, got down on his knees by his bed, and told the Lord that the pain he felt within hurt more than the pain without. He told God he was tired of this kind of abuse, and he wasn't gonna take it any more.

That night, he made up his mind that regardless of what happened, he was going to fight back. But he didn't know how he was going to do it. He also knew he wasn't fooling God, that he could see the fear in Will's heart. So he asked the man up there to help him even though he knew the Lord was against violence. But then, Will thought, didn't he destroy great armies that moved against his people? Didn't he help little David?

Sleep was slow to come that night as he prepared his mind for the coming apocalypse and the uncertain consequences of his holy rebellion against oppression and evil. Waco romped through his dreams the entire night, and his face was the first thing Will saw in his mind the next morning. Over and over, he kept telling himself that whatever physical pain he might experience, it would be better than the mental anguish that had stolen his pride and filled him with humiliation. But he wasn't fooling himself. He was scared.

By the time Will arrived at school the next morning, he was ready for anything, but it was not to be that day. Waco had skipped school, and since it was Friday, he had three more days to sweat the coming Armageddon. In his mind, Waco grew bigger and meaner over the weekend, but the remembrance of Wally being treated so inhumanly weighed heavily on Will's conscience. Will arrived at school early that Monday morning even though most conflicts usually occurred after school. Maybe he wanted to size Waco up some more, but he was late for school, and Will missed seeing him. During the lunch hour, he saw Waco and two of his cronies sneaking a smoke out behind the Boy Scout cabin at the end of the schoolyard. Waco saw Will watching and flashed a finger his way. A chill ran up Will's spine. It was going to be a long afternoon.

After what seemed an eternity, the school bell rang at three o'clock, and Will stepped into the hall to find Davie and Jerry literally shaking in their tennis shoes. "Hey, Will. We just passed Waco down the hall, and he asked us if we had our running shoes on," Davie said, his voice quivering. "Let's sneak out the gym door and head for home. It ought to give us a good head start."

"Not today, fellas. I'm going straight out the front door," Will said with somewhat shaky confidence.

"What are you talking about, Will? Are you crazy? You know he'll be waiting for us."

"I ain't running today, guys. I may get killed, but I ain't running." And with that, he headed for the front stairs with the two of them trailing fearfully behind.

Within a few seconds, he spotted Waco down by the corner where he usually waited, between the school and the safety of Will's home. He kept walking. When Will got within twenty yards of him, Waco hollered out, "Gonna fix you so your grandma won't know you, twerp." Will kept walking. Waco stepped out in front of him and said, "Where you want it, Willie? About the head? Up the gut? Don't you boys run off now? This won't take long, and then I want a piece of you two."

Will never remembered doing it himself. It was as if someone else's arm was coming around his head, his fist heading straight toward Waco's pimply nose. Waco never saw it coming either. Time slowed down. The fist mashed the nose, and it seemed to stick there in that position for seconds. Then the blood began to slowly emerge, moving down out of his nostrils in a large thick stream.

Waco staggered backward, keeping his balance. His look of disbelief was priceless. Reaching for his pocket, he pulled out a heavily soiled handkerchief and made a half-hearted attempt to stop the flow, but it was futile. Over and over, he said the words, "You're dead, punk. You're dead. Oh boy, are you ever dead."

The three boys left him there sitting on the curb with his head between his legs trying to stop the flow, looking a whole lot smaller than before, still saying those words, "You're dead. You're freakin' dead."

Will's memory of Waco didn't end there. His mind raced ahead to a confrontation they had on the football field their senior year two weeks after practice started. Will had searched everywhere for his helmet, but it was nowhere to be found. Names were taped to the back of each helmet, making them easy to identify even from a distance. But it was not where it should have been. He went out onto the playing field, and after scanning the players, spotted it on another player's head. As he approached, he could see whose head it was on. It was Waco's.

"Hey, Waco. You got my helmet." "Tough…get another one," he shot back.

"I want mine, Waco, so hand it over." He refused, muttering something under his breath, and started to walk away. Will reached out and grabbed the back of the helmet, pulling it over his head. When he did, Waco turned his head, and the helmet struck the bridge of his nose. Will didn't mean for it to happen, but for the second time, he had bloodied Waco's nose. Waco had grown a lot since their last encounter six years ago, and his reputation had grown with him; he had become the state Golden Gloves champion in his weight division. "You're dead meat, worm. You're dead. You're freaking dead." Waco told Will what he was going to do to him every time he saw Will that year, but he never did it.

One final episode with Waco centered on another meeting they had five years later, one that didn't make Will very proud. He had returned to Sikeston from Panama after having spent a year teaching jungle survival school to the Army's Ranger Forces, feeling as though he was invincible, and determined to get even for all those injustices suffered as a child.

The very first day home, Will began searching for Waco and found him in the sandwich bar of the local bowling alley. He was sitting near the far end with a couple of young ladies and didn't notice Will's arrival. Sitting down a few stools over and in a very loud voice, he boomed out, "Hey, Waco, you still chasing kids home from school?" At first, he seemed shocked to see Will, but once he composed himself, he said nonchalantly, "Hi, Will, when did you get home?" Will knew he had him flustered. He didn't look as sanguine as the last time they had met.

"I think I owe you something, don't you, Waco, something that I've been waiting to deliver for a long time. What say we step outside and even the score?" Waco was starting to sweat.

"I don't want any trouble, Will. Why don't you let me buy you a drink? Hey, Charlie, give Will a beer on me." His voice was higher than normal now.

"You know, Waco, I never saw you back away from trouble before. Could it be you've grown chicken on me? Hey, girls," Will was on a roll now, "I think you ladies are sitting with the colonel's main bird. Hey, bartender, you got any chicken feed for this chicken shit creep?" Now this is where you'd have thought the great Waco would have drawn the line, but he never said a word. He just sat there in his humiliation and kept his mouth shut.

Will thought that this would be a great moment of triumph and vindication for him to see the toughest guy in grade school brought to his knees, but he found no satisfaction in being the bully. He left the bowling alley feeling empty, even cruel. In effect, with this senseless act, he knew that had become no better than Waco.

It occurred to Will as he sat in this comfortable aircraft seat so far removed from the war that he was thinking of things he had all but forgotten. Things that had no bearing on anything, but seemed to be a part of a locomotive racing down the tracks of the past triggered by thoughts of returning home. One of those cars attached to that train contained his grandmother's family and his childhood nanny, Dough Dough.

After Will's grandfather Frank Sewell died, Mam told Dough Dough she would always have a home with her if she wanted to stay. She was a very industrious woman, always liked to stay busy, and did so by serving as Mam's housekeeper and Will's nanny. It was a blessing for Will because as a full-blooded Apache who knew a lot of their history, she could tell Will great stories about the warriors of old that had been passed down to her from her forefathers.

Because of these stories, Will always felt that somewhere in a past life, he had been an Indian. He could remember riding a broomstick horse around, not as a cowboy but as an Indian. He seemed to envy their way of life, and like the Indians, he loved the outdoors, the wild life, the changing seasons, the flocks of geese heading south, and all of nature. What a rich and glorious history they had...until the white man came along.

In between naps, Will listened to the aircraft's different audio channels until he picked up a classical one and tried to think back when the last time he had heard that type of music. Music played a major role in the first sixteen years of Will's life. He had been born with an unusually angelic soprano voice, and beginning at age seven, was frequently asked to sing at weddings and funerals. It was about the same time that Dough Dough came to live with them that Will had a problem singing at a funeral. Many of the deceased were his grandmother's friends, women who spent many hours at their house. Most of them were grandmothers themselves and were always kind and loving toward Will. It didn't take long for Dough Dough to realize that he was having a problem with death. One day, she saw him forget the words of a song he was singing at a funeral while standing at the foot of a casket [that] held one of his grandmothers good friends who had been exceptionally sweet and kind to Will. Later, Mam saw him freeze at another funeral, unable to continue.

A few days later while getting ready for bed, Dough Dough came into his room and said, "I want you to think about something, Will. We all ride into this world on a horse, and that horse is our body. And we ride that horse through out life. But sometime during our lifetime, our horse wears out. When this happens, we leave our horse behind and go on without it. This is what you must remember, that what you see there in that box is not the person you knew, but the horse they rode in on. Can you remember that, Will? That person has gone on to be with the Holy Spirit. Think you can remember that?" From then on, he would look at the person in the box and see them as a horse and was never bothered with death again until it struck closer to home.

As Will grew into his teens, he became best known as a singer and had lost all fear of performing in front of crowds. Dough Dough's teachings had given him renewed confidence. At one time or another, he sang in every church in the city as well as a number of those in surrounding towns. As a result, he developed good friends on both sides of Sikeston, from the less privileged where he lived to the influential side, where Curt Gregory lived. Will was invited to Curt's church many times to sing, which was one of the reasons he came to know Curt better than anyone else. Curt had many acquaintances but very few good friends.

To most people, Curt was an enigma. He lived on the moneyed side of town, but that didn't give a clue as to his true identity. Oh, they knew who he was on the court and what his accomplishments were in sports, but they never really knew him and Will suspected Curt wanted it that way.

His father, Lyman Gregory, devoted a great deal of time helping him develop his athletic skills, enrolling him in every sports clinic that came along. He built a full-sized basketball court in their backyard and worked with Curt year-round. Will would have given anything to have had a father like his.

Curt would have been a starter on the high school team even in the eighth grade if it had been permissible. There was nothing he couldn't do. His major asset was his speed and endurance; being part Cherokee Indian, he could run all day. Because his agility and balance were so far superior to theirs, the other Sikeston athletes found it hard to compete, so they chose events Curt didn't compete in.

During the summers, Will and Curt worked together as lifeguards at the city pool. Their first job each spring required draining the algae-infested water from the year before and scrubbing the walls and floor of the pool. On more than one occasion, Will would watch in awe as Curt sprang on the high board, over and over, higher and higher, and sometimes above an empty or partly filled pool. It was pure artistry, beautiful and rhythmic as each spring took him even higher. Not once did Will ever see him lose his balance. Along with all his other athletic abilities, he was also an exceptional diver and swimmer.

One of Will's other friends, Eddie Webber, had to try that same springboard stunt. This was a guy who usually got into more trouble than Will. The first time Will realized just how much trouble came on a Sunday during church services. No one knew for sure how Eddie made the choir, but there he was standing next to Will, three tiers up. When it came time for the choir to sing their special number, the director signaled for all to rise and the music began. While everyone was looking at the director, Eddie very carefully lifted the chair of the woman in front of him and set it up on his level.

Will wanted to say something, but he was aghast. With Eddie being so much bigger and Will being the youngest member of the choir, he said nothing. When the song ended, the director motioned for the choir to sit down. Will held his breath, and sure enough, that poor woman, thinking there was a chair behind her, sat down into thin air.

With a shriek, she tumbled into the empty space, and all that could be seen were her legs and underwear. The audience and the other choir members were shocked, and a murmur spread throughout the auditorium.

Here came the pastor, and he was hot! The first thing that struck Will was that the pastor might think he had been the culprit, but he zeroed in on Eddie, grabbing him by the ear and dragging him out the side door. That was the end of Eddie's career as a choir member.

That memory brought back another one of Eddie's errors of judgment, of him pulling the chair out from under himself, in effect. Seeing Curt, he saw no reason why he couldn't do the same thing: spring over a pool that was eighty percent dry. Will and Curt tried to warn him, but he wouldn't listen. As he began to spring over the empty pool, he started to lose his balance. Falling, his body first landed on the board, then fell off the edge. Eddie managed to grasp the board with both hands, swung under the board, lost his grip, and fell against the edge of the pool, breaking both legs.

Thinking back to Curt, he remembered how his father discouraged him from playing football; otherwise, he probably would have been a football All-American. After all, he was an All-American in track, baseball, and basketball. But it never seemed to bother him that he didn't get to play football. He loved his father so much that he never questioned his father's decisions. During one of Will's singing engagements at Curt's church, Will was afforded an opportunity to become even closer to Curt and his father. The churches in town had formed a boy's basketball league, and Curt's father was his church's coach. One Sunday after Will had sung there, Curt's father asked him if he would like to play for their church's team. Will jumped at the chance. Mr. Gregory had a way of taking kids with limited skills and making winners out of them. As long as his teammates fed Curt the ball at the right time, he would usually score. The night they played the toughest team in the league, they won, 45 to 25. Curt scored 25 of his team's points, the same as all the other players combined.

Will thought about how music was another common interest the two of them shared. Curt was an excellent pianist, and they appeared together in recitals and school concerts. Curt's version of Malagueña always brought a crowd to their feet. One day, he confided in Will that he would give anything to sing like he could. It shocked Will. Here he was wishing he could play like Curt or be the athlete he was, while all the time Curt wished, in some small measure, that he could be like Will.

But there was another compelling reason for Will buddying up to Curt. In the late forties, his father was the local candy distributor, and during World War II, bubble gum and chocolate were impossible to buy. Except from Curt, that is. His father usually received a box of Double Bubble each month, and Curt got a nickel for a one-cent piece from the kids at school. After they became friends, Will got two pieces for a nickel, which was great since most of the kids were never offered any.

Occasionally, he would share a Hershey bar with Will, and in return, Will would hustle basketballs for Curt as he practiced long shots. Will knew better than anyone why he had became such a marvelous player.

Contemplating that period, Will found himself thinking about some of the other jams he got himself into. It probably all started when he learned to drive a car. When he was twelve years old, Mam worried that she might have a heart attack or something might happen while they were on the road, and that he would be stranded with her unable to get help. So she taught him how to drive. To practice, she let him drive around the farm in her 1938 Dodge while she picked beans and corn for canning. It was a stick shift with three gears on the floor, and he was amazed at how easy it was to drive. It was also the reason he felt capable of driving Mam's car when she wasn't looking.

One day in June, close to his fourteenth birthday, Mam was invited by her friends to drive with them in their car to Cape Girardeau thirty-five miles away for an afternoon of shopping. This was rare because Mam was one of the few women in her circle that had a car and usually did the driving.

It happened that on that same day a big parade had been planned in Sikeston for the annual Cotton Carnival, and Will knew all his friends would be there. There was one young lady that he desperately wanted to impress. Her name was Peggy Myers. Remember her? The date he had when she kissed him full on the lips. Well, she had developed into something really fine and had just broken up with an upper classman. So it was now time for Will to make his move.

He saw no reason why he shouldn't drive his grandmother's car to the parade, which took place just one mile from his house since he knew she wouldn't be back for at least four hours. After all, he was an experienced driver now, and he wouldn't be driving that far. He grabbed her extra keys, swung the garage door up, started up the engine, and backed the Dodge down the driveway and out into the street. What a feeling! He was extremely nervous while at the same time elated. It was the feeling of freedom, of importance, of being big time.

One by one, Will picked up his best friends, headed down town, parked along the parade route, and sat on the hood of the car, waiting for the parade to begin. Will kept an eye out for Peggy, and sure enough, she came prancing down the street with two of her girl friends. The word was out. "Willie had wheels."

It was a beautiful day with the weather pleasant and cool for September. Will and his friends had a great afternoon enjoying their friendship and freedom as they drove around all the places the older kids frequented. Will knew he had improved his standing with this young lady sitting next to him by the way she snuggled up tight. He was in hog heaven.

As the bewitching hour approached, Will drove his friends home, got a smooch from Peggy, and headed for the house. Within minutes, he went from an ecstatic high to a heart attack low. As he approached the block where he lived, what he saw down the street made his heart stop. There, sitting on the front porch rocking away was Mam. For whatever reason, she had come home an hour early. He was in big trouble.

"Okay, Mr. Big Shot, you have just lost the right to go to your senior prom." *Lord, have mercy on me, that's three years away*, Will thought to himself. *She's gonna punish me the rest of my high school years?* About that time, the sheriff's car pulled up in front. "The scallywags home, sheriff," she said. "I'll take care of it from here." *She had called the law on him*, Will thought to himself. The sheriff smiled and drove away. It was all he could do to keep from calling him back for help, knowing what was in store for him.

The worst part of the detention was the ground he was losing with Peggy. When he would see her at school, she would want to know why he couldn't take her to a movie or to the local hangout, the Bulldog Inn. That was the most trying summer Will ever experienced when he was growing up, and it was over before he got sprung. In the meantime, Peggy had found herself a steady guy, and for Will, that was the end of that.

Mary Ann Muldune

As he fell in and out of sleep, Will's mind continued to drift back to the past, to the days of his youth that he felt were so unique. These memories had been sequestered, shut up lest they come back and cloud his thinking, his mission, and perhaps endanger his life. But now, they were finally released as he tried to think of who else he might see at the reunion. His thoughts drifted back to Sikeston High, the only high school in Sikeston. Kids from several different grade schools converged on old Sikeston High the fall of 1949, his freshman year, the year a strikingly beautiful girl moved into his neighborhood during the summer. Every day, as he rode his bike to the swimming pool, he usually saw her sunning in a lawn chair. He remembered vividly the day he met her. It was a hot, sweltering day, and he finally mustered up courage to stop and introduce himself. Her name was Mary Ann Muldune. Wanting to get something going here, he said, "You ought to come down to the city pool. You'll get a better tan around the water." Looking up from one of those Hollywood magazines, she said, "That's not a bad idea, where is it?" After he gave her directions, she replied, "I'll be down later in the day." As she got up to go inside, Will looked back and couldn't believe the shape of this girl. In his mind, the word *divine* seemed the most appropriate way to describe her.

Will didn't mention to Mary Ann that he was a lifeguard, but he fantasized about her coming to the pool and visualized the surprised look on her face as she saw him sitting high above the swimmers on his lifeguard chair. Fantasizing even more, he could see himself saving her from drowning by giving her mouth to mouth resuscitation. His dreams had no bounds.

He had been at the pool for what seemed like hours before she walked out of the girls' dressing room. Every eye in the pool stared seemingly awestruck as she strode Will's way. "You didn't tell me you were a lifeguard, Will," she said slyly, as she stood looking up at him. The view looking down her bathing suit top made him feel a little giddy and made it difficult to concentrate on their conversation. Mary Ann Muldune was definitely the girl for him, Will thought, as he watched her dive gracefully into the pool and swim away.

A few minutes later, she swam back over and said, "Hey, Will, who is that gorgeous lifeguard over there?" She was pointing to his friend Curt. Will was destroyed. Not Curt, he thought to himself, not Curt. Will had plans for this girl. Lord, not Curt. She was waiting for a response, so he told her who Curt was and that he was one of his best friends, hoping she would be satisfied with that. But no, now she wanted to meet him. So reluctantly, Will introduced them, knowing that this was the kiss of death. Good-bye, birdie. He also felt that he had led the lamb to the wolf, albeit a friend. But Will never lost his feeling for Mary Ann Muldune.

Vultures

One of the fellows sitting across the aisle from Will was blind, and the airline had permitted him to bring his Seeing Eye dog aboard. It was a beautiful breed that he had never seen before. He and the dog took a liking to each other instantly. It made him think of his childhood dog Corky and how he had died. As painful as his loss had been, it was behind him now, and refreshing his memory of their time together was no longer painful.

It was during his junior year, the weekend before school ended for the summer that Corky disappeared. He was liked by all their neighbors, so Will never tied him up or put up a fence. He became educated about crossing the street when he was a very young pup after being hit by a passing car. Luckily, he was only roughed up a bit, but he learned his lesson. So Will saw no reason to restrict him.

One sweltering Saturday, Will and his friend Buddy decided to visit the Indian mounds to dig for artifacts. He seldom went anywhere without Corky, especially to the mounds, because those little hikes were the highlight of the dog's life. So when it came time to go, Will went outside and called for him, but he didn't come. After a thorough search of the neighborhood, he left without him.

It was a typical Midwestern day, with a hot wind blowing in from across the plains, not a cloud in the sky. On the way to the Indian mounds, Will and Buddy met Curt at the rodeo grounds. Workers were busy repairing corrals and chutes in preparation for the annual rodeo scheduled in a few weeks. They crossed the dirt parking lot as the wind picked up sand, pelting their faces, stinging their eyes, and propelling them along.

Sikeston sits atop a long narrow plateau that stretches down from the Missouri Ozark foothills nearly to the Mississippi River at New

Madrid. This narrow strip of land divides a massive ancient lake or swamp that had been formed hundreds or thousands of years ago by repeated flooding of the Mississippi River and by streams flowing from the Ozarks. This swamp was called by various names such as Dark Cypress, the Big Swamp, or the Great Swamp. This gave the Bootheel another nickname: Swampeast Missouri. This swamp was drained in the early twentieth century in perhaps the largest drainage project ever attempted in the state of Missouri. In the distant past, Mississippian Indians inhabited this area, made their camps along this ridge, and hunted and fished with bow and arrows and spears. Evidence of their camps, 600 to 1,200 years old, can still be found. Small arrow points, bits of pottery, grinding stones, and other items are uncovered frequently after rain and windstorms. The ancient lake was dry now except for a few marsh areas and was rich cultivated farmland created from the sediment laid down by the prehistoric rivers, lakes, and swamps in this Mississippi Delta.

Walking along the edge of the ridge, the boys would occasionally pause to pick up anything that looked man-made. On this particular day, they were searching along an area they hadn't walked before. Over the years, erosion had washed gigantic gullies that cut deep into the ridge and trailed off to the mudflats below. The landscape looked much like a series of miniature grand canyons. As they reached the top of the arroyo, hundreds of vultures were circling overhead, observing something just out of the boy's view.

The hot, putrid smell of death blew into their faces, and Will gagged for a moment but kept moving. "Let's go see what the buzzards are having for dinner," he said, leading Buddy single file as they traced the top of the ridge down into the gully below. The trail veered off to the right, and they hadn't gone very far when Will stopped the column. What they were about to witness sent chills all over Will.

Lying on the floor of the canyon were hundreds of dead dogs. Some were mere skeletons, others appeared to have been killed recently. The stench of rotting dogs was almost unbearable. Swarms of vultures were busy at their ghastly work, looking defiantly as the boys slowly worked their way around the bodies. Then Will saw Corky and his heart sank into his stomach. There he was looking much like he did in Will's backyard, asleep on a hot summer day. He was stretched out as far as his little body could stretch, bullet wounds in his neck and stomach, and his collar with the engraved metal plate "Corky" still attached. As Will knelt beside him, Curt and Buddy stood close by. They knew how much Corky meant to him. His furry little head blurred in Will's vision as the tears poured out of his eyes onto the ground. "Now we know what the dog catcher does with dogs, Will," Curt said with disgust in his voice, "that dirty, rotten son-of-a…" As they helped Will pick him up, they carried him to the shade of one of the few trees at the top of the ridge some distance from the killing field. Will dug a hole with his hunting knife, and they laid their dear friend to rest there.

By this time, it was midday, and the heat of a Midwestern summer was at its hottest. The wind had died down a bit, but what breeze there was stung their noses and throats. They rested under the tree with Corky for a while, reminiscing about experiences and adventures they'd had with their buddy. Finally, they said good-bye to him and headed home. Knowing how much he loved that faithful dog, his friends said very little on the hike back. It was hard for Will to accept how he had died, and resentment began to fill his heart. There wasn't much he could do about all this, but for years, every time he saw the dogcatcher's truck, his mind would flash to that day, his little friend Corky, and the vision of circling vultures.

The smell of death had become commonplace since Will had been in Vietnam. The smell is different in humans than other living creatures, and he never got used to it. Like vultures, they were drawn to a village in the highland region during his first tour of duty as result of a message their command had received from a pilot who had flown over the area. He had reported that the village appeared to have been pillaged and set afire with no evidence of life. They landed in a field just outside the edge of this unknown village, and when they got within 100 yards, the unmistakable smell of death filled the air. The team counted 75 dead, some had been tortured, some had been dismembered, and some had been killed in ways that he had a hard time describing to the investigative team that was to follow.

Larry and Will grew bitter and vengeful as they set about the gruesome task of burying the dead. The hardest part was burying the children. Babies, some no more than a few months old, their little lives snuffed out before they had a chance to know life. Thinking back now, this could have been the beginning of their callousness toward the enemy. This may have been the turning point where he and Larry vowed to take full retribution, where all bets were off, and where "take no prisoners" became the order of the day.

But there were many more incidents that played a part in their vindictive attitude. One was the suicide attack they encountered while assigned to SF 22, one of the CIA's Special Reaction units that had been inserted deep within the enemy's maze of supply lanes and staging areas. This station was in the VC's heartland and was continually under attack. About every three days, they could expect the enemy to hit them hard and usually after midnight. For two weeks, this pattern continued until they could set their watches to the time they could expect the action to start. It always started with a mortar barrage followed by an infantry attack.

But one night, they caught the Americans off guard by striking earlier in the evening, which was prompted by an especially costly firefight for the VC several days before. The team had spent the day reinforcing their positions. While Larry and Will were asleep in their hooch, the enemy started a mortar barrage even while sending their own troops into the compound in the middle of the bombardment, an obvious suicide mission. The VC were so intent on wiping them out that they were willing to waste a hundred or more of their own men to destroy the American camp.

Before they knew it, they had VC pouring into their hooches running through the barrage, attacking with bayonets, machetes, and grenades. Before Will could get to his rifle, a VC came at him with his bayonet, but he was able to ward off his thrust with his flak jacket as he pulled out the Italian knife strapped to his ankle and drove it straight into the VC's stomach. Pulling the knife out brought a torrent of warm blood that instantly soaked the VC's pajama top and beyond. Larry had his hands full, firing his .45 while using one of the VC's body to shield himself from an attacker. Will stopped an intruder with a point-blank shot from his pistol just as he dropped a grenade on the floor. "Grenade!" Will hollowed, and they both dove out the door and rolled behind some sandbags as the explosion went off.

People were running in every direction, some GIs, and some VC. Will picked up a rifle from one of the dead and began to select targets, guys in pajamas, dropping one, then a second. The camp's watchtower got hit by a rocket and fell over, crashing to the ground knocking out its searchlight, but there was enough light from the explosions and flares being fired by Will's comrades to see that the enemy was now trying to retreat. Chasing after them the Green Berets and the South Vietnamese MV team pursued them with a vengeance stopping as many of the enemy as possible before they could escape.

This attack had backfired on the VC; their bodies were everywhere. Taking stock and caring for their wounded, the team counted their losses. Will's team had lost eleven men, another ten wounded but not critical. They were astounded at the losses to the enemy. Between those they had killed and those who died from their own mortars, they counted 112 dead VC and NVA.

When Will finally caught up with Larry again, he noticed he was bleeding from his side. They radioed for an airlift to airvac their dead and wounded, and Will suggested that Larry climb aboard when it arrived to have them tend to the wound properly. He argued about leaving, but one of their superiors ordered him to return. Reluctantly, he left with the others. This was his thing. This was what he lived for. This could get him killed.

Several hours after Larry's departure, Will felt a wet spot on his side. Lifting up his shirt, he discovered that he had been wounded from the bayonet charge earlier in the day. Will considered that it was grounds for a Purple Heart, but he never reported it. He wasn't there for medals, he was there to kill the enemy and stay alive.

Even now as he sat in the aircraft headed home, he could see why his thinking had become a little jaded. It was, in part, from having to put some of his closest friends in body bags: eleven courageous American Special Forces patriots that had paid the ultimate sacrifice that night. Will wanted to raise a prayer of thanks for himself and Larry coming out of that firefight alive, but the ungodly thoughts he had about the enemy far outweigh any heavenly thoughts, at least for the moment.

It was while sitting here that for the first time in over a year he had a chance to analyze his thinking away from the distractions of war… and it wasn't pretty.

The Race Track

"What are you going to do first when you get home, Will?" Larry asked, leaning over from across the aisle.

"Lie down in a nice soft bed, turn on the air conditioning so it will drown out all sound, and sleep," Will replied.

"After that?" he asked.

"After that, probably go out and visit old friends. There are a number of older people, friends of my grandmother, who I want to visit if they are still alive. Remember me telling you about my friend Curt? His father is on the top of my list. Then I want to visit the farm. I just want to walk the land, where so many of my forefathers had lived and died, and kind of renew its acquaintance if you know what I mean. I know it sounds a little hokie, but does it make any sense?"

"I guess," Larry responded, but Will doubted that he understood. *Hell, I'm not sure I understood*, he thought to himself. "Keep in mind, that farm has been in our family for over 175 years, even before the Civil War. When I was growing up, it meant nothing to me. It's only since I've been in the military that it has meant something." Even after he said those words, he had to think about that. What did it mean to him?

"Then I'm going to look up two people, Mary Ann Muldune and Waco."

Larry knew who they were. He asked, "Think she'll be living in Sikeston, Will? Or be single?" *Good question*, Will mused. Then without waiting for an answer, he asked, "What do you have in store for Waco?" Will didn't have to think about that one. He owed him an apology, make things right with him. Life is too short to be little, Will's grandmother used to say.

As the hostess arrived with another round of drinks, Will said to Larry, "This may sound weird, but I'm looking forward to going hunting. I know, you would think that after packing a rifle around all this time that the last thing I would want to do is pick up another weapon. But I always found the most peace in the field. And right now, that's what I need the most. Peace." But Will knew that while he loved to hunt and would be taking a gun, it probably would never be fired. The hunting he would be doing was for peace.

After finishing his drink, he tilted back his seat and thought about going hunting, about walking out to the pond on the Lewis farm. It was a special hunting place, and thanks to Billy Lewis, he had gotten his father to grant him permission to hunt there anytime he desired. Billy was as wild as a deer and loved to hunt as much as Will did. They didn't hunt together often when Will was entering high school because Billy was a lowly grade school kid, and that just wasn't done in those days. But Will later changed his mind because as Billy grew older, he turned into a very cool guy, and as a football teammate, he was like a brother.

Billy's father was a very successful farmer and accumulated land throughout Southeast Missouri. Being a likeable person, he had a lot of friends, but for whatever reason, he wasn't happy at home and was known to have a mistress. Billy and his father were very close, however, and he took Billy hunting in Canada and in the Far West many times. They invited Will to go pheasant hunting in Nebraska and the Dakotas once. It was a wonderful experience that afforded him a look at a part of this country he had never seen before.

Will and Billy grew much closer the year his father built a dirt stock car track on their farm. Races were held on Saturday evenings. A number of broken-down cars were left after each race to be retrieved later or abandoned permanently. This began another phase of Will's life: the world of speed.

Billy stopped in at Buddy's house one Sunday where Will was visiting and invited the two of them to come see what he had been doing all morning. After everyone left Saturday, he worked on one of the abandoned racecars and had it up and running. With a deafening roar and a cloud of dust, he was off, roaring around the track in his very own racecar. After a few laps, he pulled it off to the side and motioned Will and Buddy to join him. "Why don't we see if we can get a couple more of these junkers started," he said excitedly, "and we'll have ourselves a race?" Sure enough, after working for an hour or so, they were able to start two more cars, and the race began. They started slowly but quickly picked up speed and were having a great time until one of the cars broke down. So they stopped for the night and let the junkers return to being junkers.

On the way home that evening, Will thought about a story Dough Dough told him of how Indians would find a horse that had been ridden into the ground and abandoned by the cavalry. They would get it back on its feet and ride it another fifty miles. Now they were doing the same with these cars.

For several months, the boys continued to race, siphoning gas from farm tractors as their proficiency for racing improved day by day. Many of their friends came to see them race, filling the infield with shouting teenagers. Then one evening, Will rolled a car several times into the stands close to where some of these young fans were sitting. This accident caused Billy's father so much concern, he closed the track permanently.

Will was taken to the hospital that night with a slight concussion and a laceration of the right leg, which exposed about eight inches of shin bone. As they wheeled him into the emergency room, the first face he saw was Dr. Sargent grinning ear to ear. He wondered if the Doc would remember that scene with his dog Thor several years prior. He did.

"Well, well, well! What have we here?" he said, with glee in his voice. "Looks like Mrs. Malone's bad boy needs some stitches. Okay, tough guy, let's see how tough you really are."

The skin surrounding the wound had receded and hardened around the edges, leaving splotches of dried blood on the bone. Without anesthesia, the doctor gripped the skin just below the wound with one hand, the skin above the wound with the other, and with one mighty jerk, pulled the two together. The shock of the pain was so great that it gave Will the strength to lift both of the nurses who were holding him down. He lifted them off the ground so far, they banged their heads together in the air.

"That was great, Doc, gimme some more," Will said, through clenched teeth. This angered the doctor even more.

While the nurses were staggering about the room, trying to compose themselves, the doctor yelled out, "Bring me that needle and stitching.

So you want some more, eh?" he said, directing his eyes back on Will. "Let's give him what he wants. I said bring me that needle, damn it!"

As he continued to hold the two pieces of flesh together with one hand, he began to use the needle with the other, piercing both sides of the wound with the first stitch. Turning to Will again, he said, "How'd you like that one, Willie boy?"

"That was just right, Doc, let's have some more," Will declared through clenched teeth, sweat pouring off his face. It hurt, but not as much as it could have, probably because the tissue had been traumatized by the blow during the crash. It was also possible that Will was still out of it from the concussion.

Will's lack of emotion seemed to confuse the doctor. He expected this kid from across the street to cry for Momma, but Will wasn't about to let the doctor see him cry. With each stitch, Dr. Sargent looked for a reaction, but Will responded exactly the opposite from what he expected. "Ah, that one was just right, Doc. You're the greatest." Even the nurses were visibly shaken and would turn away rather than look at the doctor's brutal handiwork.

Will survived the doctor's retaliation, and over the years, they grew to respect one another. But it took a lot of years.

FIRST PRACTICE

Someone once said that if you live in Southeast Missouri and you don't play football, you don't have a hair on your rear. Other than the weather and the condition of the crops, it's all that people talked about. The Sikeston High Bulldogs were treated like college players. The town folks and people from the surrounding area knew all the player's names, what position they played, who their parents were, where they lived, and who their girl friends were. You were somebody if you played football at Sikeston High and nobody if you didn't…unless your name was Curt Gregory.

It was a joy for Will to think back about what happened in Sikeston during his high school years. No one would have believed that they were part of a dynasty in the making. Five years of undefeated football! It started just before Will got into high school and didn't end until he graduated. They lived in a town of 14,000 people with a high school population of only 600, but Sikeston was able to field a winning football team long before their undefeated streak began.

Southeast Missouri was a farming region that produced big farm boys, and farm boys had the work ethic as well as strength and size. The Bulldogs were the first high school team in the state to have an average 200 pound line, unheard of in those days.

The gridiron was a place you could prove yourself, where you either had it or you didn't. Daddy couldn't buy you in or bail you out, and Momma wasn't there to pat you on the head or dry your eyes. It was where everybody was equal, up to a point. It was a very exclusive club, yet even first year players were members. Seniors were worshiped and optimism sprang eternal. For some, it was a ticket to a better life. For others, it was disaster.

Will's initiation came the first week of tryouts in September of his freshman year. Few of the players were in shape and the temperature was over 100. When water break was called, the biggest players always lined up first at the water barrel. By the time the new players made it to the front of the line, the coach would blow the whistle, allowing very little time to get a drink. Few of them would forget that first week, and because of what happened to Will, he knew he never would.

While in the shower with some other guys, he was grabbed by a few seniors, and his private parts were smeared with analgesic balm, that soothing substance used on injured muscles or joints to bring warmth to an injury. It brought warmth all right. Will was suddenly on fire! Immediately, he ran under the water to scrub it off, only to discover that water actually accentuates the burning sensation, making it worse. The guys who had so generously applied this soothing balm stood by laughing as they watched Will cavort about the dressing room, looking for relief. It was still burning when he sat down at the dinner table that evening. Thank God, it was starting to subside. The only consolation he had from that experience was that the initiation was over.

The townspeople proved how much they appreciated their football players by providing the team with special sweat suits they wore when bused to a game and by offering incentives when they won. Will's father's friend Jack Lancaster guaranteed a barbecue sandwich and a soda to each player after every win. The local sporting store provided the newest equipment including all their undergarments. The owner of the bowling alley gave them season passes. They were given free admission to one of the two movie theaters in town simply by wearing their letter jacket. The florist provided corsages for their dates when a dance was planned after a game, and the list of freebees went on and on.

When players worked during the summer, the employers were instructed by the coach that time off for midsummer practices had to be allowed. Of course, they all gladly complied: this town was Bulldog crazy. Game programs were printed free gratis and resembled the kind you saw in St. Louis at a Cardinal baseball game with individual pictures, statistics, and page after page of advertising.

Will failed to make the team that first year because of his size. He was one of the smallest guys in his freshman class. Perhaps it was best because it gave Will the resolution that he was not going to be cut again.

By his senior year, he had grown to be the second tallest guy in his senior class. The one guy who was so obviously missing from football practice was Curt Gregory. Will remembered that the only time he saw Curt during the fall was either in school or when they went hunting together, but Will always knew where to find him. He would be at the gym or behind his house on the basketball court.

Curt saw the look on Will's face that freshman year and knew he hadn't made it. "Hey, buddy, you wouldn't have got to play, even if you had made the team. This gives you some time to bulk up. You'll make it next year, and besides, you can get a head start on everyone else for basketball season. What say we get started?" And started they did. Every day, they were out there dribbling and shooting up and down the court. Will didn't realize it at the time, but those months he spent trying to guard this All- American made him a much better defensive player. But it was difficult for Will to go by the football field that year when the team was practicing.

To Will, the one thing that changed his life more than anything else when he was growing up was the automobile. Up till then, it was just something you rode in to get from point A to point B. But that changed. The automobile was a way of life. It was alive and had a character all its own. Not only did it bring independence, it was liberty. It was access. It was freedom. It was manhood. It was hell.

The Bulldog Inn just outside of town was where everything was happening, and everybody in Sikeston knew it. All the girls hung out there because it was where all the jocks congregated. Every night, the place would be crawling with red and black letter jackets. It's where all of the kids wanted to be because it was the domain of the Sikeston Bulldogs. But there was a catch. You had to have a car to get there. You had to have access.

Few of Will's friends were allowed to drive on the street until their junior year. But some of the guys turned sixteen in their sophomore year, giving the rest a serious inferiority complex. Those who had a license and permission to use their parent's car were like kings. The rest of the serfs had to brownnose to the point of being pathetic just to hook a ride to the Bulldog Inn. It was too far to walk.

It was when he was surfing through his mind to remember the places he wanted to visit while he was home that he thought about their high school hangout. He could see it all now as if he were there. Off the highway, they would come, blazing into the drive around the Bulldog Inn, car after car, making the circle to check out the scene. Then back on the highway to make a few more rounds of other hangouts before returning again to the most popular place, the Bulldog Inn.

Occasionally, a crowd would gather around the raised hood of a rod or a carload of girls. But the one thing you did not see was the blue and white jackets of the Charleston Blue Jays or any other rival school. Those trespassers knew that the Bulldog Inn was a dangerous place for outsiders and very risky for athletic opponents. It was the same in Charleston for anyone wearing a Bulldog sweater, except Will. He had roots in both places because the Brandons were strongly entrenched in Charleston. It was where his father grew up and where many of his cousins still lived.

Kate Boone, a direct descendent of Daniel Boone, was Will's voice teacher and lived in Charleston. As a graduate of Julliard, Kate was the finest voice teacher in the state. As a result of him knowing most of her students and having sung in concerts in Charleston, Will became as well-known there as in Sikeston. He was in enemy territory every week, taking a voice lesson, but no one ever bothered him. In fact, he developed some really good friends there and that, coupled with his family's heritage, gave him the freedom to come and go without prejudice.

But there was one person in Charleston who gave him trouble. His name was Roland Geroud, better known as Geronimo. He hated Will, and the feeling was mutual. Worst of all, Geronimo dated Will's favorite cousin Mary Jane, one of the prettiest girls in Charleston. It was evident that he was in total control of her, and that ticked Will off.

One evening while Will was visiting his Aunt Thelma and Uncle Jimmy, Mary Jane came running in, upset at having just found out that Geronimo had gone to the Winners Circle, a secluded spot in the woods just outside of town where lovers went to park and opponents went to settle their differences. A showdown was coming between Geronimo and Mary Jane's boyfriend.

"Take me out there, will you, Will? Roland is upset at Bob for asking me out. Somebody is going to really get hurt. Please drive me out there, please?" Bob Reynolds was a guy Will really liked. He took voice lessons from Kate Boone, and the two of them had gotten to know each other pretty well. Will knew he was interested in Mary Jane, and he encouraged him to pursue those interests.

They jumped in the Plymouth and headed west. Several faster cars passed and honked, their radio's blaring, dust and gravel flying, all heading for the same place. News of a rumble travels fast. Bob Reynolds was Will's favorite Blue Jay, and he hoped Bob would do something about Geronimo. Will also knew he had very little chance against this street brawler.

The dust got worse along the dirt road generated by the cars flying by. Ahead, they saw the glow formed by dozens of headlights that lit up the circle where the action was to take place. Drawing closer, they could see the outline of two figures squaring off and sharing choice words. As they pushed their way through the crowd, her classmates saw it was Mary Jane, so they cleared a way. There appeared to be sixty to seventy people there to watch the fight.

It didn't take Will long to realize that he was the only one in the crowd not wearing blue and white. Worst of all, he was wearing red and black. The smell of alcohol in the air seemed to heighten the tension, loosen the tongue, and give false courage to those who normally kept quiet. In the middle of it was Will trying to be as unobtrusive as possible.

The fight appeared to be about even, and to Will's surprise, Bob was holding his own. That is until Geronimo kicked him in the groin, sending him face forward into the dirt clutching his privates. The crowd, even some of Geronimo's friends, began to boo and give him a hard time. "What the hell's the problem? All's fair in love and war, ain't it?" Geronimo protested.

Now Will should have known that a person wearing a Bulldog jacket keeps his mouth shut in a crowd of blue and white, but it popped out of his mouth about two decibels louder than the rest of the crowd as if another person was controlling his voice box. "You couldn't win a fair fight, you fat slob." The crowd suddenly grew silent, turning its attention to the person crazy enough to have yelled out this insult to the meanest, cruelest guy in town.

As the crowd began to recede from around Will, Geronimo recognized who he was, and a sinister smile began to spread across his face. He had been waiting for a chance at Will and here he was, ripe for the slaughter.

"Just move on back to the car, Will. I will hold him long enough for you to drive away," said Mary Jane. Oh, how he wanted to do just that, but he was wearing the Red and Black. He knew if he were to run, he would never be able to show his face in Charleston again. Moreover, all of his relatives, including his father, would hear how he had disgraced the family name. No, he had no other choice but to meet this raging bull head on. He found himself feeling like a matador without a cape and sword, bare and defenseless.

Just as Will entered the circle, someone pushed him from behind, sending him sprawling into the dirt. Geronimo rushed in and kicked Will in the collar bone. Will was lucky…he was aiming for his face. Will rolled over, trying to escape the next kick, but it caught him full in the chest, taking his breath away. "I'm gonna wipe you and that pretty letter jacket over every inch of this field, and then I'm going to run you up the Charleston High flag pole upside down!" Will had heard of this happening to some poor fool before.

Geronimo made one big mistake. He reached down to pick Will up to slug him, and when he did, Will threw a handful of dust in his eyes and the bull began to bellow. Lying beside Will was a piece of fence post. He staggered to his feet with the wood club in his hand. "All's fair in love and war, right, Geronimo? How's this for fair?" With that, he swung the weathered old post with all he had, striking the bully in the chest, sending him spinning backward and into the gravel.

Several of Geronimo's buddies stepped in indicating they were going to pick up where he had left off, but Bob and a few of his friends threatened retaliation so they backed off. "Will, you best get in your car and leave," Bob said. "I appreciate the way you stood up for me and I won't forget it. But there's a lot of resentment toward Sikeston here that is starting to be directed at you." Will knew exactly why: Sikeston had defeated Charleston the last ten times they met. "I'll take Mary Jane home, and thanks again." With that, Will was gone. Bob didn't have to suggest it twice.

Mary Jane and Bob got married a few years later. The last word on Geronimo was that while managing a liquor store in a rough section of town, he had been wounded by holdup men, but he had been able to shoot and kill both assailants. Because of death threats from family members of the deceased, he left town, address unknown.

The world Will was leaving in Southeast Asia was far different from the world he was headed. He continued to wonder how much he had changed living so isolated, so primitive. How would he act? Just watching the hostess, an Asian lady of considerable beauty, move about the cabin reminded him of desires he had long suppressed. Perhaps he had even replaced those feelings, but with what? The desire to live and an instinct to survive remained strong, of this he felt confident. It was the instinct to kill that concerned him, to eliminate anything that stood in the way. That instinct had been abnormally resolute during those last few engagements, but he didn't want anything to stop him from being a whole person in the world outside the war zone.

While thinking on these things, he suddenly thought about a friend he might see again, and that thought brought a smile to his face. Although this friend was overweight, played no sports, and was not the least bit attractive to the girls, he had learned somehow to be a part of the social circle when they were growing up. His name was Harry Cornwall, the brownnose king of Sikeston High. He had perfected mooch to a new and ultimate art form, which is how he acquired the nickname "Mooch."

Mooch never had a car, never had money, and never had a girl. In fact, he was bankrupt before he got out of high school. Yet he managed to ride more than anyone who had all those things. Somehow, he had finagled the job of sports assistant, which kept him involved in all sports as the equipment guy, the water boy, the towel man, and the right to travel on the bus to away games. He always managed to be the first one out to the Bulldog Inn. He would borrow money that he never paid back and generally freeloaded his way through high school. When he did occasionally pay back a loan, you could expect him to borrow more. Only this time, he would never pay it back. Pride meant nothing to him; he even borrowed from girls, something a self-respecting boy would never do. Since he didn't have a girl of his own, he sort of tagged along and shared everyone else's.

The only thing he did well was hustle. His father owned a pool hall/sandwich shop, and Mooch's misspent youth was in that emporium. He was the only young player who could beat Davie or Will. He hustled many a pool shark at Slade's, and several times was forced to leave in a hurry through the back door.

One night at the Bulldog Inn, Petey was playing a pinball machine while eating a sandwich. While holding it with his right hand and pushing the flipper buttons at the same time, he felt something nudging his hand. He looked down and discovered Mooch on his knees, nibbling away at his cheeseburger.

"Geez, Mooch, get your mangy mouth off my burger for Christ's sake. You got a lot of nerve. Damn," Petey said in disgust, as annoyed as a person could be finding someone else's mouth on their sandwich. "Just trying to get a taste, Pete," Mooch responded, showing not the least bit of humility. Nevertheless, he was one of them and a part of their life growing up.

The guy who always had a car was Ned "Hog Jaw" Walters. His father, a very successful businessman, made sure of that. What Will remembered most about Ned was that he was shaving when they were in the Cub Scouts. He was an exceptionally big kid who matured years ahead of everyone else. Will recalled, on the other hand, not having to shave until he was twenty-two.

With the automobile came a series of new endeavors. "Parking" was in, at least for the upper classmen. Above all other advantages, parking is the big bonus to being able to drive— because you could have your favorite girl all to yourself away from parents and others. There were certain popular spots like Hart's Graveyard or Cab Drivers Paradise, a pine grove frequented by cab drivers, or any secluded country lane or farm road. And the majority of lovers parked in the same location time after time and usually late Friday and Saturday nights.

Society had changed since Will left home, however. It was no longer safe to park in a car in a secluded area anymore. Like the radio announcer used to say, "Who knows what evil lurks in the hearts of men?" But in his teenage life, the only danger might be accidentally falling asleep with the car running and being asphyxiated by carbon monoxide.

In those days, the most exciting sport for Will and his friends was chasing parkers. When driving in the country, if their lights reflected off a car parked out in a field or up in the woods, they would pretend to drive on by, then turn around and with their lights turned off, park as close as possible without being detected. Leaving the car a short distance away, they would sneak up on the parked car and usually catch them in a compromising situation. Then they would scare the daylights out of them by bouncing a rock or dirt clod off the top of the car.

Later, they found cherry bombs worked better than rocks. Will had to smile to himself, remembering how much of a shock it must have been for lovers to have a cherry bomb go off near their car in the silence and serenity of the night. Naturally, they would either give chase or drive away, and if they did give chase, they would be lost in the dust. It was a great exciting sport, but dangerous.

One Friday night, Sam Bowman got his grandmother's new Buick to go to a teen meeting at the church where they were all members. Will laughed to himself remembering that the hood ornament on the Buick was found to be intact. That distasteful experience with Buick rings had been enough for him. Sam came by Will's with Don Baker, Tom Dunaway, and Sammy Turner to pick him up, and they headed for the country. The ruse of going to a church function always worked for getting the car from his grandmother, as it sometimes did for Will. Along the way, they stopped and bought cherry bombs before heading for Mr. Lewis's farm where they could usually find parkers.

As they drove down the dirt road, a flash of light reflected off a car parked at the far end of the farm access road. When they got close enough, they recognized it as a green Plymouth coup belonging to Hog Jaw Walters, the toughest football player on the team. But the boys couldn't resist, he was the target for the night.

Don Baker got the bright idea to find a long stick, sneak up on Hog Jaw's car, stick a cherry bomb in his exhaust pipe, light it, and then ram it home with the stick. Brilliant! So they crept up on the Plymouth, placed the cherry bomb just inside the chrome tail pipe extension, lit it, and rammed it in deep. As quiet as they were, Hog Jaw must have heard them because in the silence of the night, his car roared instantly to life. Running into each other, they ran for their car as fast as their legs would carry them.

Just as they reached for the Buick's doors, the cherry bomb exploded with such power that it blew the muffler and exhaust pipe completely off the Plymouth. Instantly, Hog Jaw's car was moving in reverse and coming fast, the noise of the car accentuated because it had no muffler. There was no time to waste; they had to move fast.

Sam Bowman's Buick was fast, and they were going way beyond a safe speed for this gravel road because they knew Hog Jaw's car was faster. Within seconds, his headlights appeared around a curve behind them. He was closing the gap rapidly.

Coming up ahead was a sharp left turn that crossed a stream at right angles. The wooden bridge that traversed the stream was narrow and had no railings, dangerous even at a sensible speed. Sam began to apply the brakes, and the car started to slide. The dust rising up behind the Buick was so thick they could barely see the headlights of the Plymouth behind. Miraculously, they made the turn and crossed the bridge with Sam picking up speed as fast as the Roadmaster would accelerate.

Hog Jaw must have been going seventy miles an hour when he drove into that cloud of dust, thinking that he would come out of it headed in the right direction, but he was wrong. His car took flight as the boys watched his headlights disappear off the bridge behind them. Now they had to decide if they should go back to see if Hog Jaw and his date were okay or keep on going. They all agreed that it would be coldhearted to leave them there, not knowing if they had survived the crash. Stepping out of the car, they could hear Hog Jaw cursing away in the darkness. Sam aimed the Buick's lights down off the road into the stream, and there was Hog Jaw and his girl friend sitting on the top of his totally submerged Plymouth.

"You guys are dead. You're dead. You're freakin dead." Where had Will heard those words before?

Another great sport they invented that year was drag racing in reverse. Since most of their parents or grandparents owned stick-shift six-cylinder cars that were relatively slow, this was a marginally appropriate activity. Racing in reverse tended to level the playing field. It wasn't how fast your car went, it was how well you could keep control. Will remembered what a challenge it was driving thirty-five miles an hour in reverse.

Another one of Will's Sunday school buddies, Burt Rowen, discovered the perfect place to race, the local airport runway. Shortly after Will turned sixteen, Mam permitted him to drive their newly acquired '49 Plymouth to Sunday School as did the parents of Burt. Sam Bowman would bring the Buick, but he would seldom race it for fear of tearing up the transmission, which was easy to do when driving an automatic in reverse. Petey brought his 1936 Plymouth, which was a relic even in 1951.

Air traffic at the Sikeston Airport was minimal to start with, but on Sunday morning at 9:30, it was practically nonexistent. Sometimes, as many as six cars would show up for Sunday morning drags, and they ran every Sunday for three months that summer.

Will's career as a dragster ended the day his grandmother heard from his Sunday school teacher that he hadn't attended Sunday school the past three months. As a result, it was a long time before he got behind the wheel of the Plymouth again. He still remembered that exhilarating feeling of looking out the window, the wind and the bugs hitting him in the face as they roared down the runway, doing all they could do to keep their cars straight. If there had been a trophy for such activity, Will thought surely he would have won one.

Contemplating how the car played such an integral part of his teenage life, the name of "Hot Rod" Moore came to mind. His name was synonymous with speed in those days. Perhaps every teenager in Missouri knew "Hot Rod" Moore. He was their hero. Hot Rod challenged the establishment and won, at least momentarily. Something all of them wanted to do, but none of them had the courage to do.

"Hot Rod" Moore lived in St. Louis, the son of a successful industrialist. With his daddy's money, he built fast cars. Will first read about him in the *St. Louis Post Dispatch* newspaper. It was reported that the Missouri State Patrol had clocked a car driven by Moore on one of the major highways leading west out of the city at speeds in excess of 120 miles per hour; very fast for that period.

Several months after this incident, another article appeared in that same paper about a similar high speed chase, and it described how Moore had outrun the police. He had been clocked at 150 mph, but later, "Hot Rod" turned himself in. As a result, his license was suspended for a year. Apparently, a newspaper reporter took an interest in this young speedster and began a series of articles that chronicled his life and his love of fast cars. To all the would-be hot rodders in Southeast Missouri, this was exciting stuff. It was one of the few common interests the kids in Sikeston and Charleston had, and they shared news and information about their mutual hero. Every day, they scanned the paper, seeking the facts of Moore's newest adventures. It was reported that he was building a special engine for his 1949 Mercury coupe, a car of the late James Dean fame.

Then one day, news came over the radio that Hot Rod's car had just left the St Louis city limits with the police in fast pursuit, destination unknown. This prompted a group of guys from both Sikeston and Charleston to maintain a vigil that week for news of his escapades as the chase continued across Missouri.

One evening in July, while socializing at the Bulldog Inn, they heard sirens approaching and looked up just in time to see his black Mercury, with flames painted over the front and down the sides, go screaming by. A loud cheer rose up from every car at the drive inn. It was the highlight of the summer.

One *Post Dispatch* article claimed that Hot Rod's sole purpose was to elude the police for as long as he could to set some kind of record. It mentioned that he had planned his route to include special hiding places along the way, such as barns, garages, woods, and even under bridges in dried-up creek beds, resting places where he had stashed food and fuel.

Among Will and his friends, Hot Rod's purpose was the center of debate. They all knew how stupid and dangerous this chase was, but they admired him anyway. His flight was a protest against the system that most of them despised.

Day and night, reports came in about Hot Rod being sighted here and there, sometimes in different parts of the state at the same time. The police set up roadblocks, but somehow, he managed to elude them. It was like he was playing chess and anticipating their next move.

Finally, that fateful day they all dreaded came: Hot Rod Moore was caught and brought back to St. Louis. It was truly a sad day for him and his followers. His license, which was already suspended, was revoked for life. He was given a sentence of six months in jail; he served four.

The last report on Hot Rod Moore came the day he was released from jail. The story read that his father had made a place for him in the family business and had hired a chauffeur to drive him to and from work each day. The boys were devastated by the news and wrote Moore off as having capitulated to the establishment. But this was not the last they were to hear of "Hot Rod" Moore. Several years later, he won the Grand National Drag Championship at Wichita Falls where he didn't need a driver's license. Knowing that he would be landing in Moore's hometown of St. Louis tomorrow, Will wonder whatever happened to his hero, "Hot Rod" Moore.

Tornado

In Will's early years, hayrides played a significant role in the lives of young people in Southeast Missouri, and Petey always had the best at Burn Brae. For those who were still not driving, a hayride under a moonlit night filled with stars and romantic music offered a chance to get close to their favorite girl.

George always drove the horse-drawn wagon and would send one of his sons ahead to the turnaround point to build a big fire and have the food ready when the wagon arrived. The setting was atop a bluff overlooking a large expanse of country and the river. From the bluff, you could see the spotlights of riverboats plying the water through the night on their way downriver to New Orleans or upriver toward St. Louis.

These were great times for Will and his friends. Life was carefree and gay, with few troubles or responsibilities to dull their senses. Relationships were light and friendships were like brotherhoods, born from years of growing up together in this close-knit community.

Changing positions in his seat, Will looked about the cabin, wondering if he had missed anything. He had been engrossed in thoughts of his teenage years for so long, he hadn't noticed that sunlight had permeated the aircraft, heralding the coming of a new day. These thoughts were too precious to interrupt, so he closed his eyes and concentrated on picking up where he had paused.

Will and his friends always seemed to fall in love on hayrides, sometimes to the same person and sometimes to someone new. It was traditional. Hayrides were synonymous with love but not in the sexual sense. Of course, sex played a part in it, but petting would be closer to a characterization of what went on in those days. There were seldom confrontations between friends. The football field and the basketball court had taught them to watch out for each other and to fight as a team, not each other. It was natural for team harmony to carry over from team sports to their social lives.

The hayride to end all hayrides came in Will's fifteenth year. It had it all the things kid's their age were looking for and more: friendship, food, romance, mystery, danger, excitement, and fun. The uninvited guest was the weather.

It all started when Hans, of lederhosen fame, brought his ukulele and was garnering all the girl's attention. It began to wear a little thin on the boys; after all, they wanted time with their sweethearts. The person that became the most perturbed was Ned "Hog Jaw" Walters. Now, everyone knows you don't disturb or perturb Ned Walters on a hayride, at least not for long.

About halfway through the night, Ned asked Hans if he could see his ukulele. Without a second thought, Hans handed it over, and Ned proceeded to place it under the turning wheels of the wagon. With a loud crunch, the little four-string instrument was smashed into smithereens. Hans squealed like a stuck pig while the rest of the boys applauded their approval.

Off in the distance, thunder could be heard and lightning lit up the western sky as thunderstorms were forming beyond the distant hills. After the barbecue was over, George turned the big wagon around and started home. They were all still singing songs and laughing, but soon, they became concerned about the sky.

Southeast Missouri is known as Tornado Alley. Every spring and summer, a number of twisters passed within sight distance of Sikeston, and occasionally, one would strike the town. People who lived there all their lives usually didn't bother to take shelter. But this time, they all became anxious about the approaching storm when they saw the intensity of the wind and the size and color of the clouds.

A lightning flash from the closest thunderhead lit up the sky just long enough to silhouette a twister a few miles away heading in their direction. George informed everyone that he was heading for an old abandoned farmhouse, which was considerably closer than the main house at Burn Brae. Located there was an old storm cellar that would provide shelter from the storm.

Within minutes, debris was flying in every direction. A piece of aluminum siding fell from the sky and landed next to the wagon frightening the horses. Dust, straw, and other trash were swirling around, making vision difficult. When they were a quarter of a mile from the old house, lightning lit up the abandoned structure, revealing the approaching tornado off to the west a short distance away, and it was heading in their direction that sounded like an approaching freight train. Even the ground seemed to shake. When lightning struck again a few minutes later, the house and outbuildings were gone.

There was nothing they could do but stop the wagon and wait to see which direction the tornado traveled. Will remembered how God was with them that night as the tornado continued passed them. Even the rain bypassed them, and within minutes, the tornado had dissipated and the entire storm was gone. Soon the sky cleared, the stars came out filling the black void above, and the storm was only a faint rumble in the distance. All was well again, and the reveling continued until time for them to go home. It was a delightful memory which caused Will to smile within himself and thank the man upstairs for bringing all of them home safely that night.

Nevada

Summer vacations were never really vacations when Will was a teenager. If he wasn't lifeguarding, he was working with a survey crew for the state highway department or, as was the case one summer, working as a horse wrangler at Boy Scout camp. Working with the survey crew along the highway gave Will a lot of practice throwing rocks, which is helpful in every sport. Usually Will's survey team was running survey lines down country roads scheduled to be turned over from the county to the state. There were plenty of ideal stones to choose from on gravel roads, and Will became an expert rock thrower with mailboxes being his favorite target. He got so good that the state issued an order forbidding the throwing of rocks at mailboxes.

More trouble came Will's way the day he had to prove how far he could throw a rock. They were surveying a winding country road that passed a large farm pond surrounded by trees. On the far side of the pond were a few enormous Duroc sows asleep in the mud. "Bet you can't hit those pigs over there, Will," one of the team members said tauntingly.

Needless to say, he couldn't resist the challenge. After carefully picking the stone that was just right, he lofted it over the trees and watched it come down on the far side of the pond, striking the largest hog in the jaw. He felt terrible about what he had done because it was evident the poor animal was in pain. Will won the bet and became legend among highway employees, but lost his job. This was one mistake the state couldn't forgive. The Duroc was a prize pedigree show hog, and Will had broken its jaw. Feeling miserable about the whole thing, he drove out to the farmer's house and confessed to the crime, offering to pay him for the animal. The owner was a Quaker and proved to be very forgiving. The animal was transported to a veterinarian that had been able to save it by wiring his jaw so that it could eat. It cost Will, but not like it could have if the pig had died.

Will concluded that thinking about Sikeston and his childhood had to be great therapy, a respite that crowded out the other memories, the horrors of war, so he continued to search his memory for the life he had unwittingly stashed away for just such occasions. The summer he worked at Boy Scout camp came to the forefront. It was the year he had become an Eagle Scout, and because he had some experience with horses, he was picked for the Wrangler's position at Camp Lewallen situated along the St. Francis River. But the recollection of that summer and the one that followed was a painful one because of a very special horse. That horse's name was Nevada.

Around Will's fourteenth birthday, he got the yen to own a horse. Many of his friends had horses, but Mam's farm was twenty-three miles from where they lived. Since no one occupied the property, keeping a horse there was not practical.

Finally, after badgering Mam for several months, she agreed that he could buy a horse, but only if one could be purchased for $100. Even in the 1950s, you couldn't buy much of a horse for $100. However, he still worked at the auction barn on Saturdays and he knew a trucker who drove west once a month to buy Mustangs, which he transported back to Sikeston to sell in the auction. Will talked the man into taking him with him on his next trip, and he got to see the real West for the first time.

Oklahoma, Texas, New Mexico, Arizona, it was an exciting trip. The last stop was in Nevada at a range camp far out in the backcountry. While Will and the trucker were sitting high on the pole fence surrounding the corral, they watched a cloud of dust rise up from the hills to the north. As the galloping herd topped the ridge, he could make them out, hear the wrangler's cry and the crack of their whips. There for the first time, Will saw real working cowboys driving wild mustangs caught on the open range.

This memory was picture perfect. From a distance, as the herd drew closer, a young buckskin was following close on the heels of the lead stallion. He was rough, but he held his head high and ran like the wind. Will's heart skipped a beat as they flew through the corral gate, with the buckskin running with a certain pride that convinced Will this was the horse he'd been looking for.

When they arrived back in Sikeston, Mam called a rancher she knew who boarded horses near town, and they took him there. Every day after school, Will would hop on his bike and ride out to the corral to work with him and usually the young stallion would be waiting there, as if expecting Will.

At first, the young horse was shy and hated the barn as he had never been in one, but before long, he fit right in with the rest of the horses. The landowner where they boarded him taught Will how to break the buckskin. He impressed upon Will the need to have patience, to have his hands on the horse as much as possible so that he would develop confidence that Will was not going to harm him. He was Will's pride and joy, and he named him Nevada.

Around and around, Nevada would trot in the training circle with Will holding his lead rope while at the same time touching him with the whip to keep him moving. It wasn't long before the young horse trusted Will completely. When the day's training exercise would end and Will would disconnect the rope and harness, the horse would follow him right up to the gate, wanting to follow him home. Within a month, Will was up and riding.

Because of his success in breaking Nevada, Will developed a false sense of confidence about training horses. Jerry Johnson was a young lady who lived fifty miles away on her father's ranch. She asked him to break a horse that her father had bought for her. He agreed to do so, knowing that it might impress her. The horse was named Rocky. With a name like that, Will should have known that this might not be the piece of cake he thought it would be.

The minute he saw her horse, he knew he had let his mouth override his rear end. This horse was several hands taller than Nevada and mean as sin. He loved to bite and would kick the daylights out of anyone he caught behind him. Rocky's disposition was ornery, and he was highly volatile. When Will told his trucker friend about this horse's habits, his advice was to keep a club handy and give the horse a rap across the nose every time he tried to bite. Rocky had tried to take a plug out of Will more than once when he wasn't looking. The other advice he gave Will was to stay clear of his rear. When Will tried to employ the same techniques he did with Nevada, Rocky would swing inside the training circle and almost run over him. He was able to cure him of his biting habits, but Will knew that he couldn't be trusted.

It finally came time for Will to mount Rocky, so he blindfolded the horse and climbed aboard. Rocky bucked only a few times, and Will walked him around the corral for twenty minutes to get him use to the idea of weight on his back. Then Will stepped down long enough to get his nerve up for the real test.

The girl who owned the horse invited some of her friends to see Will ride Rocky, so a group of teenagers had gathered hoping to see some action. At first, they were a little disappointed when he rode him blindfolded around the corral, but they were about to get the action they came for. Will climbed back up, told them to open the gate, and gingerly removed the blindfold. The horse took a minute to adjust to the light, turned around to see who was on top, and exploded straight up. Somehow, Will managed to stay aboard, but when Rocky came down, he was at a full gallop, heading straight for the open field.

There was no reining this horse in; it was all Will could do to hang on. Then Rocky stepped in a gopher hole. Down they went nose first, spilling Will over his head, and then rolling over him like a steam roller. Thanks to the rain the night before, the ground was soft, and he escaped without breaking his neck. But he was bruised from head to toe. Will's ego was also bruised, and he never tried to break a horse again.

That's when he was offered the job as wrangler at the Boy Scout camp. Camp officials had searched the area to find what they thought would be the safest horses for young scouts to ride. Some were purchased at the auction barn where Will worked. What the camp finally acquired were fourteen old nags that nobody else wanted. Will knew the first day he took them on a trail ride that they were more dangerous than more spirited animals, but this was what he had to work with.

Part of the trail on which Will took the scouts was a narrow winding path around a mountain. It was sometimes climbing and sometimes descending. The first day out, one of the horses stumbled and went to her knees. Will was leading the line when he heard a boy screaming and turned to see the old mare lying against the side of the mountain. At least, she had enough sense to fall the right direction. The boy riding her was pinned against the mountainside and hollered like he was dying, but he was not hurt, only scared.

The fun part came daily on the way back down the trail. Will always forewarned the boys that the horses would be hard to handle when they came within sight of the corral and to pull hard on the reins to hold them back. But this was a useless warning. Every trail ride ended the same way: in a stampede. The fourteen nags that minutes before had acted like they'd never make it home were now looking like they had just come out of the starting gate at the Kentucky Derby.

Why no one ever got hurt was a mystery. At full gallop, all fourteen horses would try to enter a ten-foot wide gate at the same time. Only by the grace of God was there no one ever injured. Taking care of the horses, teaching equestrian classes, and leading scouts on trail rides made that a fun-filled summer. There was never a dull moment, and Will would always cherish those wonderful memories.

Larry had moved across the aisle to talk trash with an army nurse, so Will stretched out across his seat. There he made an effort to reminisce about Camp Lewallen and his horse experiences. But invariably, his memory switched to the following year, as he knew it would, to the one he called the Horse Summer. They had a lot of summer squalls that year, more than years previous but not altogether unusual for July in Missouri. It usually came on the heels of a scorching day, whipped up dust and debris, and generated intense lightning storms and tornados.

It was one of the summers Will worked as a lifeguard. On this particular day, the lightning became so intense that he and Curt closed the pool early. They watched with awe as the storm fury drove through Southeast Missouri. As they were closing the facility, the phone rang at the desk. It was Ed Scott, the owner of the boarding stables where Will kept Nevada. "You better get out here right away, Will. Your horse is in trouble," he said, his voice trembling.

"What's happened, Ed?" Will asked.

"He jumped into the fence and has himself tangled in it. It looks bad, you better come quick."

Will called Mam to pick him up, and Ed met them at the gate. Will could see Nevada on the edge of the field out beyond the stables. "He's in bad shape, Will. I tried to reach the vet, but he's out on a call somewhere." The three of them walked out into the field, and as they approached Nevada, they could see why Ed was so upset. When the thunder and lightning had begun, Nevada became spooked. In his fear and confusion, Nevada had tried to jump the barbed wire fence but didn't make it. Instead, he came down, straddling the three strands, catching his private parts on the wire. In his fear, he had tried to fight his way free, only to pull out his insides.

There was blood everywhere, and there was nothing they could do. Will wanted to put his arms around Nevada's neck, to speak lovingly in his ear that everything was going to be okay, but he knew he would be lying. Nevada had lost most of his blood, and the distressed animal could only stand there, straddling the fence and bleed to death.

Mam reached out and brought Will into her arms, and together, they wept. Finally, they could wait for the veterinarian no longer. They couldn't let Nevada die a long and painful death, and there was no question he was going to die.

"I think we should put him out of his misery, Will. I have a gun and I can do it for you." "No, sir. He's my horse. I should be the one," Will said, his voice quivering.

Ed brought the gun, and Will asked them to back away. He stepped up to his friend and looked in his eyes. He was shaking radically now, his wonderful mane matted with sweat and blood, his tail nearly touching the ground. He looked as if he thought Will could help him. Instead, he was there to destroy him.

Will's whole body was trembling, and the gun seemed especially heavy in his hands as he raised it to the level of Nevada's head. He watched with trusting eyes as Will asked him to forgive him and pulled the trigger. His head and neck slowly slumped and his eyes closed, but he wouldn't fall. "Go down, Nevada. Go down," Will sobbed. He was still alive. "Oh, God, end this please, God."

Once more, he lifted the pistol and pulled the trigger. With this shot, the horse slowly went to his knees and fell over on his side, twitching, trembling. Will fell to the ground and crawled to him, and in his grief and anger, he cried out, "There is no God! There is no God! Why would he let this happen if there is a God?" They lifted Will from Nevada's side as he continued to cry out against God, but that night, Mam chastised him strongly. "You are so ungrateful. Don't you see? You had so many wonderful times with that horse. You were blessed. All your friends would have given anything to have had the great times you had with Nevada. This is life. You should be on your knees thanking God for all your blessing." With that, she turned and closed the door to his room.

When Mam left, Will realized that she was right. He did get on his knees to thank God that night and asked forgiveness. Will thanked him for those times they had riding across the fields and hills, those times they raced against the other riders and won, and the blue ribbon they won for the barrel race during the rodeo. The time they rode out after a pack of coyotes and stayed with them for what seemed miles, giving up only after the forest became too thick for them to keep up. He also knew he would never forget how Nevada would follow him around the barn and out to the manure pile when he would be cleaning his stall, bringing Will his bridle in his teeth as if to be begging to go for a ride. Those painful visions remained for some time until he finally remembered the words of Dough Dough, "Nevada had gone on, all that was left was the horse that he rode in on." And with that thought, he fell soundly asleep.

The next day, Will took a pen and notebook and walked to the farm where he had kept Nevada. He wanted to record his time with his horse while it was fresh in his memory, something he could look back on when he was old. And this is what he wrote:

A Horse Named Nevada
When I was just a young boy, riding was my joy, and all of
my friends had horses, but not me, all I had was toys.

Ride on, ride on, Nevada, ride on.
My family had no money to buy a horse for me. But I knew
a truck drive who brought horses in Nevada where mustangs
run free.

Ride on, ride on, Nevada, ride on.
Working as a wrangler at the cattle barn, I saved every
dollar I made and went west with the truck driver to buy a
mustang, it was my own personal crusade.

Ride on, ride on, Nevada, ride on.
They said I'd never tame him because he had lived his life
in the wild,
      But love and kindness prevailed, he was young and just
like a child.

Ride on, ride on, Nevada, ride on.
I named my horse Nevada because that's where he was from,
and he loved to go riding; when he saw me with a bridle, he
would come.

Ride on, ride on, Nevada, ride on.
It didn't take me long to realize how special Nevada was in
many ways. He ran like the wind and never tired; he could
outrun my friends any day.

Ride on, ride on, Nevada, ride on.
I put him in the rodeo, a big event in my hometown each
year, and in all the events I entered him in, he excelled and
he had no fear.

Ride on, ride on, Nevada, ride on.
I remember the time we rode after a pack of coyotes on the
prairie, until the mesquite and sage brush got too thick to
continue, it was scary.

Ride on, ride on, Nevada, ride on.
I will always remember Nevada, he was more than a horse,
he was a friend. I hope that God has a plan for me to ride
on with Nevada again.

Ride on, ride on, Nevada, ride on.

Larry did his best to convince Will to lay over a few days with him
in Hawaii, but Will's desire to get home overrode anything Larry could
say. Luckily, there was a flight leaving for LA in two hours, and they still
had time to properly say their farewells. Stepping into a nearby lounge,
they had one last drink together. There was an abundance of things they
could have talked about; after all, they had been through more together

than they would have thought possible to survive. But the shadows of Doc Tran and the friends they lost since coming to Vietnam hung over the conversation, making it distasteful to have a happy departure, so very little was said. It was not an easy parting, and Will made Larry promise that after his next tour, he would come to Sikeston for a visit. He had Larry's assurances that he would, but Will doubted that it would ever happen.

Within six hours, Will would be landing at LAX, or so he thought. The idea of being back in the USA caused him some trepidation. Returning to the United States after having been away so long was always an emotional time for him. This one was even more emotional, considering where he had been and what he had been doing the past few years. Having to say good-bye to a friend who was closer than a brother made it especially emotional.

Several hours after leaving Hawaii, the pilot came on the speaker to inform the passengers that a major storm was approaching the West Coast, and they were being diverted to Alaska. Why Alaska? This perturbed him greatly as the closer he got to America, the more impatient he was to get home. He surmised that the storm would have to be a thousand miles long to cause those in control of their flight path to send them so far out of the way. Will had only been to Alaska once before, and the memories of that experience were far from pleasant.

It was when he had just returned from the jungle in Panama that his first sergeant informed him that their unit had been chosen to be part of a major winter training exercise involving most of the 18th Airborne Corp, which includes the 82nd Airborne Division. It was called Snow Flake, which Will thought was appropriate since it never stopped snowing from the time they arrived.

The command divided each company into fifteen-man fire teams. Most of the teams' heavy equipment, such as 30- and 50-caliber machine guns, sleeping bags, tents, stoves, water, and rations were loaded into gondolas that could be pushed or pulled like sleds through snow. These were to be airdropped by parachute once the paratroopers were on the ground.

While Will was sitting there in the airliner, comfortable in his seat at 35,000 feet, contemplating that Alaskan experience, he got a sudden shiver remembering how cold he became when they opened the doors of the C-130 that day. The temperature had dropped from 70 degrees in the aircraft to below zero in less than a minute, and he instantly knew he was in for a hard time.

The temperature was a comfortable 75 degrees when they loaded the aircraft in Pope Field, just outside Fort Bragg, North Carolina. Having just returned from Panama the week before, his blood was as thin as vodka, and he was still sunburned from that last week in the jungle. All of which heightened his susceptibility to the arctic temperatures even more.

From North Carolina, they flew west to the Strategic Air Command (SAC) at Omaha, Nebraska, where they refueled, made a pit stop, grabbed some sandwiches, and then flew to an area some fifty miles north of Nome, Alaska.

Looking out at the window, Will remembered thinking how did they knew where to drop the men as they could only sporadically see the ground through the clouds, and what they could see was nothing but white with an occasional stand of pines dotting the vast wilderness.

En route, the men began to dawn their white military snowsuits, and about 100 miles from the drop area, they began strapping on their T-10 parachutes, going through the ritual of checking each other to make sure there were no line-overs or tangled rip chords. After circling the drop zone for thirty minutes, the clouds finally parted enough for a drop, and the command, "Stand up and hook up," came from the jump master. The command, "Stand in the door!" came a few minutes later, and the "stick," the name given for the men lined up to exit the aircraft, shuffled forward to wait at the door. When the doors swung open, the cold arctic wind blasted into the C-130, and Will remembered how scared he was knowing that it would be some time before he would be warm again. As soon as another break in the clouds came, the jump master commanded, "Go!" sending the men rushing through the aircraft and out the door. Looking over his jump boots to the frozen tundra below, he could make out the imprint of a frozen lake. They must have dropped the men extremely low because Will's chute made only a few oscillations before he plowed hard into the ice that was like concrete.

They had just finished recovering their chutes from the snow when the equipment aircraft arrived overhead and began dropping each fire team's gondola. Each one had a large number attached, representing the number of the fire team. To Will's dismay, their gondola, number 729, streamered all the way to the ground when its parachutes failed to deploy.

Running to number 729, the men found that their gondola had split in half, mixing fuel, water, food, weapons, and sleeping bags into one catastrophic mess. Catastrophic because where they were, they needed many of those items to survive. Moreover, it took four men to push or pull each half, where before it only took four men to move a complete gondola.

Will's platoon and fire team leaders conferred concerning the gravity of the situation and determined that there were only two solutions: either the team gets resupplied from the air, which might take days depending upon the weather, or they march to a point where snow cats could reach them from Fort Wainwright, a post at the northern most reaches of the tundra. The overall plan of Snow Flake had called for a march to Fort Wainwright at the end of the twenty-one day exercise anyway.

Slowly, each platoon began mustering its troops and then dividing up into designated fire teams. Because it would be dark soon, they started looking for an area to camp off the ice. They needed an area where they could fortify their position since this was a mock war exercise.

The troopers soon discovered that the perfect place to avoid the wind and snow was under the conifer stands of fur or spruce trees that seemed to reach up to the clouds while their branches drooped to the ground. With those branches laden with snow, they provided the only shelter in this wide-open tundra available to Will's team, which couldn't use their fuel soaked tents because of the danger of fire.

Luckily, someone in command had thought to bring extra sleeping bags from supply, and they bedded down on the soft layer of pine needles that covered the ground under those trees. Long after they were asleep, they were awakened to what sounded like a coal-fired freight train letting off steam. They jumped to their feet just as the sky lit up like it was day. Running out from under their refuge, they witnessed a gigantic pine tree explode into fire with flames billowing hundreds of feet into the air. A soldier in one of the teams had made the mistake of lighting a cigarette where ten men were sleeping, catching the pine needles on fire. Because of the resin in the tree, it was a death trap, and five troopers were burned to death and several others injured.

No one was able to sleep after that, and the following morning, they started their march to the closest outpost, a town called Taylor, as the snow continued to fall. They were given enough supplies to last for seven days while estimating the walk would take five. However, the second lieutenant in charge hoarded most of their rations and fuel to prove to his superiors that he was a responsible manager of assets. After the third day and night of going to sleep hungry and cold, he very quickly became the team's adversary. Food was parceled out like they were going to be on the tundra several weeks rather than five days. The nights were painfully cold because the lieutenant restricted the use of heating stoves to just a few hours each night. On the fourth day, the team met snow cats sent from Fort Taylor, and they still had most of their fuel and food. After this incident, Will's buddies were ready to fight over who would have the honor of shooting this SOB.

But not all of Will's experiences in the Northwest wilderness were bad ones. One he recalled with fondness happened when he was nineteen. It was the first time he saw Colorado, and the Rocky Mountains seemed awe inspiring. Buddy and his father invited Will to go big game hunting near the town of Telluride with fifteen other hunters from Southeast Missouri. A guide was hired for an early October hunt who arranged for them to have horses, motor bikes, food, and housing. He had leased an old two- story school house with two enormous fireplaces and an upper story loft. A makeshift barn had been built for the horses, and the hunting team was given last-minute advice on riding horses in the mountains and the operation of Wizard motor bikes in deep snow. Handling horses was old hat for most of the party, but the guide advised the use of Wizard motor bikes because they were better in deep snow than horses. Snow was not expected, but in Colorado, anything was possible.

Instructions were given as to the terrain, and each of them was provided area maps and compasses. Hunting in the Rocky Mountains usually requires long shots, so hunters look for a high advantage point to command a wider view.

Awakening on the first morning to the smell of breakfast being cooked by the guide and his assistant, they ate their fill and were given a few last-minute instructions.

Heading off in different directions, some were on horseback with the rest on motor bikes; Will was ready for his first hunt in the high country. Within an hour, he spotted a high ledge about 800 feet above the valley floor at approximately 7,000 feet elevation. He parked the Wizard and started to climb up a shale slide that led to the top.

After twenty minutes of climbing, he reached for a gigantic boulder to pull himself up onto the ledge only to have the boulder come away from the mountain. This sent him falling backward, head down, on the shale slide with the boulder coming down hard on his big toe. As he hit the shale, it started sliding with him as he fought the boulder to keep it from crashing into his body. There was nothing he could do but ride it out. Coming to rest close to the bottom of the slide, the boulder missed him by inches as it careened off to the side. He was in pain in several different areas. He tried to stand up, but the shale hadn't finished with him yet. He traveled yet another fifty feet on his already raw rear end. Taking stock of damage, he found the cheeks of his rear were exposed and bloody, and both elbows were sticking through his coat, slashed and bruised. The stock of his rifle had been sanded down to bare wood, and he was missing a glove and a watch.

The throbbing in Will's boot was extreme now, but it wasn't going to stop him nor was he going to let this mountain beat him, no siree. But it would have to be another day. He needed to get some first aid on that rump and have the doc take a look at his toe. Regrouping seemed to be in order, so he kicked the motor bike into action and headed back to camp, being careful to not hit too many bumps because of his sensitive rear.

Two mule deer were shot the first day, and the camp feasted on their better parts at the evening meal. The cabin was warm, and the conversation revolved around the different game the hunters had seen that day. They got a big laugh out of Will's experience and wanted to see his toe. As he took off his boot, they were shocked to see that it had turned completely black and was about twice its normal size.

One of the hunters on this trip was Will's favorite doctor, Dr. Sargent. This would have been a perfect opportunity for him to extract additional retribution, but they had made peace the year before when Will had the privilege of singing at the funeral of the doctor's mother. She was a fine Christian woman, and the doctor had expressed his appreciation many times, ensuring peace and harmony between them.

"Let me see that foot, Will," the doctor said as he shuffled a deck of cards and began dealing a round of poker. Most of the players were still eating their supper, but the doctor wanted to see it, so Will stuck his foot up on the table. "Wheeeooo," said Buddy's father. "That's some toe, Will. Looks like a gigantic blood blister. Doc, you better do something about that thing so he can go back out tomorrow." The doctor glanced over briefly between eating a plate of deer meat and beans with one hand and playing cards with the other and instructed Buddy to put his hunting knife in the fire until the tip got red hot.

"Whoa, wait a minute here," Will protested. "What do you think you're going to do?"

"Why, lance it of course," said the doctor. "Hold him, boys." When the knife got hot enough, Buddy handed it to the doctor. In between eating and dealing, he gently touched the toe, and it popped like an overripe plum, spewing across the room. A stream of it went across one guy's plate just as he lifted a spoon full of beans to his mouth. Realizing he had eaten beans laced with blood, he gagged and headed for the door. This caused a chain reaction that sent two other fellas running for the door. The whiskey they had been drinking didn't help the situation.

Instantly, the pain and throbbing ceased. Dr. Sargent poured a cup of vodka over the toe, dried it with a towel, and Buddy dressed it. He gave Will antiseptic cream for his raw rear and elbows, and Will slept like it had never happened.

The next morning, after changing the bandage, he was able to put on his boot and miraculously, except for some soreness, had very little pain. Today was going to be different, Will thought. Today, he was going to the top come hell or high water. He began the climb up the shale and halfway up recovered the glove but never found the watch. Reaching the top, it began to snow.

Positioning himself on the ledge, he began to scan the valley below with binoculars and was surprised to see so many different types of game at the same time. Off to the left, less than 200 yards away, he saw a big brown bear moseying along a game trail at the tree line. Beyond the bear, a wolverine was moving rapidly along a creek bank on his quest for food. Close to the wolverine was a pond where he could make out a large pair of beavers busily building a dam. Down in front, no more than 300 feet from where he had ended his slide, stood a small herd of mule deer within range of his Winchester. And off to the right of an aspen grove, he saw Buddy tie up his horse and enter the stand of trees.

As Will raised his rifle to his shoulder and gazed through the scope, he caught some movement off to the left. It was a herd of five elk entering that same aspen grove from the opposite end that Buddy had entered. Will knew that if he fired at the deer, the elk would spook and scatter. He also knew that if the tables were turned, Buddy would hold his fire for him so he waited.

Will watched intently waiting for the next sign of movement. Knowing Buddy as he did, he knew there was no need to try and warn him, he would know exactly how to handle the situation. Fifteen minutes passed, and the snow began to come down harder than ever, making vision difficult at long distances.

The deer were slowly moving away into a thicket now, and Will's chances of bagging one were growing slimmer. Finally, a shot rang out, then another, then another spaced a few seconds apart. He jumped from his position and began to run down the shale slide, sending the deer scampering into thicker brush. Another shot was fired and then another. Will cranked up the Wizard and headed toward the trees. The snow had already turned the ground white.

Buddy heard Will coming and met him at the edge of the trees. "Will, you are not going to believe this. Leave your bike and follow me." There, in a clearing, lay a huge pile of elk. He had killed them all. Will had never seen elk up close, and he was surprised at their size and the number of them that Buddy had killed. "I can't believe I killed them all, Will. Once I started shooting, I couldn't stop. It was like the time when we went up to dad's cabin on Current River, do you remember?"

"Yeah, I remember," Will responded. Buddy's father had decorated the walls of the cabin with plaster deer and game heads. They had driven up there to spend the night, got into his father's liquor, and Buddy started the whole thing off by throwing a knife at one of the game heads and splitting it in half. Then all the boys started throwing knives at animal heads. In the excitement of the moment, they pulled their guns out and started shooting wildly at anything that was hung on the walls.

"Well, that's how this happened. Just like in the cabin when we couldn't stop shooting, I couldn't stop shooting elk. Remember, how we ran out of the cabin in the middle of the night and headed home? That's what I wanted to do now, run for home. It was like a shooting frenzy, Will." It was obvious that Buddy was shaken up and frightened by his callous shooting of these magnificent animals.

"Did your dad ever find out who shot up his cabin?" Will asked. "No, he never did. He always thought it was vandals that had broken in and did the damage. We need to get help with these elk. I don't like the looks of these snow clouds, they look ominous. I think we're in for a bad one. Why don't you go for help, and I'll stay here. For God's sake, Will, please hurry. We might not get out of here if it gets too bad."

"Sure, Bud, I'll be back as quickly as possible."

Will jumped on the Wizard and drove as fast as he could. When he arrived, he found several hunters had come in early, anticipating the weather. When he informed the guide what had happened, he was not very happy. As the remainder of the hunters returned, he gathered them together to give them his opinion of what they should do next. "Fellas, the situation is damn serious. We've got about four inches of snow on the ground already, and that only took a little over three hours. If it continues at this rate, we will have several feet of snow before we know it, and it's snowing harder than before. We are close to blizzard conditions and can't risk losing the horses or maybe getting snowed in ourselves. It is my assessment that we have no other choice but to leave the elk where they are and get the hell out of this valley as soon as possible." Everyone agreed with his recommendation, and Will was asked to return for Buddy and bring him back as soon as possible. Back on the Wizard, he headed for the aspen grove, humping the bike over the drifts he encountered along the way.

"What do you mean leave the elk? Are you crazy? I can't waste these beautiful animals. It's bad enough that I killed them all, but to leave them to rot, come on!"

"Buddy, we don't have a choice. You're going to have problems getting your horse back to camp as it is."

"Maybe we can pull at least one back to camp, we have rope enough," Buddy said.

"Look around you, Bud. We have to leave and now. Your horse has all he can handle just getting himself back. Let's go damn it!"

Reluctantly, he saddled up and they headed back. They could see only a few feet in front of them now. Will began to wonder what would happen if they got off the trail or lost their way, but he let that thought slide quickly out of his mind. The horse was having a very difficult time now, and Buddy had to dismount and lead it. Surprisingly, it was easier to bounce the Wizard over the drifts than to lead the horse through them.

When they arrived back at camp, everyone was loaded up and waiting. The other horses were in their trailers, and once they loaded Buddy's, they sped out of the valley as fast as it was safe to drive. The area they were hunting had a record-breaking snowstorm that day, and all of the hunters agreed that the decision to break camp and leave had been a wise one. Buddy gave up any thoughts of hunting elk after that, and so did Will.

Golden Triangle Mission

The steamy jungles of Southeast Asia were a stark contrast to Will's military and hunting activities in snowy Alaska and Colorado. After mentally cooling off in his elk-hunting memories, Will suddenly had a flash of a totally different hunt- ing experience.

Will and Larry seldom had a dull, boring, or monotonous moment due to the special classification they held when they first came to Vietnam: sometimes soldier, sometimes agent. When an unusual task came up, Cecil Tighe would pull them out of whatever unit they happened to be attached and assign them to a team he was creating to complete some new assignment. That could be an airborne division, a Green Beret unit, or a ranger outfit. On several occasions, they were assigned to an all- Vietnamese outfit like the Merciless Vengence battalion of which Tom Vo had been a part. The Golden Triangle was one of those "never took place" missions, the kind the US government would deny had ever happened.

Will got a call from Cecil Tighe on their designated frequency, asking him and Larry to come in for a special meeting at Tan Son Nhut, saying that an aircraft will be picking them up at Candy's Landing, a known Air America drop-off point for agents being transported in and out of South Vietnam for activities throughout Southeast Asia. The field was close to SF 22's present base of operations. Will was surprised to see a Volpar Turbo Beech circle in to land. He had heard a lot about this aircraft but had never seen one. Volpar had converted the Beech 18 to Turbo, and with its STOL capability, it had become legend in being able to extract agents under siege.

"Thank you all for coming," Cecil began. "I know you all have pressing responsibilities out there in the field, but I've been asked to assemble a highly trained team to undertake a special mission outside of

Vietnam. We will be operating without the support of our usual army and air force back up, and because of the sensitivity of the operation, confidentiality is essential, both now and at the end of this activity. Is that understood?"

No one spoke, but most of the men present nodded in acceptance. Meeting that day with Cecil were Drew Harlow, Marshall Brant, Captain Charles Reilly, Larry Stockton, and Will. It had been a while since the six of them had been together, and Will felt pleased that whatever they were about to get involved in, they could rely on each other.

Tighe uncovered a map that was on an easel showing Southeast Asia with stickers pinned to an area known as the Golden Triangle. "As you know, this area produces more opium than any other place in the world. The sale of this drug is funding most of the operations of our buddies, the VC. Moreover, it is making its way into the veins of American soldiers as well as the arms of American youth. We are not under the illusion that we can stop this permanently. But we've been asked to interdict, to interrupt their operation, and to take out the number one warlord, Kuhn Sa."

"We have credible information that Sa's base of operations is near Si Dan Mun. We have full cooperation with the Laos and Thailand authorities, but we also know that some of the military and other officials are sympathetic to Sa's Mong Tai Army and are probably on his payroll to keep him informed about any action that might endanger him or his heroin-opium operation. So we can't trust anyone or expect any help due to the nature of what we are about to do. There are American private contractors in the area. But the kind of money heroin sales produce can make mercenaries out of the most loyal, so you will have to be careful who you work with and how much you rely on them. Some of our people will be expecting you and will lead you to the point of contact. I am instructing all of you to return to your units and be prepared to leave two days from now.

"We will leave Thursday morning and meet up in Bangkok that evening at the Pink Orchid Hotel. I'm sure some of you players have heard about the pit of vipers where naked Tai ladies dance with cobras. You will be housed there until you have been contacted by one of our operatives. I don't think I need to tell you guys to stay out of trouble. We don't need to draw attention to our presence. Yes, the place is full of Americans, but there are ears there that are paid to listen. And from what I've heard, there are some very strange people who hang out there praying on unsuspecting yanks. Do I make myself clear on this?"

Almost in unison, they responded, "Yes, sir."

"You will be provided weapons and equipment by our people on the ground, but you might want to bring a favorite sidearm anyway. I always do," he said as he smiled and raised his 1911 Colt 45 over his head.

Two days later, that same Volpar Beech, with Harlow, Reilly, and Brant aboard, picked up Will and Larry. By late afternoon, they were in Bangkok being transported by an Air America employee to the notorious Pink Orchid.

While the operation was a dangerous one, this gave the team a chance to relax a bit and to enjoy the luxury and hospitality of the Tai people. Their contact person suggested the Cobra Lounge as the place to have a drink and experience the music and culture of Thailand. They were surprised to see the place packed and jumping like a typical stateside nightclub on a Saturday night, and just as Cecil had said, there were many strange and bizarre people inhabiting the club. Will was glad he had told them they could be armed as there was a feeling that anything could happen if the people he saw were any indication of what was possible.

"Check this guy out," Drew Harlow remarked. The man he was talking about was over 350 pounds, obviously gay, and extremely aggressive. As they observed his action, he was going around grabbing men and, putting them in a bear hug, and kissing them. And he was looking the unit over like any one of them might be next. "If that SOB lays a hand on me, I'm gonna break his neck," Reilly remarked. And Reilly was big and strong enough to do it. But the big guy had his eye on Larry.

Strolling over with a fiendish smile on his face, he grabs Larry in a bear hug and plants a kiss so quickly that Larry couldn't avoid it. Without warning, Larry pulled his 45 out and shot the guy's kneecap off, sending him bloodily rolling onto the dance floor in pain. "What, are you crazy?" Marshall exclaimed, somewhat perturbed. "Weren't we given strict instructions to stay out of trouble and here you blast the guy's knee?"

To which Larry responded, "The sick bastard stuck his tongue halfway down my throat and no faggot SOB does that to me. He's lucky he didn't catch a bullet up the gullet."

Employees of the Pink Orchid carried the wounded man out of the hotel to a waiting ambulance while the unit continued to drink at the bar. But no one including the night ladies came near them after that.

The next morning, the temperature had already climbed to over 100 degrees as the team met in a private room off the lobby of the hotel to have breakfast. They dined with several plainclothes agents who provided security for them. Their contact man was a former Special Forces captain by the name of Roger Kincaid. Most of the team had heard about Kincaid before, and he completely fit the mold of what they expected. Built like a fire plug, tanned from so many hours in the bush, a résumé that included more special ops mission than a file cabinet wouldn't hold, and a steely stare that told you he was dangerous.

His presence commanded attention as he spoke. "Gentlemen, I've had my breakfast so you can go ahead and start while I bring you up-to-date on what we intend to do. There is one major change to our orders. We may need air support based upon observations we made yesterday. They know we are coming. It seems we have a mole, and he's one of us who has informed the target that a team of people from Vietnam arrived last night. They don't know the purpose of this team, only that it warranted them going on high alert status. We can't go in there the way we had planned."

Will and the other men did their best to give no indication of their concern, but it was difficult not looking around at their reactions. This would be a major fire fight, and they knew it.

"Bring him in," Kincaid ordered. A side door opened, and two men brought in an American officer who appeared to be a lieutenant wearing a uniform that had seen better days. "Gentlemen, this is your basic turncoat, Lt. Robert Howard, an officer with a *Leg* outfit or as some of you call them NAPS for non-airborne personnel responsible for shipping bodies home from Vietnam to America. While he has been drawing his full pay and hazard duty script, he has been earning a tidy sum shipping heroin home to the US with soldiers in body bags and keeping Khan Sa informed about us. If it had been up to me, he would never have seen the light of another day. But we have a plan for him, and it starts now."

The lieutenant had been roughed up, but they had been careful not to injure him in ways Khan Sa could see. He was hurt underneath his clothing, and he moved like a man in pain. He was also scared and uncertain about his future because he knew the code. The code required that he be taken out, but there might be an exception if he followed instructions. Part of that code calls for finding him and finishing the job if he tried to run. When that part of the code gets pulled into play, there is no place on earth he would be safe. Kincaid had the lieutenant removed from the room while he discussed their options.

"It will be the lieutenant's responsibility to inform Khan Sa that the Americans have returned to Vietnam and ensure us Khan Sa is where he is supposed to be when the strike goes in. We will be deploying three fire teams. The first team's responsibility is to verify that he has been eliminated. The only way to do that is to be there." The team's concern could be felt in the room. The sense the restlessness was apparent as some of the men looked around at the other team members. They knew this was not going to be easy.

"First, we are going to create a diversion. The warlord's stronghold is about a quarter mile from the fields of poppies and his processing facility. They are separated by dense jungle and are connected by a narrow road. We will strike the fields and the processing plant, which should draw most of his forces from his compound to the scene of the conflict. I've been informed that our air jockeys may be applying Agent Orange on some of the fields along with incendiary ordinance. Those of you in the second team, that is the road detail and the processing plant, should wear masks.

"The third team will be dug in along the road to set up a fire position long enough to allow the second team to make it to the rendezvous point and for the first team to come in and clean up. The first team also has to make sure Khan Sa was eliminated after the airstrike hit the compound. You will be picked up by Hueys once we get the word Khan has been identified and smoked. Our lovely lieutenant will keep us informed as to where Khan Sa should be at a given time. Concussion ordinance will be used rather than firepower so that it will be easier for identification. This will mean that not everyone will be dead, there will probably be some opposition even after the strike. But if they do survive, they will be deaf as hell."

It was a restless night for Will and Larry as the rain continued through the night. Will's thoughts centered on Lieutenant Howard. He wondered how a promising American officer could betray his country and ultimately his comrades. Was he hooked on the drugs he was transporting or was it the lure of big bucks? Perhaps it was the intrigue, the added danger to an already dangerous assignment. There was no doubt in his mind that having a twisted or warped brain came with the territory. He also knew that given enough time, no one was immune to its insidious affect.

Kincaid let the men know that because Khan Sa was probably aware of their presence and because he had informers everywhere, traveling to the target the usual way was no longer an option. Lieutenant Howard was released to make contact with the warlord to let him know that the Americans were only here just long enough to make connections for assignments elsewhere. To confirm this, the men were transported back to the airport where Air America had a hanger and several aircraft. There Kincaid let them know that they would be dropped by parachute at a remote location far enough from Khan Sa's lookouts that he should have no warning of his impending doom.

As they entered the hangar, they saw loading tables on each side of the room. The one on the left was stacked high with parachutes and other jump equipment. The one on the right contained all the necessary weapons to eliminate any resistance they might encounter. Included were their favorite CAR-15 "Colt Commando," longer M14s, a few M1919 Browning machine guns, and various grenades. There were even some M72 LAW "Light Anti-Tank Weapons," which would be great if they encountered a bunker or fortified building. They knew that Cecil Tighe would have thought of everything. Of course, every man had his own trusty Colt 1911 .45.

The men gathered in a day room to hear and see the briefing given by Kincaid. Topographic maps and photos taken by high altitude aircraft were displayed to familiarize the team with the terrain. It was decided to wait for nightfall before loading the aircraft as it was assumed they would have a better chance of going undetected. Kincaid suggested that the jumpers wait and suit up on the aircraft rather than show prying eyes that an air assault was in the making. In the meantime, the men lounged around the facility, some taking a brief siesta as they passed the time until the order was given to saddle up.

As their twin engine aircraft rose into the air and turned to the north, Larry said to Will, "Think this qualifies us for a combat jump?"

"I doubt it, pardner. We aren't even supposed to be here. How many would this be...would this be number 3?"

"Yep. You never get used to it...it's always like the very first one. At least, we don't have a long wait sitting here with all this equipment and ordinance," Larry responded.

The men on the right side of the aircraft could see the sun setting off to the west and the same question always seemed to rear its ugly head just before contact: Is this the one I won't be coming home from?

The jump master opened both side doors and gave the command, "Stand in the door." The men could feel the pilot throttling back as the aircraft slowed down. Will could see they were coming in very low, which meant that their chutes would barely have time to open, allowing only a few oscillations before they would hit the ground...hard. The jump master did his best to keep all the men within a one hundred yard grouping in case they ran into resistance early.

Marshalling together for instructions from Kincaid, they broke up into the three predetermined fire teams, and they began the airborne shuffle to get them to the target as quickly as possible. Kincaid estimated that they were less than a mile from Khan Sa's headquarters, perhaps a mile from the poppy fields and the processing plant. After coordinating their watches and instructions, each team went about getting to their positions. The time was 2100 hrs (9:00 p.m.). The assault on the fields and plant would come first at 2300 with an incendiary airstrike setting fire to the fields. A second airstrike would then come in at 2310 with concussion ordinance. Larry and Will were assigned to the team that would either take him prisoner or verify that he had been eliminated.

The first team moved slowly though the jungle until they could see Khan Sa's stronghold. After getting a glimpse of it, they crawled the last few yards and dug in to wait for the boys from "the wild blue yonder" as troopers call them. Suddenly, gunfire erupted in the direction of the poppy fields, and Kincaid's voice came over the handheld radio. Larry could hear them say that they had walked into a trap along the road to the field, and he was instructing team 2 and part of Will's team to come support them ASAP. Several of the men who had friends in the team under attack immediately volunteered to go to their aid.

Right on time, the airstrike came in, and the men who remained with Will and Larry covered their ears with their hands, knowing that Jolly Roger was about to lay down tons of ordnance designed to immobilize the opposition. What they didn't expect was seeing the Air Force drop standard ordnance, destroying parts of the stronghold and sending Khan Sa's security force running from the facility and directly at Will's team hiding nearby. While all of this was taking place, Khan Sa's headquarters was being destroyed and the noise of the concussion bombs was deafening.

Running from the bush, team 1, led by Larry and Will, met part of the security force head on. They were able to drop them where they stood, slowing down only long enough to reload. The air support finished their job and started home while Will's team began searching the remaining buildings. Some were flattened, some were on fire, and a few were still standing. Entering the walls of the compound, they searched and found the bodies of both men and women, presumably members Khan Sa's family, but no Khan Sa.

Meanwhile, Kincaid had his hands full until the strike on the poppy fields confused and disorganized Khan Sa's people. Then along with the help of the men who had come to their aid from team 1, they assaulted the processing plant running into only moderate opposition. With a few strategically positioned incendiary grenades, the plant was in flames within minutes.

During the fire fights, both teams took prisoners, and one of them was eager to tell where the warlord was hiding. The prisoner had been part of a team of construction workers that had built a bunker a few years ago to protect him against an air assault like the one that had just taken place. The entrance to that bunker was under the master bedroom's bed. Going back into the smoldering ruins, they located what was left of a king size bed. Larry and Will swept the room clean of everything, protecting the bunker's trap door, and they slowly opened it. They were greeted by Khan Sa screaming like a woman, "Ne tirez pas...s'il vous plaît ne tirez pas...je suis innocent" (Don't shoot...please don't shoot...I'm innocent).

"Yeah, right," Will said to the team with his comments directed to Khan Sa, not worrying about if he understood nor if he cared or understood that there was only one man in history that was innocent, and Khan Sa, you are not that man.

While team 1 had no casualties, the other two teams lost five men total. Was destroying a poppy field, ending a drug processing plant, and catching a drug dealer worth the lives of these men? Only God knows the answer to that question.

Their mission over, getting safely back to Bangkok was top priority!

Those Air America pilots brag that they can land and take off on a dry rug; some claim they can do it even if the rug is wet. Well, they were about to prove it. "The vacation is over," the incoming pilot said over their communications radio. "Climb aboard, time for you slackers to go back to work," which brought a smile to everyone within hearing of their radio. While the teams were thinking of how their exit would happen, they saw a C-123 come over the treetops and settle onto the grass of a very small field.

Taking their casualties, a few souvenirs, and any evidence they thought pertinent, they quickly headed to rendezvous with the C-123. True to their claims, all of them, including the troopers lost, were quickly lifted out of the Golden Triangle and headed due south to the comfort and safety of Bangkok.

Will was thankful to be among those who made it through the mission. He said a prayer of thanks and a prayer for the souls of those who were coming back in body bags. Each mission takes its toll, and this one was no different, exacting a special payment from his soul in an already empty one.

MARDI GRAS

The hostesses were serving hot toddies as a new movie came on the screen. It was about a high school football team, reminding Will of his hometown team, the Sikeston Bulldogs. The thirty-three-man team roster was posted on the bulletin board his sophomore year, and somehow, he made it. He had picked up a few pounds lifting weights with Davie who was getting bigger by the nanosecond. Because of his size, he made the team his freshman year. Their weights consisted of tin cans filled with concrete with steel bars inserted to connect them, and they worked out in Davies's garage almost every day.

It was a relatively uneventful year for Will other than Sikeston going undefeated for the third straight year. The Bulldogs rolled up scores like 50–7, 48–14, and 49–0. They beat the Charleston Blue Jays, 50–0, which discouraged Will from riding around Charleston after dark for a while. High scores afforded second- and third-string players considerable playing time, and it assured Will at least the second-string position his junior year.

Will's junior year was a duplication of the year before, except for his playing time, which increased due to the success of the first string. Again, Sikeston went undefeated. There were only two people better than Will now at the left end position, and one of them was going to graduate.

Curt turned in his usual All-American basketball performance that year, taking Sikeston to the Missouri State Championships, but the competition eliminated the Bulldogs just before the finals. College scouts were drooling over Curt even though he had a year of high school left. This attention seemed to have no effect on him. He was still the same Curt Gregory. If anything, he became more reclusive, more mysterious, and perhaps even more humble. Girls worshipped him, boys envied him, and the townspeople revered him. One day, Will asked him what he thought about all the notoriety. "Just between you and me, Will, I think it's ridiculous. It takes no virtue to be an athlete."

Basketball season ended just before Mardi Gras. Somehow, Will and his friends, Sam Tanner, Don Baker, Sam Bowman, and Jerry Guess, convinced their parents to let them go. Sam's grandmother trusted him enough to permit him to take her Buick, and they drove all night to get there. Five hundred miles and ten hours later, they arrived in New Orleans at dawn. They spotted a "Room for Rent" sign outside a Cajun's house, and they bunked down for some shuteye to get ready for the coming festivities.

Except for hunting trips or Boy Scout Camp, the boys had never been away from home without their parents. And here they were, turned loose on Bourbon Street during Mardi Gras. Will remembered how wild it was, like nothing they had ever experienced. One of his friends had told him about a world- famous place called Pat O'Brien's where they could always find beautiful women and a drink called the Hurricane. None of them had ever taken a drink before that night, but Pat O'Brien's was about to change all that. They saddled up to the bar like they had been doing it all their lives, and before they had said a word, the bartender had four Hurricanes sitting in front of them with no questions asked about age. They had heard that few grown men could consume more than two Hurricanes and remember to tell about it.

Just as they begun to sip on those so-called death-dealers, the music started and everyone's attention shifted to where a lovely young lady in a business suit had climbed onto the end of the bar and started walking in their direction. As she came down the bar, she began to disrobe, and by the time she arrived in front of the four of them, she was naked as a jaybird. Then another beautiful girl came walking toward them, disrobing as she came. They found out later that these young ladies had been recruited from an exclusive all-girls school in Gulfport, Mississippi, rich girls away from home, stripping for fun, not for money.

Within twenty-five minutes, they had witnessed twenty or more lovely young women, each seemingly more beautiful than the one before, strip to their birthday suits. In the excitement, they had wolfed down two Hurricanes and were drunk as skunks. When the show ended, they staggered back through the crowd, cradling their giveaway

Hurricane glasses, intending to take them home to prove to their friends that they had actually been to New Orleans and survived two Hurricanes. Finding a bench in the courtyard near a fountain, they sat down and ordered some coffee while trying to sober up as they observed the activities. Unknown to them, a drama was taking place in the street out front that was about to spark a riot.

A thief had been caught breaking into a car, and the arresting officer brought him into O'Brien's, handcuffed him to a pole, and went to a pay phone to call for a paddy wagon. While he was on the phone, the thief, a smooth-talking thug, convinced the crowd that he was an undercover FBI agent on the trail of a communist, and if he didn't get loose, his quarry would escape.

To understand what happened next, you need to remember that during the early fifties, communism was a big threat, perceived or otherwise. McCarthyism was the buzz word, and there was widespread national alarm. So after the thief convinced the crowd that he was an FBI agent on the trail of a communist and the policeman was interfering with his surveillance of a suspect, that was all this drunken mob needed.

When the cop returned, the drunken crowd beat him up, took his keys, and let the thief go. Somehow, the policeman got to a phone and called for backup. When more police arrived, they met tough resistance, and several members of the backup squad were beaten so severely that they had to call in the riot squad. Then all hell broke loose.

When the disturbance started, the place was wall to wall people, but they began to scatter after noticing something flying around above the heads of the crowd. People were running past them back into the building to get into the melee, and then they saw what was flying around. It was police night sticks, and people were dropping like flies. The kids from Missouri watched frozen in fear, not knowing what to do. When a tear gas canister rolled out into the courtyard and came to rest at their feet, they knew what to do—get the hell out of there. In unison, they jumped to their feet, Hurricane glasses flying, headed for the back wall, thrashed through the fountain, bounced off a bench, and ran into the alley.

Policemen were everywhere. Just as the boys would pass an alley intersection, the cops would turn the corner behind them and give chase. Will remembered it was like an old Laurel and Hardy movie.

Finally, they got lost in the crowd, but that was all the excitement they needed for one night, so they headed back to the Cajun's house and crashed.

Will always remembered his first hangover or at least the aftereffects, and it was not something that he wanted to experience again.

"Bananas! Bananas! Get your bananas." Will had the urge to feel around his head to see where the ax was imbedded. Opening one eye, an excruciating pain raced through his brain. He couldn't believe some idiot was hawking bananas at 6:00 a.m. *Please, Mr. Banana Man, don't shout so loud*, he thought to himself. "Bananas! Bananas! Get your bananas." *I got your damn banana*, he thought. The pain was almost too much to bear, and Will wasn't alone in this agony. "Anybody got any Alka-Seltzer?" Sam said, as he groped around for his backpack. "Anybody that tries to drink two of those head crushers need to get their head examined, literally" Jerry said. They were a sorry lot.

Staggering to their feet, they walked down the street to a coffeehouse to get some relief. Don spotted the headlines of the morning paper in a news stand, which read "Two Hundred People Arrested Rioting in French Quarter." In talking to their waitress, she mentioned that it was tradition to let all the drunks out of jail every morning during Carnival. They were always greeted by a cheering mob and a Dixieland band. This was something they had to see. Getting directions, they rushed over to the city jail just in time to see these forlorn wretches coming out into the sunlight to the tune of "Oh When the Saints Go Marching In." There must have been a thousand people cheering and passing them bottles of liquor to take the hair off the dog.

The Polio Bowl

The football movie had Will thinking about his old team again. In his senior year, practice started in August when the temperature and humidity in the Midwest were like those found in the Amazon. Will had tried to stay in shape and be ready for what he knew was coming, a rugged season with every team wanting to knock them off to end their four-year winning streak. Pride was the motivating factor however, and it drove players to their limit.

The season was going quite well for Will until the fifth game of the year. It was played against the toughest opponent they had, Cape Girardeau. Cape had a fullback who weighed two hundred and twenty pounds and loved to punish tacklers. In those days, many players played both defense and offense. Sometime during the fourth quarter, Cape Girardeau's fullback came around Will's end, led by a halfback whose blocking assignment was him. The halfback faked high but came in low, and somehow, Will was able to leap over him and meet the runner head on. This straightened the runner up and slowed him down long enough for Dewey Gimlin, one of several All-Americans Sikeston had on the team, to drive him into the dirt causing a fumble that the Bulldogs recovered. It wasn't until Will started to stand up that he realized he was hurt. When he threw himself over the blocker, he felt something go snap in his leg. At first, he thought it was a bone, but the pain was worse than a break. Reaching for his thigh, Will could feel two large lumps, one just above the knee and the other at the top of the thigh, about the size of his fist.

There was no getting up, and he had to be carried off the field on a stretcher. An examination revealed that he had torn the thigh muscle, causing it to knot along with the nerves at each end of the thighbone. The pain was so excruciating that it hurt his leg to blink his eye.

For all intent, this was the end of Will's sports career as he never recovered his speed, so crucial to a good athlete. The last three games of the season he was able to suit up, but now he was on the third string and played infrequently when the Bulldogs were ahead by a substantial margin.

By the end of the season, Sikeston had gone undefeated for the fifth straight year. Controversy arose over who was the number 1 team in the state. Southwestern of St. Louis had also gone undefeated and the St. Louis Globe Dispatch ranked them number 1 with Sikeston number 2. The rationale was that Southwestern's competition was stronger and their school population so much bigger than Sikeston's: 2,300 students to 600. Polio was rampant during the '50s, and Sikeston's football opponents, led by Charleston, devised a way to see the Bulldogs brought to their knees, or so they thought. The Polio Bowl was promoted as a fund-raising event to be played in Charleston on New Year's Day by the two best teams in the state, Southwestern and Sikeston, with all proceeds to be used for polio research.

The hype was incredible for a high school game with both the *St. Louis Globe* and *Post Dispatch* newspapers running front- page articles on both teams every day. It was predicted that Southwestern would win by a landslide. People from towns within their conference would caravan through Sikeston with banners on their cars supporting Southwestern. Other than the people of Sikeston, there would be a lot of happy people in Southeast Missouri if Sikeston were to lose. It was billed as country boys against city boys. The Bulldogs worked harder than ever to prepare for this game, knowing that if they won, they would in effect be beating all of their opponents again by proxy.

Though Will's leg was healing fast, he knew he was definitely slower than before. He tried to make it up by hitting harder on defense and by catching the ball better than anyone else on offense. But without speed, it was difficult to compete. He was, however, moved from the third string to the second, affording him an opportunity to play if the player ahead of him got hurt or the score was wide enough.

The day of the big game, Will received word that his father would be there. He had never attended any of Will's games or seen him play, and it was depressing to Will to know that it was highly unlikely that he would see him play that day.

The temperature was brutal, falling below zero. When the team arrived at the stadium, the ground was frozen solid, and it had started to sleet. Sikeston's fans began to cheer when the Bulldogs entered the playing field, but they were quickly drowned out by the Southwestern fans as the Southwestern players took the field. It was obvious by the roar of the partisan crowd that they had come to see the Bulldogs get blown out. Going through their pre-game drills, Will tried to scan the stadium for his father, but it was useless. To accommodate the crowd, several sections of bleachers had been added, giving the field a college bowl appearance. There were ten thousand people there that day, much larger than any crowd that had ever seen them play before.

Will remembered pausing for a few seconds as the team was running back into the dressing room, taking one last look around the stadium for his father. Knowing that this would be the last game he would ever play, if he got to play at all, he felt immense pride in being a part of this exciting event. Sikeston's coach Kenny Knox was a master at firing the team up. Comparing this game to David facing Goliath, he quoted articles from the St. Louis paper describing his players as a bunch of "Hicks from the sticks." But what motivated them the most was the impassioned last-minute talk given by their quarterback Nicholas Walker.

Nicholas was the finest athlete on the team and more respected by the players than anyone else. Time and time again, he had pulled them from the jaws of defeat. It was a tremendous confidence builder to know that he was at the helm; they had never seen him lose a game in his four years as their quarterback. "In the tradition of Sikeston High football, we honor those who have gone before us, with the torch of five years of undefeated football. It was their blood and sweat that have brought us to this moment. If we lose, their efforts will have been in vain, and we will have betrayed them, our school, our parents and friends, and our town. Bohannon, did you want to say anything?" It was appropriate that he be asked to say the prayer; he had talked about being a missionary when he graduated. He was also the guy that had beaten Will out for the left end position. "Join me in prayer, guys. We can't do it without him." The whole team was on their knees. "Dear God. Forgive us if we want to win this game for the wrong reasons. We know your will shall be done. Give us the strength to overcome our advisories just like the power you gave to David in days of old. You know what's in our hearts. Keep us free from injury. But, God, regardless of the outcome, thank you for the privilege of playing with the greatest bunch of guys that ever played the game. Amen." Will looked around the room and saw in the eyes of his teammates a certain look of determination like he had never seen before. Somehow, they knew they were going to win, they just didn't know how. The linemen began to beat on each other and became so animated, it looked like a fight had broken out.

When the Bulldogs hit the field, the crowd's noise was so intense Will couldn't hear the guy next to him talking, much less hear the announcer. Lined up on the field for the kickoff, Sikeston received the ball. Down the field, Nicholas drove his team, scoring the first touchdown on a quarterback keeper. But it didn't take long to realize how evenly matched they were. Southwestern came right back and tied it up with an impressive power-play that let the Bulldogs know this was going to be a long afternoon.

The first half was all offense, ending in a 21–21 tie. Sikeston's linemen were more exhausted than Will had ever seen them before. The burden of moving this giant defensive Southwestern line was taking its toll. Rather than a "Knute Rockne-Notre Dame" kind of rah-rah halftime speech, the coach and Nicholas spent their time just talking to each of the players individually. However, the coach never bothered to speak to Will. Perhaps Will was considered a nonissue, meaning that he wasn't going to get to play. But Nicholas did talk to Will just like he did to all of the other players.

"Think you're up for old Phantom Right, Will?" he said. With a sarcastic smile, Will replied, "Sure, in my next life. You know Knox would never call me in to play in this game. Not with the score this close."

"We'll see, Will. We'll see."

In contrast to the first half, the second half was all defense with ball possession going back and forth until Southwestern finally scored a field goal with two minutes left to play. With Southwestern now ahead 24–21, Sikeston took the kickoff back to their own forty-yard line and drove to the Southwestern thirty where they bogged down on fourth and eight with thirty seconds left to play. Nicholas called a time out and came over to the sidelines where he proceeded to get into an argument with the coach. Everyone knew you never get into an argument with

Knox. He was as tough as they come, a former Marine Corp captain with an impressive list of WWII medals. The field goal kicker and punter, Tommy Dunaway, was one of the best in the conference, but he had been roughed up earlier in the game, injuring his left leg. This made it almost impossible to set up for a field goal. In addition, his percentage from forty yards, which would be the distance of this kick, was suspect. To make matters worse, it was becoming slicker than ever as it was now sleeting harder than before.

The coach and Nicholas continued to argue, becoming very animated, occasionally looking in Will's direction. Finally, the coach signaled for him, so he dropped his parka and ran up to them. "You're taking over for Bohannon, Brandon. Get in there," Coach Knox grumbled, hardly looking in his direction as he spoke. As Will ran onto the field, a small cheer rose up from the stands above the crowd's noise. *It always pays to have friends*, he thought to himself.

The pressure was really on Will now. What could he do? he thought. Any defensive back Southwestern had could outrun him. Here he was, cold as a cucumber, with no chance to warm up and thirty seconds left to play. Don Baker, the team captain and halfback, called another time out before they were assessed a penalty for taking too much time.

Nicholas pulled the huddle together and said, "This is Will's play. We haven't run it since he got hurt. They know we won't run a play like this, they'll be expecting us to go for a first down, but we're going to take it all the way. If all of you do your jobs, we'll score. If any one of you fail in your assignment, the play will fail and we will lose. All of those years of playing together has boiled down to this one play. Remember, this is the last time we play together, guys. Let's do it for Sikeston High and for our friends, but most of all, let's do this one for us. Will, it's all yours, baby. Break!"

The sleet was coming down harder than ever now, turning the ground gray. Will went to the line and looked up at the defensive end who was so psyched, he was foaming at the mouth.

"I'm gonna squish you like a bug, skinny boy. You're dead… you're freakin dead," this big brute shouted. It wasn't the first time Will had heard those words, and they seemed comforting, like an old pair of shoes or a blister.

Firing off the ball at the snap count, Will was shivered hard by the end, but somehow, he was able to keep his balance and continue his pattern. The defensive back picked him up, and they ran stride for stride until Will faked right but broke left diagonally across center. The defensive player tried to follow his pattern, but as he made his cut, his feet slid out from under him. This sent him sprawling on the ground and out of the play, leaving Will undefended ten yards from the goal. The play had been designed to give Will the option of staying straight if closely defended or breaking deep if not, so he broke deep. As he turned to his left to look back, the ball was right there, face high, like it had been thrown on a string straight into Will's waiting hands. That was the last thing Will remembered until he woke up on the training table under the bright heat lamps with the ball still clutched against his chest.

In those days, the goal posts were placed on the goal line, not ten yards deep as they are today. Will had caught Nicholas's perfect pass only a few feet from the goal, but running into the goal post had knocked him out. Miraculously, he had kept control of the ball just as the game ended. They had won the game 27 to 24. God had smiled on the Bulldogs again.

When Will finally opened his eyes, his father was the first person he saw. He was standing beside Will with tears of concern in his eyes or perhaps they were tears of joy. He had never remembered seeing his father cry. With his big arms, he pulled Will to him, and he wept. Having his father miss all of his games, his injury, and the heartache of sitting the bench week after week was no longer important. The fairy tale ending had made it all right.

Maleguẽna

Contemplating the sound of the music being played on the aircraft's sound system, Will realized that one of the things he had missed the most about being in Vietnam was music. In the field, it wasn't wise to be listening to the radio or tape players. Charley wasn't listening to the radio; he was formulating death to GIs. Putting on headphones, the first song he heard was Maleguẽna, a classical song that was synonymous with Curt Gregory. This brought back a host of memories all centered on his friend. The first thing that came to mind were those hours they spent together in the field hunting. He reminisced.

For Curt, Buddy, and Will, that special fall hunting season had been an exceptionally productive one. They were able to squeeze in some really good hunts between Will's football practices and Curt's basketball regimen. But it had brought with it a series of incidents that should have foreshadowed some impending doom. The first incident, which Will had always considered a mini- disaster, occurred one morning on the river near Windy Bar, an island of sand surrounded by the waters on the mighty Mississippi River. After deciding to hunt a few hours before school, Will and Curt launched Curt's flat-bottom Arkansas Traveler just above Cape Girardeau before dawn and motored ten miles upriver to the bar. They then carried their equipment on foot to their pit some fifty yards from shore. It was the kind of blustery day that waterfowl seem to love. To the boys, this was a perfect day for hunting; they knew their prey would throw caution to the wind in this kind of weather. By 8:00 a.m., they had their limit of geese, so they hurriedly packed up the boat with the idea of making it to school in time for the third-hour class. As they made the last turn in the river, they suddenly found themselves facing a huge tugboat pushing a tow of twenty barges that was creating a fifteen-foot high tidal wave.

Turning the small boat toward shore, Curt throttled the ten- horse outboard to its maximum rpm. They knew what they would be in for it if they didn't beat this gigantic wave to shore, lessons learned in dealing with the treacheries of this river over the years. For a while, it looked like they were going to win the race, but about thirty yards from shore, the first massive wave rolled in over the rear of the boat, pulling them down from the stern. Curt and the motor disappeared first, and within seconds, they were completely sunk. The icy water took Will's breath away as he fought to stay above the surface. The shell-filled hunting jacket he was wearing began to pull him down. In the struggle to jettison the hunting jacket, he tried to hold on to his shotgun but lost his grip, and it was gone. At that point, it didn't matter; this was a life or death struggle.

As his eyes searched for Curt, all Will could see were decoys and debris floating on the water. He thrashed toward shore, and within seconds, he was standing up, neck deep in flotsam with still no sign of Curt. A fist thrust skyward from out of the water gripping a shotgun: it was Curt's. His hip boots, which had filled with water, had pulled him down. He told Will later that as he was going down, he took his boots off as they pulled him to the muddy bottom. When he stretched out his hands in the darkness of the river to push himself up, there lying beside him was his Magnum 12 gauge. To Curt, that shotgun was one of his most cherished possessions.

Once ashore, they surveyed the situation. The boat, motor, decoys, shells, and Will's gun were gone, and now they were about to freeze. They had taken off their heavy, water-soaked pants, and Curt was barefooted. Stumbling up the rock-strewn bank, they made it to their car, only to realize that the car keys which had been in his coat pocket had sunk with the boat. Their only choice was to head for help at the nearest house, which was several miles away. They quickly saw the look of amusement in the eyes of passing motorists, seeing two fellows trotting down the road in wet long underwear with no shoes and in subzero temperature. Since they were near a college town, passing motorists probably thought it must be some sort of fraternity hazing.

Sleeping soundly, Will was awakened by the pilot's announcement that their flight would not be going to Alaska but would be vectored to LAX. Evidently, the weather had started to break along the coast, and they were expected to arrive there in three hours. For Will, this would allow him additional sleeping time and peace from the stress of thinking about what he was leaving behind.

The hostess shook him awake, saying, "Sir, we have landed in Los Angeles. It's time to disembark." Rubbing his eyes, he gathered his gear and headed for the next gate. Finally, he was back in the States and just hours from his home. Realizing he had five hours before his next flight, he decided to catch a cab to the beach to put his tired, worn, and fungus-infected feet in the saltwater surf and enjoy just being safely back in the United States. As the taxi left the airport, they passed a demonstration of young people, protestors the driver called them, marching against the war in Vietnam. Will wondered how many of them had ever been to Southeast Asia or really knew anything about what was going on there. Remembering the many times he wondered if he would ever get home, he savored the moment as he stood on the shore and let the joy of being safely in the land of his fathers saturate his very being. The waves rolling in around his feet were tremendously invigorating, and he lay back on the sand and thought of home.

Will's up man at the agency, Cecil Tighe, had arranged first- class reservations on the next leg across the country from Los Angeles to St. Louis, and it was a pleasure to sit in an aircraft seat that actually fit his physique. Sitting by the window gave Will a chance to really see the countryside and the vastness and the majesty of America. Soon, the continental divide came into view, dotted with snowcapped peaks. Will found himself saying a prayer to God, saying the "thanks" that he had failed to say before. As it finally started to sink in that he was back home in the land of the free and the home of the brave, he felt a twinge of guilt at his lack of praying. He knew he had a lot to pray for, but it seemed to be inappropriate…when he was ending people's lives.

As he continued to think of home, he was reminded of the incident that affected him like no other until he went to Southeast Asia. Although he had tried not to think about it over the years, it never seemed to leave his thinking or at least not be far away. And here it was, back again. When it happened, it came like an avalanche without warning. But then again, is there ever a warning? The day it happened, the word of this tragedy spread throughout Southeast Missouri, leaving the community heartbroken and in a state of grief.

There had been a slow drizzle of rain for over a week, and that day was no different. Curt came by Will's house at suppertime with his boat lashed to the top of his car. It was the same one they had lost upriver, but it had later been recovered. He was very persuasive as usual, baiting Will with visions of massive flocks of geese blinded by the rain, storming into their decoys without hesitation. Curt's plan was to spend the night on Windy Bar just as they had done so many times before. This was to avoid scaring the geese that arrived during the night. It was an excellent tactic, and it had worked before. Their noisy early morning arrival usually caused them to take flight, never to see them return during the day. Curt boasted that he was going to bring home a boat load, and Will would be sorry if he didn't come along. Will's grades were in terrible condition as it was, and a test was going to be given the next day that could make the difference in him passing or failing. So he reluctantly declined the hunt to stay home and study.

Will tried to talk him out of going up there alone and spending the night on that God-forsaken bar, but this didn't faze Curt. Away Curt roared into the night as Will returned to his desk to try and study. Occasionally, his mind drifted back to Windy Bar where he could envision Curt arriving at the goose pit, setting up his spread of decoys, and settling down with his little charcoal heater to spend the night. But Curt never made it there.

The phone's sudden ringing startled Will, waking him from a restless sleep of dreaming he was in the pit on Windy Bar waiting for the sun to rise. He glanced at the clock on the desk as he picked up the receiver. It was 1:30 a.m.

"Will, it's Raymond Crews. You awake?" Mr. Crews was the mortician from Welsh Funeral Home just two blocks from Will's house. He was also the county coroner.

"I am now, Mr. Crews. What's up?"

"I need to ask you a big favor, Will," his voice serious and forlorn. "Your friend Curt has had an accident." Will could hear him breathing nervously through the phone. "He's dead, Will."

He could not move or speak. Mr. Crews was never one for mincing words. Rivers rolled out of his eyes like they had some prior knowledge that this would happen. "No, God," he pleaded. "Please no! Not Curt, God."

"Evidently, his car ran under the back of a tractor trailer, which had crossed the road in his path. The collision nearly tore the top of the car off. He's in bad shape, Will. It's a lot to ask of you, but I can't bring myself to ask his father to come and identify him. I know you were very close to him. Will you come? I can do it without anyone, but it would help, Will."

Those last few moments, just before Curt drove away, began to cross the screen of Will's mind. His face. He could see his face always so confident, usually smiling. His voice, encouraging, positive, sincere.

Mam did not hear the phone since she slept with her hearing aid off, so Will woke her up and told her the tragic news. She immediately began to cry; she had loved and admired Curt like he was her own. Will left her on her knees, praying, and walked out the front door onto the porch. The misty rain streaming down his face, mixing with the flow of tears, he ran rather than drove to the funeral home. Maybe there was some mistake. Maybe he wasn't really dead, maybe they will discover that he was breathing, and everything will be all right. He hadn't realized it, but Malegueña had started to play in his subconscious mind. It was that magnificent concerto that Curt has mastered so skillfully on the piano. He could hear it now, off in the distance from some concert grand embedded in his brain.

The lights from the funeral home portico glowed through the mist, giving it an eerie, surreal appearance, sinister and foreboding. A deep feeling of dread mounted in his soul as he tried to prepare himself for what was coming. Mr. Crews met him at the door of the big mortuary and led him down the stairs and through the darkened hallway to the morgue. The music in his subconscious intensified. If he hadn't known it was only in his mind, he would have expected anyone near him to have heard it too. The big automatic doors of the operating room swung open and there he was. Flash went the camera of his mind, a picture taken of a scene that he knew would forever be etched in his memory. He was horrified. This beloved friend, this great athlete, this great hunter now disfigured by the accident. That river of tears became a raging torrent now.

The hood and the top of his car had taken the brunt of the accident. Almost no one had installed seat belts in those days, and his face had not been spared. Will was expected to identify this fine young man who had been like a brother to him, the brother he never had. He felt ashamed. Why? Why was he confusing this terrible pain he felt deep inside his heart with shame? The flow from his eyes clouded his vision as he watched Mr. Crews and his assistant gently move Curt's head from side to side, apparently to make Will's task of identification easier, if that were possible.

Malegueña. It wouldn't stop. Oh, God, how he wanted it to stop. Why wouldn't it go away? The rhythm beat mercilessly in his temples. If he had to identify Curt by looking at his face and head, it would have been impossible. But there was no mistaking that body. This gazelle of a man, always dark and tanned, always so regal, laid almost unscarred, arms folded across his chest, the ruby from his high school ring reflecting light from the high intensity lamps above, with the initials "C. G." Will's feelings of shame intensified. He felt he had no right to invade the privacy of his nudity, especially not in death.

Now it was becoming clearer to Will. As he started trying to put this all together, he began thinking to himself, *If I had been with him, maybe this wouldn't have happened. He had all but begged me to go, but I refused. I had let him down, my best friend. Several times before, when we were driving together, he had come close to colliding with barricades as if his mind was in another dimension, swerving away at the last moment when I called out to him.*" He looked at Mr. Crews. "If I had been with him, this wouldn't have happened. He asked me to go, and I wouldn't." He began to tremble. "It's my fault. Why didn't I go?" Mr. Crews tried to console Will, but he was out of control as he ran out of the room and into the rainy darkness. The music was deafening now, and he held his ears with both hands. It felt like someone had turned up the volume or lifted the top, like the hood of his car.

All he wanted to do was run, like the many times he and Curt had run together. He remembered how Curt always held back, never running full out so not to embarrass him. Now, he would never run again.

Blindly into the rain, he trudged, vision after vision of his friend passing before him. Suddenly, he found himself in front of the high school stadium and gym. He had run across town without realizing it. The crowd noise rose out of the empty stands, and Will could see Curt leaping into the air from half court, winning the game at the sound of the buzzer as he had so many times before. And the music played on, each note of the song pounding against his brain like beats on a kettle drum.

Misjudging a curb, he stumbled and fell into the shadow of some massive, ominous object that obscured the reflected light from the street lamps. When he looked up, he had fallen into a flowerbed in front of the municipal pool, which was just across the street from the football field. Those same flowers he and Curt had planted the spring before. The shadow was that of the concrete structure that held the high diving board. He could visualize Curt there above the pool, springing higher and higher, never faltering and never afraid. He couldn't take it; he had to move on. There were too many memories here, too much pain. And that incessant concerto joined now by a full philharmonic.

Then Curt's house came into view, the lights from the front porch glowing through the mist. Slowing down, he walked up the sidewalk and saw Mr. Gregory. He had seen Will coming, and he stood up from a chair in the living room and headed for the front door. They met on the porch, and he saw what he was dreading most, the agony in this old man's face. Mr. Crews must have called ahead. They embraced, and together, they wept. There were no words exchanged. What good were words? There was very little said that entire morning. Will tried to comfort him, take some of the pain away. Mr. Gregory tried to do the same for him, but there was no real comfort to be found here. They were only sharing the grief they felt that could not be shared with anyone else. Will wanted to go home, but he didn't want Mr. Gregory to be left alone this night nor did he want to be left alone.

Will hurt deeply for this suffering old man, yet in his pain, he still had concern for Will. Mr. Crews had told him of Will's feelings of guilt and shame for not having gone with Curt, but Mr. Gregory put things in perspective by saying, "What is to be will be. We don't understand God's will. We have to trust in him. Remember also, that you could have died with Curt, but God has a different purpose for your life. Someday, when we are all together again, we will know why." Mr. Gregory then tried to assure Will that he would be okay and that he should go home and try to get some sleep. When Will left his house at dawn, the sky began to clear and the sharp rays of light heralded the coming day, proclaiming that some things are certain, even though life is not.

The phone rang incessantly that morning, Mam doing her best to shield Will from concerned friends. Late in the afternoon, after he had gotten up from a troubled sleep, he drove to where Curt's wrecked car had been taken. There was already a crowd there, and many of his friends met him as he arrived to let him know they knew how he felt. As much as he appreciated their concern, they could not possibly know how he felt.

Even knowing what had happened to Curt, it was still a shock for Will to see what was left of his car. From the condition of the exterior, there was no way anyone could identify its make any more than they could have identified its driver.

It was misting and foggy on the day of Curt's funeral much like the day he died. Mr. Gregory had asked Will to sing the Lord's Prayer, which he said was Curt's favorite. But he qualified it with an escape clause in case Will wasn't up for it. Will knew it would be difficult, but how could he say no to this dear grieving man. Members of Curt's family and those participating in the service gathered in the pastor's study of the church Curt had attended all of his life and received last-minute instructions from the minister. As they were leaving, Mr. Gregory asked Will to stay a minute, he had something to tell him.

"I just wanted you to know something about my son that you might not have known, even though you were his best friend. Did you know that he wrote poems?"

"No, I didn't," Will replied.

"Well, he did, and almost all of them spoke of an early death. I know this doesn't make your task any easier this afternoon, but because you were his best friend, I wanted you to know that somehow he had known for a long time that he was going to die soon. Here is one example," he said. With hands trembling, he handed Will a book marker with the following poem:

As I lie within my bed at night and watch the shining moon,
I oft times wonder why it is, that life must end so soon.
The tree beside my cabin door that stands so straight and tall,
    has lived nigh on a hundred years, and doesn't die at all.
The flowers that bloom each spring for me, in forest and
    in glade,
Turn their bright faces to the sky. But soon, their youth
    must fade.
Not like the tree—but like the flowers, my life on earth
    must quickly pass.
A short, fast fleeting moment here, it is as leaves or grass.

There it was again, that haunting melody off in the distance of Will's mind. And as if on cue, the barrier broke in his eyes and the torrent began again.

"But the most important thing I wanted to tell you about my son, Will, is that two years ago, he took a step of faith and became a born-again Christian. He began to get his life in order," Mr. Gregory's voice began to break, "for what he somehow knew was coming. He was ready to meet his maker, Will. I prayed, oh, God, how I prayed, that he was wrong, and I tried to convince him that this was some imaginary illusion that would soon pass." He took out his handkerchief to stem the flow. "But he was right. He is with the Lord now, Will, and they will hear you today. This means a lot to me, and I know how difficult it will be. But you are all I have left of him. You are a living link to whom and what he was. He must have planned it that way. Does any of this make sense, Will?"

As he thought about it, he began to realize that Curt had been more insistent in the last two years that he come to his house and stay over when he could. And a lot of that time had been spent with Mr. Gregory since a father's influence had been something Will craved.

From where Will was seated, he could see everyone in the huge sanctuary. He was sitting just above and to the right of Curt's open coffin, and the church was packed with people standing all the way into the street and beyond. Scattered throughout the congregation were letter jackets from every school in Southeast Missouri. Many were opponents that had come to show their respect for Curt, with the front two rows being red and black. Will began to pray for help. How could he stand beside the body of his best friend and sing without coming apart? Then the words of Dough Dough pierced his mind: "Remember, it is not the person you see in that box. It is only the horse he rode in on. He has gone on and left it behind."

The entire congregation began to grieve as he sang, but he was able to keep his composure by thinking of how Curt had prepared himself to face the next life. And Will thought of how blessed he had been, how God had given him that extra time to get his life straight, extra time that the majority of us would never have when our name is called.

Will also remembered another teaching from Dough Dough. The Apaches believed that it was the highest honor to attend to the dead. Only the most honored and revered members of the tribe were allowed to care for those who no longer could care for themselves. And that was what he was doing.

The worst appeared to be over until a flock of geese broke out of the low lying clouds above the graveside ceremony. This was a reminder to all who knew Curt of who he was, what he was, and how he died—following the wild goose.

Will's mind shut down on him that afternoon, and he collapsed, fainted they said, a safety valve to give his mind a bit of relief and to stop the incessant sound of Maleguena.

Closure at River Bend

From the moment of Curt's death, the world seemed to lose some of its luster; for Will, it seemed to have become a bigger than life atmosphere. Perhaps it was because he had finally grown up. Not gradually but instantly, he felt. After all, none of them had experienced this kind of tragedy before. Lives had been sheltered from the cares and woes of adulthood and from reality. Winter seemed to last a few months longer that year, but spring brought new hope and healing. Will was finishing his second year at Cape State, and after all that had happened, he had decided that he would not return next fall. Losing his best friend seemed to close that chapter, but there was also joy and great anticipation for the future.

Somehow, he had not just made it through that year, but he had survived his teenage years with all of their misadventures. He recalled how a commencement speaker had said that his real life was about to begin. *But is it possible…is there a chance that we had been living the real life all along? Maybe, this was the real life*, Will thought to himself. "After all, can it get any more real than what we had all just lived through?" Of course, Will knows now that it was nothing compared to what came later in Southeast Asia.

Finals! Even though Will was not returning to college, he still had to finish the semester! After his last exam, Will made his way through the crowd and caught up with Mary Ann on the campus. "Mary Ann, we made it through the semester. Free at last, free at last. There are a lot of parties tonight, what are your plans?"

"I know this is a time for celebrating, but I just don't feel like partying, Will. But I don't want to pack up and go home either." "Neither do I. I have my car. Why don't we just ride a while?"

It was a beautiful late May evening, with the sky full of moon and just enough breeze to cool the plains after a blistering Midwestern day. This was the kind of evening that makes one feel blessed to be alive. They drove north along the river where river tugboat lights perforated the sky, shinning down river, and on out into eternity. They passed the location of Cape Rock, the promontory which gave Cape Girardeau its name. Will's imagination being what it was he imagined Jean Baptiste de Girardot there trading with the Mississippian Indians. This early history was weaving itself in his memory with the history that this year will become.

Remaining silent till now, they listened to the music, enjoying the glory of creation as Will pulled into River Bend Overlook. From there, they could see Windy Bar a few miles away glistening in the moonlight. Finally, the silence was broken when Will opened with "I miss him, Mary Ann. God, I miss him."

"Me too," she replied, almost in a whisper. "We've said very little about him, you and me. I feel like I need to talk about it. Tell me if you'd rather not." He was fumbling here. Awkward, uncertain of the door he was walking through.

"It won't be easy, but I feel the same way," she answered. "It's been six months since the accident," he began. "But it's fresh in my mind. If it had happened yesterday, it wouldn't be more vivid in my memory." This was the moment to ask her the question, the question that had been eating away at his subconscious.

"Did he talk about dying to you?" Will asked.

"Yes, many times," she said. "He talked about it the same way he talked about going away to school."

"Was he afraid, to die, I mean?"

"Apprehensive is probably the better word. He had this premonition that he would die young. He didn't know why or how. But he felt like God was calling him home, I think that is how he put it. He didn't want to leave this world, nor his father or sister, however, he felt God had a reason or a purpose greater than he understood."

"Why was it he never told me?" Will asked pleadingly. "I mean, after all, weren't we like brothers? I didn't even know he was that religious, but Mr. Gregory told me he was a born-again Christian. I am totally perplexed and bewildered that there was so much of him that I didn't know."

"Maybe it was because he loved you, and he didn't want you troubled that he never told you. As to his being born-again, this was a very personal thing between him and God. But it might ease the pain for you to know that he was very much at peace with himself," she said as she reached over and took Will's hand. Her words lay heavy on his heart, yet it filled the void of empty feelings and unanswered questions that he had been carrying around like a Quasimodo hump on his back for so long.

"Can we get out and walk, Will?" He took her hand and together they walked over to the edge of the overlook and gazed up at the stars. What a glorious night it was. There was a meteor shower that night that even the light of the full moon couldn't dim. Instinctively, he put his arm around her and pulled her close. She turned and they embraced. Once he had his arms around her and felt her warmth, he didn't want to let her go. They stood this way for a long time, embracing yet saying nothing.

Will had never lost the crush he had on Mary Ann, but at the same time, he never felt antipathy seeing her with Curt. He loved them both enough to be happy for them rather than harboring feelings of resentment. In the past, he had intentionally avoided being alone with Mary Ann, but he needed her now and felt that she needed him. Not as a lover, at least not yet, but as a loving friend. One who understood his loss as he understood hers.

And on this night, Curt was still with them. Somehow, Will felt that if he knew they were together, he would be as happy for him as he was for Curt when he was alive. "What are your plans for the summer?" Will asked as they stood there in each other's arms.

"I'm working at Sterling's again this summer," she replied. "And you, Will. Did I hear you are going into the army?" "Yes," he answered. "I've been accepted for paratrooper training with the 82nd Airborne Division."

"I think you know how I feel about you. There is no one that I'd rather be with than you, but I need some time. I know Curt would approve, but the scars are too fresh. Do you know what I mean, Will?" He nodded in response as she continued.

"Can you wait for me, Will?" she asked. "If you will wait for me," he replied.

"Oh, I will, my young soldier, I will." she said, with the first smile on her face of the evening. "I will." Taking her in his arms, they embraced, absorbed in the magic of the moment, swept up in the emotion of two young people who shared what God had created, pure agape love, free from lust and sinful desires.

They sat close together the rest of the evening and the feelings of despair and hopelessness were leaving as a new day was dawning for them both. Will took one last look up the river at Windy Bar and said good-bye to his dear friend until they would meet again. Somewhere in the deep recesses of his mind, there played the haunting melody of Malagueña and beyond that, the lonesome cry of the wild goose.

Will's flight arrived in St. Louis a little after 2:00 p.m. The first thing he did was to find a pay phone to call his Aunt Bertha. Other than a few cousins, she was his only living relative. When she answered the phone, her Midwestern accent was so familiar to Will, so cheerful and warm. It hadn't changed in all those years as she spoke so excitedly about his safe return. His last letter to her was over a year ago. She had no knowledge of his whereabouts much less that he was coming home, and she was obviously moved by his unexpected call.

After promising that he would visit her now that he was home, Will walked down the corridor to the terminal, feeling excited that he was finally in his home state of Missouri and not very far from home. Approaching the terminal, he could see Petey's head above the crowd waiting for the arrival of passengers from the flight. Will had called Petey from Los Angeles, and he insisted on coming to meet his flight just as he had done so many times before. As they embraced, he said, "Damn, Brandon, you're as solid as a rock. Your system must like that gook food. How's it been living in the health spas of Saigon?" as he smiled from ear to ear.

Sikeston is located 150 miles from St. Louis and halfway between St. Louis and Memphis, Tennessee. There was no scheduled airline serving the community, so being more than a good friend, Petey was waiting to fly Will home in his restored T-6 World War II trainer. In previous returns, he had brought his Stearman, which was also a two-seater World War II trainer that had been converted to a crop duster. It was always an exciting aircraft to ride in since it was an open cockpit aircraft, and in the dead of winter, it took your breath away.

It had special significance to Petey because his father had once been a flight instructor at Malden Air Force Base in Southeast Missouri where Stearman biplanes were used to train pilots for the war. The significance to Will was that it was the first aircraft from which he had made a parachute jump when he was home on military leave. Being in an airborne unit, he had to jump a few times when he was home to leave his mark.

Following the Mississippi, the T-6 flew south over and sometimes under the bridges that spanned this great river. Sitting in the forward seat, Petey pointed ahead to Windy Bar, Curt's favorite hunting ground. Dropping low, he buzzed this barren sand bar and scared up a small flock of geese. It was early October and still warm, but the great migrations of Canada geese would soon be moving into the area, and Windy Bar would be their temporary habitat as they made their way south for the winter.

The landscape was very familiar to Will. He had hunted and fished the river many times and knew every twist, turn, and intersecting stream from the Missouri foothills to the Arkansas state line. Coming up on their right was the riverfront college town of Cape Girardeau where Will went to school. Except for its size, the town hadn't changed much in the last hundred and fifty years. At one time, it had been a crossing point for settlers heading west.

Shortly after passing Cape, Will saw another familiar cove ahead and the small town of Commerce. This had been the starting point for the Louis and Clark Expedition where they had loaded supplies aboard before heading up to Saint Louis and the crowds that would be waiting to send them up the Missouri River and into the unknown. Petey made a sharp bank to the right and pointed down. There, below them was the farm of Will's ancestors. So many times, he had wondered if he would ever see this place again or Southeast Missouri for that matter. He was the sole remaining survivor of his great-grandfather, Frank Sewell, one of the area's first settlers. This farm was his legacy to Will.

As they turned to the southwest, Will could see Sikeston off in the distance, and within minutes, they were making their final turn, passing over a little sand farm where one of his buddies, David Dye, had grown up. He hoped his friend would be at the reunion. He and several of his friends had joined the Marine Corp, and Will wondered if he had ended up doing what he had been doing, chasing Chi-Coms in Vietnam.

As Will looked down, he could see the old house and the watermelon fields. It brought back memories of the night Will and his friends attempted to steal a car load of watermelons from David Dye's father. Evidently, he got wind of this caper and took a shot at them with his shotgun, not realizing his son was one of the thieves. Some of the fellas got peppered by the rock salt with which Mr. Dye had loaded his shells, but the boys were just far enough away to escape any serious injury.

Petey flew the trainer over Sikeston below the legal altitude. They crossed over the entire town, buzzing the high school, the football field, the swimming pool, and Will's old home place. The old T-6 was well-known in this town, and Will could see people waving from the ground and from cars as they made their final approach into the great city of Sikeston, Missouri, population 14,000.

After they had pushed the T-6 into the hangar, they got into Petey's pickup truck and drove into town. "She's back," Petey said, glancing Will's way as he drove. He didn't have to ask who Petey was referring to. He was talking about Mary Ann Muldune.

"It's been ten years, Petey. The last time I heard anything about her she had married some guy she met at Cape State."

"Your news is a little stale, Will. That marriage ended two years ago."

"Any children?" Will asked. "Nope."

"How does she look, Petey?"

"I'll let you be the judge of that," he said with a silly smile on his face.

It wasn't until they drove into the familiar surroundings of Sikeston that Will realized how much he had missed this one horse town. He saw people he knew on the street and in the shops. While sitting at a stop light, a loud voice hollered out, "Willard!" Only one person ever called Will that. It was Alan Stewart, standing at the corner across the street. Recognizing Petey's truck, he had spotted his passenger, Will Brandon.

Pulling over to the curb, Will jumped out. He met Alan in the street, embracing and laughing at anything the other said whether it was funny or not. It was a great way to be greeted on his first day home, a friend he had been close to since they were kids.

"Have you seen her yet?" Alan asked.

One thing about Sikeston, your business was everybody's business. "No, Alan. I understand she's in town, but no, I haven't seen her."

"You're gonna flip, Will," he answered. "You're gonna flip."

After saying good-bye and promising to have a drink with him tonight at the reunion kickoff party at the Country Club, they drove out to Burn Brae. It hadn't changed much except that new housing construction was encroaching upon its boundaries. Petey's aunt and uncle owned it now, and he lived with them when he wasn't flying crop dusters or flying forest fire suppression missions out of state.

Driving up the long drive past the barn, Will could see the corral. It was empty now. Hattie, Old Frank, Smokey, Blind Jack, Lucie, Jessie, Pop Eye, and Thunder were all gone. To some degree, he was afraid that this would be the theme of his return home. It saddened him to realize that many of the people, including the animals and things that were such an integral part of his childhood would be gone.

Driving around the circular drive in front of the big house, Will thought about the Bakers. They were gone too and so was their era. "I guess you know George died last year?" Petey asked. He didn't know why, but somehow, he thought George would always be there. He must have been ninety or older when he died. "No, I didn't, Petey. This is the bad part of coming home. I've had so little news about Sikeston the past ten years that I get it all in one lump. How about Velma," he continued, "is she still alive?"

Just at that moment, the screen door opened and Velma stepped out onto the porch. "Masta Will, you come here and greet your ol' black mammy," she said, a big smile across her face. They held each other, rocking back and forth, and now, he knew he was home. *Thank God some things hadn't changed*, he thought.

There in the shade of a massive cypress tree, just off the veranda, Velma had laid out an appetizing lunch, or dinner—the noon meal is called in the South and parts of the Midwest. Poke salad, surrounded by deviled eggs and large chunks of country- cured ham, kidney bean salad, a plate of sliced tomatoes, and Velma's home-cooked bread. It was delightfully southern and so typical of Velma and Burn Brae.

After they ate, Petey took Will out to one of the garage-like outbuildings and opened wide the double wooden doors. There it was:

the DeSoto Adventurer. Will was stunned. "I thought I told you to sell it, Petey. Why did you keep it?"

"I knew what it meant to you, Will. And I knew you'd be coming home someday, so why sell it?'

"But it looks just like it did when she died."

"George kept it clean and in running order while he was alive Will, and other than starting it occasionally, I haven't done much to it since. I'll get one of the farmhands to clean it up and get it started this afternoon, and you can take it for a ride if you like." Will looked at that beautiful machine for quite a while, thinking of all the memories it brought back until finally Petey said, "Let's go up to the house and get you settled in."

They walked back to the house and up the winding stairs to the guestroom where Petey opened the sliding doors that lead out to the balcony. From there, Will could see across the expanse of corn, soybean, wheat, and cotton fields and into the woods and beyond to the river. "Well, Will, I guess you're pretty beat from your trip. I'm going to let you rest awhile. I'll call you about 6:00 p.m. to get ready for the reunion, which starts with a cocktail hour. The liquor cabinet is packed, and the little refrigerator is full of beer, so relax and I'll call you."

Will cracked a beer, laid down on the massive mahogany four poster, and looked out through the sliding doors across the balcony to the harvest fields and beyond to the tree line. He recalled the many summers he had driven a tractor out there in those fields to help the Bakers when they were shorthanded, the hayrides, the quail hunts, the close call when George had saved him, and the ice pick in George's back. Jet lag was taking its toll now, and he very quickly fell asleep. He was safe here. There were no threats. He was home.

The Prodigal Returns

On their way to the reunion, Will could see the cemetery up ahead and asked Petey to drive in for just a moment.

The Malones and the Brandons occupied a significant portion of this graveyard, and there they stood in the middle of them. Will's grandmother, grandfather, and mother were on their left, and next to his father, his great-grandparents were on their right. Just beyond his great-grandparents were his uncle's and aunt's graves and all the proceeding generations of Brandons back to the early 1800s.

Disease and weather took its toll on the little ones in those days, as proven by the small headstones that lay at the foot of the patriarchs. The infant death rate then was astounding. It must have been difficult to have children that you came to know and love only to have them die, many times before they learned to walk. It was not unusual to see as many as six or eight infant graves at the foot of their parents' graves. There was no birth control then, no inoculations, and life was difficult.

From a very early age, Will always felt at home here among his forefathers just as he did today. This was where he would come when he was troubled, depressed, or lonely. Many times, he had driven in here in the middle of the night to share his troubles with the dead. Just before returning to Vietnam for his second tour of duty was one of those times. As he scanned the graves, there among the Brandons was the patriarch of the family, Francis Mallett Brandon, marked with a large ten-foot high triangular tombstone.

Francis was a true pioneer, arriving here in the early 1800s, first as a farmer, but he later opened one of the first saloons along the west bank of the Mississippi. The Lewis and Clark expedition had stopped in for one last grog of beer before heading north to the mouth of the Missouri River. His unusual story had been told to Will when he was very young by his uncle James Brandon. It seems that his wife, Eleanor Brandon, became sick and needed constant care. With his business being many miles from the farm where they lived, he was in need of a nurse to stay with Eleanor while he worked the saloon. But to take another woman who he was not married to into the house far out in the country would have been unthinkable. So he married another younger woman and moved her into the house with them. This was the only acceptable solution in those days. According to the story, the two women became like sisters, and the younger woman grieved greatly when the older woman finally died. There, on this three- sided tombstone are the names of Francis Mallett Brandon, husband and father, then on one side the name of Eleanor Mallett Brandon, wife of Francis, and on the third side of the stone the name of Margarette Mallett Brandon, consort to Francis Mallett Brandon. And the three of them are buried head to the stone.

Curt Gregory's grave was just a short distance away, and the two of them walked over to his site and stood silently for a few minutes as the memories once again began to take shape. Breaking that silence, Petey said, "It's hard to believe that it's been fourteen years since his death."

"I know." Will couldn't help but think how appropriate it was that on the night of their class reunion he would be standing here, near his beloved friend.

"I guess we'd better go, they'll be looking for you," Petey said, turning toward his truck.

"What do you mean, looking for me?" Will asked.

"Because they heard about your exploits and know you're in town," he answered.

This unnerved Will a bit. They knew nothing of his life since graduation. What could they be expecting from him? After all, he was no different than them and hopefully no different than when he left, but the verdict was still out on that.

Will realized that his life might seem exciting and glamorous to some, but they have never been in a war zone. They've never gone weeks in the same wet dirty clothes or eaten what he's had to eat. Nor have they ever seen their buddies blown up or been in fear of losing their lives for weeks on end. They've never had to face wave after wave of VC running straight at them with a bayonet or a grenade, ready to die for the glory of killing an American. Nor have they ever killed their fellow man. He wondered if they would have found anything glamorous about the massacre of Doc Tran.

They arrived at the country club to find some of his friends waiting outside to greet him. Abruptly, he saw the facial expressions of his friends change, and then he felt a warm hand on his shoulder. He turned, and there she was. He couldn't believe his eyes. It was Mary Ann Muldune. He was stunned. She was always beautiful, but now…now she was gorgeous. He remembered her as a well-developed cheerleader type with all the enthusiasm of an eighteen-year-old co-ed, but now she was a full-bodied mature woman who caused his heart to race like he had just finished a marathon.

Without speaking a word, she jumped into his arms, and he lifted her off the floor as smiles broke out on all those around. This sudden meeting, seeing this beautiful Venus that was the girl of his dreams, and feeling her gorgeous body next to his lifted Will's spirits sky high. Finally, she whispered, "Thank God you're home safe."

As if on cue, Doris Day's "When I Fall in Love" began to play. This was one of the most popular songs when they were seniors. How many times when he was trying to fall asleep in the jungles of Vietnam had he thought of it as "their" song. How appropriate, and the words said it all: "When I fall in love, it will be forever, or I'll never fall in love." Then it ended with: "And the moment I can feel that you feel that way too, is when I fell in love with you." Will and Mary Ann blended in with the other couples on the dance floor, holding each other closely. Lights were lowered, and Will was so blissfully happy that he thought this was heaven on earth. The second song was perfect. "No Other Love" was sung by a popular crooner whose name Will couldn't remember at that moment. But he remembered holding Mary Ann those warm sultry evenings when the stars seemed to blink just for them, when the world seemed peaceful, and hope filled their hearts as they looked forward to a bright future.

Later that night, they began showing slides of their high school days, and they laughed and joked about the clothes they were wearing then, the cars they were driving, their teachers, and the football team. It was delightful, and it brought back many more memories. At one point, a slide of Curt Gregory came up, a picture of him making his classic game-winning jump shot as the crowd cheered. There was total silence in the room until Nicholas Walker broke the silence and proposed a toast.

"To the greatest athlete this town has ever known." They raised their glasses and remained silent for a moment. Then his slide was gone, replaced by a picture of the school's cheerleaders.

Mary Ann stuck to Will like bark on a tree and he observed her reaction when one of Will's friends asked what he had been doing the past fifteen years. He tried to give his standard answer. "Living the good life in the tropics." or "Flying around the world on the taxpayers' money." But once in a while, someone would ask a more direct question like "Did I hear that you worked for the CIA, Will?" or "What's this I heard about you being a spy?" or "Have you ever killed anybody, Will?" Ignoring that question, he tried to change the subject. Although Mary Ann remained quiet, he could tell she was contemplating his every response.

Once they had a moment alone, they walked out to the pool area to get some relief from the smoke and heat of the ballroom. It was a night a little like the last one they shared, full of stars and moon, and a cool breeze that swayed the trees along the golf course.

"Do you have a car?" he asked.

"Yes," she said smiling, anticipating his next remark.

"Let's drive out to River Bend Overlook. I flew over it this morning. I haven't been there since you and I were there last. Shall we?"

Mary Ann's car was a convertible, and she asked Will if he'd like to drive. After giving it just a moment's thought, he declined. He wanted the pleasure of watching her and enjoying this beautiful night. And watch her he did. He knew then what the expression "sight for sore eyes" really meant. She was the picture of grace and femininity and a joy to behold.

Aware that he was watching, she looked over and, with a pixie little smile, asked, "Have I changed much, Will? The way I look, I mean?"

"Oh yes, you've changed all right," he responded.

"How?" she asked.

"When I left you were a pretty girl. Now…well, now you are a woman…a very desirable woman. But I guess you know that already." She blushed but remained silent.

Pulling into River Bend Overlook, they got out of the car. Taking her hand, they walked to the same spot where they stood the last time they were there. This was the culmination of a fantasy Will had dreamed so many times back there in the jungle. He thanked God they were here because that dream had begun to fade the last couple of years. If he had a fantasy wish, it would be that this night would last forever.

Eventually, he asked her the question that had been nagging at him all night. "I understand that you got married?"

With a faint look of pain, she answered, "Knowing that I would have to answer that question sooner or later, I've been rehearsing what I would say to you, and now that you've asked it, the answer seems inadequate." She sighed, took a deep breath, and while looking up at the heavens, continued, "Will, I haven't heard from you for more than three or four times in the last ten years, and nothing the past five." She turned and, looking very serious, said, "Five years, Will. Five years. I finally had to take a look at the reality of things and tell myself that I didn't mean that much to you or you would have called or written me. And then I began to feel that I was foolish to wait any longer." She grew sad as tears began to well up in her eyes.

As she slowly began to walk toward the overlook, Will followed. "Yes, I got married," she said demonstratively, turning suddenly Will's way. Looking back and forth from him to the river, she said, "Why didn't you write or for that matter why didn't you come home?" She was becoming emotional. Will kept quiet. "For God's sake, Will, did you expect me to wait forever?" And with that, she really began to cry.

Putting his arms around her, he drew her close. Many times throughout his Southeast Asian tour, he had questioned his unswerving, unfaltering allegiance to his country. Was it outdated? Was it justified? Was it too demanding? Was it necessary? Now, thousands of miles from the conflict, he found reason to question this loyalty. Here in his arms was a casualty of this blind allegiance.

Will believed at the time that it was his duty to do what he was doing, to be where he had to be. It was part of the brainwashing so necessary in his line of work. He didn't want her to know what he was doing or where he was for a number of reasons. Nor could he be worrying about someone back home lest it took his mind off his missions for one fatal second.

She looked up into Will's eyes for answers, and by some miracle, she must have found some of them because she said, "You've been through a lot, haven't you, my darling?" not really expecting a response. "I have no way of knowing and maybe I'm not supposed to know. But whatever it was, it has changed you. You are not the young lifeguard I used to know. What I see in your eyes frightens me." She moved closer into his arms again and buried her face in his chest. Will wanted to tell her, God knows he wanted to tell her about that other world out there that most people don't know exists. Especially about the last ten years of his life, about what he had been doing, and about what he had become. But where would he begin? The vows of silence had been ingrained into his psyche. It was not something he could suddenly forsake.

Will suspected that those who knew him when he was growing up might have considered him a motormouth kid, never quiet, always jabbering. But now, he was beginning to realize that he had become the opposite. He had become silent now or perhaps even sullen. He had been so isolated from the civilized world that the metamorphoses had sneaked up on him, transformed him without his knowing it. Yet he knew that until he could release this anger, frustration, and yes, guilt, he could not be the real Will Brandon. Did the person exist that he thought he was? Until he exposed all this intrigue to the light, he had no doubt that it would be a dark invisible barrier between the two of them, and he would be only the shell of a man romantically worthless to any woman.

As they stood there in each other's arms, he could feel her shivering now. The night air had dropped several degrees since leaving the club. "Let's go back and sit in the car," Will said, keeping her wrapped tightly in his arms as they walked. Putting up the top and rolling up the windows, they sat silent for a moment, looking at each other.

She reached in her purse for what he thought was a handkerchief, but it was a piece of paper. Unfolding it, she said, "This was in the last letter you sent me, Will." It was the prayer that he had sent her shortly after he graduated from Special Forces school. She began to read:

> Almighty God, who art the author of liberty and the champion of the oppressed, hear our prayer. We the men of Special Forces, acknowledge our dependence upon thee in the preservation of human freedom. Go with us as we seek to defend the defenseless and to free the enslaved. May we ever remember that our nation, whose oath "In God We Trust," expects that we shall requite ourselves with honor, that we may never bring shame upon our faith, our families, or our fellow men. Grant us wisdom from thy mind, courage from

thine heart, and protection by thine hand. It is for thee that
we do battle and to thee belongs the victor's crown. For thine
is the kingdom, and the power, and the glory, forever. Amen.

"Will, this prayer has been with me ever since the day I received it. It was with me the day I got married." His throat got suddenly dry when she told him that she had actually carried it down the aisle the day she married another man. "It comforted me during the hard times and made me feel connected to you. Then when I didn't hear from you for so long I could only assume…" She turned her face away and looked toward the rising moon so far beyond the horizon. "I had wanted to save myself for you, that you would be the one and only lover in my life. I wanted you to be proud of knowing that your woman…your bride, would be pure and chaste. And now…" Will could see her slump in despair as if all of her strength had left her body. "I'm not the same girl you invited to the pool that day," she said, her face twisted in sorrow.

"And I'm not the same boy that invited you either, my darling." Will tried to think of what he could say that would let her know that while those things have value, they're also unimportant now. "Mary Ann, the only thing that matters or is important is that they we're finally together, here and now, and by the grace of God, we have a great future ahead of us. The love you have kept in your heart for me is the greatest gift any man could ask for. Maybe you need to know who Will Brandon is now, Mary Ann. I'm not the same innocent kid in the lifeguard's chair you once knew. I need to tell you about my life, and maybe you can understand why I couldn't communicate with you. Let me tell you about the real Will Brandon."

Relaxing back in the seat, he continued, "When I left Sikeston, I went through the Army's eight weeks of basic training before going to Fort Bragg, North Carolina, for four weeks of airborne jump school and four more weeks of airborne heavy drop school with the 82nd Airborne Division. Wanting to learn all I could, I volunteered for every special training course being offered. Sometime during that first year, I applied for the Special Forces, and a year later, I was accepted. After going through their training, I was sent to the Jungle Warfare Center in Panama for jungle survival training. Because of my ability to adapt well to the jungle and the oppressive heat, I was offered an instructor's position, which I readily accepted."

A slight breeze picked up the dust around the car as he continued, "After I had been an instructor for a while, a group of nonmilitary people came to the school for training. I later found out that they were from the CIA. They were evidently impressed with me and interviewed me for an assignment with the agency. I heard nothing from them for over nine months, and during that time, the army sent me to intelligence and language school where I learned Vietnamese. Just before completion of those schools, I had a visit from those same people I had trained in Panama. They informed me that they had an opening for which I was qualified if I was interested in a foreign assignment with the agency. The also hinted that Vietnam was that assignment."

Another car pulled into River Bend and parked about twenty-five yards away. He waited to see what they were going to do before he continued. It became obvious that they were lovers. Before Will had a chance to pick up where he had left off, Mary Ann said, "Will, you don't have to tell me this. I can see that it's a sensitive area and very painful. I'm sure that whatever you did, you did the right thing."

"It is painful, but until you have an understanding of what's going on over there and the part I played, you will never know me. And even after I've told you, you still might not know me. You see, Mary Ann, the American people have no idea what is going on in Vietnam. I'm not going to tell you why we should or should not be there. Personally, I've always felt we should be there, but my opinion is not important. What I want to tell you is why I think the stars in the American flag have lost their glitter, and why I have not always been proud to be an American soldier." Mary Ann looked bewildered by this story, but he continued not knowing where he was going or where he'd end up.

"I was attached to a Special Forces unit called an SOG for Special Operations Group, which patrolled an area in the Mekong Delta containing a number of villages loyal to the South Vietnamese regime. Although our primary mission was reconnaissance, we had been spending a lot of time in villages like Doc Tran where we rebuilt an irrigation system that had been destroyed by the VC. We taught them modern methods of farming, sanitation, and precautions they could take against disease. I became good friends with many villagers because I spoke their language. They came to me, knowing I understood not only their language, but also their problems and their fears. The patriarch of the village, an old man by the name of Ho Bein, became my very close friend, and I knew his whole family. One of his granddaughters, a six-year-old named Mei Rai, followed me around like a puppy every time I visited the village. On one of my trips into Saigon, I bought a small gold cross and chain and gave it to her. It was a distinctive cross because it was in the shape of Christ, with his arms out holding on to a rope that was tied to a cross. I had never seen one like it. I doubt that anyone had ever given her anything, especially a religious symbol because the villagers were very poor. Now she really followed me around, and eventually, after she had asked me a hundred times who the man was on the cross, I told her the whole story. She was a beautiful child, so inquisitive, and she shared the story of baby Jesus with everyone she met. Although we knew Charley was active in this sector, we had other villages to support as we were trying to teach all of them to be independent and self-reliant."

The moon was coming up now, full and bright. The same moon Will had seen rising above the rice paddies of Doc Tran. He began visualizing the scene he was about to relay. "One morning, just a few days after leaving the village, we received a radio transmission from an air force pilot saying that he had spotted a large fire and smoke emanating from Doc Tran. We were about twenty miles away on foot, and to get there quicker, we called for a gunship from another unit operating some fifty miles north. Within the hour, we were in the air heading for Doc Tran. No sooner had we reached a safe flying altitude, then we saw that the column of smoke rising from the jungle off in the distance was more than one column indicating that something major had happened at Doc Tran."

Changing positions, it was easier for Will to study Mary Ann's reactions to what he was telling her. "The pilot sat the big gunship down about two clicks from the village in the only visible clearing safe enough to land without fear of an ambush, and we ran the rest of the way on foot. As we approached the village, we stopped and surveyed the site. We then spotted the special greeting that had been set up by the VC. It was a narrow bamboo post about six feet high driven into the ground with a young girl attached to it in the most sadistic manner. She was facing us, eyes open, arms bound to a post tied diagonally to the main one in the manor of a cross. They had crucified her. What they had done to her I will only partially describe. It was too barbaric. It was Mei Rai and she was still alive. She was trying to speak, but no words could be heard. Yet it was not difficult to read her lips. She was saying the word Jesus, over and over. At the foot of the post lay five other children laid out neatly like the spokes of a wheel, their throats cut. In front of this hideous altar, on their knees bent over forward were the bodies of the girl's mother and father, shot in the head. The VC had made them watch as they cruelly crucified their daughter, leaving her there alive to die alone."

Swallowing hard, he took a deep breath and continued, "There was nothing we could do. We debated among ourselves if we should kill her to put her out of her misery, and if that was our decision, who would do it? Mercifully, she died shortly thereafter. It is a scene I will never forget. Even now, half a world away, my blood boils as the image of what they did burns away in my brain." Mary Ann's face clouded up as she tried to keep her composure. She was shaken by Will's story but asked him to continue. "There had been seventy-five people living in Doc Tran, but we only found forty-five of them…all dead. The rest had either been taken prisoner or had fled into the jungle. I found the old man of the village, Ho Bein, the man who had called me son, lying facedown near his wife in the irrigation ditch we had helped him build. He was so proud of that little ditch. There were many other atrocities throughout the village including the stripping of all of the victims' clothing. Viet Cong consider this the supreme humiliation." Tears began to well up in Will's eyes as he relived the tragedy, but he quickly brushed them away.

"They had also shot and killed all five of the village's water buffalo and set fire to everything they couldn't carry. We buried the dead, including Mei Rai, in a mass grave and took a few minutes to give them a farewell. I was asked to say the prayer, but it was difficult. I was furious, Mary Ann. Furious with God so I made it short. Prayers are supposed to contain thanks. I felt I had nothing to be thankful for at that moment, and what we had in mind didn't match up with the prayers I was expected to say. No, we had work to do, and it wasn't God's work. But then again, maybe it was."

The sounds of the night were broken occasionally by the sounds of a riverboat reminding them of where they were so far removed from the scenes Will was portraying. He knew he had to continue while he still had the valiancy to bare more of his inner secrets. "Mary Ann, this is hard to explain, but I saw a frightening rage began to build among my fellow soldiers. A determination if you will. Something I hadn't witnessed before, but something of which I was now a part. It was happening to me as well. No one had to say a word. We all knew that it was time to do what we do best…kill VC. It was now time to avenge these senseless atrocities, and it was damn personal. As the anger continued to build, my comrades prepared to chase down the perpetrators."

"Larry and I conferred with the Green Beret commander, Captain Reilly, a West Point grad, and after a wide sweep by the helicopter, which turned up nothing, we decided to track them down. It was getting dark and tracking would be difficult. They had a half-day's start on us, and it would be light before we would engage them so we wasted no time in preparing."

The memories of this episode came vividly into focus as he relived every moment of the team's pursuit. "I had never seen men so earnest about preparing for war. There would be no Geneva Convention here. What we had in mind was below the level of human thought…below the lowest level of human decency. Most of the Green Berets stripped to the waist, covered their bodies with mud to protect against the mosquitoes and to blend into the landscape, and wrapped camouflage headbands tightly about their heads. One of the men was a full-blooded Arapaho who painted our faces like warriors of old. It was a ritual dating back to the western plains of America. Many of them wrapped bandoliers across their chest, loaded packs with ammunition magazines, and took extra weapons from the Huey.

"Within minutes, we were being led on a quick jog by the Indian down the path leading from the center of the burning village. I now understood why the men had given him the nickname of 'Jim Thorpe.' Once he started, he could run all night. The helicopter crew became very agitated when they were told to remain with the gunship in case we needed air support. They had seen the carnage, and they wanted to kill their share. After we had been on the move for almost an hour, we came upon our first hostage, a middle-aged woman lying in a stream. She had been disemboweled. The VC were not very imaginative. It only served to strengthen our resolve that not one of these creeps would go home alive to see their mama san." Will's fury became so visual that he realized that he was about to lose control over his emotions so he began to speak more calmly, more matter-of-factly.

Seeing the dead woman, the commander became concerned about trip wires, especially because of the pace we had set. Unwittingly, the VC had done us a favor by killing the woman. As bad as we wanted to kill the SOBs, it made us stop and think. We were a prime target for a bobby trap or ambush. For a moment, we had forgotten all about those months of training that had made us the professionals that we were. We needed to slow down, think this thing through, and come up with a new strategy, a strategy born more from calm resolve than from blind revenge. After all, the VC are not exactly Boy Scouts. We knew that the closer we came, the more hostages they would kill. The captain and his officers finally came up with a plan. We were to return to the village, load up in the Huey, and fly over the hidden VC. This would give the appearance that we were leaving for good. After we had disappeared beyond the horizon, we would then return from a different direction and lay our own ambush.

"The VC have a habit of leaving a squad of troops behind their main party, salting their trail with mines and pitfalls. Then, when they hear a mine blow up behind them, they move ahead to set up another series of traps, repeating this over and over again until their enemy finally gives up. Our plan's success depended upon the captain's ability to predict the direction the VC had taken and then interdict that path to setup our ambush. It meant a lot of scouting, but it paid off. I won't go through all the details, Mary Ann, but we positioned ourselves along the path they were predicted to take and we waited.

"It was very early in the morning when they appeared through the fog. We were totally concealed just off their path, so close we could smell them. Once you've smelled a VC, you never forget what they smell like." Will's heart was beating so loud he was sure Mary Ann could hear it. "As they moved closer, we could see that the prisoners were tied to a long rope and were guarded front and rear. This exercise required precise timing or we would lose our village friends in the crossfire. The VC appeared sleepy, groggy from a night of heroin. They had probably been celebrating our departure. They had no idea we were within twenty miles of this lonely, fog-shrouded clearing. Opening fire, we cut them down like standing corn. Our automatic weapons sounding like thunder bolts, the barrels of our weapons blazing out red flames as our magazines disgorged their projectiles. Some of the VC managed to break out of the clearing into the jungle as they ran for their lives. The Green Berets swept over those caught in the crossfire like demons. There would be no prisoners taken.

"Larry and I ran to join three other soldiers as we gave chase after those remaining survivors, each of us picking a target to pursue. All I could think about was revenge, to make them pay for what they had done to Doc Tran and my helpless friends. I keep Mei Rai in my memory, her arms outstretched as if begging us to stop the agony. Looking back, I can see I had lost contact with humanity, with right and wrong. And at this point, I also lost count of my comrades of who was where.

"As I ran through a thick stand of trees, I caught a glimpse of someone out of the corner of my eye standing behind a tree I had just passed. He must have tripped me with a limb or something because I went down. But I twisted around as I fell and saw him coming after me. Without thinking, I was pulling the trigger on my M-16, and it stopped him cold. I was close enough to see the efficiency of the rifle round as it streaked around inside his body, turning his internal organs into mush. It was a familiar scene. I had seen its gruesome results before. When the M-16 round strikes a hard bone, the bullet will break up, sending fragments into other parts of the body, causing still more damage."

She was looking at Will differently now, almost unbelieving. Although she wanted to hear the rest of his story, this was more than she had bargained for. She was frightened. He then realized that his emotions had gotten away from him. He had gone too far with his description of the slaughter that had taken place. She was seeing someone she didn't recognize, someone she might even be afraid of. But Will was determined that she was going to hear it all regardless, immediately picking up where he had left off.

"I jumped to my feet and gave chase. There was gunfire all around me, but it didn't faze me. My mind was on nothing but killing. I know it sounds terrible to you that I could forget about my own safety just to kill and get even, but that's the way it came down. Running ahead, I spotted three VC heading down a stream bed off to my left, and I followed."

Will could see that he was becoming animated now pointing to the right as if he were there reliving this drama. The fact was, he was reliving it. "When I had cut the distance to about fifty feet, I stopped and fired a full magazine of ammunition, dropping one of them facedown in the stream. He was moving when I ran up, so I shot him with my pistol."

"Didn't you feel any remorse?" Mary Ann asked. She was looking intently at him now as if she was uncertain that this was really Will.

"Not in the least," he answered, pausing for a moment and then continuing. "I struck out again down the stream bed and hadn't gone far before I noticed Larry off to my right running at about my same pace. He fired at targets ahead of us sending one man rolling down the bank into the stream, another jumped to his feet in flight with me right behind." He knew she was seeing him now for what he had become, but for better or for worse, this was what had happened.

"As the distance between the man ahead of me narrowed, he stopped to take a stand, firing his weapon just as I dove behind a rise in the terrain. We continued to exchange fire until it appeared he had expended his ammunition. He then threw down his weapon and began to run again. I made a decision to catch this one alive and make him regret the day he ever saw Doc Tran. It didn't take long for me to run him down. Taking him by the collar, I flipped him around to face me and pulled my survival knife out of its sheath on my ankle. I was gonna make sure this guy was going to suffer for his part in the village massacre. Mary Ann, when her blouse came open, I suddenly realized that this was not a guy at all, but a girl, a very young woman, maybe fifteen or sixteen. She began to plead, 'Mau-chay-nhieu' (have mercy, have mercy). It disarmed me, set me back. I had all this hate and evil inside of me that I wanted to vent on this VC, but I was uncertain, even bewildered. Then Larry and another Green Beret came running up the stream shouting, 'Kill him, Will. Kill him.' I called back, 'She's a girl.' Larry responded, 'Kill her anyway, damn it. She was one of them. Kill her anyway.' We debated back and forth, standing there over her. Finally, Larry reached down and took her by the shirt, pulling off the buttons and exposing her chest. There, tied to a string around her neck was the gold Christ which I had given Mei Rai. 'See,' Larry shouted. 'Do you need anything more to convince you she was a part of this?'

"The girl was on her knees now, crying again, 'Mau-chay- nhieu' (have mercy). 'She might even be the one that killed Mei Rai's parents.' he said. Are you going to let her live? Stand back. I'm going to blow her stinkin VC head off,' he screamed, more agitated than ever. Mary Ann, I could have stepped in, but I wanted her dead. We stepped back, the three of us pointed our pistols at her, and in Vietnamese, Larry yelled, 'This one is for Doc Tran.' With that, each of us pulled the trigger."

"Will, you're trembling," she said. He hadn't noticed, but he had broken out in a cold sweat and was trembling uncontrollably. It was as if he were there experiencing the same horrible moment all over again. He buried his face in his hands. The scene was too authentic, too real. He wanted to cry but couldn't, he just felt numb. There had just been one other time in his life that his memory was photographic: the night he had to identify Curt Gregory's body.

Mary Ann's arms were around Will now, and he felt her tears dripping on his neck. He wondered if they were being shed for him or for something they once had but may have lost. Hearing a car start, both of them looked up as the couple drove away, their passion complete. How simple, just two people, young lovers, with uncomplicated lives. Perhaps the deepest thing they had to worry about was the girl getting pregnant.

Sensing Mary Ann's emotional state, Will drove back to Sikeston. Few words were spoken on the drive back into town. Arriving at the country club, the grounds were dark, the parking lot empty. The breeze blowing in from across the fairways blew bits of paper across the blacktop, and an occasional discarded corsage or boutonniere could be seen drifting with the rest of the trash in the wind. "I guess you'll have to drive me to Burn Brae," he remarked, breaking the silence that had gone up like a wall between them.

As they turned into the tree-lined drive leading up to the big house, he could see the light Petey had left on, shining its lonely light on the veranda. For just a moment, he felt like he was returning from a high school dance as he had many times so long ago. He opened the door, got out, and held the door for her to come around and get behind the wheel. Just as she started to slide into the seat, she hesitated, looked intently into his eyes, took his hand, saying, "We've waited too long to be together to end the night this way." At that very moment, a flock of Canada geese began to honk in unison as they set their wings to glide over the house and into the field beyond the corral. It was just the ice breaker they needed, and she rushed to Will, tears in her eyes. They kissed, grasping for one another as if the other might escape. This was their night and nothing short of God himself was going to spoil it.

The morning sun began to creep up beyond the cottonwood trees down by the river, catching them huddled together in a chaise lounge on the porch. This had been the night of their dreams, the one they had been waiting for since that night along the river before Will went into the army. Will held Mary Ann close to him as they talked between moments of silence. They erased, at least for the moment, the hideous thoughts that had been the topic of conversation earlier.

Velma opened the door and stepped out onto the veranda but jumped back suddenly, startled by their presence out there at such an early hour. Once she realized who they were, she smiled happily, saying, "Massa Billy, it's jus like ole times, finding you here on da porch. Ms. Mary Ann, would yo like to freshen up a bit? I'll have coffee and som breakfas ready b'fore you knows it." After they had eaten, Mary Ann and Will lay down on the game room couch and quickly feel asleep. A few hours later, Will awoke to find her gone. Lying on the coffee table in front of him was a note, which read, "You are home where it's safe. I pray it's for good. We can work it out. MA."

Sliding open the patio door, Will decided to take a stroll. It started with the barn and corral. Climbing up the tall fence, he sat near a weathered old post, exactly the place where he had sat so many times before. Thinking of those days, he could see and hear the horses and mules swatting flies, snipping at each other now and then just like it was. Old Frank, Hattie, Smokey, Blind Jack, and Lucie were all gone. Jessie, Popeye, Thunder, they were gone too. This was the place George had pulled Will from the stampede.

From the corral, he walked to the back fence that separated the mowed grass from the cultivated farmland and stood for a moment thinking of the hours he and Petey had spent riding tractors back and forth across the farm. They always had an enviable tan, but it was a tough way to get it.

Returning, Petey spotted Will at the tool shed and joined him where he was observing the heavy equipment hung on the walls which they had used during those long days of toil. "I guess it's a miracle we didn't lose an arm or something when we were working out there," he said.

"That's for sure," Will replied.

In the tack room hung the animal work equipment that to Will represented the sweat and toil of horses and mules from a bygone era. The long difficult days the beasts of burden spent, never complaining, just following the commands of their drivers until the day they died or were finally put out to pasture. It caused Will to contemplate how similar men are to the animals toiling throughout their lifetime, and those who are fortunate enough to survive their working years to retire, unless some adversary bent on destruction might end their lives prematurely.

Walking back to the house, Will could see Petey's Stearman crop duster sitting so regal, so adventurous, as if waiting for the first daredevil to climb aboard and roar away into the blue. "Remember how we planned to go into the crop dusting business when we were little, Will?"

"How could I forget," he answered. "Foolish dreams by foolish people," Will said absentmindedly, as he inspected Petey's oil-streaked aircraft.

"It doesn't have to be just a dream. I've been building up a pretty good client base of farmers who have come to rely on me every year. There's no need for you to look elsewhere for work. You don't intend on return to Southeast Asia, do you, Will?" Before he could answer, Petey continued, "Together, we can have a pretty good living. I need someone to help me administratively and logistically. You are good with people, Will. Personally, I hate dealing with people. What do you say? We can do this together." He knew Petey was sincere and he knew they could work well together. But his offer caught Will unprepared. He hadn't considered what he would do if he left the agency. Without a response, Petey added, "Just remember, Will, if you went back to Vietnam, there's no guarantee that you'd ever come back." Will knew he was right. More than he knew.

At that moment, Velma stuck her head out the back door and hollered, "Masta Will, you got a long distance call, a Mista Larry I believe he said it was."

Larry's call irritated him a bit. After all, Will asked himself, he had only been out of the war zone a few days. *Had he forgotten that I was through with all the problems of Southeast Asia, that I wanted a rest free from conflict?*

"Hi, Larry, can't live without me, eh, buddy? What's up?" "You enjoying life, compadre?" Larry asked.

"Yeh. Nobody shooting at me out here, at least not yet, anyway," Will replied with a chuckle. "How about you? Find anybody to share that pent-up aggression with?"

Without answering, he said, "I just got a call from Cecil. One of our projects has been compromised." Larry loved to speak in spook talk, play the role so to speak.

"Which one?" Will asked, afraid of the answer.

"Lo Dow," he answered. They both were silent for a moment, contemplating the friends they knew there.

"There were no survivors," he volunteered. "They even killed the dogs and the chickens."

Will could feel his blood pressure rising as he hesitated to ask the next question. "How about the Special Forces contingency stationed there?"

"Like I said, no survivors. There is one other thing, they haven't found Callaway."

Every hair on his body stood erect. He knew a number of the villagers and all the soldiers personally, but Callaway was unique. A former Delta Force colonel, he was the agency's special operations field commander, perhaps one of its most valuable assets. And Lo Dow had been his pride and joy. They had cleared a large section of jungle near there and had just harvested their second annual crop of vegetables.

Larry continued, "Intelligence tells us they have him in a stronghold on the Cambodian border. Cecil has arranged a military aircraft to take me into Saigon tomorrow. I know you have pretty much washed your hands of Vietnam, but I thought you might want to know. Who knows, you may want to join me there. Or maybe Callaway doesn't mean that much to you?"

"You know he's a dead man, Larry. They'll get what they want out of him and waste him, or they will keep him as bait, knowing we'll come after him. Either way, there will be a heavy price to pay. No, I'm not coming, Larry. Why should I?"

"Because he would for you," Larry retorted. That one hurt. It hurt because he was right. Callaway would never turn his back on either one of them if the situation were reversed.

"Larry, you and I have given our best to this stupid war. I said good-bye to it, and I meant it. It hurts me what has happened, but it will continue to happen. There's not a thing in the world we can do that will make a difference. I'm staying here. I appreciate your call, but I'm tired of the killing. If you're smart, you'll stay put in Maui and enjoy that well-earned vacation."

"You know I can't do that, Will. As far as I'm concerned, this is unfinished business. I'll see you, Will. Good luck in your new life." He wanted to plead with Larry, but he was gone before he could say what he needed to say.

He stood up and looked at the phone receiver as the open line tone continued to sound. Seeing him visibly shaken, Petey took the phone from Will's hands and placed it on the hook, silencing the sound abruptly. "Will, you've got to tell me what's going on. I'm too close to you to not know." Will knew he was right.

"Let's drive. I need to think. I wanted to visit the farm, so let's drive over there, and I'll tell you about the whole thing."

"Want to take the DeSoto?" Petey asked. "Why not?" Will answered.

The car was amazing, driving almost like the day Will's grandmother drove it off the show room floor. They arrived at the entrance road to Will's farm just as he finished telling the Callaway story. He had told it all, but unlike the way he told it to Mary Ann, with Petey, he left nothing out.

Petey was dumbfounded and searched for something to say to console Will. Sitting there in the entranceway, Will contemplated how ironic it was that at this moment, facing possibly the most difficult challenge of his life, he found himself there on the land of his forefathers. He had come full circle.

They drove onto the property, and ahead of them off to their left stood the foundation of the old house where his grandmother grew up. Battered now, it outlined the size of the structure, which was huge even by today's standards. The remaining building had been vandalized, leaving just a shell of what had been one of the outbuildings from that era so long ago.

The old barn had collapsed, leaving only a pile of rubble, but the chicken coops, corral, hog houses, and outbuildings were still standing. The perimeter of pecan trees still stood, just as they had when Mam was a child. With a little imagination, one could perceive what life must have been like here at the end of the Civil War. The slave buildings had been washed away during a major flood even before Will was born, leaving no trace of that life.

They drove out to a knoll that stood higher than any point on the farm, giving them a view of the entire property right down to the river. Will's family had always believed that this had been an Indian burial ground as they had found several artifacts, including a large grinding stone, hollowed out from the grinding of grain, a stone ax point, and many fish arrow points. Out of respect or maybe out of superstition, his great-grandfather had decided not to build his home there even though it was the highest point on the property and well above flood stage.

"What are you going to do, Will?" Petey asked, as they leaned against the roof of the DeSoto and watched the mighty Mississippi roll by.

"I wish to hell I knew, Petey," he answered. "I wish I knew." It was peaceful here, so far removed from the jungles of Southeast Asia. But Will could feel Vietnam pulling him back, and the pledge that tied all Green Berets together and that had meant so much to him tugged away at his conscience because of Callaway. Could he now ignore it?

They tarried on the farm for some time, driving through the fields and woods, and finally down to the river's edge. "We've had some great times out here, haven't we?" Will asked.

"Some really great hunts, that's for sure," Petey responded. "I remember the time we killed so many ducks back there on the slough we couldn't carry them all." He was pointing toward the big cypress trees that identified the swamp. "And the time we tried to drill a well so that we could flood the slough one summer when it went dry."

"Yes," Will replied. "I remember. We worked all day in the heat with some rental drilling equipment that only produced a dribble of water. We finally gave up and had a dirt clod fight. We picked up pieces of the dried mud that had cracked from baking in the sun after years of being underwater. We threw those clods at each other to release our frustrations."

As the sun began to set, they drove out of the fields, back past what remained of the place Will's grandmother called the old home place. He felt sadness leaving this place, but his main thoughts were on Callaway.

Final Mission

This was the big night, the class reunion banquet. Mary Ann drove around the Burn Brae circle, stopping at the walk leading up to the veranda where Will was waiting. If she was beautiful last night, she was a queen tonight. Her perfume permeated the car as he got in on the passenger side where he could continue to admire this Venus in all her loveliness.

"Velma said you got a call from Larry. Anything important?" she asked as she drove through town toward the club. There are no secrets at Burn Brae. When Will told her, she grew silent, afraid to ask what he was going to do.

"Don't worry, I'm not going anywhere. I could spend the rest of my life trying to help other people and for what, a medal, or worse a bullet? No, I've come home to get a normal life back." He wondered if she believed him. He wasn't sure he did. He had always thought of himself as a patriot, but his definition of one may have changed. Or rather than changed, become less relevant. Will remembered hearing someone say that a patriot is "One for whom no partial ties can prevail to act traitorously to the team, and sacrifice the interest of the whole to that of a part. On the contrary, the patriot pursues nothing less than the good of the team or the country, setting aside personal interests. For the patriot, duty to country is the highest calling…next to the duty we owe the Supreme Being."

Arriving at the entrance to the club, they were greeted by several of their friends who were outside taking a smoke or just getting fresh air. They had missed seeing some of them at the party the night before because of their late arrival into town. Will and Mary Ann needed some pleasure and some laughter, and the reunion held the promise of both.

One of the first guys Will saw was the "Greaseman," Willy Deschamp. He was the only guy from their class that seemed to have mastered the slide rule while at the same time was always close to being kicked out of school due to his bad grades, a very strange paradox. "Hey, Will, run any road blocks lately?" he said as he gave Will a big bear hug. Everyone that heard him knew what he was referring too. It was an incident that both of them would always remember because it was a turning point for them both.

It all started when Will bought his first car just after he got out of high school, a 1949 Plymouth. He wanted a V-8, but his grandmother made him buy a six-cylinder Plymouth coup from an elderly lady down the street. Although it had a few years behind it, this reliable set of wheels had only been driven 14,000 miles, had always been kept in a garage, and was pristine in every way.

Will wasn't happy with a six-cylinder car, but he made the best of it by dropping the body down low to the road, shaving the heads to give it more compression, and adding dual exhausts, fender skirts, and spotlights. It was the "cat's meow" as they used to say. Even more so after he had put half-moon disks on the headlights and slanted them, giving the car a cat-like appearance as you saw it coming down the road at night.

One day, Greaseman came by the house and asked Will if he wanted to sell the car. He was a drag car enthusiast and had built a reputation as the guy who knew race cars better than anyone largely because he had learned to employ his slide rule in that endeavor. When he set his mind to it, he could do almost anything with cars and his slide rule, and he did time and time again.

"Not really," Will answered. To sell it meant replacing it, and he saw no prospects that excited him.

"Can I take a look at your car?" the Greaseman asked. "Sure," Will replied. So they went outside, lifted the hood, and he proceeded to climb in on top of the engine with his measuring tape and slide rule. When he finished, he was even more insistent that Will sell him the car to which he answered, "Not interested." Finally, when he realized he was getting nowhere, he asked the question, "Would you be interested in letting me put my engine in your car and use it only for going to the races at Wichita Falls, Texas?" This would leave Will with an extremely fast car to drive from then on.

The engine Willy wanted to put in Will's Plymouth was from a hopped-up 1952 Chrysler Saratoga club coupe that he had rolled into a field a few weeks earlier. This accident destroyed the car, but the 331 cubic inch FirePower "Hemi" engine was salvageable. This was the same engine that was later used in the first Chrysler 300 Letter Series, the C-300. That 1955 automobile was the first American production car to have a 300 horsepower engine, and they may have taken some of their performance tips from Willy.

"That big engine will never fit in my car, Willy. It's way too big."

"My calculations indicate that with a few modifications, I can make it fit."

"What, are you crazy?" Will shot back. "The engine will hit the front wheels and never let you turn the car except in a big field or parking lot. Plus the rear end would have to be replaced because it would never handle the power your engine will generate. And how about the oil pan? Won't it drag the ground? You need to forget that idea."

"I can change all that. Come on, Will, let's give it a try." The idea of driving a car that looks like an old-maid six-cylinder, but with a hemi engine that would probably have close to 300 horsepower by the time he got finished with it, was so exciting there was no way he could say no.

It was amazing what Greaseman did, starting with redesigning the oil pan, reducing its capacity from five quarts to four, adding an additional oil pump to keep oil circulating through a specially designed cooling unit, lifting the frame of the car so that it could house larger wheels and tires, installing real dual exhausts, and the changes went on and on.

For four months, Will walked, got his grandmother or friends to take him around, or rode with Willy in his car while he worked on getting the engine to fit. Willy cursed, cried, and banged his head on the wall for four months. Finally, he was ready to take it out on the road. They didn't go more than a block before he had a universal joint failure, requiring them to push the car back to his shop.

A few days later, they were back out on the road. This time, they got a few more miles until he put his foot into the accelerator, and the '49 Plymouth stick shift transmission came apart. As they began to push the car to turn it around, Will realized that he would have to be cautious where he parked this thing because the turning radius was as horrible as he had expected.

Finally, after several additional modifications that included putting a heavier rear end in the car, a bigger transmission, and jacking up the car for those larger tires and wheels they were ready for its first full-blown test. Driving out to the edge of town on Salcedo Road, Willy gradually took it up to 70, 80, 90, and then 100. Will looked at the speedometer, and it was stuck on 100 because that was all the speedometer was designed to register. Meanwhile, they were speeding faster and faster when the speedometer cable broke.

The next day, Willy put a new cable in the speedometer, took a chisel and knocked the peg off the speedometer, and back out on Salcedo road they went. This time, they were going so fast the speedometer needle disappeared down below the lower part of the dashboard and started showing up again on the left coming up against the peg where the needle starts at zero. This car was unbelievably fast.

The Greaseman went on to win the Grand National Championship that year, and Will was delighted to have a car that was a true sleeper. Guys who didn't know the car would pull up alongside him at a stoplight, look over with a sneer, and try to take off ahead only to find themselves staring at Will's tail lights. But that's just half the story. The real story comes a year later when Willy wanted to buy the car from Will again. Will had a girl friend that lived in Poplar Bluff, about fifty miles from Sikeston. Coming home late one night as he was crossing a five- mile causeway that traversed a swamp, he got stuck behind a line of slow-moving traffic that was being led by a self-propelled combine. It was close to midnight, and he had been burning the candle at both ends by staying out late and trying to keep a job that required early hours. Although there was a law against passing on a causeway, he needed to get home and get some rest. He could see up the road for miles and there was no oncoming traffic so he pulled out to pass. As luck would have it, one of those cars was a State patrolman. As Will roared by him, the officer turned on his red light and gave pursuit. It wasn't long before Will could no longer see his headlights as he reached speeds well in excess of 120 miles per hour.

At some point, Will slowed down to 85 mph and kept driving for about thirty minutes when he saw something a few miles ahead. It was a road block! As he approached the police cars that were stretched nose to nose across the roadway, he made a last- minute decision to swerve off the right side into the drainage swale where tall grass belayed the rain water from the day before splashing mud and grass across his windshield, blocking his vision. By the time he had his windshield wipers going fast enough to clear the mixture from his vision, his car had come back up onto the road and was heading in the right direction, dragging pieces of a fence post and barbed wire attached to his rear bumper. This new accessory left a trail of sparks like a Roman candle.

Revving back up to over 100 miles an hour, he approached Sikeston and took a detour around town in the event another roadblock had been set up to stop him at the city limits. Fortunately, Mam had left her car out in the drive that night, and he flew into the garage, closing the door just a few seconds before the police drove up, shining their spotlights at the garage. Everyone in town knew who owned the Plymouth, especially the police. But in those days, the law never came onto your property without a warrant, so he was safe for the moment.

The following day, a Sunday, Willy knocked at Will's door early in the morning and was invited in for coffee. He was even more insistent that Will sell him the car and was willing to pay double what Will had paid for it. Perhaps it was because Will had been looking at a Ford convertible that he could buy for cash if he sold the Plymouth, or perhaps it was because he knew that with his lead foot, sooner or later, he would be in big trouble. In any case, he decided it was time to move on so he sold him the car. A deal was struck, Willy wrote out a check for the full amount, and Will promised to get the title for him the following day from his grandmother's safe deposit box at the bank.

Walking out to the garage, Will wondered what they were going to see when he raised the garage door. When the door came up it looked like Willy would have a heart attack. "Jeesss Brandon, what the hell have you done to my car?" The first thing he saw was about six feet of fence and a piece of a fence post hung on the back bumper, and there was mud and grass from one end to the other. Although the car was metallic green, you would not have known it.

After Will got Willy calmed down, they moved the car out of the garage into the yard to hose it down. After removing the fence post and wire, and much to Will's surprise, there was only a small dent in the middle of the front bumper and a few scratches on the back where the fence had bounced off the pavement as it followed behind. Although he wasn't thrilled about the road block episode, he took the car anyway. Willy never liked the color of the car and already had plans to repaint it once it was his.

Will watched from the porch as Willy roared away happy as a pig in slop, leaving a streak of rubber all the way to the corner stop sign. About an hour later, the phone rang, and it was Willy. "What have you done to me, man? They got me down here in the slammer charged with fifteen violations, and they've confiscated my car and license. Come on, Will, you got to help me out here."

So he borrowed Mam's car and drove down there to confess to all these terrible crimes. The police knew who had been driving the car anyway. Hell, everyone in Southeast Missouri knew who owned that car. So he paid the fines, and that was it. Will knew that if he did that today, they wouldn't lock him up and throw away the keys.

When Will and Mary Ann entered the ballroom, Nicholas Patrick, their old team's quarterback, appeared to be holding court off to one side. Seeing each other, they moved toward the middle of the room where they embraced and began laughing uncontrollably. Nicholas's four years of college football had made him bigger and stronger, but his personality hadn't changed. He was still the class president and rightly so.

After the banquet, everyone was given an opportunity to speak on what they had been doing since graduation. Will had no desire to speak nor did he believe anyone there would be interested in what he had to say so he chose to remain silent. But Nicholas, being the master of ceremonies, wasn't about to let him off that easily. "There's one guy who's been to the far ends of the earth who we haven't heard from tonight. And we all know that he hasn't been away to seminary school. Let's welcome our class mystery man to the podium. Will Brandon."

Not knowing what to say, Will was reluctant to speak but they insisted, so he finally moved to the stage and began. "Fellow classmates, how wonderful it is to be back home again. There were moments that I doubted I would ever see you guys again. I don't know about you, but I feel that we had a unique experience growing up together here in Sikeston. And through that unique experience, we were bound together closer than we might have been if we had grown up somewhere else. Like you, my memories of Sikeston High, our teachers, our ball teams, our joys, and yes, our sorrows, made our teenage years unforgettable. I wouldn't trade those years for anything.

"Some of you have wanted to know what I've been up to the past fifteen years. Well, a significant part of that time I was in Southeast Asia. And the best way to describe my job is to say that I have been an observer." That word seemed to stick in his throat. What a joke. "And what I have been witnessing is man's inhumanity to man. Even now, as we celebrate this joyous occasion, whole villages are being destroyed and families are being killed or tortured."

Looking around the room, people appeared frozen, remaining quiet and still while hanging on his every word. "I do not intend to put a damper on such a joyous occasion. But I think that we need to say a prayer tonight to thank God that Sikeston is not a village in South Vietnam, that our hometown is a safe place to live and raise kids, and that we can all go to sleep tonight in the comfort of knowing that this town will still be here when we get up in the morning."

Nicholas said one of his usually inspiring prayers. It was a wonderful evening, and Will was able to forget, at least for a moment, all that grief back there in Vietnam. He held Mary Ann as close as he could as they danced around the ballroom to the tunes of the '50s. Will and Mary Ann said they loved each other many times during the evening, and he thanked God for this night which had turned out exactly the way he had prayed it would.

As they approached Burn Brae, Will pulled off the main road into the field, drove back to the river, and parked. Walking around to the front of the car, Will lifted Mary Ann up on the fender, and they watched the moonlight bounce on the ripples in the water. He had picked something up in Saigon especially for this moment. Taking it from his pocket, he opened the black case and presented it to Mary Ann. It was a small diamond ring, set in gold, a simple yet elegant piece. "Mary Ann, I wasn't certain that this was something I would want to do when I came home or that you would have anything to do with me. But I have been praying that you would be here, that we would reunite, and that we could pick our lives up where we left off. God has answered those prayers. Will you marry me?"

Her eyes had shown excitement and happiness before but never like this. She jumped down from the fender and began to prance like a pony, hugging the box and its contents. "Here, let me put it on you and see if it fits." She could hardly hold her hand still. She had the look of complete bliss as he slid the ring on to her finger, a perfect fit.

"Well? What's your answer, Mary Ann?"

"You silly guy. What do you think my answer is?" she answered as she jumped back into his arms. As they kissed, he could feel the warmness of her tears that flowed down her cheeks onto his.

The next few weeks, Will divided his time between planning the wedding with Mary Ann, looking for a place to live, and working out the details of joining Petey in his crop dusting business. But his thoughts were never far from Callaway or Larry.

The leaves had begun to change now, and there was crispness to the air. Large flocks of geese dotted the sky as the fall migration began to arrive on their way south. Will was invited to go goose hunting, but his desire to hunt, which had always dominated his thinking in the fall as a boy, had left him. Perhaps he had seen enough killing that the thought of shooting geese left him cold.

Having no place to spend money in Vietnam, Will had saved a considerable sum, enough to buy into Petey's business and to purchase farm equipment. Will's contract farmer was close to retirement, and he offered his equipment at a fair price. He had never farmed the land he had inherited from his grandmother other than as a helper or tractor driver for the tenant farmer. Since Petey had offered him a full partnership in his business, he offered him the same in his farm. He knew more about agriculture than Will did anyway.

To celebrate their betrothal, Petey held an old-fashioned hayride. The kind they had when they were teenagers. Although most of those who came were married, it was still a romantic moonlight event, and it conjured up wonderful memories of their youth. The hayride culminated with a barbecue back at Burn Brae with everyone sitting around a big bonfire singing school songs. The highlight of the night was seeing their class cheerleaders lead them in cheers and their high school song, "The Red and the Black." What joy and bliss Will felt realizing that his God had blessed him by returning him from the chaos of war to the peace and serenity of his hometown.

Around midnight, Velma sent a message to Will that he had a long distance call. Petey and Mary Ann both looked in Will's direction, an expression of concern on their faces as Will jogged back to the house.

"Hello."

"Is this Will Brandon?"a female voice said, somewhat formally. "Yes," Will replied.

"I have a call for you from Cecil Tighe. Please hold." It had to be bad news, Will thought to himself. Cecil would not call him if it weren't. After all, Will had resigned from the agency with his blessings.

"Good evening, Will. How's the civilian life treating you?" "Great, Cecil. I haven't heard a gunshot or helicopter in weeks. What's happening?"

"We got a problem. Are we secure?" "Yes. Is this about Callaway?"

"Yes and no. Will, we haven't heard from Larry in a week. He left Camp 222 last Friday with eleven other team members on a tip we had from one of our spotters, which was later confirmed by an Air Force surveillance aircraft. We were relatively certain where they were holding Callaway. The team was dropped by helicopter about five miles from the VC stronghold. That was four days ago, and we haven't heard from them since. We've sent reconnaissance aircraft in there as well as a recon team, but not a trace. It appears the VC have moved their stronghold across the border into Cambodia. We should have some confirmation of that within the next twenty-four hours."

Will began to feel sick, deep in his gut. "Why are you calling me, Cecil?" as if he didn't know.

"Because I need your help," he answered. "You know that area better than anybody. If there is one man that could lead a team in there and rescue them, it's you."

"But, Cecil, you don't even know if they're alive. You know as well as I that it's pretty slim that they are. And even if they are alive, it might take a battalion to free them because they will know we're coming. And I'm sure our guys would be killed if they even got a hint we were in the neighborhood. I'm sick about the men, but I get even sicker thinking about leaving my future wife and my new life, only to find out our team has been killed. No, you'll have to do this one without me."

"Don't give me a final answer, Will, until we get some more intelligence. I'm going to call you sometime tomorrow. We expect some answers then. Fair enough?"

"Whatever," Will answered, perturbed knowing that Cecil never gives up. Just as he hung up, he looked up to see Mary Ann standing in the doorway.

"You're going back, aren't you, Will?" "No, Mary Ann, I am not."

"But Larry's your friend," she retorted in a tone that was asking a question, but not really wanting to hear the answer.

Will mumbled some response to try and reassure her, but he knew it wasn't very convincing. There was a struggle going on inside of him involving common sense, telling him Larry and Callaway were dead and strong emotions that told him to disregard all that and go anyway.

After all the guests had gone, Will, Mary Ann, Petey, and his girlfriend Linda Paris gathered around the dwindling fire and toasted to the upcoming marriage and the new "AG AIR" partnership, the name Petey called their new crop dusting company. Will had just returned from taking Mary Ann home so she could drive to Cape Girardeau early the following morning to pick out a wedding gown. That is when Cecil's call came. He had left the details of the wedding entirely in her hands, the gown being just one of them, and she was busy making preparations.

Cecil began on a serious note, "Information gained from informants along with Cambodian agents operating in the field have helped the agency get a spot on where the VC might be holding Callaway and now perhaps Larry as well. One report indicates a blond American being guarded with other prisoners where we have known for some time that a regiment of North Vietnamese have their field headquarters. High altitude surveillance has given us some other data including strength of our opposition."

"This is my last call, Will," Cecil said. "Our time is short. The company's jet is available and currently parked at Pope AFB adjacent to Fort Bragg. We can be there to pick you up by 0700 hours tomorrow and be in Saigon the day after tomorrow. There's a bonus for you when you get back that could come in handy for the upcoming wedding. What do you say, Will? Are you with us on this?"

It's Not Over Till It's Over

The sun was just beginning to rise above the horizon as Will and Petey watched the unmarked jet bank and turn to make its final approach into the Sikeston Airpark. Will wondered what the townspeople would be thinking when they heard a jet come in right over the center of the town this early in the morning or at anytime for that matter. He also wondered if Mary Ann had heard the noise and if she would connect the jet's arrival to his departure. He hadn't told her he was leaving. There would be no emotional good-byes. He knew it would be too painful.

While the crew loaded his gear, he took a moment to say good-bye to Petey. Their lifelong friendship was being interrupted once again, and Will knew Petey had great concern for his well- being. Although Will had downplayed the danger, Petey knew this was no ordinary mission.

Standing on the tarmac, Petey watched as the aircraft taxied down the runway, turned, and roared by him, lifting into the air until it finally disappeared behind the clouds. Thinking of what lay ahead, he shivered at the thought of what he might have to go through, then he said a prayer and got in his pickup and drove away, thankful he was safe in good old Southeast Missouri.

Will watched Petey from the window as the aircraft passed him standing on the tarmac, waving with his hat. And as Sikeston began to get smaller below, they turned to the northwest passing over the old farm, allowing Will one last look at the fields of corn and soybeans and the old homestead foundation. Will had chosen to leave without saying good-bye to Mary Ann, knowing that she might persuade him to stay rather than return to Vietnam. He hoped she would understand and forgive him, and he prayed that she would be waiting for his return… if he ever did.

The Gulfstream Jet turned due west now, heading for the coast. It was going to be a beautiful day here in the heartland of America, and Will began to think about the people below. They were sleeping happily secure in their beds, oblivious to what was happening half a world away. He also began to think about his state of mind. Unwittingly, he began to assume old thought patterns, visualizing the jungle and the danger he would face. To offset what lay ahead, he began to think of what lay behind. She had never given up on him all those years, never knowing where he was or if he was even alive. And yet she continued to keep him in her thoughts and her prayers. How blessed he was to have the love of a woman that devoted. After her divorce, she continued to hope and pray. And now she would have to wait again.

After refueling in San Diego, they were back in the air, the dark blue Pacific Ocean falling away beneath them. The young hostess offered Will a cocktail and gave him a choice of movies. He smiled when he realized they were all war movies and wondered if the company psychologist had recommended them over a comedy or a romantic movie. He smiled again when he thought how the Agency always thought of everything.

It appeared to Will that there was an unusual amount of activity at the Tan Son Nhut Air Base when they arrived. A steady stream of aircraft flights in and out accompanied by heavy helicopter movement was taking place. A young special forces captain by the name of Harris met Will's flight and directed him to the briefing hut across the tarmac. *Soldiers make captain earlier these days*, Will thought.

As they stepped into the Quonset hut, he was greeted by old friends Marshall Brant and Drew Harlow. There were several other members of the operations team assembled, each with special knowledge or capabilities. It pleased Will to see the attention the rescue operation was receiving. He had known of instances where other personnel had been left out to dry with no official acknowledgement that they even existed because of their involvement with the agency. But this was different.

After Will greeted everyone, Marshall Brant began the briefing with an assessment of the enemy's perceived strength followed by Drew Harlow's review of the terrain.

It was just after dark when Will arrived at Camp 222. There, standing in the glow of the ground fires was Tom Vo, waving in the chopper with a flare. "I'm out of here the minute you unload the ordnance, Brandon," the helicopter pilot shouted. "I don't like the looks of this place at all." It took only five minutes, and the helicopter was back in the air, streaking across the jungle and out of sight.

"I knew you'd come, Will," Tom said as they embraced. "I knew you'd come."

"He'd come for me, Tom. And so would you." "What took you so long?" he said smiling.

Whatever It Takes

"Tom, where is everyone?"

"They be here soon. When they hear copter, they come. We have perimeter secure. No surprises tonight."

Within a few minutes, the first one to reveal himself was Jim Thorpe, and Will was glad to see the Indian. First, it was good to know that he was still alive, and second, with him around, it would be near impossible for the enemy to ambush the team. He was also a bit of a comedian. Walking up to Will, he began a war dance, singing, "White man come, sweep across plain, kill all buffalo. Nothing left but buffalo chips. But we got good news. We got plenty of buffalo chips." The team laughed as Jim Thorpe continued his little war dance. But no one relaxed or got comfortable. Charley was out there. How close and how many, Will thought to himself, we shall see what we shall see.

One by one, the Special Forces team members emerged from the jungle to welcome Will and to devise a plan to free Larry and Callaway, if they were still alive. There were forty-five Green Berets, all experienced special operations veterans, men who didn't just go out at night to get their exercise. Throughout the Vietnam Conflict, the regular army had often planned their strategies like all previous wars where there was a battlefield front and where you judged your day's work on how much you had advanced. These men fighting this war were not like that! No, they had been trained to judge their day on how many confirmed kills they had versus casualties they had sustained and how much terror they had created. It was a pride thing and they were good at it.

The rest of the team consisted of Marshall Brant and Drew Harlow, CIA operatives with years of special warfare experience in a number of theaters around the world. For ordnance, there were four Special Warfare experts who were also Special Forces trained. They carried their bags of equipment like they contained remnants of the Holy Grail. For communications, Cecil Tighe had made sure the team had the best electronic surveillance experts in Vietnam. These men were trained to interpret data that would be relayed to them from a high altitude reconnaissance aircraft. They had also brought with them the newest agency issue: small handheld satellite phones programmed to our government's newest satellite perched in an orbit that brought it directly over South Vietnam several times a day. The one thing they all knew was that the agency took care of their own, and when one of them was in jeopardy or was compromised, they would pull out all the stops. The schedule of satellite passovers would tell the team when they could use them and when they would be out of communications only a few hours each day.

Commanding this operation was Captain Reilly. He had been the platoon leader who had run down the perpetrators of Doc Tran, and he had asked to be assigned to this operation. The plan would not be finalized until aerial photographs of the enemy camp had been scoped out, their numbers calculated, and the place where the prisoners were being held had been determined. Standing by some 100 miles away would be a wing of ten gunships ready to move in their direction at a moment's notice once the assault of the enemy camp began. There was also available other aircraft, fighter jets and B-52s standing at alert. Cecil was well connected.

Captain Reilly gave orders for the team to move up closer to the stronghold and, from there, await additional intelligence from command. They were on the move before the first trace of dawn, moving slowly until it was light enough to spot trip wires or other antipersonnel devices. Intelligence had indicated that Larry was wounded but still walking when his captors forced him to march to their stronghold, a place with map coordinates but no name. While the camp was new, it had been spotted and photographed by the agency's high altitude reconnaissance aircraft, the Raven. To insiders, it was called Blackbird because of its color and because it usually only flew at night.

There were no roads to this mountain fortress, and the jungle was thick and treacherous. Will knew the Viet Cong would be expecting an air assault, but he also knew Larry would be the first casualty if their presence were detected. This made attacking from the air impractical.

They had to approach the enemy camp in an unusual manner, knowing the camp would be on alert and expecting a rescue.

Just before nightfall, the team found a clearing where they could camp for the night. A perimeter of security was set up, and scouts sent out to ensure the force would not be discovered. A low-level hutch was erected and Captain Reilly laid out a map of the camp that detailed the area around the enemy's position. For hours, different strategies of the operation were discussed, but nothing could be decided. Late in the evening, new aerial photographs arrived and were relayed electronically from a Blackbird that passed high above the enemy camp. The aerial photos were spread across the ground under a hanging lamp. The pilot informed them that they were about five miles away from the target area.

Two facts stood out in Will's mind while surveying the enemy's fortifications. First, it was surrounded by jungle grass that appeared to be exceptionally dry. Second, there was a stream running across the front of the camp, which was lined with that same grass. His mind raced through the different options, and he began to consider an idea that had started to formulate in his mind. This was a bold option and perhaps a little too far out, but who had a better idea? It was Larry's life on the line, not to mention the lives of those on the team.

"Does anyone know how deep the stream is or could reconnaissance aircraft determine the stream's depth?" Will asked, starting to add the details required to transition his idea to a real plan. No one knew its depth, but the answer was yes to the aircraft's ability to analyze the stream's depth.

As the team leaders considered the options, Will was still thinking through this crazy idea he was considering. "What is the possibility of getting some scuba gear sent up here?" he asked. There was a moment of silence. He let them in on his radical idea, but it was the best plan yet. They all agreed that it just might be crazy enough to work. Details would be formulated later.

All eyes looked toward Marshall Brant and Drew Harlow for their reaction to the plan. The two of them looked at each other, and Marshall was the first to speak. "Can we reach Cecil? We need his okay on the plan. He's the only one that can pull it off and get the equipment up here by tomorrow."

Drew injected, "I'll contact Blackbird and ask for a status on the stream." Capt. Reilly commanded, "Get on it."

It wasn't until Marshall pulled it out of his backpack that the men realized that he carried a satellite phone. "Cecil sleeps with his," said Marshall. The satellite was scheduled to pass over within a few minutes, and before long, he was on the air with Cecil. Between the two of them, they began to discuss the needed equipment and the details of the delivery. "He wants to talk to you, Will," as he handed Will the phone.

Cecil greeted Will and wished the team success. Then he asked, "Do you remember the substance we nicknamed Krypton?"

"Vaguely." Will had heard about this new gas, named after the Krypton of Superman fame discussed at Langley, but he always thought it was still in an experimental stage. "Why do you ask?" "Because it's no longer a concept, it's a reality, Will. It is clear, odorless, and can put you to sleep in seconds. Depending on how it's administered, the person may have no side effect other than a headache. The problem is it only lasts for a short time, say only ten to fifteen minutes, and then the body becomes immune to it. Also, if there is no wind, it has a tendency to reside in a small area. In other words, it won't help you if your victims are fifty yards away or out of the wind drift. Use it with discretion. It can help, but don't rely too heavily on it. I'm sending the gear Marshall requested, and I'll try to have it there by noon tomorrow." There was a pause then Cecil said, "I'm sending some new gas masks that have built in night vision and also some underwater masks that have the same capability. You'll like these: they cover your eyes, nose, and mouth and give you better underwater vision in poor light. By the way, can you use a UWTV?"

"What in the world is a UWTV? Some new TV we haven't heard about?" Will asked.

"It's an under water transport vehicle. It's light, silent, fast as hell… and good for about two hours of operation. Our Frogmen have been using them lately and few people are aware of them, especially Charley. It would help you get Larry or anyone else out when you're in a hurry, which could be very important if they are wounded. Shall I send it with the drop?"

"Why not? I'm sure it will get nasty by the time we leave the camp."

"Good luck and tell Larry when you see him that his vacation is over, and it's time to go back to work." Will laughed to himself, knowing how true that statement was.

At 1100 hours, the C-130 came in over the encampment, dropping the equipment by parachute in a stand of scrub trees, making only one pass, and then it was gone. The team broke out the new equipment and distributed it to the men. The UWTV was tested and running smooth. Jim Thorpe said it reminded him of a walrus, and the nickname stuck. It would take two men to carry it, and it would be destroyed and sunk when they left. After inspecting the equipment to make sure everything was intact, Capt. Reilly gathered the strike force together to discuss the plan. Everyone not going in the water was assigned the special gas mask. Drew voiced his hope that Blackbird would be able to tell them which way the wind would be blowing based on the smoke raising from the enemy camp. This was important for the placement of Krypton. Will and two other soldiers were to enter the water about a mile upstream, fully equipped to swim underwater with the Walrus the last 100 yards. They knew it would be an easy swim downstream. It was the extraction of Larry and Callaway, if he were there, and the trip back upstream with the Walrus that would be critical.

The jungle changed significantly as they marched toward the encampment. The landscape transformed from thick undergrowth to rolling hills and thinner vegetation with taller trees housing small but rambunctious monkeys. Between the birds and the monkeys, there was more noise than downtown Saigon. This was a critical time for the team. Their success or failure depended upon stealth. They were getting closer now, and there was concern for the men on reconnaissance that moved ahead of the force.

Just before dusk, two scouts returned with news of the camp, now less than a mile away. It was discouraging to hear that they saw no evidence of a prison or prisoner being guarded. The news sent trepidation throughout the team. It meant going back for a closer look, and that could jeopardize their mission.

Capt. Reilly called Marshall, Drew, Tom, and Will together, asking, "What do you think? Do we take a second look, do we abort, or do we just go in there and blow the hell out of the place?" This comment was uncharacteristic of the captain who was a pragmatist, but it revealed his frustration.

"I don't think we have a choice," Will said. "We've got to go in close, look for a small prison, or possibly a decoy prison. They know we are coming, they just don't know when or how. They want us to come. And they know we won't use airpower for fear of losing our men."

"Then you go, Will," Capt. Reilly responded. "Take a couple of people, get up close, and let's get some answers."

The smell of human waste confirmed how close they were to human habitat. Tom directed Jim Thorpe off to the left, and Will went to the right. Somewhere ahead, they could hear the sound of commands being given in Vietnamese. They had to be extremely cautious here as Viet Cong usually surround their permanent camps with mines and booby traps. Slowly, Will parted the brush just a fraction to see their camp below, about a hundred yards away. He checked his watch. They had agreed to meet at the separation point in twenty minutes. Will searched the camp with binoculars for signs of a prison cell but saw none. His spirits began to fade at the possibility that Larry was not there, and it began to override his thinking. Just as he was about to back out of his observation point, he noticed two guards stop and point toward the ground at an object just out of his vision. If it's what he thought it might be, he had to know what had their attention. Changing his position, he crawled along the ground through the dry grass and up a small rise in the turf. Moving to his right, he could see what they were talking about. It was a pit covered by a bamboo top large enough to hold one or more people. It was just about fifty feet from the stream on a knoll between two large pine trees. His spirits rose again over the thought that this could be Larry's and Callaway's prison. But how could he be sure?

Tom and Will arrived at the starting point at about the same time, with Jim Thorpe arriving a few minutes later. They hadn't observed anything unusual but became excited when Will told them what he had seen. Although they had told Capt. Reilly they'd be back in four hours, they all agreed that their questions warranted them taking a better look. Jim was sent back to report to the captain what Will had seen and to tell him that they would be returning to their observation position to wait and watch.

Even though they had taken compass readings before starting for the stronghold, they knew it would be difficult finding their camp in the dark, not to mention the danger of stepping on a mine or a trip wire. As they contemplated heading back to camp, Will noticed another Viet Cong carrying what looked like food and water. Sure enough, the guard standing nearby reached down and lifted the cover while the soldier with the objects handed them down to two outstretched arms.

They arrived back in camp about two hours after dark. Capt. Reilly was preparing to send a team to find why they had been an hour late. Other than those on guard, all of the rescue team gathered around the three observers for a briefing.

"Did you see them, guys?" Capt. Reilly asked. "Did you see Larry or Callaway?"

"We couldn't be certain," Will replied. "All we saw were someone's arms."

"It had to be them," Tom declared.

"But how do you know?" Capt. Reilly threw the question back at Will. "What if it isn't him, then what?" The Indian spoke up, "Then some poor slob will be the happiest SOB in Vietnam."

Tom and Jim Thorpe entered the water with Will just as the sun set behind the trees on the distant hills. The thought of what might be in the water with them entered Will's mind for a moment, but he quickly disregarded it. After all, it was a little late to be worrying about that now. Tom placed an underwater marker where he knew the rescue team wouldn't miss it. They would be coming back in a hurry and wouldn't want to miss their exit point. This was the trail back to safety. It was also important because they would need to exit the stream and double-time it out of there before they got caught in the barrage from the planned air strike that was to follow.

By the time they reached the point where they were to go in the water, darkness had started to set in. They checked their watches. They were where they were supposed to be at the designated time. Within minutes, the current took the three- man team, now submerged, downstream to the point adjacent to where they thought the subterranean prison cell would be. Watches were checked again. They were fifteen minutes ahead of the coordinated assault on the camp. Coming up on the opposite side of the stream in marsh reeds they waited, peering through reeds at the camp. A Vietnamese soldier was leaning against a tree, smoking a cigarette as he stood guard over the prison cell. About twenty yards away, a group of soldiers were crowded around a small cooking fire, enjoying the cool breeze that lifted the camp fire smoke away from their area.

Will looked at his watch again, and it was time to start breathing from their tanks as Krypton would soon be silently snaking its way through the camp. The first guy to drop was one of the guards around the fire, and then the rest fell out on the ground, one directly over the fire. The soldier standing guard saw the soldiers fall, and he began hollowing at the others just as a burst from an automatic weapon broke the silence of the camp. The three men swam the short distance to the camp side of the stream, and as they came up out of the water, all hell broke loose. Mortar rounds began to fall like rain from one end of the camp to the other. Small arms fire increased and the sky lit up from flares and exploding mortar fire.

On a dead run, the three rescue men headed for the prison cell. The guard leveled his AK-47 directly at them just as they turned their weapons loose. Water sprayed from their M-16 muzzles like lawn sprinklers and the VC's weapon never fired as he was cut down. Tom tore back the cage-like top and crouching there were two very surprised men: Larry and Callaway. Immediately, Callaway started boosting Larry out of the pit as Will reached down to lift him out. Larry winced with pain since his shoulder was somewhat dislocated, but there was still a look of smiling optimism on his face.

Jim Thorpe placed masks over their faces, informing them of the importance to not breathe the night air. "Who in the hell are you, guys? You look like stand-ins for the Phantom of the Opera." Will pulled down his mask to show him who he was being careful not to breathe, and when Larry saw who it was, he smiled through his pain and said, "What's for dinner, Will?"

The sound of gunfire seemed to come from every direction, confirming that the fire team had their hands full. As they ran for the stream, the incoming rounds were buzzing by at an increasing rate. A squad of enemy soldiers who had been out of the wind drift zeroed in on the men, intent on making sure they didn't live out the night. Then Will noticed a change in the sound of gunfire and an occasional tracer streaked toward the VC. It was a 50 caliber being fired by a team member, and in the wet night air, it sounded like a cannon. Approaching the water, Will looked back and saw a company size force swarming down through the camp, heading in their direction less than 150 yards away. At that moment, he realized that they might not make it; that this might be their last day on earth. But that thought didn't survive long. As they entered the water, slowed down by a wounded man, Will realized how extremely vulnerable they were to rifle fire, grenades, and mortar shells.

It was now time to swim or die. Although Larry was an experienced diver, he was having trouble with his breathing gear while Callaway looked more like a serious diver. Meanwhile, Will and the team hugged the bottom, expecting the worst. The water conducted the sound of explosions, and it confirmed that there was a major conflict taking place on the surface. Will wondered if the Special Forces team was taking casualties from that barrage above and if they would be at their rendezvous point. As they reached the submerged UWTV and released it from its tether, it sank to the bottom just as a VC standing a short distance away began firing directly into the water. The rounds went streaking by Will and the other men, carrying air bubbles along with them. Jim Thorpe turned and swam downstream a few yards and came up firing. That problem was now solved.

They were moving fairly fast now, Tom and Will holding on to the Walrus with Callaway and Jim Thorpe holding on to their legs. Larry was hanging onto the backpacks of Jim and Callaway, looking something like a circus act. There was a loud splash on the surface behind them as a grenade fell to the bottom of the stream. Somehow, Jim was affected the most by the exploding grenade and appeared somewhat dazed by it. Blood was coming from within the hood of his wet suit. Tom and Will swam to him and pulled him to the Walrus. Concerned that Jim might be taking in water instead of air from his tanks, Will pulled him up to check his mask. Good, bubbles rising from his mask indicated he was breathing normally. Once Will saw that Jim was okay and had a good hold on his ankles, he started the UWTV again and turned the throttle to full speed.

They had escaped the camp, but the danger wasn't over. Mortar shells began to fall with ever increasing frequency. One exploded on the bank close by raining shrapnel on the water twenty yards ahead of them. Then another fell into the water perhaps thirty yards behind. Another hit the water midstream drifting lazily to the bottom until it exploded, sending a shock wave that lifted the Walrus on its tail. At least, the small arms fire was diminishing. VC are expert mortar men, but Will could tell they were just guessing at their position from a distant emplacement. Guessing or not, there was always a chance that they could get lucky. Stopping for a moment to check on Jim's breathing apparatus, Will looked at Tom for a sign as to whether they should continue or lie low. Looking back at Will, he paused, listened for gunfire, then motioned onward.

The team came out of the water at the marker, sabotaged the Walrus, and sank it in the deepest part of the river. They took stock of the wounded. Knowing the enemy would be pursuing them, they moved a safe distance from the stream to observe any enemy troop movements that would be tracing the stream's edge. The Americans had snatched Larry and Callaway right out of the lion's mouth. VC pride and honor was at stake here. They would be coming, but how far behind they were was the question.

The sound of the air strike echoed through the jungle, and they watched the sky come ablaze with explosions, sending burning debris into the heavens. The American pilots were giving them hell, but the surviving pursuers would be coming; they had no doubt about that.

Jim was semiconscious and bleeding more now that he was out of the water. When they pulled the top of his wet suit over his head, they could see that the blood had been emanating from his ears. Getting him to his feet, they forged ahead until they found the stash point where water, rations, additional ammunition, and weapons for Larry and Callaway were hidden.

Not knowing what had happened back there, they could take no chances. They moved with haste to the pick-up location. Placing Jim's arms around their necks, Tom and Will moved as fast as they could with Callaway and Larry struggling hard to keep up. Their incarceration in a small damp pit had taken its toll. They were as emaciated as you would expect for prisoners of the VC.

It was a harrowing night that never seemed to end. Every shadow was suspected of being a VC; every pair of trees there could be a trip wire or mine strategically placed. They knew Charley would be out there, following their trail probably on a dead run. There was no dallying around, it was time to call upon those years of training and conditioning or be run down by a ruthless foe.

After several hours, Will stopped the group so they could take a breather while he went back up the trail about a hundred yards.

Stepping off the path into the underbrush, he waited to see if NVA had done what he expected they would do: send runners ahead to take an assessment of their strength and condition. Within minutes, he heard them coming and they passed just a few feet in front of him, running about ten yards apart. The last one heard Will come out of the brush and tried to stop his charge, but he wasn't fast enough. Will's ever-so-efficient survival knife had cut his throat from ear to ear before he knew what had happened.

Thrashing around in the tall grass, it alerted the lead runner who came running back, attacking Will with his rifle-mounted bayonet. Neither of them wanted to use firepower as it would alert the other team of their proximity. Will was able to ward off the bayonet, but the VC very skillfully swung the butt of his rifle around, hitting the left side of Will's chest causing him to drop his knife and knocking him off the path into the tall grass.

He wasted no time coming after Will with his bayonet, but Will had gone for his Colt .45 automatic, firing several rounds just as he hit the ground. At least one round hit his midsection, and for a moment, he hesitated looking at Will before he fell bleeding profusely at his feet.

Will knew that the sound of his discharged Colt was not good, that his NVA's buddies would be coming full speed now that they knew where the Americans were, but Will had no choice in the matter. He ran back to where Larry, Tom, Callaway, and Jim were waiting, and immediately, they began a slow trot, helping each other along as fast as possible toward the rendezvous.

Just before dawn, they reached the pick-up point, an LZ selected because of its openness, a strategic place to land helicopters, usually UH-1s which they called slicks. As they laid Jim down against a large tree, he was beginning to act normal again, and Larry sat down beside him to give him water and rations.

It was dawn now, and with the sun came the heat. Not knowing how long it would be before their team joined them, they started looking for a more defensible position. As they circled back toward the stream, Tom grabbed Will's arm and motioned silence. He had heard the sound of men walking through dry grass very close. As the men crouched in the grass, two NVA came out of the tall glass walking directly toward them. Will saw Tom click his safety off.

For a moment, Will was thrown back in time to a scene so long ago when he and his friend Edward Malone were crouching in the grass near the pond they loved so well, waiting for the Canada geese to come in closer.

Tom was now reaching for his knife rather than his weapon, knowing that if he fired it, the North Vietnamese would come running to their position. Together, they sprung up from the tall grass right in the face of their pursuers, surprising them so much that they didn't have time to bring up their weapons before the men were on top of them. Will's knife sought out a mortal position as he came up from the ground, thrusting the blade upwards. Halfheartedly, the NVA reached for his safety, but it was too late; for him, it was all over. Tom had spun his victim around, and from his rear, very quickly cut the enemy's throat. Will and Tom were both covered with blood and visibly shaken. It confirmed what they knew all along that VC were fighting with NVA when they were able to see the perpetrators up close. It had been too easy, taking those lives. It had been heartless. But it had been necessary.

Rushing back to the pick-up point, the other men were shocked when they saw Will and Tom with blood-streaked clothing, fearing that they had been mortally wounded. Tom spoke up, "We are certain the main NVA force is coming. We need to build up protection with logs, dirt, anything." They had an entrenching tool so they dug in.

While scanning the tree line, Will caught a glimpse of a man emerging from the right about 200 yards away, then another. Before long, there was a line of soldiers followed by another line. It was the Green Berets! Tom stood up and motioned to them, and they waved back.

Capt. Reilly was in front of the team and was the first to reach the group. "Where is that sandbagging SOB that went out and got himself caught? Doesn't he know we got better things to do than rescue his sorry ass?" Lifting Larry up, careful not to hurt his fragile body, he gave him a warm hug, and Larry responded.

Will counted the guys as they came in. Was it possible, he thought to himself, that not a man was lost? It was too good to believe. There were some wounded, seventeen according to Captain Reilly, who spoke up and said, "I called ahead for extraction several hours ago. We should hear our slicks (UH-1 troop transports) coming within the next ten minutes. They are bringing medics and medical supplies. I need spotters at the western edge of the clearing. Send up a flare if you see trouble." He spoke up again a few minutes later, "We were lucky, but it ain't over 'till it's over. They're coming. They have to. We hurt them bad. The thing is we don't want to be here when they arrive." He looked to the sky, searching the horizon for those little black dots that will tell them that Puff the Magic Dragon was on the way.

The radio began to crackle as contact was made with Blackbird. "You got 'em coming at you from the southwest, a company size group. Your transportation is on the way, but it's gonna be close."

"I called for additional air support two hours ago," their radioman reported. "I would think they'll be here soon. Keep us informed, Blackbird."

The helicopter pilot's voice leading the extraction wing came in clear. "I think we can see the LZ ahead of us, maybe five to ten minutes out. What's it like down there?" "It's quiet, but Blackbird tells us that's about to change."

Suddenly, a burst of automatic rifle fire broke the silence. "Geez…I heard that up here," the helicopter pilot said clearly over the radio. Rap, rap, rap, rap…there was that 50 caliber talking the same language it was talking back at the encampment. Then it really got hot. Their comrades had set up claymores where they anticipated Charley would be approaching, and they began detonating them. Those who had stayed back to assist the wounded immediately ran to reinforce their comrades. Tom started to join them, but Will hollered for him to stay to help load the wounded once the slicks landed.

Without advanced warning, four mean looking F-4 Phantoms screamed across the clearing and banked to the left to come around again. "This is Ant Eater," the jet pilot radioed in. He must have heard the remark by Blackbird. "I'm gonna fry up some ants for dinner, boys. Stand by." The radio man confirmed the coordinates, and with that, they came down the tree line about a hundred feet off the deck, dropping their napalm load of death and setting the woods on fire for a quarter mile.

Like the dragons they were named after, eight choppers came in full bore. Lifting the leaves and grass into a vortex of debris, they slowed down and began auto rotating. As they loaded the wounded in the first two, Will looked around for instructions from Captain Reilly, but he had joined his troops. When the other choppers landed, Will could see the Green Berets standing up to look over the battlefield before abandoning the clearing. He sighed with relief when he saw the last soldier, Captain Reilly, board the remaining chopper.

Looking down now at the clearing and the burning jungle that bordered its western edge, Will marveled at how close the napalm had come to them and how devastating that bombing run had been. Still, there was a significant force that had survived, which was firing up at them as they climbed out of range. Later, they discovered that Ant Eater had a little something planned for Charley following their departure. Arclight, the acronym for a B-52 bomb strike, came in behind the F-4 Phantom napalm run, and it eliminated any opposition from that sector. From the open door of the gunship, Will could see the fires from the burning camp that had lit up the smoke-filled western sky. Miraculously, they had faced a battalion of North Vietnamese regulars and an undetermined number of VC, and they had not lost a man. Will turned and looked around the aircraft and said a prayer to thank God that they were out of danger and heading for the safety of Tan Son Nhut.

After an hour in the air, the radio began to buzz with activity, reporting some civil unrest in the capital city of Saigon. The news was garbled and chaotic, and the pilots seemed perplexed by what they heard. Will stuck his head up between the pilots and asked what was going on.

"The North Vietnamese forces have been involved in another phase of the Tet Offensive, and they are striking Saigon again," the pilot said. "We're uncertain what this means, something about a possible evacuation." This was troubling news for everyone aboard the helicopter.

One of the younger soldiers asked Will what he thought was happening. "It appears they are ordering all units to return to their commands. It's unusual to say the least," Will answered.

"Do you think they are bracing for a fight or preparing to pull out?" the young soldier asked.

"I guess we'll soon know."

Air traffic increased as they approached Tan Son Nhut: C-119s, C-123s, and C-130s were landing every few minutes. Helicopter Cobra gunships and UH-1 troop transports were landing on every available helipad. Flight crews were directing troops who were disembarking as quickly as they landed. Captain Reilly was able to get through on the radio to Special Operations Group and was instructed to land in a designated field outside the air base near the SOG headquarters.

Off in the distance heavy artillery, 50 caliber machine guns, and the unmistakable sound of the AK-47 could be heard as the team disembarked. A Navy Medevac helicopter was standing by, and the wounded including Callaway, Larry, and Jim Thorpe were loaded aboard for transfer to an offshore hospital ship. Will shouted, "Keep your hands off those beautiful navy nurses, Larry!" "Don't worry about me, my buddy. It's you we have to worry about. What is going on anyway?"

"How the hell do I know? I don't like the sound of those cannons and that rifle fire we are hearing. They are pretty close. I hope to see Cecil in a few minutes, and maybe I can get some answers," Will replied, stepping back from the closing door as the pilot started the engine.

Larry shouted above the scream of the turbochargers, "Keep your ass out of trouble, Will," he said with a smile on his face. "I won't be there to save it for you." He was hurting, but he would never let it show.

Watching from the window, Larry waved as Tom and Will walked to the SOG compound with the other Green Berets. The dust, scraps of paper, and leaves were whirling around from the prop wash as the chopper lifted off.

Cecil Tighe greeted the men nervously as they stepped into the Quonset hut. "Well done, men," he said as he shook hands with every man. "I'm going to recommend special commendations for all of you." *What a joke*, Will thought to himself. *Who gives a damn about metals?* After Cecil had spoken personally with each one of them, he instructed a young second lieutenant to get everyone a beer and asked Marshall Brant, Drew Harlow, and Will to join him in his private office.

"I guess you wonder what's going on here. While you were out there taking care of business, North Vietnamese forces were hitting a bunch of places along the border with Cambodia and Laos. Apparently, the VC was not involved in this one. In fact, those ants that were fried were probably some of the troops who were involved in this thing.

"I think they were trying to draw us away from Saigon and the air bases. You remember the Battle of Kham Duc back in May. They just about destroyed that place. If you remember, it got so bad that Westmoreland ordered Kham Duc to be evacuated.

"Well, after hitting along the border, they have struck Saigon again. Everyone is getting pretty antsy! No one seems to know what the long-range plan is anymore."

"This doesn't sound like our version of the picnic. Are we gonna let those bastards move in and take over?" the captain spoke out, an exclamation more than a question.

"What can I say, Will? Hell, you know me. I'd vote we go all the way to China. After all, we're gonna have to take them on sooner or later, you know that. Meanwhile, this CIA operation is shutting down, and we are leaving for sure."

Sipping his beer, Will found himself frowning as he asked, "What about our allies? What about guys like Tom Vo out there? You know what they'll do to him."

"Oh, we'll take care of Tom, Will. Don't worry about that."

Cecil showed no emotion, no evidence that what he just said wasn't true. But Will knew how old, hard-line operatives can control their emotions. Years ago, Cecil had bragged how he had beaten the lie detector, and he did it by teaching himself that the lie was the truth until he started to believe it. But Will suspected he had another solution. The agency had developed a pill that gave the lie detector a fit, but nobody ever talked about it. His answer about Tom made Will very uneasy. There was no way he could tell whether Cecil was lying or telling the truth.

"One of my officers will take you boys over to the officers' mess and get you a good dinner and a room so you can get some rest. It's about 1900 hours. I'm waiting for instructions from command. If we are to evacuate, I'll make sure our orders include Tom and anyone else who fought for us. Take it easy for a while, and I'll send for you when I know something."

Incoming and outgoing air traffic had further increased at the largest airbase in South Vietnam since they landed. The mess hall was crowded, and everyone carried their weapons in the dining area. This had been forbidden in the past. Small arms fire and occasional heavy weapon reports were heard off in the distance as they talked about the possibility of going home.

Militarily, the Tet Offensive had been a bigger disaster for the North Vietnamese than Little Big Horn was for Custer, but it had some very unintended consequences for the United States. First, when the troops were pulled back to defend Saigon and the military bases, the rural areas and villages were left undefended. The VC moved back into those areas with dire consequences for those who had supported us. Once pacification became inoperative, the South Vietnamese realized that they could not be protected even with US support. It was mindful of the old expression, "If you can't be with the one you love, love the one you're with." The countryside was a dangerous place.

Secondly, aside from 1968 this as been the deadliest year of the war for US forces. That combined with the Johnson administration's failure to convince Americans that the Tet Offensive had been the disaster it was for North Vietnam, this led to a rapid decline in public opinion and a rapid increase in antiwar protests.

"What you think, Will? Will I be leaving with you?" asked Tom.

"That's what Cecil says, Tom," Will answered, doing his best to conceal his concerns.

"But what you think, Will?"

"I think I'm not going home without you, Tom. That's what I think. How about you, Marshall…Drew, what are your thoughts?" "I don't feel comfortable about the situation, Will," Marshall said with a worried look on his face.

"Me neither, Will. But we're with you. Before we leave Vietnam, Tom will be with us."

After eating their first hot meal in several days, they headed to the hooch to get some sleep. The incessant sound of helicopters and fixed wing aircraft continually arriving and taking off, and the bombardment in the distance, made it difficult for the men to fall asleep immediately, but exhaustion finally took control.

Shortly before daybreak, they were awakened by the increased sound of heavy artillery fire. It was still off in the distance but closer than the day before. Looking at his watch, it was 0530. Will had slept for eight hours. He couldn't remember a time when he slept for eight hours in Vietnam. Rubbing his eyes, he noticed that the air traffic had not subsided. On a helipad nearby, a helicopter was idling, drowning out all other sounds in the vicinity except the occasional thud of artillery fire.

Stepping out of the building, Will noticed several comrades were also awake, and he joined them to stroll down to the mess hall for a cup of coffee. Around 0700 hours, the same lieutenant that had escorted them to the officers' mess informed the group that they were to be picked up just after noon at the parade ground near the helicopters assigned to the 77th Special Forces Brigade. Some of these flyers had been in on the extraction of the troops after they had freed Larry at the stronghold. "May I speak to you privately, Mr. Brandon?" The young officer led him over to the recreation room and closed the door. "Mr. Tighe asked me to speak to you alone because of the sensitivity of the subject. He cannot help your friend Tom Vo leave the country." Reaching in his pocket, he pulled out a brown envelope and handed it to Will. "Mr. Tighe regrets that he cannot do anything at this time because of pressure from his agency. It has something to do with Mr. Vo's security clearance and him being an 'undesirable.'"

A hot flash of anger welled up throughout Will's body. "Have they forgotten all that this guy has done, or how many times he has laid it all on the line for us? Have they forgotten what the North Vietnamese or VC will do to him? And now you tell me he is 'undesirable'?"

"Sir, I've heard about this man, and I can't believe they are doing this either."

Will was fuming. "He couldn't deliver this message himself.

He couldn't face me. He had to send someone else." "What are you going to do?"

"Who the hell knows?"

After the lieutenant left, Will took Tom aside and broke the news to him. "Cecil sent this envelope to you." Tom opened it and saw what appeared to be several thousand dollars of US currency in one hundred dollar bills.

"There nothing you could do?" he asked. "Don't they understand, they signed my death warrant? I thought you my friend. You promised me. You know I would die for you. Americans no different than VC. At least you know VC have no honor. I thought Americans were honorable. I don't want money. What good is money?" And he threw it on the ground.

"Tom, we'll do something. I'm not sure what right now… but something. You are like a brother. I won't leave you here, my brother, trust me."

"I did trust you, but what I get. You go home, Will, you marry pretty girl, you live in peace, happily ever after." Tom turns and walks away a few feet and turns back. "I really thought you were my brother." With that, he walked out the gate, turned the corner by a guard shack, and was quickly out of Will's sight.

He assembled the men and told them what had happened. Once the shock of Cecil's decision had passed, they very quickly turned into an armed mob, a very hostile armed mob. These were battle-hardened Green Berets. They wanted to take out Cecil Tighe and were willing to pay the price, whatever it took.

Finally, Will got them to calm down and listen to him. "What I am about to do may cost me prison time or worse, but I can't do it alone. I'll need help. I don't have the right to ask any of you because you haven't fought beside Tom as long as I have. But I owe this guy, big time. More than once, Tom was there when we needed him. Some of us are alive today because of him. Now I'm gonna stick my neck out for him like he's done for me. If we aren't shot, we could be incarcerated for a long time. Those of you who want to walk away will have no problem with me. You have a perfect right to stay out of this, and this war appears to be in chaos, I wouldn't blame you one bit. If you want to stay out of this, you may leave right now, no problem. But if you are with me"—he paused, looking about the room—"just follow me." With that, he walked out the door. For a few seconds, they just looked at each other and then, as if on cue, they all jumped to their feet and ran to follow.

Their first problem was to find Tom. The second was to get him out of the country. As they began to discuss ideas, Capt. Riley, who had been attending a briefing of the extraction mission, walked up to join the discussion. Knowing that he knew nothing of their plans, they were reluctant to involve him, but he sensed they were up to something. "What's going on here? You guys look like you are about to rob a bank. I know you guys pretty well, speak up."

"You need to stay out of this, Captain, for your own sake," Marshall Brant offered.

"Let me be the judge of that. Spill it. What the hell are you planning?"

Drew Harlow, who had been quiet during the discussions, spoke up. "They've denied our request to take Tom Vo with us, Captain, and we can't leave him. You know what they will do?"

"So you're going to go against orders and take him anyway, is that it?"

"You damn right!" a voice spoke out strong from the fringe of the group. All of the men turned to see who it was, and it was the lowest ranking enlisted man on the team.

Another soldier spoke out, "Right is right." "Yeah," they cried out in unison.

They turned back to Capt. Riley, who was silent for a moment, and then he said, "What the hell are we waiting for?" A cheer rose up, and the men thrust their fists into the air. It reminded Will of a cheer of resolve his high school football team had given just before the beginning of the second half of the Polio Bowl game. Being the highest ranking officer, Capt. Riley took control, and they began making plans for a mission that could prove more devastating personally than any of the firefights they had experienced since coming to Vietnam.

At 1000 hours, the airbase alarms started going off, and the team noticed a smoking C-130 circling to land at Tan Son Nhut. In Vietnam, when an emergency such as a disabled aircraft occurred it became a top priority. Fire-fighting equipment could be seen moving in every direction. People were running toward the runway, and above the noise and confusion was the deafening sound of chopper blades.

Just as directed by the Special Operations Group command, helicopters from the Special Forces wing began landing to pick up the Green Beret teams at the parade field. Those who had been in on the rescue of Larry and Callaway started loading the choppers and immediately began to take over the aircrafts. The pilots had been ordered to pick up the team and transport them to a Marine aircraft carrier designed especially to accommodate troop helicopters, but they were now under the command of Capt. Riley to find Tom and escort him with the team to the carrier, by force if necessary. Once the pilots were told of the reasons behind the abrupt commandeering of their aircraft, most of the pilots voluntarily went along with the plan. Others voiced their opposition, but being Green Berets, they went along anyway.

The sound of heavy artillery grew closer as the day went on. They searched every hamlet on the outskirts of Tan Son Nhut, reckoning that Tom may have sought shelter nearby with relatives or friends. Helicopters were landing in villages throughout the surrounding area where the team members questioned people about their commando friend who had become a legend among the South Vietnamese people.

Just as they were about to give up the search, a call came in from one of the teams that Tom had been spotted walking in a market not far from the airbase with his M-16 slung over his shoulder. They were there within a few minutes, and Tom recognized Will from the ground, waving from the door of the Cobra gunship. But he kept walking, looking up only occasionally as he made his way through the crowd of people in the village.

"Can you let me down?" Will shouted to the pilot. "I don't see any place to land, and I need to talk to him."

"Do we have a repel line and harness aboard?" Marshall Brant called out to the pilot.

"Yeah, just under the forward seat. We also have a winch to bring you back, but only one at a time," he replied.

Once on the ground, Will began working his way through the crowd, taking hand signals from above as to Tom's position. The people were antagonistic toward Will now, demanding that he do something to protect them against the approaching NVR force. Moving as fast as he could, he spotted Tom about thirty yards ahead and quickly caught up to him.

"You're coming back with us, Tom," Will said. "Who says?"

"I do. And so does Capt. Riley and all the other Green Berets." "You crazy. They not let me go. Tighe told you I not go. You think he now say okay?"

"We don't care what Cecil says, Tom. We won't go if you don't go. It's that simple."

"You crazy, Will Brandon. Why you do this?" "Because you would for me."

With that a smile spread across his face. "I always know…you crazy, Will Brandon."

An artillery shell hit the village less than a quarter of a mile away, sending the people into a panic as they began running down the crowded street in the direction of the main gate at Tan Son Nhut. "Are you with me?" Will shouted amid the confusion.

"I ready," he replied, that smile still on his face.

The chopper stayed over them till they came to an open spot surrounded by huts where they lowered a line. Will asked Tom to go first, but Tom insisted that he go first. As he was being lifted, small arm rounds began to hit the aircraft. "Get him up here. We're taking fire. Somebody's got us in their sights," the pilot hollowed out.

When Will was aboard, they began lowering the line for Tom. *Paanng*! A bullet whizzed past Marshall's head. "Damn, it's getting hot. Where's that coming from."

"Back of that building on the main street," one of the soldiers pointed out. "I saw some guys with weapons taking pot shots."

"Call in a gunship," Marshall instructed the pilot. "Gotcha," he replied.

Just as they lifted Tom off the ground and started to move away, a series of bullets hit the helicopter and it began to auto- rotate. "The pilot's hit. Somebody get up there that can fly this thing and help the copilot or we're going down," Marshall cried out.

Will looked down from the door to see Tom swinging wildly out of control. "He may be hit. We got to get him up here fast." As the helicopter made a wide circle, it passed over a church. In horror, they saw Tom swing into the church's steeple, tearing off the cross and its parapet. The copter took more hits, and suddenly, the aircraft was full of smoke. "We're going in. Hang on," the copilot called from the flight cabin.

Tom hit the ground hard just before the helicopter settled in, destroying its landing gear. Fearing a fire, the soldiers bailed out the door followed by Marshall, Will, and the two pilots. They rushed to Tom who was injured but conscious. They were taking fire from several directions, but the soldiers were answering back with M-16s and one 50 caliber. Their response provided cover for Marshall and Will as they drug Tom to a small levee used for irrigation where they assessed his injuries. His right boot was pointing in the wrong direction; obviously, Tom had a broken leg, and blood was oozing through the front of his shirt. When they ripped it open, they saw that he had been shot, the bullet entering the left edge of his abdomen and exiting out the right.

Just at that moment, the Cobra gunship arrived on the scene, spewing fire and death from machine guns on both sides. Within seconds, the snipers were destroyed and the soldiers finished the cleanup. One of the team's helicopters landed in the church playground and waited for them to board. "We're going to make it, Tom, just hang on," Will said, as one of the medics bound Tom's wounds.

Marshall and Will began carried Tom to the chopper, carrying him in the sitting position on their intertwined arms while one of the Green

Berets carried his foot to avoid additional damage to the ankle. He was in intense pain, but he never cried out.

As the aircraft gained altitude, all of the Special Forces helicopters lined up in formation. Looking out the doors of the UH-1, the men could see fires off in the distance and powerful explosions could be felt in the air. The war was coming closer, and they contemplated how fortunate they had been to complete the rescue of Larry out there on the Cambodian border. Had they been a few days later, they might never have left Vietnam alive.

"You got a guy on the radio demanding to speak to you, sir," the young Green Beret pilot said to Will, "says you'll know who it is." He was right. Will knew it would be Cecil.

The pilot handed Will the transmitter just as Cecil said, "Before you get in any deeper, Brandon, you tell your pilot to land at SOG right now. Do you hear me? That's a direct order."

Choosing his words carefully, he responded stoically, "Before you go any farther, Cecil, let's understand one thing. He's going home with us. We are prepared to go all the way on this, make no mistake about it. There is a platoon of Green Berets that feel exactly as Marshall, Drew, and I feel. If you persist and create a problem for us, all bets are off. We are no longer bound by the code of silence so important to the company. And you know, as operatives, we were insiders to more atrocities than you would care to explain to your friends on Capitol Hill. So back off. Have I made myself clear?" The radio suddenly went dead.

The sun was starting to slip below the horizon as off in the distance, the troop carrier came into view. Tom's condition had worsened so they radioed ahead for medical support to be at the ready once they landed on the deck.

Will also wondered how the Marines would receive several helicopters, which had been commandeered by the Green Berets and were shot full of holes. It might be hard to explain.

Medics were there to take charge of Tom, attaching oxygen and plasma as they rushed him to the ship's hospital. He had lost consciousness, and there was great concern among the Green Berets for his life. Will followed his gurney, vowing to stay with him till the danger had passed, but Drew Harlow, who had arrived on one of the other aircraft, talked him into joining him in the pilot's lounge for coffee and to relax. Tom was now in good hands, and there was nothing more Will could do.

There was one thing Will and Drew could do and that was to pray for their friend and wait. Soon Capt. Riley, Marshall Brant, and the other soldiers joined them in their vigil. It was a long night and most of them fell asleep in lounge chairs. But Will couldn't sleep for fear of waking up to the news that Tom was gone.

Around 0500 hours, a doctor came out to inform the team that Tom was out of immediate danger. He was not entirely out of the woods, but he had a better than 75 percent chance of survival. Will walked up to the flight deck and strolled to the fantail. Aircraft arrivals had ceased, but observation helicopters were warming for patrol. The ship appeared to be dead in the water, but the waves were pounding against the side, sending a stream of ocean spray in ten-second intervals. As he watched the first evidence of light sneak up from behind the horizon, his thoughts ranged from the stronghold on the frontier to his hometown in the heartland of America. Somewhere in the direction of the rising sun, over the horizon, across the Pacific, past the West Coast, and the mountain ranges, somewhere out there was the woman of his dreams.

The spray helped clear Will's thoughts, bringing the events of the past two weeks into sharper focus. He felt a new anointing of his spirit and mind. In spite of what he had been through, he now felt that he could leave all of this behind. Finally, death would no longer be in the forefront of his consciousness. Now he could think those pure thoughts that had been absent from his thinking for so long. And there, alone on the flight deck, he thanked God.

Watching the sun rise fully in the sky, the thought occurred to him that regardless of what he and his comrades had been through these past few years, life goes on as always. And win or lose, they had done what they had been trained to do to the best of their ability, and they had done it with honor.

That sunrise also brought a surprising feeling of redemption within himself, a knowledge that for whatever reason, God had brought him through, and he was going home for the last time. At that moment, he watched the carrier crew push the "borrowed" Special Forces helicopters off the side of the ship and into the sea, and the last one to go was the horse he rode in on.